How to Find Love in a BOOK SHOP

Veronica Henry

First published in Great Britain in 2016
by Orion Books
This paperback edition published in 2016
by Orion Books,
an imprint of The Orion Publishing Group Ltd,
Carmelite House, 50 Victoria Embankment
London EC4Y 0DZ

An Hachette UK Company

17 19 20 18 16

A CIP catalogue record for this book is
available from the British Library.

ISBN 978 1 4091 4689 6

Typeset at The Spartan Press Ltd,
Lymington, Hants

Printed in Great Britain by Clays Ltd,
Elcograf S.p.A.

www.orionbooks.co.uk

Veronica Henry worked as a scriptwriter for *The Archers*, *Heartbeat* and *Holby City*, amongst many others, before turning to fiction. She won the 2014 RNA Novel of the Year Award for *A Night on the Orient Express*. Veronica lives with her family in a village in north Devon.

Find out more at www.veronicahenry.co.uk or follow her on Twitter @veronica_henry

Also by Veronica Henry

Wild Oats
An Eligible Bachelor
Love on the Rocks
Marriage and Other Games
The Beach Hut
The Birthday Party
The Long Weekend
A Night on the Orient Express
The Beach Hut Next Door
High Tide

THE HONEYCOTE NOVELS
Honeycote
Making Hay
Just a Family Affair

This book is dedicated to my beloved father,
William Miles Henry
1935—2016

'Reading is everything'

NORA EPHRON

Prologue

February 1983

*H*e would never have believed it if you'd told him a year ago. That he'd be standing in an empty shop with a baby in a pram, seriously considering putting in an offer.

The pram had been a stroke of luck. He'd seen an advert for a garden sale in a posh part of north Oxford, and the bargain hunter in him couldn't stay away. The couple had two very young children but were moving to Paris. The pram was pristine, of the kind the queen might have pushed – or rather, her nanny. The woman had only wanted five pounds for it. Julius was sure it was worth far more, and she was only being kind. But if recent events had taught him one thing it was to accept kindness. With alacrity, before people changed their minds. So he bought it, and scrubbed it out carefully with Milton even though it had seemed very clean already, and bought a fresh mattress and blankets and there he had it: the perfect nest for his precious cargo, until she could walk.

When did babies start to walk? There was no point in asking Debra – his vague, away-with-the-fairies mother, ensconced in her patchouli-soaked basement flat in Westbourne Grove, whose memory of his own childhood was

1

blurry. According to Debra, Julius was reading by the age of two, a legend he didn't quite believe. Although maybe it was true, because he couldn't remember a time he couldn't read. It was like breathing to him. Nevertheless, he couldn't and didn't rely on his mother for child-rearing advice. He often thought it was a miracle he had made it through childhood unscathed. She used to leave him alone, in his cot, while she went to the wine bar on the corner in the evenings. 'What could go wrong?' she asked him. 'I only left you for an hour.' Perhaps that explained his protectiveness towards his own daughter. He found it hard to turn his back on her for even a moment.

He looked around the bare walls again. The smell of damp was inescapable, and damp would be a disaster. The staircase rising to the mezzanine was rotten; so rotten he wasn't allowed up it. The two bay windows either side of the front door flooded the shop with a pearlescent light, highlighting the golden oak of the floorboards and the ornate plasterwork on the ceiling. The dust made it feel other-worldly: a ghost shop, waiting, waiting for something to happen, a transformation, a renovation, a renaissance.

'It was a pharmacy, originally,' said the agent. 'And then an antique shop. Well, I say antique – you've never seen so much rubbish in your life.'

He should get some professional advice, really – a structural survey, a quote from someone for a damp course – yet Julius felt light-headed and his heart was pounding. It was right. He knew it was. The two floors above were ideal for him and the baby to live in. Over the shop.

The book shop.

His search had begun three weeks earlier, when he had decided that he needed to take positive action if he and his

2

daughter were going to have any semblance of normal life together. He had looked at his experience, his potential, his assets, and the practicalities of being a single father, and decided there was really only one option open to him.

He'd gone to the library, put a copy of the Yellow Pages on the table, and next to it a detailed map of the county. He drew a circle around Oxford with a fifteen-mile radius, wondering what it would be like to live in Christmas Common, or Ducklington, or Goosey. Then he worked through all the book shops listed and put a cross through the towns they were in.

He looked at the remaining towns, the ones without a book shop at all. There were half a dozen. He made a list, and then over the next few days visited each one, travelling by a complicated rota of buses. The first three towns had been soulless and dreary, and he had been so discouraged he'd almost given up on his idea, but something about the name Peasebrook pleased him, so he decided to have one last look before relinquishing his fantasy.

Peasebrook was in the middle of the Cotswolds, on the outer perimeter of the circle he had drawn: as far out as he wanted to go. He got off the bus and looked up the high street. It was wide and tree-lined, its pavements flanked with higgledy-piggledy golden buildings. There were antique shops, a traditional butcher with rabbit and pheasant hanging outside and fat sausages in the window, a sprawling coaching inn, a couple of nice cafés and a cheese shop. The Women's Institute were having a sale outside the town hall: there were trestle tables bearing big cakes oozing jam and trugs of mud-covered vegetables and pots of herbaceous flowers drooping dark purple and yellow blooms.

Peasebrook was buzzing, in a quiet way but with purpose, like bees on a summer afternoon. People stopped in the street and talked to each other. The cafés looked pleasingly full. The tills seemed to jangle: people were shopping with gusto and enthusiasm. There was a very smart restaurant with a bay tree outside the door and an impressive menu in a glass case boasting nouvelle cuisine. There was even a tiny theatre showing The Importance of Being Earnest. Somehow that boded well. Julius loved Oscar Wilde. He'd done one of his dissertations on him: The Influence of Oscar Wilde on W.B. Yeats.

He took the play as an omen, but he carried on scouring the streets, in case his research hadn't been thorough. He feared turning a corner and finding what he hoped wasn't there. Now he was here, in Peasebrook, he wanted it to be his home – their home. It was a mystery, though, why there was no book shop in such an appealing place.

After all, a town without a book shop was a town without a heart.

A book shop could only make things better – for everyone in Peasebrook. Julius imagined each person he passed as a potential customer. He could picture them all, crowding in, asking his advice, him sliding their purchases into a bag, getting to know their likes and dislikes, putting a book aside for a particular customer, knowing it would be just up their street. Watching them browse, watching the joy of them discovering a new author, a new world.

'Would the vendor take a cheeky offer?' he asked the estate agent, who shrugged.

'You can but ask.'

'It needs a lot of work.'

'That has been taken into consideration.'

Julius named his price. 'It's my best and only offer. I can't afford any more.'

4

When Julius signed the contract four weeks later, he couldn't help but be amazed. Here he was, alone in the world (well, there was his mother, but she was as much use as a chocolate teapot) but for a baby and a book shop. And as that very baby reached out her starfish hand, he gave her his finger to hold and thought: what an extraordinary position to be in. Fate was peculiar indeed.

What if he hadn't looked up at that very moment, nearly two years ago now? What if he had kept his back to the door and carried on rearranging the travel section, leaving his colleague to serve the girl with the Rossetti hair . . .

And six months later, after weeks of dust and grime and sawing and sweeping and painting, and several eye-watering bills, and a few moments of sheer panic, and any number of deliveries, the sign outside the shop was rehung, painted in navy and gold, proclaiming 'Nightingale Books'. There had been no room to write 'purveyors of reading matter to the discerning', but that was what he was. A bookseller.

A bookseller of the very best kind.

I

Thirty-two years later...

What do you do, while you're waiting for someone to die?

Literally, sitting next to them in a plastic armchair that isn't the right shape for *anyone's* bottom, waiting for them to draw their last breath because there is no more hope.

Nothing seemed appropriate. There was a room down the corridor to watch telly in, but that seemed callous, and anyway, Emilia wasn't really a television person.

She didn't knit, or do tapestry. Or sudoku.

She didn't want to listen to music, for fear of disturbing him. Even the best earphones leak a certain timpani. Irritating on a train, probably even more so on your deathbed. She didn't want to surf the Internet on her phone. That seemed the ultimate in twenty-first-century rudeness.

And there wasn't a single book on the planet that could hold her attention right now.

So she sat next to his bed and dozed. And every now and then she started awake with a bolt of fear, in case she might have missed the moment. Then she would hold his hand for a few minutes. It was dry and cool and lay motionless in her clasp. Eventually it grew heavy and made her feel sad, so she laid it back on top of the sheet.

Then she would doze off again.

From time to time the nurses brought her hot chocolate, although that was a misnomer. It was not hot, but tepid, and Emilia was fairly certain that no cocoa beans had been harmed in the making of it. It was pale beige, faintly sweet water.

The night-time lights in the cottage hospital were dim, with a sickly yellowish tinge. The heating was on too high and the little room felt airless. She looked at the thin bedcover, with its pattern of orange and yellow flowers, and the outline of her father underneath, so still and small. She could see the few strands of hair curling over his scalp, leached of colour. His thick hair had been one of his distinguishing features. He would rake his fingers through it while he was considering a recommendation, or when he was standing in front of one of the display tables trying to decide what to put on it, or when he was on the phone to a customer. It was as much a part of him as the pale blue cashmere scarf he insisted on wearing, wrapped twice around his neck, even though it bore evidence of moths. Emilia had dealt with them swiftly at the first sign. She suspected they had been brought in via the thick brown velvet coat she had bought at the charity shop last winter, and she felt guilty they'd set upon the one sartorial item her father seemed attached to.

He'd been complaining then of discomfort. Well, not complaining, because he wasn't one to moan. Emilia had expressed concern, and he had dismissed her concern with his trademark stoicism, and she had thought nothing more of it, just got on the plane to Hong Kong. Until the phone call, last week, calling her back.

'I think you ought to come home,' the nurse had said. 'Your father will be furious with me for calling you. He doesn't want to alarm you. But . . .'

The 'but' said it all. Emilia was on the first flight out. And when she arrived Julius pretended to be cross, but the way he held her hand, tighter than tight, told her everything she needed to know.

'He's in denial,' said the nurse. 'He's a fighter all right. I'm so sorry. We're doing everything we can to keep him comfortable.'

Emilia nodded, finally understanding. Comfortable. Not alive. Comfortable.

He didn't seem to be in any pain or discomfort now. He had eaten some lime jelly the day before, eager for the quivering spoons of green. Emilia imagined it soothed his parched lips and dry tongue. She felt as if she was feeding a little bird as he stretched his neck to reach the spoon and opened his mouth. Afterwards he lay back, exhausted by the effort. It was all he had eaten for days. All he was living on was a complicated cocktail of painkillers and sedatives that were rotated to provide the best palliative care. Emilia had come to hate the word palliative. It was ominous, and at times she suspected ineffectual. From time to time her father had shown distress, whether from pain or the knowledge of what was to come she didn't know, but she knew at those points the medication wasn't doing its job. Adjustment, although swiftly administered, never worked quickly enough. Which in turn caused her distress. It was a never-ending cycle.

Yet not *never*-ending because it *would* end. The corner

had been turned and there was no point in hoping for a recovery. Even the most optimistic believer in miracles would know that now. So there was nothing to do but pray for a swift and merciful release.

The nurse lifted the bedcover and looked at his feet, caressing them with gentle fingers. The look the nurse gave Emilia told her it wouldn't be long now. His skin was pale grey, the pale grey of a marble statue.

The nurse dropped the sheet back down and rubbed Emilia's shoulder. Then she left, for there was nothing she could say. It was a waiting game. They had done all they could. No pain, as far as anyone could surmise. A calm, quiet environment, for incipient death was treated with hushed reverence. But who was to say what the dying really wanted? Maybe he would prefer his beloved Elgar at full blast, or the shipping forecast on repeat? Or to hear the nurses gossiping and bantering, about who they'd been out with the night before and what they were cooking for tea? Maybe distraction from your imminent demise by utter trivia would be a welcome one?

Emilia sat and wondered how could she make him feel her love as he slipped away. If she could take out her heart and give it to him, she would. This wonderful man who had given her life, and been her life, and was leaving her alone.

She'd whispered to him, memories and reminiscences. She told him stories. Recited his favourite poems.

Talked to him about the shop.

'I'm going to look after it for you,' she told him. 'I'll make sure it never closes its doors. Not in my lifetime. And I'm never going to sell out to Ian Mendip, no matter what he offers, because the shop is all that matters. All the diamonds in the world are nothing in comparison. Books are more precious than jewels.'

She truly believed this. What did a diamond bring you? A momentary flash of brilliance. A diamond scintillated for a second; a book could scintillate forever.

She doubted Ian Mendip had ever read a book in his life. It made her so angry, thinking about the stress he'd put her father under at a vulnerable time. Julius had tried to underplay it, but she could see he was upset, fearful for the shop and his staff and his customers. The staff had told her how unsettled he had been by it, and yet again she had cursed herself for being so far away. Now she was determined to reassure him, so he could slip away, safe in the knowledge that Nightingale Books was in good hands.

She shifted on the seat to find a more comfortable position. She ended up leaning forwards and resting her head in her arms at the foot of the bed. She was unbelievably tired.

It was 2.49 in the morning when the nurse touched her on the shoulder. Her touch said everything that needed to be said. Emilia wasn't sure if she had been asleep or awake. Even now she wasn't sure if she was asleep or awake, for she felt as if her head was somewhere else, as if everything was a bit treacly and slow.

When all the formalities were over and the undertaker had been called, she walked out into the dawn, the air morgue-chilly, the light gloomy. It was as if all the colour had gone from the world, until she saw the traffic lights by the hospital exit change from red to amber to green. Sound too felt muffled, as if she still had water in her ears from swimming.

Would the world be a different place without Julius in it? She didn't know yet. She breathed in the air he was no longer breathing, and thought about his broad shoulders, the ones she had sat on when she was tiny, drumming her heels on his chest to make him run faster, twisting her fingers in the thick hair that fell to his collar, the hair that had been salt and pepper since he was thirty. She held the plain silver watch with the alligator strap he had worn every day, but which she had taken off towards the end, as she didn't want anything chafing his paper-thin skin, leaving it on the table next to his bed in case he needed to know the time, because it told a better time than the clock over the nurse's station; a time that held far more promise. But the magic time on his watch hadn't been able to stop the inevitable.

She got into her car. There was a packet of buttermints on the passenger seat she had meant to bring him. She unpeeled one and popped it in her mouth. It was the first thing she had eaten since breakfast the day before. She sucked on it until it scraped the roof of her mouth, and the discomfort took her mind off it all for a moment.

She'd eaten half the packet by the time she turned into Peasebrook high street and her teeth were furry with the sugar. The little town was wrapped in the pearl-grey of dawn. It looked bleak: its golden stone needed sunshine for it to glow. In the half-light it looked like a dreary wallflower, but in a couple of hours it would emerge like a dazzling debutante, charming everyone who set eyes upon it. It was quintessentially quaint and English, with its oak doorways, mullioned and latticed windows, cobbled pavements, red letterboxes and the row of pollarded lime trees. There were no flat-roofed monstrosities, nothing to offend the eye, only charm.

Next to the stone bridge straddling the brook that gave

the town its name was Nightingale Books, three storeys high and double fronted, with two bay windows and a dark blue door. Emilia stood outside, the early morning breeze the only sign of movement in the sleeping town, and looked up at the building that was the only home she had ever known. Wherever she was in the world, whatever she was doing, her room above the shop was still here; most of her stuff was still here. Thirty-two years of clutter and clobber.

She slipped in through the side entrance and stood for a moment on the tiled floor. In front of her was the door leading up to the flat. She remembered her father holding her hand when she was tiny, and walking her down those stairs. It had taken hours, but she had been determined, and he had been patient. When she was at school, she had run down the stairs, taking them two at a time, her school bag on her back, an apple in one hand, always late. Years later, she had sneaked up the stairs in bare feet when she came in from a party. Not that Julius was strict or likely to shout: it was just what you did when you were sixteen and had drunk a little too much cider and it was two o'clock in the morning.

To her left was the door that came out behind the shop counter. She pushed it open and stepped into the shop. The early morning light ventured in through the window, tentative. Emilia shivered a little as the air inside stirred. She felt a sense of expectation: the same feeling of stepping back in time or into another place that she had whenever she entered Nightingale Books. She could be whenever and wherever she wanted. Only this time she couldn't. She would give anything to go back, to when everything was all right.

She felt as if the books were asking for news. He's gone,

she wanted to tell them, but she didn't, because she didn't trust her voice. And because it was silly. Books told you things, everything you needed to know, but you didn't talk back to them.

As she stood in the middle of the shop, she gradually felt a sense of comfort settle upon her, a calmness that soothed her soul. For Julius was still here, amidst the covers and the upright spines. He claimed to know every book in his shop. He may not have read each one from cover to cover, but he understood why they were there, what the author's intent had been and who might, therefore, like to read them, from the simplest children's board book to the weightiest, most indecipherable tome.

There was a rich red carpet, faded and worn now. Rows and rows of wooden shelves lined the walls, stretching right up to the ceiling – there was a ladder to reach the more unusual books on the very top shelves. Fiction was at the front of the shop, reference at the back, and tables in the middle displayed cookery and art and travel. Upstairs, on the mezzanine, there was a collection of first editions and second-hand rarities, behind locked glass cases. And Julius had reigned over it all from his place behind the wooden counter. Behind him were stacked the books that people had ordered, wrapped in brown paper and tied with string. There was an old-fashioned ornate till that tinged when it opened, which he'd found in a junk shop and, although he didn't use it any more, he kept it as decoration and sometimes he kept sugar mice in the drawer to hand out to small children who had been especially patient and good.

There would always be a half-full cup of coffee on the counter that he'd begun and never finished, because he would get into a conversation and forget about it and leave it to get cold. Because people dropped in to chat to Julius all the time. He was full of advice and knowledge and wisdom and, above all, kindness.

As a result, the shop had become a mecca for all sections of society in and around Peasebrook. The townspeople were proud of their book shop. It was a place of comfort and familiarity. And they had come to respect its owner. Adore him, even. For over thirty years he had fed their minds and their hearts, aided and abetted in recent years by his assistants: warm and bubbly Mel, who kept the place organised, and lanky Dave the Goth, who knew almost as much as Julius about books but rarely spoke – though once you got him going it was impossible to stop him.

Her father was still here, thought Emilia, in the thousands of pages. Millions – there must be so many millions – of words. All those words, and the pleasure they had provided for people over the years: escape, entertainment, education ... He had changed minds. He had changed lives. It was up to her to carry on his work so he would live on, she swore to herself.

Julius Nightingale would live forever.

Emilia left the shop and went upstairs to the flat. She was too tired to even make a cup of tea. She needed to lie down and gather her thoughts. She wasn't feeling anything yet, neither shock nor grief, just a dull heavy-heartedness that weighed her down. The worst had happened, the worst thing possible, but it seemed the world was still turning. The gradual lightening of the sky told her that. She heard birdsong, too, and frowned at their chirpy heralding of a new dawn. Surely the sun wouldn't rise? Surely the world would be grey forever?

All the rooms seemed drained of warmth. The kitchen, with its ancient pine table and battered old units, was chilly and austere. The living room was sulking behind its half-drawn curtains. Emilia couldn't look at the sofa in case it still held the imprint of Julius; she couldn't count the number of hours the two of them had spent curled up on it with tea or cocoa or wine, leafing through their current read, while Brahms or Billie Holiday or Joni Mitchell circled on the record player. Julius had never taken to modern technology: he loved vinyl, and still treasured his Grundig Audiorama speakers. They had, however, been silent for a while now.

Emilia made her way to her bedroom on the next floor, peeled back her duvet and climbed into the high brass bed that had been hers since she could remember. She pulled a cushion from the pile and hugged it to her, for warmth as much as comfort. She drew her knees up and waited to cry. There were no tears. She waited and waited, but her eyes were dry. She thought she must be a monster, not to be able to weep.

She awoke sometime later to a gentle tapping on the flat door. She started awake, wondering why she was in bed fully clothed. The realisation hit her in the chest and she wanted nothing more than to slide back into the oblivion she had been in. But there were people to see, things to do, decisions to be made. And a door to answer. She ran downstairs in her socks and opened it gingerly.

'Sweetheart.'

June. Stalwart, redoubtable June, arguably Nightingale Books' best customer since she had retired to Peasebrook three years before. She had stepped into Julius's shoes when he went into the cottage hospital for what looked like the final time. June had run her own company for more than forty years and was only too willing to pick up the reins along with Mel and Dave. With her fine bone structure, her thick dark hair and her armful of silver bangles, she looked at least ten years younger than her three score years and ten. She had the energy of a twenty-year-old, the brain of a rocket scientist and the heart of a lion. Emilia had at first thought there might be a romance between June and Julius – June was twice divorced – yet their friendship had been firm but purely platonic.

Emilia realised she should have phoned June as soon as it happened. But she hadn't had the strength or the words or the heart. She didn't have them now. She just stood there, and June wrapped her up in an embrace that was as soft and warm as the cashmere jumpers she draped herself in.

'You poor baby,' she crooned, and it was only then Emilia found she could cry.

'There's no need to open the shop today,' June told Emilia later, when she'd sobbed her heart out and had finally agreed to make herself some breakfast. But Emilia was adamant it should stay open.

'Everyone comes in on a Thursday. It's market day,' she said.

In the end, it turned out to be the best thing she could have done. Mel, usually loquacious, was mute with shock. Dave, usually monosyllabic, spoke for five minutes with-out drawing breath about how Julius had taught him everything he knew. Mel put Classic FM on the shop radio so they didn't feel the need to fill the silence. Dave, who had many mysterious skills, of which calligraphy was one, wrote a sign for the window:

> *It is with great sadness that we have to tell you*
> *of the death of Julius Nightingale*
> *Peacefully, after a short illness*
> *A beloved father, friend and bookseller*

They opened a little late, but open they did. And a stream of customers trickled in throughout the day, to pay their respects and give Emilia their condolences. Some brought cards; others casseroles and a tin full of home-baked muffins; someone else left a bottle of Chassagne-Montrachet, her father's favourite wine, on the counter.

Emilia had needed no convincing that her father was a wonderful man, but by the end of the day she realised that everyone else who knew him thought that too. Mel made countless cups of tea in the back office and carried them out on a tray.

'Come for supper,' said June, when they finally flipped the sign to CLOSED long after they should have shut.

'I'm not very hungry,' said Emilia, who couldn't face the thought of food.

June wouldn't take no for an answer. She dragged Emilia up and took her back to her sprawling cottage on the outskirts of Peasebrook. June was the sort of person who always had a shepherd's pie on standby to put in the Aga. Emilia had to admit that she felt much stronger after two servings, and it gave her the fortitude to discuss the things she didn't want to.

'I can't face a big funeral,' she said eventually.

'Then don't have one,' said June, scooping out some

vanilla ice cream for pudding. 'Have a small private funeral, and we can have a memorial service in a few weeks' time. It's much nicer that way round. And it will give you time to organise it properly.'

A tear plopped onto Emilia's ice cream. She wiped away the next one.

'What are we going to do without him?'

June handed her a jar of salted caramel sauce.

'I don't know,' she replied. 'There are some people who leave a bigger hole than others, and your father is one of them.'

June invited her to stay the night, but Emilia wanted to go home. It was always better to be sad in your own bed.

She flicked on the lights in the living room. Against its deep red walls and long tapestry curtains, there seemed to be more books here than there were in the book shop. Bookcases covered two of the walls, and there were books piled high on every surface: on the windowsills, the mantelpiece, on top of the piano. Next to that was Julius's precious cello, resting on its stand. She touched the smooth wood, realising it was covered in dust. She would play it tomorrow. She was nothing like as good a player as her father, but she hated to think of his cello unplayed, and she knew he would hate the thought too.

Emilia went over to the bookcase that was designated as hers – though she had run out of space on it long ago. She ran her finger along the spines. She wanted a comfort read; something that took her back to her childhood. Not Laura Ingalls Wilder – she couldn't bear to read of big, kind Pa at the moment. Nor Frances Hodgson Burnett – all her heroines seemed to be orphans, which Emilia realised she was too, now. She pulled out her very favourite, in its red cloth cover with the gold writing on the spine, warped with age, the pages yellowing. *Little Women*. She sat in the wing-backed chair by the fire, slinging her legs over the side and resting her cheek on a velvet cushion. Within moments, she was by the fire in Boston, with Jo March and her sisters and Marmee, hundreds of years ago and thousands of miles away . . .

By the end of the following week, Emilia felt hollowed out and exhausted. Everyone had been so kind and thoughtful and said such wonderful things about Julius, but it was emotionally draining.

There had been a small private funeral service for Julius at the crematorium, with just his mother Debra, who came down on the train from London, Andrea, Emilia's best friend from school, and June.

Before she left for the service, Emilia had looked at herself in the mirror. She wore a long black military coat and shining riding boots, her dark red hair loose over her shoulders. Her eyes were wide, with smudges underneath, defined by her thick brows and lashes. Her colouring, she knew from the photo kept on top of the piano, was her mother's; her fine bone structure and generous mouth her father's. She put in the earrings he had given her last Christmas with shaking fingers and opened the gifted Chassagne-Montrachet, knocking back just one glass, before putting on a faux fox fur hat that exactly matched her hair. She wondered briefly if she looked too much like an extra from a costume drama, but decided it didn't matter.

The next day, when they had put Julius's mother back on the Paddington train – Debra didn't like being away from London for too long – Andrea marched Emilia over the road to the Peasebrook Arms. It was a traditional coaching inn, all flagstone floors and wood panelling and a dining room that served chicken kiev and steak chasseur and had an old-fashioned dessert trolley. There was something comforting in the way it hadn't been Farrow and Balled up to the rafters. It didn't pretend to be something it wasn't. It was warm and friendly, even if the coffee was awful.

Emilia and Andrea curled up on a sofa in the lounge bar and ordered hot chocolate.

'So,' said Andrea, ever practical. 'What's your plan?'

'I've had to jack in my job,' Emilia told her. 'They can't keep it open for me indefinitely and I don't know when I'm going to get away.' She'd been teaching English at an international language school in Hong Kong. 'I can't just drift from country to country forever.'

'I don't see why not,' said Andrea.

Emilia shook her head. 'It's about time I sorted myself out. Look at us – I'm still living out of a backpack; you're a powerhouse.'

Andrea had gone from manning the phones for a financial adviser when she left school, to studying for exams at night school, to setting up her own business as an accountant. Now she did the books for many of the small businesses that had sprung up in Peasebrook over the past few years. She knew how much most people hated organising their finances and so made it as painless as possible. She was hugely successful.

'Never mind comparisons. What are you going to do with the shop?' Andrea wasn't one to beat about the bush.

Emilia shrugged. 'I haven't got any choice. I promised

21

Dad I'd keep it open. He'd turn in his grave if he thought I was going to close it down.'

Andrea didn't speak for a moment. Her voice when she spoke was gentle and kind. 'Emilia, deathbed promises don't always need to be kept. Not if they aren't practical. Of course you meant it at the time, but the shop was your *father's* life. It doesn't mean it has to be yours. He would understand. I know he would.'

'I can't bear the thought of letting it go. I always saw myself as taking it over in the end. But I guess I thought it would be when I was Dad's age. Not now. I thought he had another twenty years to go at least.' She could feel her eyes fill with tears. 'I don't know if it's even viable. I've started to look through the accounts but it's just a blur to me.'

'Well, whatever I can do to help. You know that.'

'Dad always used to say *I don't do numbers.* And I don't either, really. It all seems to be a bit disorganised. I think he let things slip towards the end. There're a couple of boxes full of receipts. And a horrible pile of unopened envelopes I haven't been able to face yet.'

'Trust me, it's nothing I haven't dealt with before.' Andrea sighed. 'I wish people wouldn't go into denial when it comes to money. It makes it all so complicated and ends up costing them much more in the end.'

'It would be great if you could have a look for me. But no mate's rates.' Emilia pointed a finger at her. 'I'm paying you properly.'

'I'm very happy to help you out. Your dad was always kind to me when we were growing up.'

Emilia laughed. 'Remember when we tried to set him up with your mum?'

Andrea snorted into her wine glass. 'That would have been a disaster.' Andrea's mother was a bit of a hippy, all joss sticks and flowing skirts. Andrea had rebelled completely against her mother's Woodstock attitude and was the most conventional, aspirational, law-abiding person Emilia knew. She'd even changed her name from Autumn when she started up in business, on the basis that no one would take an accountant called Autumn seriously. 'They would never have got anything done.'

Julius was very easygoing and laissez-faire too. The thought of their respective parents together made the two girls helpless with laughter now, but at the age of twelve they had thought it was a brilliant idea.

As they finished laughing, Emilia sighed. 'Dad never did find anyone.'

'Oh come off it. Every woman in Peasebrook was in love with your father. He had them all running round after him.'

'Yes, I know. He was never short of female company. But it would have been nice for him to have met someone special.'

'He was a happy man, Emilia. You could tell that.'

'I always felt guilty. That perhaps he stayed single because of me.'

'I don't think so. Your dad wasn't the martyr type. I think he was really happy with his own company. Or maybe he did have someone special but we just don't know about it.'

Emilia nodded. 'I hope so . . . I really do.'

She'd never know now, she thought. For all of her life it had just been the two of them and now her father had gone, with all his stories and his secrets.

2

The book shop was in Little Clarendon Street. Away from the hurly-burly of Oxford town centre and just off St Giles, it was bedded in amongst a sprinkling of fashionable dress shops and cafés. As well as the latest fiction and coffee-table books, it sold art supplies and had an air of frivolity rather than the academic ambience of Blackwell's or one of the more cerebral book shops in town. It was the sort of book shop that stole time: people had been known to miss meetings and trains, lost amongst the shelves.

Julius Nightingale had started working there to supplement his student grant since he'd first come up to Oxford, just over four years ago. And now he'd completed his Masters, he didn't want to leave Oxford or the shop. He didn't want to leave academia either, really, but he knew he had to get on with life, that his wasn't the sort of background that could sustain a life of learning. What he was going to do he had no idea as yet.

He'd decided to spend the summer after his MA scraping some money together, working at the shop full-time. Then maybe squeeze in some travel before embarking upon the gruelling collation of a CV, job applications and interviews. Apart from a brilliant first, there was nothing much to mark him out, he thought. He'd directed a few plays, but who hadn't? He'd edited a poetry magazine, but again – hardly unique. He liked live music, wine, pretty girls – there was nothing out of the ordinary about him, except the fact that most people seemed to like him. As a West London boy with a posh but penniless single mother, he'd gone to a huge inner city comprehensive. He was streetwise but well mannered and so mixed easily with both the toffs and the grammar school types who had less confidence than their public school peers.

It was the last weekend in August, and he was thinking about going up to his mother's and heading for the Notting Hill Carnival. He'd been going since he was small and he loved the atmosphere, the pounding bass, the pervasive scent of dope, the sense that anything could happen. He was about to close up when the door opened and a girl whirlwinded in. She had a tangle of hair, bright red – it couldn't be natural; it was the colour of a pillar box – and china-white skin, even whiter against the black lace of her dress. She looked, he thought, like a star, one of those singers who paraded around as if they'd been in the dressing-up box and had put everything on.

'I need a book,' she told him, and he was surprised at her accent. American. Americans, in his experience, came in clutching guidebooks and cameras, not looking as if they'd walked out of a nightclub.

'Well, you've come to the right place, then,' he replied, hoping his tone sounded teasing, not tart.

She looked at him, then held her finger and thumb apart about two inches. 'It needs to be at least this big. It has to last me the plane journey home. Ten hours. And I read very fast.'

'OK.' Julius liked a brief. 'Well, my first suggestion would be *Anna Karenina*.'

She smiled, showing perfect white teeth.

'"All happy families are alike. Each unhappy family is unhappy in its own way."'

He nodded.

'OK. What about *Ulysses*? James Joyce? That would keep you quiet.'

She struck a theatrical pose. '"Yes I said yes I will yes."'

She was quoting Molly Bloom, the hero's promiscuous wife, and for a moment Julius imagined she was just how Molly had looked, before reminding himself Molly was a work of fiction. He was impressed. He didn't know many people who could quote Joyce. He refused to be intimidated by her apparently universal knowledge of literature. He would scale his recommendation down to something more populist, but a book he had long admired.

'*The World According to Garp*?'

She beamed at him. She had an impossibly big dimple in her right cheek.

'Good answer. I love John Irving. But I prefer *The Hotel New Hampshire* to *Garp*.'

Julius grinned. It was a long time since he had met someone as widely read as this girl. He knew well-read people, of course: Oxford was brimming with them. But they tended to be intellectual snobs. This girl was a challenge, though.

'How about *Middlemarch*?'

She opened her mouth to respond, and he could see

immediately he'd hit upon something she hadn't read. She had the grace to laugh.

'Perfect,' she announced. 'Do you have a copy?'

'Of course.' He led her over to the bookshelf and pulled out an orange Penguin classic.

They stood there for a moment, Julius holding the book, the girl looking at him.

'What's your favourite book?' she asked.

He was flummoxed. Both by the question and the fact she had asked it. He turned it over in his mind. He was about to answer when she held up a finger.

'You can only have one answer.'

'But it's like asking which is your favourite child!'

'You have to answer.'

He could see she was going to stand her ground. He had his answer – *1984*, small but perfectly crafted, never failed to chill and thrill him – but he wasn't going to give in to her that easily.

'I'll tell you,' he said, not sure where his boldness had come from, 'if you come out for a drink with me.'

She crossed her arms and tilted her head to one side. 'I don't know that I'm that interested.' But her smile belied her statement.

'You should be,' he answered, and walked away from her over to the till, hoping she would follow. She was capricious. She wanted a tussle and for him not to give up. He was determined to give her a run for her money.

She did follow. He rang up the book and she handed over a pound note.

'There's a band on tonight,' he told her. 'It'll be rough cider and grubby punks, but I can't think of a better way for an American girl to spend her last night in England.'

He slid the book into its bag and handed it to her. She was gazing at him in something close to disbelief, with a hint of fascination.

Julius had always been quietly confident with girls. He respected them. He liked them for their minds rather than their looks, and somehow this made him magnetic. He was thoughtful, yet a little enigmatic. He was very different from the rather cocky public school types at Oxford. He dressed a little differently too – a romantic bohemian, in velvet jackets and scarves, his hair lightly bleached. And he was pretty – cheekbones and wide eyes, which he occasionally highlighted with eyeliner. Growing up in London had given him the courage to do this without fear of derision from those who didn't understand the fashion of the times.

'Why the hell not?' she said finally.

'I'll be there from eight,' he told her.

It was twenty past eight by the time he got to the pub. She was nowhere to be seen. He couldn't be sure whether she was late too or had been and gone. Or simply wasn't going to turn up at all. He wasn't going to let it worry him. If it was meant to be . . .

He ordered a pint of murky cider from the bar, tasting its musty appleness, then made his way out to find a bench in the last of the sunshine. It was a popular but fairly rough pub he loved for its unpretentiousness. And it always had good bands on. There was a sense of festiveness and expectation in the air, a final farewell from the sun in this last week of summer. Julius felt a change coming. Whether it would be to do with the girl with the red hair, he couldn't be certain, but he had a feeling it might.

At nine, he felt a sharp tap on his shoulder. He turned, and she was there.

'I wasn't going to come,' she told him. 'Because I didn't want to fall in love with you and then have to get on a plane tomorrow.'

'Falling in love is optional.'

'Not always.' She looked serious.

'Well, let's see what we can do to avoid it.' He stood up and picked up his empty pint glass. 'Have you tried scrumpy yet?'

'No.' She looked doubtful.

He bought her half a pint, because grown men had been known to weep after just two pints of this particular brew. They watched the band, a crazy gypsy-punk outfit that sang songs of heartbreak and harvest moons. He bought her another half and watched her smile get lazier and her eyes half close. He wanted nothing more than to tangle his fingers in her pre-Raphaelite curls.

'Where are you staying tonight?' he asked, as the band started packing up and tipsy revellers began to make their way out of the pub into the warm night.

She put her arms around his neck and pushed her body hard against his. 'With you,' she whispered, and her mouth on his tasted of the last apples of summer.

Later, as they lay holding each other in the remains of the night's heat, she murmured, 'You never told me.'

'What?'

'Your favourite book.'

'*1984*.'

She considered his answer, gave a nod of approval, closed her eyes and fell asleep.

*

He woke the next morning, pinioned by her lily-white arm. He wondered what time her flight was, how she was getting to the airport, whether she had packed – they hadn't discussed practicalities the night before. He didn't want to wake her because he felt safe with her so close. He'd never experienced such a feeling before. A feeling of utter completeness. It made so many of the books he had read start to make perfect sense. He had thought he understood them, on an intellectual level, but now he had a deeper comprehension. He could barely breathe with the awe of it.

If he stayed very still and very quiet, perhaps she wouldn't wake. Perhaps she would miss her flight. Perhaps he could have another magical twenty-four hours with her.

But Julius was responsible at heart. He didn't have it in him to be so reckless. So he picked up a tress of her hair and tickled her cheek until she stirred.

'Hey,' he whispered. 'You have to go home today.'

'I don't want to go,' Rebecca murmured into his shoulder.

He trailed a hand across her warm, bare skin. 'You can come back.'

He touched each of her freckles, one by one. There were hundreds. Thousands. He would never have time to touch them all before she left.

'What time is your flight? How are you getting to the airport?'

She didn't reply. She picked up his arm and looked at the watch on his wrist.

'My flight's at one.'

He sat up in alarm. It was gone ten. 'Shit. You need to

get up. You'll never make it. I can drive you, but I don't think you'll get there in time.'

He was grabbing for his clothes, pulling them on. She didn't move.

'I'm not going.'

He was doing up his jeans. He stared at her.

'What?'

'I made up my mind. Last night.' She sat up, and her hair tumbled everywhere. 'I want to stay here. With you.'

Julius laughed. 'You can't.' He felt slight panic.

She looked up at him from the middle of the bed, wide-eyed.

'You don't feel the same as me? As if you've met the love of your life?'

'Well, yes, but . . .' It had been an incredible night, he had to admit that. And he was smitten, if that was the right word. But Julius was sensible enough to realise you didn't make momentous decisions off the back of a one-night stand.

Rebecca, it seemed, thought differently.

'It makes perfect sense. I want to major in English. I want to do it in the best place in the world. Which is here in Oxford, right?'

'Well, yes. I suppose so. Or Cambridge.'

'I'm smart enough. I know I am. If I can get into Brown, I can get into Oxford.'

Julius laughed again. Not at her, but at her confidence. The girls he knew were never as brazen about their abilities. They were brought up to be modest and self-effacing. Rebecca wore her brilliance with pride.

She crossed her arms. 'Don't laugh at me.'

'I'm not. I just think you're being a bit rash.' That was an understatement.

'I'm not getting on that plane.'

Julius gulped. She was serious. Besides, there was no way she was going to get her plane now. And as far as he knew, she had nowhere else to go.

'What are your parents going to say?'

'How can they argue?'

'Easily, I'd have thought. Aren't you supposed to be going to college?'

'Yes. But you know what? It never felt right. I was just going because that's what I was expected to do. But this feels right. I can *feel* it here.'

She pressed a fist to her heart. Julius looked at her warily, not sure if she was serious. He knew plenty of fanciful girls but they usually had a limit to their capriciousness. He felt anxious: clever, wilful and rich was a deadly combination, and he was pretty sure Rebecca was all of those. He'd got enough insight into her life to know it was very privileged.

Which was why she felt entitled to the ultimate privilege.

'It's what I deserve.' She scrambled out of bed. 'I'm going to get a job. Right here. In Oxford. And I'm going to sit the entrance exam and get a place to study here next year.'

She looked a little crazed. He wasn't sure how to handle her. She was alien to him. The usual arguments weren't going to work. He decided to pretend he thought she was joking.

'It's the scrumpy,' said Julius. 'It does that to you.'

'You think I'm kidding, right?'

Julius scratched his head. 'I'm not sure you've thought it through.'

'Sure I have. I mean, what's the problem? Why not? Seriously, tell me why not. It's not like I'm running off with the lead singer of a rock band. I want to go to the best university in the world. Surely that's a good thing?'

She was one of those infuriating people who made the craziest of ideas seem utterly plausible.

'Look, let me drive you to the airport. You can change your ticket, go home and talk to your parents. If they agree, you can come back.'

'Am I freaking you out?'

'Well, yes, actually. A bit.'

She came over and put her arms around his neck. He breathed her in, his heart pounding. He felt weightless from lack of sleep and too much of her. He felt electrified, but he also felt responsible, because he knew his reaction would dictate what happened next: their future. He should take control; slow things down a bit.

'This is the most amazing thing that's ever happened. You and me. Don't you feel that?' she demanded.

'Well, yes. It actually is. Amazing. I am . . . amazed.' Julius could see she was carried away. Would there come a moment when she stopped to think and realised she was fantasising? That her vision was riddled with complications? 'But I still think you should talk to your parents.'

As he said it, he thought how boring he sounded. But he wasn't going to be responsible for her screwing her life up, or incurring the wrath of her family.

'I'm going to. Right now.' By Rebecca's reaction, it didn't seem to occur to her they might not think it a good idea. 'I think they'll be really excited. My dad loves

England – he did an exchange when he was just a bit older than me and spent six months here. It's why he sent me over for the summer. Where's the nearest phone?'

'There's a pay phone downstairs in the hall,' said Julius. 'But you'll have to reverse the charges. And do you think they'll appreciate being woken up? Maybe you should wait until this afternoon?'

'Maybe you're right. It's three in the morning. Let's go and get something to eat while we wait. I'm starving!'

He took her for a traditional English fry-up – the ultimate hangover cure – and prayed that after some sustenance the combined effects of the scrumpy and their torrid night might recede a little. No such luck. By three o'clock that afternoon she was as determined as ever to see her plan through. She was resolute as she phoned them – he imagined her parents in their perfect New England kitchen being shocked to discover that they weren't going to be driving to the airport that afternoon to collect her after all. He wondered if they were used to flights of fancy from Rebecca. Whether she would come upstairs in a few minutes, crushed and dissuaded.

He listened to her voice floating up the staircase.

'Oxford is me, Daddy. As soon as I got here I knew. This is where I want to be. This is where I want to study. It's in my bones and my blood and my heart and my soul . . .' Julius raised an eyebrow. She was very convincing. 'You *know* how wonderful it is. You told me yourself. You'll just have to come back here and see for yourself. If you don't agree with me, I'll come home with you. That's the deal, Daddy.'

Wow. She was a fierce negotiator all right.

She came back up the stairs and jumped into the middle of his bed.

'Daddy's coming over. He thinks it's a fabulous idea, but he wants to see everything for himself.'

Julius looked around his room. 'He's not going to be too impressed with this.'

Julius loved his bedroom, but it wasn't the sort of room that would gladden a father's heart. He'd painted the walls inky dark purple. They were smothered in postcards he'd collected over the years, of his heroes and heroines, from Hemingway to Marilyn Monroe. There was a record player in the corner – his biggest investment – and a stack of records four feet long. A mattress on the floor served as both a sofa and a bed. His clothes were hung on a makeshift rail: charity shop suits and a collection of hats. He was quite the dandy. In another corner were a kettle and a gas ring. Despite his best intentions there were more empty Pot Noodle pots in the bin than he could count. There were so many more interesting things to do than try and conjure up something nutritious in the health hazard that was the kitchen downstairs. Julius liked food, and cooking, but he didn't want tetanus.

'It's fine. I don't have to show him this. I'll tell him I'm staying in some all-girls' hostel and I'm looking for accommodation. And we need to make sure you stay out of the way.'

'Oh.' Julius was a little stung.

She put her arms around him.

'I didn't mean that like it sounded. If my dad thinks there's a guy involved, he'll drag me back home by the scruff of my neck. Give it a few weeks. Then I can casually mention you. Maybe you could come to New England for Christmas!'

Julius nodded, not a little daunted by the plan. It was all going a bit too fast for him. He had, after all, only met her the day before, and she had turned her whole life upside down on the basis of one night together. Yet he had to agree: the attraction between them was undeniable. He was enchanted by her; she was besotted with him. It was physical and mental and spiritual. All-consuming and intoxicating. He was secretly delighted by her nerve. He was fairly sure he wouldn't have the same mettle. He, after all, had nothing to lose by going along with her plan.

By the time Rebecca's father arrived the following Thursday and checked into the Randolph, Rebecca had persuaded Julius's manager to give her a part-time job in the shop. On her first day of work there, she sorted through all the miscellaneous boxes of old books in the stockroom and either returned them or put them out on the shelves, a job no one ever wanted to do.

And she had worked her way through the colleges and grilled several of the admissions tutors as to the likelihood of her getting a place to study. She came back with a sheaf of past papers to revise with. She had less than two months to get up to speed for the entrance exam.

Julius was impressed. When this girl wanted something, she went all out to get it.

'I knew my life was going to change as soon as I met you,' she told him. 'This is the most exciting thing that's ever happened to me. I can't believe I could be packing to go to the most boring college on the planet right now.'

When Julius answered the door to her after her visit to

her father, he didn't recognise her. She was dressed in a pair of grey trousers ('pants') and a white blouse, her hair parted in the middle and tied back in a neat ponytail. She burst out laughing when she saw his puzzled face.

She pulled her hair out of its band and started to undo her shirt as she pushed her way past him and headed up the stairs.

'He thinks I'm a genius,' she told Julius. 'We walked around all his old haunts and he's totally fallen back in love with Oxford. And it will be such a status symbol – none of his friends will have a daughter at college in England. He's paying my rent, and my fees if I get in. I have to go home for Thanksgiving and Christmas and Easter. That's the deal. It's a small price to pay.'

The two of them fell back onto the rumpled sheets, laughing in delight, at each other and the thrill of her new adventure. Julius couldn't resist Rebecca's enthusiasm or her guile or her body. There was a tiny little voice that warned him to be careful, but as he raked his fingers through her red hair to mess it up again, and ran his mouth over her small, round breasts, it was easy to ignore it. He was older and wiser than she. He could manage her.

Couldn't he? Julius knew this was something different: attraction on another scale to anything he had experienced before. Was it infatuation, he wondered, or would it become true love? And if so, which kind? Love, he knew from books, was not always a force for good, but he would do his best to make his so.

Yet he had a feeling Rebecca would not be able to control her feelings in the same way he could. She was far more passionate and impetuous. In just a short time, he could see she was a little bit of a fly-by-night, and the last thing you did with fly-by-nights was try to pin them down. He would give her his heart, and his head.

In the meantime, he showed her more of her new world. It was wonderful, rediscovering Oxford through someone else's eyes. He'd been there over four years now, and he'd stopped seeing the beauty and the wonder in quite the same way. He'd begun to assume everyone lived in a cosy bubble of cobbles and cloisters and grassy greens and bicycles. But he was fiercely proud of it, and showing Rebecca the landmarks made him realise why he had been dragging his feet, how he hadn't wanted to make a decision about his future in case it involved leaving Oxford, and now he didn't have to.

He showed her his room in his old college, and she gasped at its antiquity and its rudimentary facilities and the fact it was straight out of *Brideshead Revisited*.

'Where is your teddy bear?' she demanded, laughing.

'I promise you: I couldn't be less like Sebastian Flyte. There's no stately home to take you back to.'

'Oh,' she said, feigning disappointment. 'And there was me imagining myself as the lady of the manor.'

'We'll get our own little manor,' he said, pulling her to him. 'It might not be Brideshead, but it will be ours.'

He took her to a concert he was playing in. He played the cello, and the orchestra was decidedly third rate, because Oxford was stuffed with brilliant musicians and players and he wasn't up to one of the more elite outfits, but she thought he was incredible, sitting in the front pew of the church and not taking her eyes off him once during Fauré's *Requiem*.

'Is there anything you can't do?' she asked. 'I've never met anyone who can do so many things.'

'Scrape out a tune on the cello and make a chicken casserole?' he laughed, self-deprecating to the end. She was even impressed with his cooking skills, which were self-taught and based on years of trial and error brought about by his mother's utter disinterest in anything on a plate.

They worked out they could stay together in Oxford for the next four years, while she studied. Julius was going to look for something that paid better than the book shop, so they could find a little house of their own to rent.

'You're not to worry too much,' said Rebecca. 'I only have to wire home for more cash if we get short.'

Julius looked at her, appalled. 'We will do no such thing.'

He didn't believe in sponging off your parents. It was one of the first things he taught her, the idea of standing on your own two feet. And she understood the principle, even if he knew she was still being subsidised. He couldn't expect her to break the habits of a lifetime straight away.

Summer turned to autumn, and was even more idyllic. They took long walks by the river and ate sausages and chips in the pub, wandered through all the curious exhibits in the Pitt Rivers museum – she exclaimed incessantly over the stuffed dodo – and went to more concerts. Her musical knowledge was scanty, but Julius introduced her to string quartets and garage bands, choral works that made tears course down her cheeks, and lazy Sunday afternoon jazz.

And Julius coached her for her exam, pushing her to read texts and memorise quotes and write essay after essay. Not that she needed pushing. She was more motivated than any student he'd ever met, and her memory was seemingly infallible. She could quote reams after just one reading.

'I'm a freak,' she told him. 'I could recite the whole of *What Katy Did* by the time I was seven.'

'You *are* a freak,' he teased her, but in fact he was more than a little daunted by her brain power. He thought she could probably take over the world. Yet she wasn't wrapped up in scholarship. She wanted as much fun as the next student. He nursed her through her first hangover, let her try her first joint, gave her a driving lesson in his ancient brown Mini around a disused airfield – she had her American license, but gears were a mystery to her, and he was secretly pleased when it took her a little while to understand clutch control.

'So you're not perfect,' he remarked, and she was furious with him.

She took the entrance exam and was confident she'd passed (yet again Julius was bewitched by this confidence of hers and explained to her that everyone in England always insisted they had failed every exam they sat). She told her parents she'd moved out of her digs and into a shared house, without going into too much detail about whom she was sharing it with.

'They trust me,' she told Julius.

'That's their first mistake,' he replied, and she pretended to be outraged.

Socially, they were a king and queen. Everyone wanted their company, at the most Rabelaisian of parties. They were young, and they ran on very little sleep and very little money. Wine and music were all that mattered, and good conversation, and books. They talked about books day and night. They were allowed to take books from the book shop and return them once read, as long as they didn't damage them. They read a book a day each, sometimes two. It was bliss. She fell upon Muriel Spark and Iris Murdoch and was entranced by her namesake, *Rebecca*, devouring every other Daphne du Maurier she could lay her hands on. On her recommendation he discovered John Updike and Philip Roth and Norman Mailer. He wrote her his ultimate list of cult classics; she made him read *Middlemarch* when he admitted he hadn't.

More than once, it occurred to Julius to ask Rebecca to marry him, but something stopped him. He wanted them to be financially secure, and to be able to afford a house of their own. Although he fantasised about a discreet wedding in a registry office followed by a wild party to celebrate on the banks of the Cherwell, marriage was definitely for grown-ups and they weren't grown up yet. Instead, he began to put away some of his wages into a building society account, to save for a deposit, and if it meant just one bottle of red wine instead of two to go with the spaghetti on a Friday night, she didn't notice.

'You're my princess,' he told her.

'Princess is not such a good thing where I come from. It's a pejorative term, for a woman who wants her own way all the time,' Rebecca told him.

'Like I said,' replied Julius. 'You're my princess.' And she laughed.

He knew his mother, Debra, would be tolerant of the situation, because Debra was broad-minded and he didn't think she had told him off, ever, in his life.

They drove up to London and Debra took them out for lunch at a wine bar in Kensington. The walls were covered in a mural of grape vines, and they ate chicken cacciatore and chocolate fudge cake.

Rebecca was fascinated by Debra, with her strings of amber beads and endless St Moritz cigarettes and her husky drawl. Debra had a world-weariness about her. You got the sense she had seen and done everything, even though she now lived a very tame existence. She wasn't in the least intimidated by Rebecca's fierce IQ or force of personality or brazen dress sense. They were a match for each other in their own inimitable ways.

When Rebecca went to the loo at the end of lunch, Debra lit another cigarette.

'Be careful, darling,' she said. 'The bubble won't last forever.'

Julius told himself his mother was just being protective. Which was odd, because she hadn't been when he was young. She'd left him to get on with it much of the time. He wondered what had changed.

He sighed. 'Better to have loved and all that.'

'I just don't want to see you hurt if things go wrong.'

'What can go wrong?'

Debra blew out a plume of smoke. 'Any number of things.'

Julius was determined not to be unsettled by his mother's warning. And when Rebecca came back to the table and put her arm around him and called him her guardian angel, he smiled at Debra as if to say 'See?'

'Your mom is so cool,' said Rebecca as they trundled back down the A40.

Julius rolled his eyes.

'My mum's never had to worry about anyone except herself,' he said, trying to shake off the sense of foreboding

Debra had given him. He was cross: just because she was world-weary didn't mean she had to spoil it for everyone else, did it? 'She doesn't care what anyone else thinks.'

'She's the exact opposite of mine, then,' said Rebecca. 'My mom cares what everyone thinks. Right down to the mail man.'

Debra was right, though.

Julius supposed he should have seen it coming. But then, why should he?

The thing was, all the girls he'd ever dallied with had been on the pill. It was almost a given – most girls put themselves on it when they went off to university, if they weren't already. A quick trip to their local doctor and they were covered. It had never occurred to him that Americans might be different. That Rebecca might have landed on English soil without organising contraception before she left. Of course, everyone at Oxford was pretty casual about sex. There was a fair amount of bed-hopping. Julius had been as guilty as anyone, but not once he met Rebecca. He knew the love of his life when he saw it. Yet he'd forgotten the key question.

So when she sat up one morning, looking green at the gills, then bolted to the bathroom, he was shocked into silence when she told him why.

'I think I'm pregnant.'

'Aren't you on the pill?'

She shook her head.

'Why didn't you tell me?' He was appalled – at both his negligence and hers. 'I just assumed . . . Surely you realised this might happen?'

She put her face in her hands. 'I guess I just hoped.'

'Hoped?'

'For the best.'

'That's not the most reliable form of contraception.'

'No.' She looked utterly forlorn. She sat in the middle of the bed, holding her stomach.

'Well, I suppose we should go to the Family Planning Clinic.'

'What's that?'

'It's where you go for contraception. Or, um...'

She held up a hand.

'Don't say it. Don't say that word.'

He didn't want to say the word. 'They can arrange... things for you.'

She stared at him. 'It's out of the question.'

He blinked. It hadn't occurred to him that wasn't the route she would want to go down. 'Oh. Right. OK. Um...' He scratched his head. 'So what is the plan?'

'What do you mean?'

'You want to go to university. We live in one room. We don't really have any money.'

She lay back on the bed and stared at the ceiling. 'We don't have any choice. I'm not getting rid of it. I'm not getting rid of our baby.'

Julius wasn't sure what to think or feel. This was an eventuality he hadn't prepared for. He didn't really know anyone else who'd been in this situation. He knew a couple of girls who'd been caught out, but they'd sorted things quickly and quietly and learnt their lesson. He certainly didn't know anyone who'd gone ahead and had a baby. But he wasn't going to force Rebecca into anything she didn't want to do.

'What are you going to tell your parents?'

She gave a heavy sigh. She didn't answer for a moment.

'I'll tell them when I go home for Thanksgiving. At the end of the month.' She sat up, and to his surprise, she was smiling. 'A baby, Julius. I knew when I saw you, you were going to be the father of my children.'

'Well, that's lovely,' said Julius, thinking that was all very well but he would have liked to wait a little longer. He didn't say that, though. 'We're going to have to find somewhere better to live. And I'll have to get a decent job.'

Bugger, he thought. It was his own stupid fault. It was his responsibility as much as hers. He should never have assumed.

Rebecca got up to be sick again. And Julius looked around the room that had been their home for the past few months and thought: I'm going to be a father.

Rebecca didn't tell her family when she flew back to New England for Thanksgiving. She was still as slim as a reed, because she wasn't even three months gone, and she had thrown up every morning and every evening like clockwork, despite devouring sugary, fatty lardy cakes Julius brought her from the bakery.

'There just wasn't a good time. I wasn't there for long enough, and there were so many visitors. I'll tell them at Christmas.'

By Christmas, she was putting on weight, but it was cold, so she was able to wrap herself in swathes of baggy clothing. She still didn't reveal her secret.

'I didn't tell them. I didn't want to ruin the holiday.'

'It's getting a bit late.' Julius was anxious. He had told his mother, who had expressed no surprise. But nothing surprised or shocked Debra, who'd been there and seen it and done it all.

'Just don't expect me to babysit,' was all she told him, and he laughed, but didn't say she was the last person he would leave a child with.

By the time Rebecca was four months pregnant, she found out she had got a place at Oxford and finally told her family. Julius realised it was because before then she'd been afraid they might force her into something she didn't want to do. She had a will of iron, but pregnancy had made her vulnerable and pliable and she'd feared that on home territory she might be brainwashed.

'You? Brainwashed?' Julius was disbelieving.

'I'm not as tough as I make out,' she told him. 'And you don't know my family.' She made a face. 'Daddy's flying over.'

'I thought you had your dad wrapped around your little finger?'

'There's a difference,' she said, 'between wanting to study at the best university in the world, and having a baby at nineteen.'

'It'll be fine,' Julius told her. 'I'm here to back you up.'

She was frightened, Julius realised, despite her fighting talk. And he thought perhaps she feared she might capitulate, because it would be the easy option. How awful, he thought, to fear manipulation by your own family. Debra might be on her own planet, but she was never interfering or controlling. In that moment, he swore to himself that he would never try and control his own child. That he would be supportive without being manipulative.

He wondered if Thomas Quinn was going to turn up with a shotgun. He was ready for him, if so. Julius didn't much care about how Thomas Quinn felt – he was only concerned for Rebecca and his unborn child. There was

46

a limit, in certain situations, as to how many people's sensibilities you could address.

Thomas Quinn was surprisingly measured and calm about the situation. Rebecca came back from meeting him a little subdued, but relieved that there hadn't been a scene.

'It would have been different if my mom had come over,' she told Julius. 'Dad says she can't even speak about it. I know Mom. She'll turn it round to be her crisis. Her drama.'

'She sounds awful,' said Julius.

'She just doesn't like anything that doesn't fit into her vision of how things should be.'

'I suppose she's not alone in that.'

'No. But boy, do you know about it if it's your fault.'

'Well, it's lucky she's not here.'

'Yes,' agreed Rebecca. 'Dad wants to meet you, though.'

'No problem,' said Julius. 'I think we should meet.'

He wanted to reassure Thomas Quinn as much as he could.

Rebecca eyed him with interest. 'You're very brave.'

Julius shrugged. 'I've done nothing wrong.'

'You do know most guys would have totally freaked out.'

'There's no point in getting hysterical. Or pretending it hasn't happened. You've just got to get on with it.'

Rebecca hugged him. 'You know what? You make me feel safe. I never knew that's what I wanted...'

Julius met Rebecca's father Thomas the next day in the drawing room of the suite he had hired. Rebecca had decided to keep out of the way.

'I'll only get emotional if he says something I don't want to hear. Don't let him bully you.'

'Don't worry,' said Julius. He wasn't nervous, though he was apprehensive. He didn't want to make a tricky situation turn nasty.

Thomas Quinn was scrupulously polite, ushering him in and ordering coffee. It was a little bit surreal, thought Julius, sitting in opposing armchairs in this formal setting. He felt like a head of state about to discuss foreign policy.

'I want to make this situation as least disruptive as possible,' Thomas told him. 'You know, of course, what a smart girl Rebecca is. She has a very bright future.'

'Yes,' said Julius. 'She's very clever. Far cleverer than I am.'

'And, as her father, it would be wrong of me not to want her to make the most of her potential.'

'I'm sure that's what we all want for our children.'

Julius held his gaze.

Thomas Quinn cleared his throat.

'I appreciate that you have been a gentleman and agreed to stand by her. Rebecca tells me what a tower of strength you are. How supportive. I'm very grateful.'

This wasn't quite the tack Julius had expected. He'd anticipated disapproval. Criticism.

'Thank you,' he replied, wondering what was coming next.

'However, I think you're both being idealistic. I don't think either of you really have any idea of the impact having a baby will have on your careers, your lifestyle, your economic circumstances. I mean, you don't actually have a career, as yet – do you? You're working in a book shop?'

Julius stared, intense dislike starting to boil up inside him. He'd thought it was too good to be true. He remained calm and polite.

'Yes. But I have a good degree. I'm quite confident—'

'Your confidence is charming. But you're being naïve. Take it from me. I've had three children. Good intentions are all very well in theory. Admirable. But you will find the reality a very different story.'

'Mr Quinn, people have children every day and bring them up perfectly well—'

Thomas Quinn cut him off again. 'I don't want to see my daughter's potential wasted. I want her to be the best person she can be. I don't think having a baby at nineteen is going to enable that. No matter how much support she has from you.'

'She can carry on her studies. We'll find a way.'

Thomas gave a dismissive snort.

'Look, I'm not going to pretend I think this is a good idea on any level. Rebecca is a pistol, on the surface. But underneath, she's actually very vulnerable. And not as strong as she comes across. Believe me, I'm her father. I know Rebecca. Which is why I'm so very concerned. I know you think this is about her mother and me, but it isn't. I'm very worried. And I can see she thinks the world of you, and would listen to what you have to say.'

Julius felt a growing sense of horror. 'It's too late for an abortion. If that's what you're thinking.'

He was pleased to see Thomas flinch. Julius wasn't going to mince his words to spare this man's feelings.

'I know that,' said Thomas carefully. 'But it's not too late to give the baby up for adoption.'

Julius couldn't hide his shock. He wasn't sure he'd heard right. 'What?'

He crossed his arms and stared at the man who, in theory, had things gone in the right order and more happily, might have been his father-in-law.

Thomas walked over to the latticed window of the hotel room. Julius stared at his broad back and wondered what he was actually thinking. Was he really doing the best for his daughter, or was there another agenda? Was this all about saving her reputation? Protecting the family name?

'Let me make a deal with you.' Thomas turned back, walked across the room and sat down. 'If you can persuade Rebecca to give the baby up for adoption, I will write you a cheque for fifty thousand pounds. And I will help find the very best family possible.' He held up his hand. 'Don't say anything for at least a minute. Please know that this comes from a desire to do the best for my daughter.'

Julius walked over to the window and stood where Thomas had stood. He looked out at the buildings, the colleges; the hopes and dreams of so many young people, himself included, Rebecca included, were held inside those walls. Eventually he turned.

'I suppose there aren't many problems you don't think can be solved by money.'

Thomas gave a smile.

'I am sure one day you will understand my need to protect my child,' he said. 'Especially if it's a girl.'

'I would let my daughter make her own decisions. With my guidance.'

'If you turn this offer down, I won't be giving you and Rebecca any financial support. You do understand that?'

'It hadn't even occurred to me that you might. It wasn't something I was relying on.' Julius stood up and held out his hand. 'Please, be assured that I will look after your daughter and grandchild to the best of my ability.'

'If you change your mind, the offer is there until the end of the week. Until I go back.'

'I won't be telling Rebecca about our conversation,' Julius told him. 'I don't want her upset. I'll just tell her you wished us the very best.'

Thomas Quinn didn't look shamefaced in the slightest as he shook Julius's hand.

In the end, he did tell her, because she pestered him to reveal what they had discussed.

'Did he offer you money?' she asked. 'I bet he did.'

'He wanted me to persuade you to give the baby up. For adoption.'

Rebecca was furious. 'He is *so* manipulative.'

'I think it's because he cares. I tried to put myself in his situation.'

Julius wasn't sure why he was trying to protect Thomas Quinn, but it was mostly because he didn't want Rebecca upset. He was feeling more and more protective of her, especially now the baby was showing. And so he suggested they get married.

After a certain amount of laborious paperwork, they left the registry office one sunny spring afternoon.

'You know what we should do? We should open our own book shop,' Rebecca said as they walked home, hand in hand.

Julius stopped in the middle of the pavement. 'That,' he said, 'is the best idea I've heard for a long time.'

'Nightingale Books,' said Rebecca. 'We could call it Nightingale Books.'

Julius felt a burst of joy. He could see it now, the two of them with their own little shop.

In the meantime, he got a managerial position at the book shop, which gave him a slightly higher wage, and found them a house of their own to rent: the tiniest two-bedroomed terrace in Jericho. The second bedroom was only a box room, but at least they had their own space. He spent all his spare time painting it, until it was bandbox fresh. He put up shelves and hooks so they had plenty of storage. He took Rebecca to Habitat to choose them a sofa.

'Can we afford it?' she asked.

'We'll use it every day, for the next ten years at least, so it's worth spending money on it.'

He didn't tell her Debra had given him five hundred pounds to make their lives more comfortable. He didn't want to get into comparing parents. He didn't consider taking her money to be sponging, either: Debra had offered it happily. Debra was infuriating in her own way, but she had a generous streak, and she hadn't said 'I told you so'. Just knowing she was there made him feel secure, so he understood that Rebecca must find it difficult, being semi-estranged. He wondered how her parents would react once the baby was born. He suspected they were just playing a waiting game, hoping she would crack. Hoping, no doubt, that perhaps he would abandon her when the going got tough.

Which it did.

By her third trimester, Rebecca changed in front of his eyes. She swelled up. Not just her tummy, but everything:

her fingers, her ankles, her face. She was miserable. Fretful. She couldn't sleep. She couldn't get comfortable. She stopped working at the shop and lay in bed all day.

'You have to keep active,' Julius told her, worried sick. She no longer seemed enchanted by the idea of a baby, as she had been at first. She was frightened, and fearful.

'I'm sorry. I don't feel like I'm me any more. I guess I'll be better when the baby gets here,' she told him one night, and he rubbed her back until she fell asleep.

She woke one night, three weeks before the baby was due, writhing in pain. The bed sheets were soaked.

'My waters broke,' she sobbed.

Julius phoned for an ambulance, telling himself that women went into labour early all the time and that it would be fine. Giving birth was the most natural thing in the world. The staff at the hospital reassured him of the same thing. Rebecca was put in a delivery room and examined.

'You've got an impatient baby there,' said the midwife, smiling, not looking in the least perturbed. 'It'll be a little preemie, but don't worry. We have a great track record.'

'Preemie?'

'Premature.' She put a hand on his arm. 'You're in safe hands.'

For eighteen agonising hours, Rebecca rode the waves of her pain. Julius was privately horrified that anyone should have to go through this, but if the noises coming from adjoining suites were anything to go by, it was the norm. None of the staff seemed disconcerted by Rebecca's howls as the contractions peaked. Julius did his best to keep her distress at bay.

'Does she really have to go through this?' he asked the

midwife at one point, who looked at him, slightly pitying, as if he knew nothing. Which was true – until now, he had never been in close contact with anyone pregnant, let alone watched them give birth.

Then suddenly, as if it couldn't get any worse, the complacency of the staff turned to urgency. Julius felt cold panic as the nurses compared notes and a consultant was ushered in. It was almost as if he and Rebecca didn't exist as the three of them conferred, and a decision was made.

'The baby's distressed. We're taking her into theatre,' the midwife told him, with a look that said 'don't ask any more'.

The system swooped in. Within minutes, Rebecca was wheeled out of the delivery room and off down the corridor. Julius ran to keep up with the orderlies as they reached the double doors of the theatre.

'Can I come in?' he asked.

'There's no time to gown you up,' someone replied, and suddenly there he was, alone in the corridor.

'Please don't let the baby die, please don't let the baby die,' Julius repeated, over and over, unable to imagine what was going on inside. He imagined carnage: blood and knives. At least, he thought, Rebecca's screams had stopped.

And then a nurse emerged, with something tiny in her arms, and handed it to him.

'A little girl,' she said.

He looked down at the baby's head, her shrimp of a mouth. She fitted into the crook of his arm perfectly: a warm bundle.

He knew her. He knew her already. And he laughed

with relief. For a while there he had really thought she was in danger.

'Hello,' he said. 'Hello, little one.'

And then he looked up and the surgeon was standing in the doorway with a solemn expression and he realised that he had been praying for the wrong person all along.

They kept the baby in the special care baby unit, because she was early and because of what happened.

They left the hospital two weeks later, the smallest family in the world. The baby was in a white velour Babygro, warm and soft and pliant. Julius picked up a pale yellow cellular blanket and wrapped her in it. The nurses looked on and clucked over them, as they always did when sending a new little family out into the world.

There was still a plastic bracelet on her wrist. *Baby Nightingale*, it said.

He really hoped that this was as complicated as his life was ever going to get as he stepped out of the hospital doors and into the world outside.

The baby snuffled and burrowed into his chest. She'd been fed before they left the ward, but maybe she was hungry again. Should he try another bottle before getting in the taxi? Or would that overfeed her? All this and so many questions was his future now.

He put the tip of his finger to her mouth. Her tiny lips puckered around it experimentally. It seemed to placate her.

She still hadn't got a name. She needed a name more than she needed milk. He had two favourites: Emily and Amelia. He couldn't decide between the two. And so he decided to amalgamate them.

Emilia.

Emilia Rebecca.

Emilia Rebecca Nightingale.

'Hello, Emilia,' he said, and at the sound of his voice her little head turned and her eyes widened in surprise as she looked for whoever had spoken.

'It's me,' he said. 'Dad. Daddy. I'm up here, little one. Come on, let's take you home.'

'Where's the missis, then?' the taxi driver asked him. 'Still a bit poorly? Aren't they letting her out?'

'It's just me, actually,' said Julius. He couldn't face telling him the whole story. He didn't want to upset the driver. He didn't want his sympathy.

'What – she's left you holding the baby?'

The driver looked over at him in surprise. Julius would have preferred him to keep his eyes on the road.

'Yes.' In a way, she had.

'Bloody hell. I've never heard of that. Picked up plenty of new mums whose blokes have done a runner. But never the other way round.'

'Oh,' said Julius. 'Well, I suppose it is unusual. But I'm sure I'll manage.'

'You're not very old yourself, are you?'

'Twenty-three.'

'Bloody hell,' repeated the driver.

Julius sat in the back as the taxi made its way through the outskirts of Oxford and wondered why on earth he didn't feel more scared. But he didn't. He just didn't.

He had met Thomas Quinn very briefly a few days after Rebecca's death. The Quinns were flying her body home, and Julius didn't argue with their wishes. She had been their daughter and he felt it was right for her to be buried in her homeland.

Their meeting was bleak and stiff, both men shocked by the situation. Julius was surprised that Thomas didn't blame him for his daughter's death. There was some humanity in him that made him realise anger and resentment and blame would be pointless.

Instead, he gave Julius a cheque.

'You might want to throw this back in my face, but it's for the baby. I handled everything wrongly. I should have given you both my support. Please put it to good use.'

Julius put it in his pocket. Protest and refusal would be as pointless as blame.

'Should I keep you informed of her progress...? A photo on her birthday?'

Thomas Quinn shook his head. 'There's no need. Rebecca's mother would find it too distressing. We really just need to move on.'

Julius didn't protest. Though he was surprised anyone could turn their back on their own flesh and blood, it would be easier for him, too. To have no interference.

'If you change your mind, just get in touch.'

Thomas Quinn gave a half nod, half shake of his head that indicated they probably wouldn't, but that he was grateful for the offer.

Julius walked away knowing that he had made the final transition from boy to man.

He got back to the house. It was mid-afternoon. It felt like the quietest time of day. He made himself a cup of tea, then made up a fresh bottle of baby milk and left it to cool. He put Nina Simone on the record player.

Then he lay on his bed with his knees crooked up and put Emilia on his lap so her back was resting against his thighs. He held her in place carefully and smiled. He picked up his camera and took a photo.

His baby girl, only two weeks old.

He put the camera down.

As the piano played out he pretended to make Emilia dance as he sang along.

He'd never really met a baby before, he realised. Not to pick up and hold. How funny, he thought, for the first baby he'd ever met to be his own.

JULIUS NIGHTINGALE

3

It was a delicate balance, trying to hit the right note between a tribute and a shrine. The last thing she wanted to be was mawkish, yet she couldn't think of a nicer memorial than filling the book shop window with all of Julius's favourite books. But at the rate she was going, thought Emilia, every book in the shop would be in here.

Amis (father and son), Bellow, Bulgakov, Christie, Dickens, Fitzgerald, Hardy, Hemingway – she was going to run out of space long before she got to Wodehouse.

She had resisted the temptation for a black backdrop, instead opting for a stately burgundy. Nor had she put up a photo or his name or any kind of pronouncement. It was just something she wanted to do: capture his spirit, his memory.

And it took her mind off the fact that she missed him.

The shop had been busy over the past week, busier than usual, with people dropping by. Every time the bell tinged, she looked up expecting it to be him, walking in with a takeaway coffee and the day's newspaper. But it never was.

Her eye was caught by a large car drawing up and parking on the double yellow lines outside the shop. She raised her eyebrow: the driver was taking a risk. The traffic warden in Peasebrook was notoriously draconian. No one usually dared flout the rules. When she looked closer, however, she realised this particular driver had no regard for the rules. It was an Aston Martin, with a personal plate.

Ian Mendip. Her stomach curdled slightly as he got out of his car. He was tall, shaven-headed, tanned, in jeans and a leather jacket. She could smell his aftershave already. He stood for a moment looking up at the shop, eyes narrowed against the sunlight. She could imagine him calculating the price per square metre.

It was ironic he had chosen not to use the book shop car park, as that was what he was after. Nightingale Books fronted onto the high street next to the bridge over the brook. Behind it was a large parking area owned by the shop, with room for at least ten cars. And adjacent to the book shop, behind the high street and backing onto the brook, was the old glove factory, disused and rundown, which Ian Mendip had snapped up for his portfolio a few years ago. He wanted to turn it into luxury apartments. If he had the book shop car park, he could increase the number of units; without the extra allocated parking his hands were tied, as the council wouldn't grant him permission without it. Parking was enough of an issue in the small town without extra stress being put on it.

Emilia knew Ian had approached Julius, who had quietly shown him the door. So she wasn't surprised to see him, though it was a bit soon, even for someone as hard-bitten as Ian. She knew him of old: he'd been a few years above her at Peasebrook High. He'd never looked at her twice then. He'd been a player, a chancer; there'd been an air of mystique about him that Emilia had never bought into, because she could see how he treated women. Not well. He had a trophy wife, but there were always rumours. He turned her stomach slightly.

She clambered out of the window so as to be ready for him. The bell tinged as he came into the shop.

'Can I help?' She smiled her widest smile.

'Emilia.' He held out his hand and she really had no choice but to shake it. 'I've come to give you my condolences. I'm really sorry about your dad.'

'Thank you,' she said, wary.

'I know this might seem a bit previous,' he went on. 'But I like to strike while the iron's hot. You probably know your dad and I had conversations. And I thought it was more polite to come and see you in person to discuss it. I like to do business out in the open. I like a face-to-face chat. So I hope you're not offended.'

He gave what he thought was a charming smile.

'Mmm,' said Emilia, non-committal, not giving him an inch.

'I just want you to know the same offer I gave your dad is open to you. In case you're wondering what to do.'

'Not really,' said Emilia. 'I'm going to be running the shop from now on. And trust me – no amount of money will change my mind.'

'It's the best offer you'll get. This building's worth more to me than anyone else.'

Emilia frowned. 'I don't understand why you don't understand: I'm not selling.'

Ian gave a smug shrug, as if to say he knew she would come around in the end.

'I just want you to know the offer is still on the table.

You might change your mind when things have settled down. I think it's great that you want to carry on, but if you find it's a bit tougher than you first thought...' He spread his hands either side of him.

'Thank you,' said Emilia. 'But don't hold your breath. As they say.'

She was proud to stand her ground. Proud that her father had taught her there was more to life than money. The air felt tainted with the scent of Mendip's wealth: the expensive aftershave he wore that was cloying and overpowering.

Seemingly unruffled, he held out his card.

'You know where to find me. Call me any time.'

She watched as he left the shop and climbed back into his car. She rolled her eyes as it glided off down the high street. Dave loped over to her.

'Was he after the shop?'

'Yep,' she replied.

'I hope you told him where to get off.'

'I did.'

Dave nodded solemnly. 'Your dad thought he was a cock.'

With his dyed black hair tied back in a ponytail, his pale skin and his myriad tattoos, Dave wasn't what you'd expect to find in a book shop. All she really knew about him was he still lived with his mum and had a bearded dragon called Bilbo. But his knowledge of literature was encyclopaedic, and the customers loved him. And Emilia felt a surge of fondness for him too – for his loyalty and his kindness.

'I just want you to know, Dave, I don't know exactly what I'm doing with the shop yet. Everything's a bit upside down. But I don't want you to worry. You're really valued here. Dad thought the world of you . . .'

'He was a legend,' said Dave. 'Don't worry. I understand. It's tough for you.'

He put a gentle paw on her shoulder. It was heavy with skull rings.

Emilia gave him a playful punch. 'Don't. You'll make me cry again.'

She walked away to the shelves, to choose another tranche of books. She hoped desperately that things could stay the same. Just as they were. But it was all a muddle of paperwork, probate and red tape. She had gone through her father's paperwork and bank statements and handed them all over to Andrea with a sinking heart. She wished she'd discussed things with him in greater depth, but when someone was on their deathbed the last thing you wanted to talk about was balance sheets. The problem was it didn't look as if they were balancing.

It couldn't be *all* bad, she thought. She had the shop itself, loyal staff, hundreds of books and lovely customers. She'd find a way to keep it all afloat. Perhaps she should have come back earlier, instead of mucking about travelling the world and trying to find herself. She didn't *need* to find herself. This was her – Nightingale Books. But Julius had insisted. He had as good as kicked her out of the nest when she'd had a disastrous fling with a man from Oxford, whose ex-wife had turned out not to be so very ex after all when he had realised how much the divorce was going to cost him. She'd been in no way responsible for his marriage break-up, and thought she was doing a good job of getting him over it, but it seemed she was not sufficient compensation. Emilia had thought herself heartbroken. Julius had refused to let her mope and had bought her a round-the-world ticket for her birthday.

'Is it one way?' she'd joked.

He was right to make her widen her horizons, of course he was, because she'd realised very quickly that her heart wasn't broken at all, but it had been good to put some distance between herself and her erstwhile lover. And she'd seen amazing things, watched the sun rise and set over a hundred different landmarks. She would never forget feeling as if she was right amongst the clouds, on the eighteenth floor of her Hong Kong apartment block, overlooking the harbour.

Yet despite all her adventures and the friends she had made, she knew she wasn't a free spirit. Peasebrook was home and always would be.

Once a month, Thomasina Matthews would go into Nightingale Books on a Tuesday afternoon – her one afternoon off a week – and choose a new cookery book. It was her treat to herself. The shelves of her cottage were already laden, but to her mind there was no limit to the number of cookery books you could have. Reading them was her way of relaxing and switching off from the world, curling up in bed at night and leafing through recipes, learning about the food from another culture or devouring the mouth-watering descriptions written by renowned chefs or food lovers.

Until recently, she had spent these afternoons chatting to Julius Nightingale, who had steered her in the direction of a number of writers she might not have chosen otherwise. He was fascinated by food too, and every now and then she would bring him in something she had made: a slab of game terrine with her gooseberry chutney, or a piece of apricot and frangipane tart. He was always appreciative and gave her objective feedback – she liked the fact that he wasn't afraid to criticise or make a suggestion. She respected his opinion. Without Julius, she would never have discovered Alice Waters or Claudia Roden – or not as quickly, anyway; no doubt she would have got around to them eventually.

'It's not about the pictures,' Julius had told her, quite sternly. 'It's about the words. A great cookery writer can make you see the dish, smell it, taste it, with no need for a photograph.'

But Julius wasn't here any more. She had read about his death in the *Peasebrook Advertiser* in the staffroom. She'd hidden behind the paper as the tears coursed down her cheeks. She didn't want anyone to see her crying. They all thought she was wet enough. For Thomasina was shy. She never joined in the staffroom banter or went on nights out with the others. She was painfully introverted. She wished she wasn't, but there was nothing she could do about it. She'd tried.

Julius was one of the few people in the world who didn't make her feel self-conscious. He made her feel as if it was OK just to be herself. And the shop wouldn't feel the same without him. She hadn't been in since she'd heard the news, but now, here she was, hovering on the threshold. She could see Emilia, Julius's daughter, putting the finishing touches to a window display. She plucked up the courage to go in and speak to her. She wanted to tell her just how much Julius had meant.

Thomasina had been three years below Emilia at school, and she still felt the awe of a younger pupil for an older one. Emilia had been popular at school: she'd managed to achieve the elusive status of being clever and conscientious but also quite cool. Thomasina had not been cool. Sometimes she had thought she didn't exist at all. No one ever took any notice of her. She had few friends and never quite understood why. She certainly wasn't a horrible person. But when you were shy and overweight and not very clever and terrible at sport, it turned out that no one was especially interested in you, even if you were sweet and kind and caring.

Food was Thomasina's escape. It was the only subject she had ever been any good at. She had gone on to catering college, and now she taught Food Technology at the school she had once attended. And at the weekends, she had A Deux. She thought it was probably the smallest pop-up restaurant in the country: a table for two set up in her tiny cottage where she cooked celebratory dinners for anyone who cared to book. She had been pleasantly surprised by its success. People loved the intimacy of being cooked for as a couple. And her cooking was sublime. She barely made a profit, for she used only the very best ingredients, but she did it because she loved watching people go out into the night glazed with gluttony, heady with hedonism.

And without A Deux, she would be alone at the weekends. It gave her something to do, a momentum, and after she had done the last of the clearing up on a Sunday morning she still had a whole day to herself to catch up and do her laundry and her marking.

She was used to being on her own, and rather resigned to it, for she felt she had little to offer a potential paramour. She had a round face with very pink cheeks that needed little encouragement to go even pinker and her hair was a cloud of mousy frizz. She had been to a hairdresser once, who had looked at it with distaste and said with a sniff, 'There's not much I can do with this. I'll just get rid of the split ends.' She had come out looking no different, having gone in with dreams of emerging with a shining mane. She did her own split ends from then on.

To her surprise, her students loved her, and her class was one of the most popular, with girls and boys, because she opened their eyes to the joys of cooking and made even the most committed junk food junkie leave her class with something delicious they had cooked themselves. When she spoke about food she was confident and her eyes shone and her enthusiasm was catching. Outside the kitchen, whether at home or school, she was tongue-tied.

Which was why she had to wait until the shop was empty before approaching the counter and giving Emilia her condolences.

'Thomasina!' said Emilia, and Thomasina blushed with delight that she had been recognised. 'Dad talked about you a lot. When he was in hospital he said he would take me to your restaurant when he got better.'

Thomasina's eyes filled with tears. 'Oh,' she said. 'It would have been an honour to cook for him. Though it's not really a restaurant. Not a proper one. I cook for people in my cottage.'

'He was very fond of you – I know that. He said you were one of his best customers.'

'You are staying open, aren't you?' asked Thomasina anxiously. 'It's one of the things that keeps me going, coming in here.'

'Hopefully,' said Emilia.

'Well, I just wanted to tell you how... how much I'll miss him.'

'Come to his memorial service. It's next Thursday. At St Nick's. And if you want to say a few words, it's open to everyone. Just let me know what you'd like to do – a reading, or a poem. Or whatever.'

Thomasina bit her lip. She wanted more than anything to say yes, to honour Julius's memory. But the thought of standing up in front of a load of people she didn't know petrified her. Maybe Emilia would forget about the idea? Thomasina knew from experience that if she protested about things, people became fixated, whereas if she concurred in a vague manner very often their ideas faded away.

'It sounds a wonderful idea. Can I have a think and let you know?'

'Of course.' Emilia smiled, and Thomasina was struck by how like her father she was. She had his warmth, and his way of making you feel special.

She drifted back over to the cookery section, and spent a good half-hour browsing. She had narrowed it down to two books, and was holding them both, considering them, when a voice behind her made her jump.

'The Anthony Bourdain, definitely. No contest.'

She turned, and felt her cheeks turn vermilion. She recognised the speaker, but struggled to place him. Had he been to A Deux? He was as tall and thin as she was short and round. She was mortified that she couldn't recognise him, for she was certain she should.

'It's the best book about food I've ever read,' her unknown observer went on. And then she remembered. He worked in the cheesemonger. She didn't recognise him without his white hat and striped apron – he was in jeans and a jumper and she realised she had never seen his hair properly: it was curly and fair and he looked a bit like a cherub, with his cheeky baby face. She always bought her cheese from there – she always included a cheese course, with home-made oat biscuits and quince jelly and rhubarb chutney – and he had served her a couple of times, cutting little slivers of Comté or Taleggio or Gubbeen for her to try, depending on the theme of the meal she was cooking that night.

'Sorry,' he went on, and she saw his cheeks went as pink as her own. 'I didn't mean to interrupt you, but it's one of my favourite books.'

'I shall have it, then.' She smiled, and put the other one back. 'I didn't recognise you at first.'

He pulled his curls back from his face and made the shape of a hat with his hands. She laughed. For some reason, she didn't feel awkward. Yet she couldn't think of a thing to say.

'Do you like books, then?' was all she could manage. How ridiculously lame.

'Yes,' he said. 'But I couldn't eat a whole one.'

She frowned, not sure what he meant.

'It's a joke,' he said. 'A bad one. It's supposed to be *do you like children?*'

She looked at him blankly.

'I love books,' he clarified. 'But I hardly ever have time to read. You have no idea how hectic the world of cheese can be.'

'No,' she said. 'I don't. But I think it must be fascinating. Have you always been in cheese?'

He looked at her. 'Are you taking the mickey?'

'No!' she said, horrified that he might think so. 'Not at all.'

'Good,' he said. 'Only people do. They seem to find the idea of working in cheese hilarious. Whenever I go out, I just get cheese jokes.'

'Cheese jokes? Are there any?'

'What kind of cheese do you use to disguise a small horse?'

Thomasina shrugged. 'I don't know.'

'Mascarpone. What type of cheese is made backwards?'

'Um, I don't know. Again.'

'Edam.'

Thomasina couldn't help laughing. 'That's terrible.'

'I know. But I have to tell the jokes before anyone else does. Because I can't bear it.'

She looked at him. 'There must be a camembert joke in there somewhere.'

'There is.' He nodded gravely. 'But let's not go there. Anyway,' he looked around the shelves, 'I've come to get a present for my mum. She loves cookery books, but I think I've bought her just about every book in this shop. So I'm a bit stuck for ideas.'

'Does she like novels?'

'I think so . . .' He wrinkled his nose in thought. 'She's always reading. I know that.'

Thomasina nodded.

'You could get her a food-related novel. Like *Heartburn*. By Nora Ephron. It's kind of funny but sad and with recipes. Or maybe *Chocolat*? You could get her a big box of chocolates from the chocolate shop to go with it.' Thomasina was getting carried away. 'If it was me, I'd love that.'

He looked at her, impressed. '*She'd* love that. You're a genius.' He looked around the shop. 'Where do I find them?'

Thomasina led him over to the fiction shelves and found the books in question.

'These two are keepers,' she told him.

He looked puzzled.

'You know, some books you lend or lose or give to a charity shop, but these are books for life. I've read *Heartburn* about seventeen times.' She blushed, because she always blushed if she ever talked about herself. 'Maybe I need to get out more.'

More? To misquote *Alice in Wonderland*, how could she go out *more* if she didn't go out at all?

He patted her on the shoulder and she felt all fizzy inside. Fizzy and fuzzy.

'Well, you're a star and no mistake. I'll see you in the shop?'

She smiled at him and wanted to say more, but she didn't know what to say, so she just nodded as he sauntered off to the counter. She realised she didn't even know his name.

She watched him chatting to Emilia while he paid. He was so warm and friendly and open. And she realised something. He hadn't made her feel shy and tongue-tied. She had almost felt like a normal person when she spoke to him. It had been easy. Yes, she'd gone pink, but she always went pink. It was just what she did.

The only other person who hadn't made her feel self-conscious was Julius. Maybe it was the shop? Maybe there was something in the air that made her the person she wished she were? Someone who could actually hold a conversation.

She went to pay for her books and plucked up the courage to ask Emilia.

'You don't know what that bloke's name is? The one I was just talking to? I know he works in the cheese shop.'

'Jem?' said Emilia. 'Jem Gosling. He's a sweetheart. He always used to bring my father the last of the Brie when it was running out of the door.'

Thomasina looked down at the counter. She couldn't, she just couldn't, ask if he had a girlfriend. She knew there were women, more brazen than she, who would be bold enough. But that just wasn't the sort of person Thomasina was.

Emilia was looking at her. She looked knowing. But not in an unkind way.

'As far as I know,' she said casually, 'he's unattached. He had a girlfriend but she went off to Australia. He used to come and talk to my father about it, when she first left. But I think he's probably over it.'

Thomasina felt flustered. She didn't know what to say. She didn't want to protest that she didn't need to know any of that, because it would seem rude. But she was mortified that Emilia thought she was after Jem. She hoped Emilia wouldn't say anything to him if she saw him, even in jest. The very thought made her feel ill. She changed the subject as quickly as she could, hoping Emilia would forget she'd ever mentioned him.

'By the way, I'd love to do a reading,' she found herself saying. 'At the service.'

'That's wonderful.' Emilia smiled. 'If you can let me

know what you're going to read, I can put it into the order of service.'

Thomasina nodded, hot blood pounding in her ears. What on earth had she said that for? She couldn't stand up and speak in public, in front of a full church. It was too late now, though. Emilia was writing her name down on a list. She couldn't back out, not without looking disrespectful to Julius.

Feeling slightly sick, she paid for her book as quickly as she could and left.

'The Desprez à Fleur Jaune is going to have to come out. It's just not thriving. It'll break my heart. It's been there ever since I can remember. But I don't think there's any hope.'

Sarah Basildon spoke about her rose as if it were a beloved animal she was having put down. Her fingers moved gently over the space on the planting plan taken up by the sick flower, as if she were stroking it better.

'I'll take it out for you,' said Dillon. 'You won't have to know about it. And once it's actually gone, perhaps you won't notice.'

Sarah smiled a grateful smile. 'Oh, I'll know. But that's good of you. I'm just too much of a wimp.'

Of course, Sarah was far from a wimp in reality. She was redoubtable, from her wellington boots to her chambray denim eyes. Dillon Greene thought the world of her.

And she him. They were as close as could be, the aristocrat and the horny-handed son of toil, thirty years apart in age. They loved nothing better than sitting in the dankness of the garden room, drinking smoky builders' tea and dunking custard creams. They could easily get through a packet in a morning as they put the world and the gardens to rights.

Sarah's planting plans for the next year were spread on a trestle table in the middle of the room, the Latin names spidered all over the paper in her tiny black italics. Dillon knew the proper names as well as she did now – he'd been working with her at Peasebrook Manor since he left school.

As stately homes went, Peasebrook was small and intimate: a pleasingly symmetrical house of Palladian perfection, built of golden stone topped with a cupola, and set in two hundred acres of rolling farmland. When Dillon joined as a junior gardener in charge of mowing the lawns, he quickly became Sarah's protégé. He wasn't sure what it was she had recognised in him: the shy seventeen-year-old who hadn't wanted to go off to university as his school had suggested, because no one else in his family ever had done. They'd all worked outdoors: their lives were rugged and ruled by the weather. Dillon felt comfortable in that environment. When he woke up, he looked at the sky, not the Internet. He never lay in bed of a morning. He was at work by half seven, come rain or shine, sleet or snow.

One teacher had tried to persuade him to go to horticultural college, at the very least, but he didn't see the point of sitting in a classroom when he could learn hands-on. And Sarah was better than any college tutor. She grilled him, tested him, taught him, demonstrated things to him, and then made him show her how it was done. She gave praise where it was due and her criticism was always constructive. She was brisk and always knew exactly what she wanted, so Dillon always knew exactly where *he* was. It suited him down to the rich, red clay on the ground.

'You really have got green fingers,' she told him with

admiration and increasing frequency. He had a gut feeling for what went with what, for which plants would flourish and bloom together. To supplement his innate ability, he plundered her library and she never minded him taking the books home – Gertrude Jekyll, Vita Sackville-West, Capability Brown, Bunny Williams, Christopher Lloyd – and he didn't just look at the pictures. He pored over the words describing their inspiration, their visions, the problems they faced, the solutions they came up with.

Dillon, Sarah realised one day, knew much more than she did. More often than not these days he questioned her planting plans, suggesting some other combination when redesigning a bed or coming up with a concept for a new one. He would suggest a curve rather than a straight line; a bank of solid colour instead of a rainbow drift; a bed that was conceived for its smell rather than its look. And he used things he found around the estate as features: an old sundial, an ancient gardening implement, a bench he would spend hours restoring. It was reclamation at its best.

Her greatest fear was losing him. There was every chance he would be headhunted by some other country house because the gardens at Peasebrook Manor had become increasingly popular over the past few years. There were three formal rose gardens, a cutting garden, a walled kitchen garden, a maze, and a miniature lake with an island and a ruined temple for visitors to wander around. There had been a flurry of articles in magazines, many of them featuring pictures of Dillon at work, for there was no doubt he was easy on the eye. More than once her own heart had stopped for a moment when she'd rounded a corner and seen him in his combat shorts and big boots, his muscles coiling as he dug over a bed. He'd be television gold.

She would do anything in her power to keep him. She couldn't imagine life at Peasebrook without him now. But there was a limit to how much she could afford to pay him. Times were hard. It was always a struggle to balance the books, despite all their best efforts.

But today, at least the stress took her mind off her grief. Her secret grief. She'd had to put her heart in a straitjacket and she'd hidden her heartbreak well. She didn't think anyone was any the wiser about how she was feeling or what she had been through.

Six months, if you counted it from the beginning. It had ripped through him, devoured him with an indecent speed, and she could do nothing. They had snatched as much time together as they could but—

She shut off her mind. She wasn't going to remember or go back over it. Thank God for the gardens, she thought, day after day. She had no choice but to think about them. They needed constant attention. You simply couldn't take a day off. Without that momentum she would have gone under weeks ago.

'What about the folly?' asked Dillon, and Sarah looked at him sharply.

'The folly?'

'It needs something doing to it. Doing up or pulling down. It could make a great feature but—'

'We'll leave it for now.' Sarah used her *don't bring up the subject again* voice. 'That's a long-term project and we don't have the budget.'

He looked at her and she held his gaze, praying he wouldn't push it. Did he know? Is that why he'd brought it up? She had to be careful, because he was perspicacious. More than perspicacious. He almost had a sixth sense. It was one of the things she liked about him. Sensitive wasn't quite the right word, she thought. Intuitive, maybe? He'd once told her his grandmother had 'the gift'. That kind of thing could be hereditary. If you believed in it. Sarah didn't know if she did, but either way she wasn't going to give anything away at this point.

He was right, though. The folly did need attention. It was on the outer edge of the estate, high on a hill behind a patch of woodland. An octagon made of crumbling ginger stone, it was straight out of a fairy tale, smothered in ivy and cobwebs. It had been neglected for years. Inside, the plaster was falling off the walls, the floorboards were rotten and the glass doors were coming off their hinges. There was just an old sofa, steeped in damp and mildew. Sarah could smell it now, its comforting mustiness mixed with the scent of his skin. She'd never minded the insalubrious surroundings. To her, it could have easily been the George V or the Savoy.

She didn't want anyone else going in there.

'Let's just shut off the path to the folly for the time being,' she told Dillon.

She thought of all the times she had been along it, the tiny woodland path that led up the hill to their meeting place. He would park his car in the gateway on the back road, behind a tumbledown shed. The road was barely used except by the odd farmer, so with luck no one had ever noticed. Although sometimes drunk drivers used it as a rat run from the pub, and it only took one person to put two and two together . . .

She couldn't worry about it. It was almost irrelevant

now, and certainly no one could prove anything. She tried to put it out of her mind and concentrate on the wedding instead. As the mother of the bride, it should be her priority. But it seemed to be organising itself. There didn't seem to be the usual hysteria that accompanied most weddings. They had plenty of experience, after all: Peasebrook Manor had had a wedding licence for some years, and it was one of the things that had filled the gaping coffers, so when it came to organising a wedding for one of their own, they were well prepared. And Alice wasn't a highly strung, demanding bride-to-be. Far from it. As far as Alice was concerned, as long as everyone she loved was there, and there was enough champagne and cake, it would be a perfect day.

'I don't want fuss and wedding favours, Mum. You know I hate all that. It's perfect to be getting married at home, with everyone here. What can go wrong? We can do this with our eyes shut.'

Alice. The apple of her eye. Alice, who treated life like one long Pony Club camp, but with cocktails. Alice, whose sparkle drew everyone to her and whose smile never seemed to fade. Sarah could not have been more proud of her daughter, and her need to protect her was primal. Though Alice was quite able to look after herself. She was charmed. She strode through life, plumply luscious, in her uniform of too-tight polo shirt, jeans and Dubarrys, her flaxen hair loose and wild, face free from make-up, always slightly pink in her rush to get from one thing to the next.

There had been a couple of years of worry (as if she'd needed more worry!) when Alice had gone off to agricultural college to do estate management – she was, after all, the heir to Peasebrook Manor, so it seemed logical, but she failed, spectacularly, two years running. She had never been academic, and the course seemed beyond her. Of course there was too much partying going on, but the other students seemed to manage.

So Alice came home and was put to work, and it suddenly became abundantly clear that running Peasebrook Manor was what she had been put on earth to do. She had vision and energy and a gut feeling for what would work and what the public wanted. Somehow the locals felt included in Peasebrook Manor, as if it were theirs. She had been the mastermind behind converting the coach house in the middle of the stable yard into a gift shop selling beautiful things you didn't need but somehow desperately wanted, and a tea room that sold legendary fruit scones the size of your fist. And she was brilliant at orchestrating events. In the last year there'd been open-air opera, Easter egg hunts, and a posh car boot sale. She was thinking of running children's camps the following year: Glastonbury meets Enid Blyton.

And the most exciting upcoming event, of course, was Alice's own wedding, to be held at the end of November. She couldn't have a summer wedding, because they were too busy holding them for other people.

'Anyway,' said Alice, with typical optimism, 'I'd much prefer a winter wedding. Everything all frosty and glittery. Lots of ivy and lots of candles.'

She was to marry Hugh Pettifer, a handsome hedge fund manager who set hearts a-flutter when he raced through the lanes in his white supercharged sports car, bounding from polo match to point-to-point.

If Sarah had her doubts about Hugh, she never voiced

them. He was perfect on paper. And utterly charming. She supposed it was her maternal need to protect Alice that made her wary. She had no evidence that Hugh was anything other than devoted. His manners were faultless, he mucked in at family events, he was thoughtful, and if he partied hard, then all Alice's crowd did. They were young and beautiful and wealthy – why shouldn't they have fun? And Hugh worked hard. He earned good money. He wasn't a freeloader. And anyway, if he was looking for a meal ticket, he wouldn't get one from the Basildons. They were classic asset rich/cash poor. If anything, they needed him more than he needed them.

So Sarah kept any doubts about Hugh to herself. She had to learn to let go. It was time to hand Alice over. She would still be very much part of life at Peasebrook Manor – it would fall apart without her – but she was a woman in her own right. And Sarah wasn't gold-digging on Alice's behalf. It would be nice for her to have a husband who could support her when the time came for her to have children. Sarah was in no doubt of her daughter's capabilities, but she knew how deep the pressures dug. And nobody could deny that money didn't make things easier, especially when it came to motherhood.

'I'll put a gate up, shall I?'

Dillon's voice startled Sarah and dragged her back to the matter in hand.

'Yes. And put a lock on it for the time being. I don't think the folly's safe. We don't want anyone getting injured.'

Dillon nodded. But he was eyeing her with interest. Sarah started to doodle on the edge of one of the planting plans. She couldn't quite look at him. He knows, she thought. How she wished she could talk to someone about it, but she knew the importance of keeping secrets. And if you couldn't keep your own secret, how on earth could you trust someone else to keep it?

'Right.' Dillon stood up. 'I better get on. It's starting to get dark early. The days are getting shorter.'

'Yes.' Sarah couldn't decide which was worse. The days or the nights. She could fill her days with things to do but she had to pretend to everybody, from Ralph and Alice down to the postman, that nothing was wrong, and that was wearing. At night she could stop; she didn't need to pretend any more and she could sleep. But her sleep was troubled and she couldn't control her dreams. He would appear, and she would wake, her face wet with tears, trying not to sob. Trying not to wake Ralph because what could she say? How could she explain her distress?

She sighed, and took another custard cream. Her brain had no respite these days. Everything whirled around in her head, day and night; a washing machine filled with thoughts, fears, worries that seemed to have no answer.

And she missed him. God, she missed him.

She picked up their used mugs and took them back to the kitchen. On the kitchen table was a copy of the *Peasebrook Advertiser*. Ralph must have been reading it, or one of the staff. Sarah kept her kitchen open to the people who worked for her, because she felt it was important for them to feel part of the family. The kitchen was enormous and there was a back door out into the courtyard so they didn't have to traipse through the rest of the house, and there were just less than a dozen full-timers working in the estate office, the tea room and the shop, and in the grounds. They were usually all gone by five o'clock so it

84

wasn't too much of an imposition, and she was convinced it was an advantage.

She looked down at the paper. There was a picture of him on the left-hand page. His dear face; his kind smile; that trademark sweep of salt-and-pepper hair.

Memorial service to celebrate the life of Julius Nightingale...

She sat down, reread all the details. Her head swam. She knew about the funeral – it was a small town, after all. It had been tiny, but this memorial was open to anyone who wanted to come. Anyone who wanted to do a reading or a eulogy was to go and see Emilia at the shop.

A eulogy? She would never be able to begin. Or stop. How could she put into words how wonderful he had been? She could feel it coming, a great wave of grief, unstoppable, merciless. She looked up at the ceiling, took deep breaths, anything to stop it engulfing her. She was so tired of being strong; so tired of having to fight it. But she couldn't afford to break down. Anyone might come in, at any moment.

She gathered herself and looked down at the page again. Should she go? Could she go? It wouldn't be odd. Everyone in Peasebrook knew Julius. Their social circles overlapped in the typical Venn diagram of a small country town. And in her role as 'lady of the manor' Sarah attended lots of funerals and memorials of people she didn't know terribly well, as a gesture. No one would think it odd if she turned up.

But they would if she broke down and howled, which is what she wanted to do.

She wished he was here, so she could ask his advice. He always knew the right thing to do. She imagined them, curled up on the sofa in the folly. She imagined poking him playfully, being kittenish. He made her feel kittenish: soft and teasingly affectionate.

'Should I go to your memorial service?'

And in her imagination, he turned to her with one of his mischievous smiles. 'Bloody hell, I should think so,' he said. 'If anyone should be there, it's you.'

5

Jackson had been dreading his meeting with Ian Mendip. Well, meeting made it sound a bit formal. It was a 'friendly chat'. In his kitchen. Very informal. Ian had a proposition.

Jackson suspected it would mean doing something he didn't want to do yet again. Breaking all the promises he had made to himself about getting out of Ian's clutches and getting some backbone. He had no alternative though. He had no qualifications, no references, no rich dad to bail him out like so many of the kids he'd been at school with.

That was the trouble with this area, thought Jackson, as he took his seat at Ian's breakfast bar: you were either stinking rich or piss poor. And while he had once been filled with ambition, and optimism, now he was resigned to a life of making do and being at Ian Mendip's beck and call. Somewhere amongst it all he'd lost his ambition and his drive. The galling thing was he knew it was his own fault. He'd had the same opportunities as Mendip: none. He just hadn't played it as smart.

He looked around the kitchen: white high-shine gloss units, a glass-fronted wine fridge racked up with bottles of vintage champagne, music coming as if from nowhere.

There was a massive three-wick scented candle oozing an expensive smell, and expensive it seriously was – Mia had wanted one, and Jackson really couldn't get his head around anyone thinking spending hundreds of pounds on a candle was a good idea.

Ian hadn't got all this and the Aston Martin parked outside by being nice. Next to it was Jackson's ancient Suzuki Jeep, the only set of wheels he could afford now, what with the mortgage payments and the maintenance for Mia, which took up nearly all his salary. His mates told him he'd been soft, that he'd let Mia walk all over him. It wasn't as if they were even married. He didn't have to give her a penny, they told him. But it was about Finn. Jackson had responsibilities and a duty to his son, which meant he had to look after his mother. And to be fair, Mia hadn't actually asked for anything. He'd known it was his duty.

Which was why he was still running around after Ian instead of setting up on his own, which had been his original intention. But you needed cash to start up, even as a jobbing builder who just did flat roof extensions and conservatories. That's how Ian had begun. Now he did luxury apartments and housing developments. He was minted. He had proven that you could claw your way up from the bottom to the top.

Jackson was Ian's right-hand man. He kept an eye on all his projects and reported back. He scoped potential developments: it was Jackson who had given Ian the heads-up on the glove factory, which meant Ian had been able to swoop in and get it at a knock-down price before it went on the market.

Which was why Jackson knew he was capable of

achieving what Ian had. He could spot the potential in a building. He had the knowledge, the experience, the energy; he knew the tradesmen who could crew it. He just didn't have the killer instinct. Or, right now, the money he needed to invest in setting up on his own. He'd missed the boat. He should have done it years ago, when he was young and had no responsibilities. Now he was trapped. Not even thirty and he'd painted himself into a dingy little corner.

He hunched down in the chrome and leather barstool opposite Ian. Ian was spinning from side to side in his, smug and self-satisfied, tapping a pencil on the shiny black granite. In front of them were his development plans for the old glove factory: line drawings of the building and its surroundings.

'So,' said Ian, in the broad burr he hadn't lost despite his millions. 'I want that book shop. That is a prestige building and I want it as my head office. It's classy. If I do that up right, it'll do more for my reputation than any advert.'

Ian was obsessed with how people perceived him. He longed for people to think he was a class act. And he was right – the book shop was one of the nicest buildings in Peasebrook, right on the bridge. Jackson could already see the sign hanging outside in his mind's eye: Peasebrook Developments, with its oak leaf logo.

'And I've gone over the drawings for the glove factory again and done a bit of jiggling. If I get the book shop car park, I can have parking for four more flats. Without it, I'm down to eight units, which doesn't make it worth my while. Twelve will see me a nice fat profit. But you know what the council are like. They want their allocated parking. And that's like gold dust in Peasebrook.'

He tapped the drawing of the car park with his pencil.

'Julius Nightingale wasn't having any of it,' Ian went on. 'One of those irritating buggers who don't think money's important. I offered him a hefty whack, but he wasn't interested. But now he's gone and it's just his daughter. She insists she's not interested either. But now the dad's gone, she's going to struggle to keep that place afloat. I reckon she could be persuaded to see sense. Only she's not going to want to hear it from me. So . . . that's where you come in, pretty boy.'

Ian grinned. Jackson was, indeed, a pretty boy, slight but muscular, with brown eyes as bright as a robin's. There was a little bit of the rakish gypsy about him. His eyes and mouth were wreathed in laughter lines, even though he hadn't had that much to laugh about over the past few years. With his slightly too long hair and his aviator sunglasses, he looked like trouble and radiated mischief but he had warmth and charm and a ready wit. He was quicksilver – though he didn't have a malicious bone in his body. He just couldn't say no – to trouble or a pretty girl. Although not the pretty girls any more. His heart wasn't in it. He wasn't even sure he had a heart these days.

Jackson listened to what Ian was saying and frowned. 'But how am I going to get to know her? I've never read a book in my life.'

'Not even *The Da Vinci Code*? I thought everyone had read that.' Ian wasn't a great reader himself, but he managed the odd thumping hardback on holiday.

Jackson shook his head. He *could* read, but he never did. Books held no thrall for him. They smelt bad and reminded him of school. He'd hated school – and school had hated him. He'd felt caged and ridiculed and they had been as glad to see the back of him as he had been to leave.

Ian shrugged.

'It's up to you to work out how to do it. But you're a good-looking boy. The way to a girl's heart is through her knickers, surely?'

Even Jackson looked mildly disgusted by this. Ian leant forwards with a smile.

'You get me that shop and you can manage the glove factory development.'

Jackson raised his eyebrows. This was a step up, letting him manage an entire project. But Ian's offer was a double-edged sword. He was flattered that Ian thought him capable of the job. Which of course he was.

But Jackson wanted to be able to do what Ian was doing for himself. He needed money if he was going to do that. Proper money. Right now, Jackson couldn't even put down a deposit on a pigsty.

Ian was smart. He knew he'd got Jackson by the short and curlies. He was taking advantage of him. Or was he? He paid him well. It wasn't Ian's fault that Jackson had screwed up his relationship. Or that keeping Mia was bleeding him dry. He only had himself to blame for that. If he hadn't been such an idiot ...

Ian opened a drawer and pulled out a wad of cash. He counted out five hundred.

'That's for expenses.'

Jackson pocketed the cash, thinking about what else it could buy him.

He'd love to be able to take Finn on holiday. He

imagined a magical hotel on a beach, with four different swimming pools and palm trees and endless free cocktails. He longed for warmth on his skin, and the chance to laugh with his son.

Or he could put it towards a decent van. He'd just need one job to get him started. If he did it well, there would be word of mouth. He could move onto the next job, start saving, keep his eye open for a house that needed doing up . . . He could do it. He was certain.

In the meantime, he had to keep in with Ian. Ian was his bread and butter, and he wouldn't want to let Jackson go. He had to play it smart.

Emilia Nightingale shouldn't take him long. Once Jackson had a girl in his sights, she was a sitting target. He had to muster up some of his old charm. He used to have them queuing up. Pull yourself together, he told himself.

Jackson held out his hand and shook Ian's with a cocky wink that would have done credit to the Artful Dodger.

'Leave it with me, mate. Nightingale Books will be yours by the end of the month.'

After his meeting with Ian, Jackson drove to Paradise Pines, where he was living with his mum, Cilla. He wasn't going to tell her about the deal, because she wouldn't approve.

He hated the park. It was a lie. It was advertised as some sort of heavenly haven for the over fifty-fives. 'Your own little slice of paradise: peace and tranquillity in the Cotswold countryside.'

It was a dump.

Never mind the rusting skip in the car park, surrounded by untaxed cars and wheelie bins and the mangy Staffie tied up in the corner that represented the 'security' promised in the brochure ('peace of mind twenty-four hours a day, so you can sleep at night').

He slunk past the Portakabin where Garvie, the site manager, sat slurping Pot Noodles and watching porn on his laptop all day. Garvie was supposed to vet visitors, but Ted Bundy could have floated past arm in arm with the Yorkshire Ripper and Garvie wouldn't bat an eyelid. He was also supposed to take deliveries for the residents, deal with their maintenance enquiries and be a general all-round ray of sunshine for them to depend upon. Instead he was a malevolent presence who reminded each resident that he was all they deserved.

Garvie was obese, with stertorous breathing, and smelt like the boy at school no one wanted to sit near. He turned Jackson's stomach. Cilla said she was fond of him, but Cilla liked everyone. She had no judgement where people were concerned.

Jackson wondered how he could have turned out so differently from his mother. He didn't like anyone. Not at the moment, anyway.

Except Finn, of course. And Wolfie.

He ploughed on along the 'nature trail' that led to his mother's home. It was an overgrown path with a very thin layer of bark to guide you. There was no nature apparent, though more than once Jackson had seen a rat scuttle into the nearby undergrowth. He should let Wolfie loose up here one day, even though you were supposed to keep dogs on a lead on the site. He would have a field day, rooting out the vermin. But there was no point. The residents left their garbage rotting. The rats would be back in nanoseconds.

The fencing that surrounded the little patch of grass belonging to each home was rotting and the grass itself was bald and patchy. There were lamp-posts lighting the paths, but hardly any of them worked, and the hanging baskets hanging from them trailed nothing but weeds.

Maybe it had been all it had proclaimed in its brochure once upon a time. Maybe the grass *had* been lush and manicured, the grounds tended immaculately. Maybe the owners had taken pride in their own homes.

Jackson had felt utter despair the day his mother told him what she had done. She had been conned. Taken into a show home and given a glass of cheap fizzy wine and bamboozled by a spotty youth in a cheap suit and white socks, who had convinced her this was the best place for her to invest her savings. She'd had a fair old nest egg, Cilla, because she'd always been a saver. And Jackson was shocked by her naiveté. Couldn't she see the park homes would lose value the minute the ink was dry on the contract? Couldn't she see the management fee was laughably high? Couldn't she see that the park owners had absolutely no incentive to keep their promises once all the homes were leased? As a scam it was genius. But it made him sick to his stomach that his mother was now going to be forced to live out her days here. No one wanted to buy on Paradise Pines. Word was that you went there to die. It was one step away from the graveyard.

And now here he was, living with her in the place he had come to hate. It had only been supposed to be temporary. When Mia had first thrown him out, two years ago, when Finn was three, he had thought it wouldn't be long before she allowed him back. He knew now he'd been useless, but he just hadn't been ready to be a dad.

It had been a shock, the realisation that a baby was there around the clock. It had been too easy for him to slide out of his share of the childcare, coming home late from work, stopping off at the pub on the way, having a few too many beers.

And to be fair to him, Mia had changed. Motherhood had made her overanxious, sharp. She fussed over Finn too much, and Jackson told her repeatedly to stop worrying. It had caused a lot of friction between them. He spent more and more time out of the house, not wanting to come back to arguments and disapproval and crying (usually Finn's, sometimes Mia's). He tried to do his best but somehow he always managed to end up displeasing her. So it seemed easier to stay out of her way.

Then she'd booted him out, the night he'd come back half cut at one in the morning, when she'd been dealing with a puking Finn for four hours and had to change the sheets twice when she'd taken him into bed with her, desperate for a moment's respite. Jackson had protested – how was he to know the baby had a tummy bug? But he knew he was in the wrong and had got everything he deserved.

He thought it was only going to be temporary, that Mia was just giving him a short sharp shock. But she didn't want him back.

'It's easier without you,' she said. 'It's easier to do everything all on my own, without being disappointed or let down. I'm sorry, Jackson.'

He didn't bother knocking on the flimsy white door, just pushed it open. There was his mum, in the gloom of the caravan. Wolfie lay at her feet but jumped up as soon as Jackson came in. At least someone was glad to see him. He'd got Wolfie once it was clear Mia wasn't going to have him back. He'd gone to the dog rescue place and looked at everything they had: Jack Russells and collies and mastiffs. At the far end was a Bedlington lurcher, far too big to be practical and ridiculously scruffy. But he'd reminded Jackson of himself. He was a good dog, deep down, but sometimes he couldn't help himself... How could he resist?

His mum was as delighted to see him as Wolfie was. Her face lit up, her eyes shone. He still couldn't get over how frail she looked. He didn't want to admit to himself that his mum wasn't getting any younger. He was going to cook her a decent dinner. He was no chef, but he'd bought some chicken pieces and some vegetables with the cash he'd been given.

She'd always taken pride in cooking them proper meals when they were young but somewhere, between husbands three and four, she'd lost interest in food.

He didn't want to look at his once beautiful mother, sitting in her chair, bird-like and frail. He didn't want to look at the hair that had once been dark and lustrous, tumbling over her shoulders. Now, the black dye she used to recreate her former glory had grown out, showing three inches of grey.

It was depression at the root of it. Obviously. Which wasn't surprising when your looks and your husband left you at the same time. Was it easier, Jackson wondered, not to have been beautiful in the first place? He knew he'd got by on his looks more than once. His looks and an easy charm.

'Shall we go out somewhere?' he asked, knowing what the answer would be. He wanted her to surprise him and say yes, and yet he didn't. He didn't want to see her out in the real world, because it made her situation even more depressing.

'No, love,' she replied, just as he'd thought. 'It's enough for me to have you here.'

He sighed and made the best he could of the food he had bought with the facilities available. He dished it up, coating it all in a glistening layer of packet gravy.

They ate it together at the tiny table. Jackson had no appetite, but he wanted to set an example. He forced more carrots on her. Gave her the rest of the Bisto. At least now he knew she'd had some vitamins, some calories.

He'd bought a ready-made apple pie and a carton of custard, but she declared herself full.

'I'll heat it up for you later.'

'You're a good boy.'

She'd always said that to him. He could remember her, lithe and vibrant, dancing in the kitchen, holding him in her arms. 'You're a good boy. The best boy.' He would touch her earrings with his tiny fingers, entranced by the glitter. He would breathe in the smell of her, like ripe peaches.

Where had she gone, his mother? Who had stolen her?

He did the washing up in the sink, which was too small to put a dinner plate in flat. He tried to suppress his despair for the millionth time. He washed all the cups and glasses that were lying around, and wiped down the surfaces.

He could imagine Mia's voice: 'You never did that for me.'

He had. Once upon a time. But nothing was ever right for Mia; she was a control freak. He couldn't even breathe right.

'I'm off to see Finn, Mum.' He bent down to kiss her, not leaning in too close. 'I'll be back in a bit.'

'Ta ta. I'm going to have a snooze now.' She settled back in her chair with a smile. He whistled for Wolfie and the dog jumped to his feet. He was like a cartoon, his eyes coal black and inquisitive, his legs and tail too long, his shaggy grey coat like a backcombed teddy bear. He loped beside Jackson, amiable and eager.

Jackson lugged the bin bag back down the path and hurled it over the side of the skip. The Stygian gloom of the caravan stayed with him.

'Oi!' shouted Garvie from his lair, but Jackson knew he was safe. Garvie wouldn't bother to chase after him, or to fish the bag out.

He left the park and broke into a run, gulping in gusts of fresh air, trying to expel the stifling staleness of the past two hours. Wolfie ran beside him, joyful, his ears streaming behind him.

There's got to be something better out there for us, he thought.

He walked back into Peasebrook with Wolfie, then along the main road that led to Oxford. Eventually he reached the small cul de sac of houses where Mia and Finn lived. And where he had once lived. It had been one of Ian's most lucrative projects, a mix of executive four-beds and the low-cost housing he was obliged to build as part of the deal. The homes that only locals were allowed to buy. It was one of the reasons Jackson remained loyal to Ian, because he'd let him have one of them cheap. Ian had flashes of generosity, though there was usually something in it for him. This had been an act of pure selflessness, as far as Jackson could make out, though he was always waiting for Ian to call the favour in. He was convinced one day he'd have to get rid of a dead body.

Of course, Jackson's plan *had* been to get his hands on something that needed doing up. A project for him and Mia. They could make some money on it, sell it on and buy something bigger. Keep doing that until they had a total palace. But then Mia had got pregnant and they'd needed a place of their own quickly, somewhere suitable for a baby. You couldn't bring a baby up in a building site.

So it had been a compromise. Nevertheless, Jackson had been proud to get on the property ladder. He remembered Mia's face when he led her over the threshold. They were pretty little faux mews houses, built in imitation of the weaver's cottages traditional in the town. He'd chosen everything off-plan: the pale blue Shaker kitchen, the silver feature wallpaper in the lounge, the pale green glass sink in the downstairs toilet. Mia had been speechless.

'Is it ours?' she had whispered. 'Is it really ours?'

Now there was no 'ours' about it.

He knocked on the pale cream front door. He remembered choosing the colour and being so proud. Mia answered. Her dark curly hair was tied back; she was wearing a baby pink sweatshirt and grey yoga pants and eating a low-fat yoghurt.

'Can Finn come out for a bit?'

She sighed. 'Don't you ever listen? He does tae kwon do on Tuesdays. At the leisure centre.'

Jackson nodded. 'I'll walk over there and pick him up.'

'It's OK. I've got it covered. The coach is bringing him back.'

'I can tell him not to worry—'

'No. He's bringing me some protein powder for my training.'

'Training?'

'For the triathlon. I was supposed to be going for a swim, but . . .'

Mia had become a fitness freak since he'd left. She was obsessed. Jackson thought she'd lost way too much weight. Her curves had gone; she looked angular and her face had lost its softness.

He looked at her. On closer inspection, she seemed positively drawn.

'Are you OK?'

She looked startled. They never expressed concern for each other in their current relationship. They avoided the personal.

'Course,' she said. 'Just, you know, wrong time of the month.'

She'd always suffered. He used to make her tea and hot water bottles and rub her back. Before he'd become a total twat. He opened his mouth to commiserate or console her but wasn't sure what to say. Anything seemed too personal now, to this woman who had become a stranger to him.

She spooned in some more yoghurt, still on the doorstep, no intention of asking him in.

'You didn't come to Parents' Evening.'

Her voice had that horrible accusatory edge. He was glad he hadn't sympathised.

'What?' He frowned. 'When was it? You didn't tell me.'

'It was last Thursday. I shouldn't have to tell you.'

'How am I supposed to know?'

'By taking an interest?' She glared at him. 'You never have a clue what he's doing.'

'I have.'

'Really? What's his topic this term, then?'

Jackson couldn't answer.

'Vikings, Jackson. It's Vikings.'

He sighed. 'I'm a loser, Mia. We know that. You don't have to prove it.'

'It's a shame for Finn, that's all.'

'We have a laugh, Finn and me. We have a great time when he's with me.'

'It's not all about the laughs.'

He looked at her. When had she become so bitter? And why?

'Are you happy?' he asked suddenly.

She looked startled, as if he'd caught her doing something she shouldn't.

'Of course.'

'Really? Only happy people don't try and make other people feel bad.'

She looked away for a moment. Jackson couldn't tell what she was thinking. He never could. Since Finn had been born, he felt as if the real Mia was somewhere else.

When she spoke, he could hardly hear her.

'I'm just tired, that's all.'

That was what she used to say when he was with her. She was tired all the time.

'It must be the training. It's no wonder. Give yourself a break, Mi.'

He stepped towards her. He wanted to give her a hug. Tell her it was going to be all right. But she sidestepped him.

'I'm fine.' She gave him a half-smile. 'The training's what keeps me going.'

'I don't understand, Mi. You've got this house. You've got our lovely boy. You've got rid of me. What more could you want?'

She rolled her eyes. 'You can have him tomorrow after school. Don't be late.'

She put another spoonful of yoghurt in her mouth and shut the door with her foot. Jackson stood on the step for a moment, unable to believe that she had the power to make him feel worse every time he saw her. It was obvious she thought little of him. Obvious she thought he was a shit dad. Well, he wasn't a shit dad. They *did* always have a laugh, him and Finn. He took him fishing. Took him to the skate park and taught him tricks. Bought him decent food, not that rubbish she kept feeding him: lentils and quinoa. And Finn loved Wolfie with a passion.

What did he have to do to prove himself?

He turned and walked back along the drive to the main road, Wolfie trotting along by his side, looking up at him every now and again. Dusk was falling, and he mulled over the events of the day. And gradually, as he walked, an idea emerged. He could do Ian's bidding *and* prove he was a good father. And if all went according to plan, maybe he could get himself out of this mess.

6

'It's a can of worms, Em,' Andrea told her. 'You'd better come to my office. But don't panic. We can sort it. That's what I'm here for.'

Emilia felt her heart sink. She felt grateful she had Andrea. She couldn't have asked for a better friend, even though they were so different. Andrea called her every day to see how she was. And she brought her thoughtful presents: last week she'd given her a Moroccan rose-scented candle, expensive and potent.

'Just lie on the bed and breathe it in,' Andrea instructed. 'It will make you feel better at once.'

Strangely, it had. The scent was so soothing; it had wrapped itself around her and made her feel comforted.

Emilia walked from the shop to Andrea's office in a slick modern block built from glass and reclaimed brick, and was ushered in to a room with sleek Scandinavian furniture, a Mac and a space-age coffee machine. There wasn't a scrap of paper in sight.

Andrea swept in, with her figure-hugging navy blue dress and designer spectacles that ensured she missed nothing. Emilia immediately felt as if she should have dressed more formally. She was in jeans and Converse and her favourite old grey polo neck jumper – not very businesslike.

Then Andrea hugged her, and Emilia felt her strength. They got straight down to business, though: Andrea brooked no nonsense, took no prisoners and pulled no punches. She sat behind her desk and brought up Nightingale Books on a computer screen that was the size of a kitchen table.

'It's taken me quite a while to trawl through everything and make sense of it,' she said. 'I'm not going to pretend. It looks as if the shop's been in financial trouble for quite a while. I'm so sorry. I know that's not the sort of news you need at the moment, but I really felt you should be put in the picture as soon as possible. So you can decide what you want to do.'

She handed Emilia a neatly bound sheaf of papers.

'Here are the balance sheets for the past two years. Balance not being the operative word. There's been far more going out then coming in.' She gave a rueful smile. 'Unless your dad was operating in cash and we don't know about it.'

'Dad might have been useless with money but he was honest.'

'I know. I was joking. But look, he hadn't even been drawing much of a salary for himself for the past few years – he was only ever worried about paying his staff. If he'd been paying himself properly there'd be an even greater loss.'

Emilia didn't need a huge understanding of numbers to see that none of this was good news.

'If he hadn't owned the building outright he'd have

been in even bigger trouble. He would never have been able to afford the rent or the mortgage repayments.'

'Why didn't he say anything?'

Andrea exhaled. 'Maybe he wasn't bothered. It's not all about profit for some people. I think the book shop was a way of life for him, and as long as it was ticking over he was happy. It's a shame, because with a bit of professional help, he could have made it much more efficient without changing the way he did things too much.' She clicked through a few more pages of depressing numbers. 'He made a lot of classic mistakes, and missed a lot of tricks.'

Emilia sighed. 'You know what he was like. Dad always did things his own way.' She looked down at the floor. 'He was always sending me money. I didn't realise he couldn't afford it. I would never have taken it off him...'

She couldn't cry in Andrea's office. But the tears leaked out.

'Sorry.' She looked up and to her surprise Andrea was crying too. Well, just a bit misty-eyed.

'Oh, I'm sorry too,' Andrea said. 'How unprofessional of me. But I was really fond of your dad. I used to pretend he was mine when we were kids, you know. He was just so... *there*. Unlike mine.' Andrea's father was a flaky figure who appeared once in a blue moon, usually when he had run out of money and had come to beg off her mother.

She pulled open a drawer and brought out a box of tissues. 'These are for bankruptcy proceedings. Even grown men cry at those.'

'So,' said Emilia, when she'd mopped up her tears and felt a bit stronger. 'Are you saying the shop needs to close?'

Andrea had composed herself now.

'No. Not at all. It really depends on you, and what you want to do. But it will take a great deal of hard work to turn it round and make it profitable.'

Emilia nodded.

'You're sitting on a valuable piece of real estate. The building was bought in your name, which is one good thing, so there would be no capital gains. And he made you a director of the company as soon as you were eighteen, so that makes things easier too, once we get probate. You're free to do whatever you want.' Andrea paused. 'You *could* sell that building straight away and be very well off. And save yourself a lot of trouble.'

'I've already had an offer. From Ian Mendip.' Emilia hadn't mentioned his visit to Andrea, because she'd had a sneaking feeling Andrea might think it was a good idea.

Andrea looked awkward. 'Ah.' She cleared her throat. 'I've got to admit to a slight conflict of interest here. I do Ian's accounts. I should tell you that before we go any further.'

Emilia had forgotten how everything in Peasebrook connected up in the end. Suddenly she felt unsettled and slightly paranoid.

'Did he tell you he'd made me an offer?'

'No. But I'm not at all surprised. I know he's got the glove factory and I was going to suggest you asked him what he would offer you. But he's ahead of me.' She breathed a sigh. 'I'd have thought he'd have waited a bit. It's a bit predatory even for Ian.'

Emilia shrugged. 'I think he wanted me to know the offer was there. For all he knows I might want to sell up. He'd talked to Dad about it a few times but Dad wasn't interested.'

'It was one of the lovely things about your dad, that he wasn't interested in money. Not like Ian, who's obsessed with it.' Andrea laughed, then looked a bit shamefaced. 'Sorry. I shouldn't talk about my other clients like that. It's very indiscreet. And don't worry. I'm not going to influence you either way. I just want to help you stand back and look at the options. Without being sentimental or emotional.'

Emilia leafed through the balance sheets Andrea had given her. She felt her heart sink. She didn't feel equipped to make an informed decision. She understood enough to know the figures weren't good, but not how to come up with a solution.

'So – do you think I can make the shop work?'

'Well. It would have to be a very different shop. You would have to invest quite considerably. And the problem is there's not a lot of ready cash in the coffers. Of course, you could take out a loan. You've got plenty of equity.'

Emilia chewed the side of her thumbnail while she thought.

'I don't understand why it's in such trouble. I mean, he's got masses of customers. The shop's always full of people.'

'Yes. Because it's a lovely place to come in for a chat and a browse and wander around. But those customers don't always buy. And when they do it's not much. And I know for a fact he was always giving people discount, because he used to offer it to me. I told him off about it more than once.' Andrea sat back in her chair and breathed out. 'Nightingale Books was a wonderful, warm place to be. He made people feel welcome and want to stay in there for hours. But it was a terrible business model. He'd make them cups of coffee and talk to them for hours and they'd wander out without buying anything. Then they'd go up the road and spend twenty quid on lamb chops or cheese. He was very easy to take advantage of.'

'I know,' sighed Emilia. Her lovely father, who was as kind and easy-going as a man could be.

Andrea drummed her French-polished fingernails on the glass tabletop.

'But there's nothing I hate more than seeing a potentially good business go down the pan. I'm very happy to give you my advice. But it's no good just listening. You have to be proactive.'

'Well, I'm very happy to take your advice,' said Emilia. 'And I want you to be honest with me. Do you think it's salvageable?'

'OK,' she said. 'Here's the thing. I know Peasebrook and how it works. My guess is at the moment, it's really only locals and old customers who go in the shop. People who'd built up a relationship with Julius. And they are still valuable. Of course they are. What you need to do is widen your net. Make it an attractive destination for tourists, weekenders and people who live further out. Diversify. Find different revenue streams. Monetise!'

Emilia could already feel rising panic. She forced herself to carry on listening. Andrea was smart.

'You should open on a Sunday for a start. There are lots of people who come to Peasebrook for a weekend break from London. Or who drive here for Sunday lunch. There's nothing much else for them to do but spend money. So you need to find a way to pull them in. The shop is slightly out of the way, being at the end of the high street, so if you're from out of town and you don't know it's there you might miss it. You need to make it a little more eye-catching. And do some marketing and advertising. Get a decent website and start a database – send your customers a newsletter. Put on events and launches and—'

Emilia put her hands over her ears. She couldn't take it all in.

'But all this costs money,' she wailed. 'Money I don't have!'

'I've got an idea there. The obvious thing to do would be to rent the flat out. That would bring in a regular income – at least a thousand a month if you're clever. There's a huge demand for holiday accommodation in Peasebrook. I've got an agency on my books. I can introduce you – get them to give you an estimate. You'd need to spend some money on it, though. People expect luxury.'

'I'd have to find somewhere to live myself.'

'Well, yes.'

Emilia's head was spinning with all the possibilities.

'I can't think straight.'

'I'll help you as much as I can,' said Andrea. 'There's nothing I would love more than to see Nightingale Books turn a healthy profit. But we've got to be realistic. You need to do a watertight business plan.'

'I wouldn't know where to start! I've never done a spreadsheet in my life.'

'Well, that's what I'm here for. I love spreadsheets.' Andrea grinned at her. 'But it won't be easy. It's a question of whether you want to live, breathe, sleep and eat books for the foreseeable future.'

'It's how I was brought up.'

'Yes, but you won't be able to float around plucking novels from the shelf and curling up in a corner.' Andrea laughed. 'Every time I went in your father had his nose in a book, away with the fairies. That's not going to work. You're running a business. And that means being businesslike.'

Emilia nodded. 'I understand,' she said. 'But I need to get the memorial service out of the way first. I feel as if I can't move on until that's happened.'

'Of course,' said Andrea. 'There's no rush. The shop will tick over for a few months yet. And in the meantime, if you've got any questions, just pick up the phone. I want to help you make the right decision. But the right decision for you, not one made out of sentiment or a sense of duty.'

The two women hugged. Emilia left Andrea's office, not for the first time gratified by how kind people were, and reassured at how perceptive and caring Andrea was. She felt that whatever decision she made, she'd be in safe hands.

Later, Emilia sat in the familiarity of the kitchen.

On a shelf were rows of glass jars, with stickers on, their contents carefully stated in Julius's copperplate handwriting: basmati rice, red lentils, brown sugar, penne. Below them were smaller jars containing his spices: bright yellows and brick reds and burnt oranges. Julius had loved cooking, rustling up a huge curry or soup or stew and then freezing it in small portions so he could pull whatever he fancied out in the evening and heat it through. Next to the food was his collection of cookery books: Elizabeth David, Rose Elliot, Madhur Jaffrey, all battered and stained with splashes. Wooden chopping blocks, woks, knives, ladles.

She could imagine him in his blue and white apron, standing at the cooker, a glass of red wine in one hand, chucking in ingredients and chatting.

Never had a room felt so empty.

She had an A4 pad in front of her on the table. She picked up a pen and began to make a list of ideas.

Staff rota
Open Sunday (extra staff?)
Website - Dave (She was pretty sure Dave would be
    able to help.)
Redecorate
Relaunch. Party? Publicity?

It all looked a bit vague and nebulous. The problem was Nightingale Books had been the way it was for so long she couldn't imagine it any other way. She completely understood Andrea's concerns, and that it couldn't carry on the way it was. But did she have the wherewithal to turn it around?

She had no idea what to do for the best. She tried to empty her mind and focus, so she could identify what she wanted, but it was impossible, because what she wanted was for everything to still be the same, for her father to be here, and for her to be able to drop in whenever she liked; have coffee with him, a meal with him, just a chat with him.

She sighed. It was only half past two, and she felt as if she could go to bed now and not wake up until tomorrow.

She couldn't though. Julius's friend Marlowe was

coming over to give her a lesson on Julius's cello. She desperately wanted to play 'The Swan' by Saint-Saëns at his memorial, but she hadn't played for so long, and she'd sold her own cello when she went abroad.

Julius had been a founder member of the Peasebrook Quartet, along with the formidable Felicity Manners, who had retired from the quartet a couple of years ago when her arthritis became too bad for her to play the more intricate pieces. Marlowe, who had been second violinist, had taken over as first and now did a wonderful job of choosing and arranging pieces that pleased both the hoi polloi and the music snobs (of which there were quite a few in Peasebrook).

The quartet was affiliated to Peasebrook Manor and played a variety of concerts in the gardens every summer, and at half a dozen carefully chosen weddings, as well as a popular Christmas carol service in the chapel. That way the quartet didn't take over their diaries, and left them room to get on with other things. They were respected and enjoyed, and although they were never going to make millions, they were all passionate about the music they made.

And Marlowe fuelled that passion. Marlowe was a true renaissance man. He quietly earned a small fortune composing music for adverts, and he was an exquisite violinist. He was one of those understated people who made you believe anything was possible. He was never still for a minute, yet he had time for everyone.

Although Marlowe was nearer Emilia's age – mid-thirties, she thought – he and Julius were as thick as thieves, sitting at the kitchen table for hours drinking bottles of New World Cabernet while they decided on the programmes for the quartet. They'd watched every series of *Breaking Bad* together, fuelled by tequila and tacos, and compiled an annual New Year's Eve quiz for the Peasebrook Arms, with fiendishly difficult questions.

Emilia had always been drawn to him, and occasionally wondered if there could be more between them, but somehow, over the years she had known him, either she or Marlowe had always been attached to someone else. He had a string of glamorous girlfriends, usually musicians, whom he treated with benign absent-mindedness, always preoccupied with his latest project.

When Emilia had phoned and asked Marlowe for help to practise the piece she wanted to play at Julius's memorial, Marlowe hadn't hesitated.

'That is quite wonderful,' he told her on the phone. 'Your father would be delighted. I can't tell you what a loss to the quartet he is. We've asked Felicity back pro tem, though it will limit what we can play. Petra's still on viola, of course. Delphine's going to take over from Julius, though cello's not her first instrument and so she won't be a patch on him. But don't tell her I said so or she'll have my balls for earrings.'

Delphine was the French mistress at a nearby prep school and Emilia was fairly sure that Marlowe and Delphine were an item. Julius had intimated so, expressing the merest hint of disapproval, which surprised Emilia. Her father was rarely judgemental, but he found Delphine terrifying.

'She stands too close. And I never know what she's thinking.'

'She's very attractive,' Emilia had pointed out. She'd met Delphine briefly on several occasions, but knew instinctively they would never be kindred spirits. Delphine was a fashion plate, always perfectly made-up, inscrutable, with a hint of the dominatrix that Emilia knew she could never pull off in a million years.

Julius shook his head. 'She's scary. And she doesn't eat. I'm not sure what Marlowe sees in her.'

Emilia could see exactly. Delphine was the stuff of male fantasy.

'She's very demanding,' added Julius. 'Maybe Marlowe will get fed up with it in the end.'

Emilia laughed. 'Just don't criticise her,' she advised. 'Or you'll only make her more attractive to him.'

Marlowe arrived promptly. He gave Emilia a huge hug. He felt warm and comfortingly solid in a big cashmere overcoat, his curls stuffed underneath a bobble hat.

'How've you been?' he asked.

Emilia just shrugged. 'You know. Vacillating between grief and despair.'

'It's awful for you.'

'It is.'

'I bloody miss him. I keep thinking *I'll drop in and have a drink with old Julius*. And then I remember . . . So I can't imagine how you must feel.'

Marlowe took off his coat and threw it on the sofa. Underneath he wore black skinny jeans, a grey cable-knit sweater and a pair of oxblood Chelsea boots. When he took off his hat his black curls sprang free, wild and untamed.

He looked at Julius's cello, standing in the corner of the room.

'May I?' he asked, mindful of its significance.

'No, please – go ahead.'

He strode across the room and lifted the cello off its stand. He ran his long, slender fingers over the strings, expertly listening to see if it was in tune, adjusting the pegs until the notes were just as he wanted them. Emilia felt a pang, wondering about the last time Julius had played it: what had he played? He had played every day. It was his way of switching off. He never considered it a chore.

She watched Marlowe tune up, fascinated, always intrigued by the way a true musician handled an instrument: with absolute confidence and mastery. She could never take her playing to the next level because she was always slightly afraid the instrument was in charge, rather than the other way around.

He picked up Julius's bow and ran it over a small block of resin until the fine hairs were as smooth as silk. Then he sat down and let the bow dance over each string and the notes rang out loud and true in the stillness of the living room. He began playing a tune, short sharp staccato notes, and Emilia smiled in delight as she recognised it. 'Smooth Criminal'. Not what one would expect from a cello.

Then he segued into something sweeter, something she didn't recognise. He finished with a flourish, stood up and pointed her to the seat.

'Let's see how you are.'

'I haven't played for years. I meant to practise before you got here—'

'Ah. The fatal words. *I meant to practise*. I don't want to hear you say that again.'

Emilia blushed. Now he had pointed it out, it did

sound lame. Brilliant musicians were brilliant because they practised, not just because they had talent.

She warmed up, playing a few scales. It was surprising how well she could remember. It was almost instinctive as she moved her fingers up and down the strings, stretching and curling them to capture just the right note, then moving on to arpeggios to reignite the muscle memory.

'There you are, you see?' Marlowe looked delighted. 'It doesn't go away. It's like riding a bicycle. You just need to put the time in now.'

She took out the sheet music for 'The Swan' from the pile on the piano. She began to play. She had done it years ago for one of her grades. She couldn't remember which – six, she thought. She had been note perfect then, and had got a distinction. But after all this time, her playing was dreadful. She scraped and scratched her way through it, determined not to stop until she got to the end.

'It's awful,' she said. 'I can't do it. I'll do something else. I'll read a poem.'

'No,' said Marlowe. 'This is perfect for your father. And yes, it was bloody awful. But you can do it. I know you can. I'll help you. If you practise two hours a day between now and the memorial, it will be the perfect tribute.'

He started breaking the music down for her, picking out the fiddly bits and getting her to master them before putting them back in, marking up the manuscript with his pencil. After an hour and a half of painstaking analysis, he asked her to play it through again.

This time it sounded almost like the tune it was. Not perfect, far from perfect, but at least recognisable. She laughed in delight, and he joined in.

'Bravo,' he said.

'I'm exhausted,' she told him.

'You've worked hard. We better stop now. There's only so much you can take in.'

'Would you like a glass of wine before you go?' she asked, hoping he'd say yes. 'It's going to take me years to work my way through Dad's wine collection if I don't have help.'

He hesitated for a moment. 'Go on then. Just a glass. I mustn't be late.'

She couldn't help wondering if it was Delphine he mustn't be late for, but she couldn't really ask.

She flicked on the sound system in the kitchen. Some Paris jazz sessions flooded the room: cool, smooth sax and piano with an infectious beat. It took her breath suddenly. It must have been the last thing Julius listened to.

Marlowe found his way around the kitchen, pulling a bottle of red from the rack, opening the drawer to find Julius's precious *bilame*, the corkscrew favoured by French wine waiters. He opened the bottle effortlessly and poured them each a glass.

He looked at her, and she couldn't hide her tears.

'I'm sorry,' she laughed. 'You just don't know when it's going to get you. And it's always music that does it.'

'Tell me about it,' said Marlowe, handing her a glass. 'But it's OK to cry, you know.'

Emilia managed to compose herself. She wanted to relax, not grieve. As she drank her wine, Emilia managed to unwind properly for the first time since she'd come home. The kitchen felt alive again, with the music and the company, and she found herself laughing when Marlowe told her about the disastrous impromptu poker school he and Julius had set up the winter before last.

'We were rubbish,' he told her. 'Luckily the maximum stake was only a fiver, or you probably wouldn't have a roof over your head.'

Emilia didn't mention that she was slightly worried she might not anyway.

When he left, after two glasses of wine not one, the flat seemed a slightly dimmer place. He ruffled her hair as she left, an affectionate gesture, and she smiled as she turned and shut the door. People were kind; people were loving. At least, the people her father had attracted were.

When Emilia went to bed that night, her head was spinning with accidentals and spreadsheets and pizzicato and bank loans and opening hours and crescendos. And the running order for Julius's memorial – everyone in Peasebrook wanted to do something, it seemed. But despite all the things whirling around in her brain, she thought how lucky she was to have the support of such wonderful people – June and Mel and Dave, and Andrea, and Marlowe. Whatever she decided, she was going to be all right.

EMILIA NIGHTINGALE

EPONYMOUS LITERARY HEROINES

Pamela Samuel Richardson

Jane Eyre Charlotte Brontë

Lolita Vladimir Nabokov

Zuleika Dobson Max Beerbohm

Emma Jane Austen

Anna Karenina Leo Tolstoy

Madame Bovary Gustave Flaubert

Mrs Dalloway Virginia Woolf

Moll Flanders Daniel Defoe

Matilda Roald Dahl

7

On the morning of Julius's memorial, the staff gathered in the middle of the book shop just before it was time to set off. Emilia felt filled with pride. June, who still insisted on coming in every day to help out, was in a deep pink wool dress with a matching wrap. Dave, as a Goth, always wore black anyway, but he had on a splendid velvet frock coat and a black ribbon in his ponytail. Mel had changed three times but settled on a purple satin Stevie Nicks skirt and a plunging top that showed off her impressive cleavage. Emilia had gone for traditional black, in a high-necked dress with lace sleeves and a full skirt that fell almost to her ankles but would enable her to play. Her dark red hair was tied in a chignon.

'We look like something out of Dickens.' June smiled. 'He'd be very proud.'

They'd decided to shut the shop, as a mark of respect, but Dave and Mel were coming straight back to open up. Emilia wasn't providing anything afterwards. She felt as if she had already made everyone in Peasebrook tea over the past few weeks, and she didn't have the emotional energy left to host any sort of wake. The memorial would be uplifting and that, she hoped, would be it. She could start looking ahead to the future and make some concrete decisions.

'I just want to say, before we go, how grateful I am. You've been diamonds, all of you. I wouldn't have got this far without your support. I'd have fallen apart.'

June put her arm around her. 'Rubbish. You're made of stern stuff. And you know how much we all thought of your father.'

'Come on, then,' said Emilia. 'Let's go and see him off. Give him the send-off he deserves.'

She was trying to be brave, but inside she felt small, and really all she wanted was her father here to tell her it was going to be all right, but he was never going to do that again. It was up to *her* to make everything all right. And not just for herself, she was starting to realise. For everyone. Julius had left behind so much: so many friendships, so much loyalty.

She shut the door of the shop with a ceremonial flourish and set off down the high street with her little entourage. Marlowe had taken the cello to the church and was going to tune it so it was ready for her. The quartet was going to play too – Elgar, one of Julius's great loves. Marlowe had arranged the 'Chanson de Nuit' especially for the four of them.

St Nick's was at the other end of the high street, fronted by an ancient graveyard. It was a bright autumn day, the sky a brisk blue, the sharpness of the air cutting through the smell of fallen leaves. Emilia arrived at the church door and stepped inside. She gasped. The service wouldn't start for half an hour but already the pews were full to bursting.

'Oh,' she said, putting her hand to her mouth. 'Look how many people there are.'

June touched her shoulder gently.

'Of course, my darling girl,' she told her. 'Of course.'

Sarah loved her kitchen in the mornings. There was an estate office, but she liked to hold her briefings around the table in here: run over any problems they'd had with visitors, talk about upcoming events, discuss any brainwaves the staff had. The kettle was on the Aga top non-stop, and there was always a tray of brownies or flapjacks or date slices sent over from the tea room. This time of year was their quietest. They always took some time in autumn to take a breath after the furore of summer and before the mayhem of Christmas.

Sarah had been auditioning Father Christmases for the grotto all week. It was more difficult than she had anticipated. Their old Father Christmas had finally decided to hang up his boots, but finding someone good-natured and jolly and bearded (she had no truck with false beards: Peasebrook Manor was all about authenticity) was a challenge. Still, it had taken her mind off the impending memorial service.

But now the day had come. The service was at twelve o'clock. No one ever questioned what Sarah was doing or where she was – she knew that from years of discreet vanishing – but today she felt self-conscious, exposed and slightly vulnerable, as if today was the day she was finally going to get caught for her transgressions, because of her emotions.

Of course, the safest thing to do would be not go. To take herself off somewhere and have her own private memorial. But she wanted to be there for him. He would want her there, she was sure. She wished she had a friend, a stalwart who could come with her, but she had never confided in anyone. It was the only way to be sure.

If she could get through today, she would have got away with it.

She felt slightly giddy with the risk. Perhaps it was better to focus on that than her grief, a little black bundle she only opened when she knew no one was around.

She also knew it was easier to get away with things if you were open. She had never pretended not to know Julius. If she was with Ralph and they bumped into each other in Peasebrook at a social function, or in the supermarket or simply in the street, she always made a point of talking to him. So it wasn't in the least odd that she was going to pay her respects.

Ralph was reading the paper, and the two girls who worked in the office were comparing text messages.

'Right – I'm off into Peasebrook. I'm going to Julius Nightingale's memorial.' Sarah said it as casually as she could. Never had three words struck such coldness into her heart.

Ralph didn't flicker. He didn't take his eyes away from the paper.

'Sure. See you later.'

Sometimes, she had wondered if he knew, or suspected, but judging by his reaction, he hadn't a clue. And now he never would know.

Sarah had never set out to be an adulteress. But like all adulteresses, she had found a way to justify her infidelity. The one thing she was glad of was that at least Julius wasn't married, so she was only causing potential harm to her own marriage, not her lover's. The only person who ever gave herself grief about her infidelity was herself, because no one else knew. And when she backed herself into a corner over it, Wicked Sarah told Pious Sarah that Ralph was lucky she hadn't left him. He should be grateful that the only knock-on effect of his behaviour was her affair.

It was fifteen years ago now, but she could remember the shock as if it was yesterday.

In retrospect, Sarah supposed that it was a testament to the strength of her marriage that Ralph was able to confess the extent of his debt to her. A lesser man might have driven them to the brink of ruin. Ralph stopped short of that. Just. And for that Sarah was, if not grateful, then thankful. For she would never have forgiven him if it had meant selling Peasebrook. Never.

It was unusual for a house like Peasebrook to be passed down the distaff side, but Sarah's parents handed it over to her when she turned thirty and scarpered off to live in the Scilly Isles, and she took on the responsibility with gusto. Ralph was working in the City as a financial analyst and making plenty of money for them to maintain the house and have a good life. But when the pressure of that became too much, he took early retirement. He claimed to have done the maths, and assured her there was enough in the coffers to keep them in Hunter wellies and replace the roof tiles when necessary. He had the rent from his bachelor flat in Kensington and he still played the stock market.

'We'll never be helicopter rich,' he told her, but he knew helicopter rich wasn't Sarah's bag. And it meant a much more relaxed life, having him around instead of up in London during the week, and he was there for Alice – whom they both adored – and somehow it was as it should be. They both did their own thing, and agreed it had been the right thing to do when they met in the kitchen for coffee or were able to turn up as a couple to Alice's nativity play or when they went off to the White Horse for lunch just because they could. When Ralph had worked, they had barely seen each other, and that was no way to run a marriage.

It was the horses that did for Ralph. He couldn't help it. He was used to taking risks with money, and missed the adrenalin. Sarah knew he had a flutter every now and again, but she didn't mind. It was important for men to have an interest, and if that meant Ralph poring over the *Racing Post* at breakfast and trotting off to the races with his cronies, she didn't mind – she liked the occasional trip to Cheltenham or Newbury herself if there was a decent meeting or a horse they knew running.

Until one day she came into the kitchen and saw Ralph sitting at the table. In front of him were a bottle of Laphroaig and a set of keys. With a lurch, Sarah recognised them as the keys to the gun cabinet.

'Take them away,' said Ralph, his voice thick with whisky.

'What's going on?' Her heart was hammering as she picked them up. 'You're drunk.' Ralph wasn't the type to get drunk at eleven o'clock in the morning. Eleven o'clock at night, yes.

He rubbed his face in his hands and looked up. His eyes were bloodshot.

'I'm sorry.'

'You're going to have to spell it out.' Sarah was crisp. 'What's going on?'

'I should have quit while I was ahead. I was at one point. But I couldn't resist, could I? And I should know, better than anyone. The only one that wins is the bookie.'

Sarah sat down at the table opposite him.

'You've lost money?'

He nodded.

'Well, at least you've told me. We can deal with it. Can't we?'

'I don't think you understand.'

Ralph put his hand on the neck of the bottle to pour another drink, but Sarah stopped him.

'That's not going to help. Come on. Tell me.'

'I've lost the lot,' he said.

'What lot?' Sarah felt fear.

'All my money. Everything I had.'

Sarah swallowed. All his money? She had no idea how much that was. Not that Ralph would have hidden it from her, but his assets went up and down every day. Sarah had her own bank account, with her own family money, and they had a joint account for bills and house-keeping, but they didn't really get involved in each other's financial matters.

'I don't understand.'

'It's all on my account on the computer if you want to look at it.' There was a bleakness in his eyes Sarah found harrowing. 'I broke all my own rules, didn't I? I let emotion get in the way.'

'How much?'

He turned the laptop screen towards her. She thought she might be sick.

'What do we do?'

He could only manage a shrug.

She tried to think. Her brain couldn't take it in: the staggering sum, or how she could have missed what he was doing. She'd been too engrossed in Alice and Peasebrook to notice.

'It was going to be all right.' His voice was cracked. 'I would have stopped.'

'Ralph. You know better than anyone . . .'

'That's why I thought I was being clever.'

Sarah's mind raced. It settled on the most logical conclusion.

'You'll have to sell the flat.'

The flat was their safety net.

He looked at her. His eyes said it all.

'Oh God!'

She stood by him, of course she did. She still loved him, and she didn't want to destroy their little family, or what they had together. Her support of him was unstinting: practical and no-nonsense. She made him face up to the fact he had an addiction. She cut up his credit cards, took away his laptop, made him give her access to his online bank accounts – all with his permission; she wasn't trying to emasculate him. They needed a strategy to stop him being tempted, ever again, and if that meant she had to police him, then so be it.

And it was then she decided to make Peasebrook work for them and open it to the public. It was the best chance they had of a steady income. It would be hard work, but Sarah certainly wasn't afraid of that. After all, Peasebrook was her life already, so it might as well be her living too.

But her trust in Ralph had gone, and she didn't know if she would ever be able to get it back. He had risked everything he had because he was a fool, and she felt sure Peasebrook had only been spared because it was a step too far. It made her blood run cold to think of what might have happened. Her respect for him had gone too. He was weak. And no matter how he tried to excuse it, or explain it, he just wasn't the man she thought he was. In no way did she blame herself for what had happened. She was a good wife, and she wasn't insecure enough to start looking for imperfections or ways in which she didn't measure up. She bloody well did. It was Ralph who didn't.

She didn't share what had happened with many people. She hated gossip and speculation. She didn't want Ralph being a public spectacle, for Alice's sake as much as anything. Sarah was a very private person. It was a huge burden to shoulder all alone. Every now and then she longed for a friend to share the truth with, but she didn't trust anyone. A few glasses of wine and your private business was public knowledge. She'd heard enough intimate secrets splurged at dinner parties to know that. So she kept quiet.

The first Christmas was awful. They had to tighten their belts. They didn't send out invitations to their usual Christmas Eve party and Sarah ended up fabricating an excuse involving a tricky and unpleasant varicose vein procedure to stop people thinking they had been left off the guest list because the party had become a tradition locally. She found the pretence dispiriting and exhausting, and all the excitement of Christmas was tainted. Tainted by the stupid, awful, ridiculous debt. She still didn't understand why Ralph had felt the need, because there'd always been sufficient, or so she thought, but when he tried to explain that gambling wasn't driven by any logic, she got upset. And tried not to get angry.

But when there wasn't enough money for Christmas presents, because every last penny was going into the development fund for Peasebrook, she felt resentful. All those bloody acres, she thought, and no cash in the kitty. She was determined that Alice should have what she wanted, and not have any sense of the crisis they were in, so she bought everything on her list to Father Christmas – more than she would usually – and everyone else was going to have books.

Books, after all, were her escape from the horror she had been through. At night she could curl up with Ruth Rendell or Nancy Mitford and the stress melted away, and for a couple of hours she could be somewhere else. Reading gave her comfort.

She went into Nightingale Books. Until now, she had been working her way through the books in the library at Peasebrook, but she wanted to choose specific books for everyone in the family.

Julius Nightingale was behind the counter when she walked in, wearing a distinguished pair of half-moon glasses and peering at a catalogue. She gave him a smile.

'Can I help?'

'I've come to do my Christmas shopping. I'm just going to have a wander round.'

'Shout if you need me.'

She saw a pile of Dick Francis novels on one of the tables and thought how in previous years she would have bought one for Ralph. Not this year though.

As she browsed, she found the horrors of the recent past fading away. She lost herself somewhere in amongst the shelves as she chose for her friends and family: a thick, weighty historical biography for her father; a sumptuously illustrated cookery book for her mother; the Narnia Chronicles for Alice; the latest escapist fiction for her younger sisters; jokey books for the downstairs loo for her brothers-in-law. Choosing the books was soothing her soul.

The pile was enormous. As she handed over her debit card, she hoped there'd be enough in the account to cover it. She thought she'd probably overdone Alice's stocking. She was definitely overcompensating. Sarah busied herself looking at a rack of Penguin classics while he processed the payment, her heart hammering.

'I'm so sorry,' said Julius. 'It's been declined. It happens a lot at Christmas,' he added kindly.

Sarah felt her cheeks burn. She was mortified. She was going to cry, she realised with horror. Thank goodness she was the only person in the shop at that moment. And then it struck her that, throughout all the turmoil and the trauma and the chaos and the fear and the panic, she hadn't cried once. Ralph had, great snivelling, gulping sobs of self-pity, and it made her want to scream, because the whole situation could have been avoided if only he hadn't been such a fool. He had brought it on them through his own stupidity. But Sarah wasn't a shouter; she was a stiff-upper-lip-and-get-on-with-it sort of person who came up with solutions rather than wallowing.

Only now, suddenly, she felt as if she were six years old and the world had come crashing down around her because she'd smashed her piggy bank on the kitchen floor. She swallowed back the tears.

'I'm so sorry,' she stammered.

'Take them anyway. You can pay me later,' Julius said, and he grinned. 'I know where you live, as the Mafia say.'

'No, I can't possibly,' said Sarah, and this time she couldn't stop the tears.

Julius was the perfect gentleman. He made her an industrial strength cup of tea and sat her down. And he was so understanding and so unjudgemental she found herself spilling out everything that had happened.

'What a horrible time you've had,' he sympathised.

Sarah put her face in her hands. 'Please. Don't tell anyone. I shouldn't have said anything.'

'I won't breathe a word,' he promised solemnly. 'Honestly, sometimes I feel like a priest in here. People tell me all sorts of extraordinary things. I *could* write a book. But I'm too busy selling them.'

In the end, he made her laugh so much the world seemed a better place.

'Look,' he said. 'Take the books. Pay me when you can. It's honestly no skin off my nose.'

He was so insistent that it was easier to take them than to refuse. And it gave her an excuse, a few days later when she'd managed to scrape together some cash, to go in and pay him. And she stayed nearly an hour and chatted, because the great thing was you could stay in a book shop talking about books for as long as you liked and nobody thought it strange.

The books she'd chosen made Sarah's Christmas brighter. Even the book she had chosen for Dillon, the lad she had taken on to help with the garden, went down better than she had expected. She'd given him a copy of *The Secret Garden*. It was a book she herself returned to time and again, and she never failed to find the story one of hope.

She wrapped it in white tissue with a dark green ribbon and gave it to him.

'You probably think this is a really weird and inappropriate present,' she told him. 'But this book means the world to me. And I want you to know how much I appreciate what you're doing here at Peasebrook. You make me feel as if I can achieve what I want to.'

He was so polite when he opened the book. He thanked her effusively, and assured her he didn't think it was a boring present. It was the only present he'd had that was actually wrapped. His mum and dad had got him some safety goggles and a bottle of Jägermeister.

'I wasn't expecting anything at all from you, to be honest,' he told her.

She thought he would probably take it home and shove it away somewhere, never to be seen again. But to her surprise he came to her a few days into the New Year and told her how much he'd enjoyed it.

He might have just been being polite, but the next time she went past Nightingale Books, she went in and told Julius, and he was delighted.

'It must happen to you all the time,' said Sarah. 'People telling you how much a book has meant.'

'Yes,' said Julius. 'It's why I do what I do. There's a book for everyone, even if they don't think there is. A book that reaches in and grabs your soul.'

And he looked at her, and she felt a tug deep inside, and she thought – that's *my* soul.

She looked away, flustered, and then she looked back, and he was still looking at her.

She could remember every detail of that moment as she took her navy coat off the peg in the cloakroom and then tucked a silk scarf around her neck. The last one he had given her. They had always given each other scarves at Christmas. After all, no one ever questioned a new scarf the way they might a piece of jewellery, yet they were pleasingly intimate. Sarah cherished the feel of the silk against her skin, as soft and caressing as her lover's fingers had once been.

She buttoned up her coat and walked briskly to her car.

Thomasina was grateful, for once, for the distraction of her unruly class. Trying to keep them in check kept her mind off the stress. They were particularly skittish today: clearly the rigours of making a béchamel sauce weren't enough to hold their attention. They liked things they could take home and share, like pizza or muffins or sausage rolls. And béchamel sauce was tricky: difficult not to burn, even harder to get rid of the lumps. It took practice and patience, neither of which came naturally to her Year Elevens.

Her star pupil, Lauren, proffered her saucepan, showing her a glossy smooth sauce, and Thomasina smiled.

'Perfect,' she said.

The result particularly pleased her because Lauren was one of the school's problem pupils. She'd been threatened with exclusion on more than one occasion for disruptive behaviour. Lauren took bubbly to a new level. She was incapable of keeping quiet or concentrating for any length of time. Thomasina had sat in on endless staff meetings to discuss Lauren's behaviour, and had heard every teacher express exasperation.

'She's either going to end up in prison or on the *Sunday Times*' Rich List,' sighed the head.

For some reason, Lauren behaved impeccably in Thomasina's class. She was the only member of staff who seemed to have any influence over her. Which was odd, because Thomasina usually found people took no notice of her whatsoever.

She'd taken a risk two months before, and with the head's permission asked Lauren if she would like a Saturday job with her at A Deux.

'Good idea,' the head agreed. 'She'll only be out shoplifting or drinking cider otherwise.'

She wasn't stereotyping. Lauren had been cautioned for both in the past. Thomasina was surprised at how pleased she was when Lauren agreed to the job.

'What do you want me to do?'

'Help me prep. Lay the table. Make sure the glasses and plates and cutlery are spotless. Run to the shops if I need anything. And wait at the table while I do the cooking.'

'Be your bitch, you mean,' grinned Lauren.

'If you like,' said Thomasina. She knew she was taking a big risk, but she had seen something in Lauren the other staff had overlooked. She'd seen her concentrate while she was cooking, her total absorption in the process. Lauren wasn't interested in the written theory, but she threw herself into the practical work with something bordering on passion, and she wanted to please Thomasina – again, something none of the other teachers had ever experienced. Thomasina wanted to capture that passion and do something with it, and giving Lauren a job out of school, where she didn't have the rest of the class to show off to, was a step in the right direction.

Thomasina was halfway out of the classroom door when Lauren stopped her.

'Do you need me this weekend, miss?'

'Yes, please. I've got an anniversary dinner booked in.' She looked at Lauren. 'But you know the drill. Short nails. No scent. Hair tied back.'

Lauren came to school with glittery fake nails, her blonde hair backcombed into a bouffant mane, drenched in noxious perfume.

She rolled her eyes. 'Yeah, yeah.' She looked at her nails – silver with black lightning streaks appliquéd on. 'Do you know how long these take?'

'It's non-negotiable.' Thomasina was putting on her coat. Her stomach was churning. Why had she said yes? She was starting to hope for a natural disaster – a hurricane, perhaps? It was too early for a snowstorm. Or maybe her car wouldn't start? It wouldn't be her fault, then, if she didn't turn up.

'You all right, miss?' Lauren was looking at her.

'I'm nervous about something.'

'What?'

'I promised to do a reading at a friend's memorial.'

Thomasina couldn't even begin to think about it. If she thought about it, she wouldn't do it. She had the book in her bag – *Remembrance of Things Past*, by Proust. It had seemed obvious to her, to do the most famous literary passage about food. She had practised it over and over and over at home. But practising at home was worse than useless, because there was only ever her there.

Lauren was staring at her, puzzled.

'What are you scared of? You'll be ace, miss. Knock 'em dead.' She made a face when she realised what she had said. 'Well, you know what I mean.'

Thomasina couldn't help laughing. And she felt a little bit cheered by her pupil's faith in her.

'Thanks, Lauren,' she said.

'That's all right,' said Lauren. 'You tell me I can do things I don't think I can do all the time. No one minds if you mess up, that's what you say. But you have to try.'

Thomasina was touched by Lauren's logic. She hadn't realised her words of encouragement went in. It gave her the courage she needed.

Sarah arrived at the church door just before the service was about to begin. She slipped inside and her eyes widened in surprise at the size of the congregation. She scanned the pews for a space, hoping that no one would turn and notice her. She reminded herself there was no reason for her not to be here, but nevertheless she didn't want to be under scrutiny. There was a space next to a pillar. She wouldn't have the greatest view, but in a way the pillar gave her protection. She sat down as the vicar stepped forwards to begin his welcome.

Oh Julius, she thought, and clasped her hands in her lap tightly.

Thomasina's reading was one of the first. With terror, she read her name on the order of service and realised there was no time to back out now. On the other hand, her ordeal would be over more quickly. She was in the front row, along with the others who were doing a reading or a performance. Her heart raced, and her palms felt sweaty. She wanted to run out, but she couldn't make a spectacle. She had to go through with it.

And then suddenly, the preceding hymn – 'Fight the

Good Fight' – came to an end and it was her turn. She made her way out of her pew, and walked across to the pulpit as if she was walking to her execution. She climbed up the winding steps. She felt as if she was high up, in the clouds. She put the book down on the lectern, open at the page she was going to read. She'd underlined the words in red and they swam in front of her. She couldn't look out at the congregation. The thought that every single person in the church was looking at her, waiting for her to start, made her feel hot with fear. She was trembling. Just begin, she told herself, and then it will end. Before you know it.

She started to read, but her voice was barely there. She paused, cleared her throat, ignored the little demon inside her that was telling her to run down the steps and down the aisle and out of the door, and forged on. Her voice found itself. As she read on, it became clear and true:

'She sent for one of those squat, plump little cakes called "petites madeleines", which look as though they had been moulded in the fluted valve of a scallop shell. And soon, mechanically, dispirited after a dreary day with the prospect of a depressing morrow, I raised to my lips a spoonful of the tea in which I had soaked a morsel of the cake. No sooner had the warm liquid mixed with the crumbs touched my palate than a shudder ran through me and I stopped, intent upon the extraordinary thing that was happening to me. An exquisite pleasure had invaded my senses, something isolated, detached, with no suggestion of its origin. And at once the vicissitudes of life had become indifferent to me, its disasters innocuous, its brevity illusory – this new sensation having had on me the effect which love has of filling me with a precious essence; or rather this essence was not in me it *was* me.

I had ceased now to feel mediocre, contingent, mortal. Whence could it have come to me, this all-powerful joy? I sensed that it was connected with the taste of the tea and the cake, but that it infinitely transcended those savours, could not, indeed, be of the same nature.

'Whence did it come? What did it mean? How could I seize and apprehend it?'

By the time she reached the last three sentences, she had hit her stride. She lifted her eyes and looked out as she spoke the words. The congregation was rapt, and she felt a surge of joy that she had managed to do for Julius what had seemed impossible. She smiled as she finished, and closed the book, calm, composed. And confident. She felt confident.

Luckily for Sarah, there wasn't a dry eye in the church when Emilia played her piece on Julius's cello.

She stood at the front of the church and spoke before she began.

'My father gave me a love of books first and foremost, but he also gave me a deep passion for music. I was five when he first let me play his cello. He taught me to play "Twinkle, Twinkle, Little Star" one Sunday afternoon, and I was hooked. I went on to do my grades, though I was never as good as he was. We played together often, and this was one of his favourite pieces. It's "The Swan", by Saint-Saëns.'

She gave a little nod, sat in her seat, picked up her bow and began to play. The notes were achingly sad, their melancholy sound echoing around the church, sweet and lingering. Sarah could feel them make their way into her heart and break it. She fell on her knees onto the prayer stool in front of her and buried her head in her arms, trying not to sob. She breathed as deeply as she could to calm herself until the last note died away. There was a silence, punctuated only by other members of the congregation sniffing and clearing their throats and wiping away their tears, and then someone began to clap, until the entire church was united in their applause. Sarah gathered herself, sat up, and joined in. She knew how very proud Julius would have been, how much he had loved his daughter, and she wished she could tell Emilia of the way his eyes had shone when he spoke of her.

Emilia felt elated when she finished playing. She had spent the last two weeks rehearsing every night until she was note perfect, but she was still afraid that she would freeze midway through, or her fingers would betray her. But they hadn't. And then she sat and listened to the quartet play Elgar's 'Chanson de Nuit'. Somehow, under Marlowe's direction, they made the music not sad but uplifting. Emilia didn't think her battered little heart could take it, but as the last notes faded away she was still breathing. She was still alive.

Thomasina was making her way out of the churchyard, through the toppled gravestones. She needed to be back at school to teach the last lesson of the day. She felt a hand on her arm. She turned, and saw Jem smiling at her.

'That was a really great reading,' he told her. 'I wish I'd had the nerve. But there aren't many readings about cheese, and that's all we had in common.' He made a lugubrious face, but it was obvious he was joking.

Thomasina laughed.

'Thank you. I was really nervous.'

140

'You didn't look it.'

'Really?' Thomasina was surprised. She'd thought her fear would have been apparent.

'Not at all. My mum loved those books, by the way. Thank you . . .'

'I'm really pleased.'

They stood for a moment, the autumn leaves scuttling around their feet.

'I've got to go,' said Thomasina. 'I've got a class.'

'Yeah, and I've got to get back to the shop.' He held up a hand. 'See you.'

He strode off down the path towards the town and Thomasina watched him go, feeling as if she should have said more – but what more could she have said?

After the service, Emilia was putting away her cello in the vestry. She was glad to have something to occupy her. It had all been so perfect, and all she could think of was how much her father would have enjoyed everyone's contributions. She reminded herself she would have to send everyone a thank you letter.

'You played beautifully.'

She jumped, and turned.

There was Marlowe, smiling. 'You see? I told you. Practice makes perfect.'

'I don't know about perfect.'

'It was at *least* a merit.'

She pretended to pout. 'I got a distinction when I did it. For Grade Six, I think.'

'Good. Because there's something I want to ask you.'

He looked a bit awkward. Emilia felt her cheeks go slightly pink. Was he going to ask her out? Surely not, just after her father's memorial service? But a little bit of her hoped he might. She could do with a drink, she liked Marlowe, and her father had thought a lot of him. He was interesting and fun and—

'I wondered if you'd take your father's place in the quartet.'

'*What?*' This wasn't what Emilia had been expecting.

'Poor old Felicity is so limited with what she can do now and I don't want to put her under pressure. If you join, Delphine can go back to second violin, which will make her happy.' He gave a rueful grin. 'Which makes my life easier, I can tell you.'

Delphine. Of course. She had been at the service today, demure in a black shift dress. How on earth had she thought Marlowe might be interested in her?

Emilia shook her head. 'No way am I good enough. Look how long it took me just to get one piece right.'

'No way would I be asking you if I thought you weren't up to it. It's my reputation at stake. I wouldn't risk it.'

'I don't know what's happening. I don't know how long I'll be around. I don't know what I'm doing with the shop.' She was gabbling excuses.

'Just join till the end of the year. It's quiet for us, except for a few carol concerts. And Alice Basildon's wedding.' He was looking at her, his brown eyes beseeching behind his glasses. 'I can give you some lessons. Get you up to speed.'

Emilia could feel herself weakening. Of course she wanted to join the quartet. But it was daunting.

'I don't want to let you down.'

'We'll just be doing carols, and the usual wedding repertoire. No Prokofiev or anything too fiddly.'

She looked at him. How would she resist that disarming smile? Being in the quartet would be the perfect distraction from the stress of the shop and all the decisions she had to make. And even if she were to close Nightingale Books tomorrow, she would be tying up the loose ends for a few months yet. Most importantly, Julius would be so proud and pleased to think she had taken his place. She remembered his patience as he had taught her to pick out her first notes, shown her how to hold the bow correctly. They had played duets together, and Emilia remembered being transported by the music, the joy of being in sync with someone else. She missed that feeling. The quartet would give that to her.

'Promise me that if I'm not up to it, you'll say.'

'I promise,' said Marlowe. 'But you'll be fine. Is that a yes?'

Emilia thought for a moment, and then nodded.

'It's a yes.'

Marlowe looked delighted. 'Your dad would be so proud. You know that, don't you?'

He hugged Emilia, and she felt a warm glow.

She told herself it was the pleasure of doing something she knew her father would have wanted.

Sarah drove back to Peasebrook Manor feeling dry-eyed and hollowed out, numb with the effort of trying not to feel. She had suppressed her emotions so ferociously she thought she might never feel anything ever again. A wave of gloom hit her as she turned into the drive. Oh God, Friday night fish pie and false smiles. That was what the evening held. Could she really live the rest of her life like this?

8

That evening, Dillon stopped off at the White Horse. He always dropped in on a Friday. He and a few mates met for a pint of Honeycote Ale, a bag of cheese and onion crisps, and a chat about how their week had gone, before they all drifted off home for a shower and their dinner. Some of them had wives and girlfriends to go home to; some of them came back later, for a few more beers and maybe a game of darts or pool.

The White Horse was the perfect country pub. Perched on the river just outside Peasebrook, on the road to Maybury, it was rough and ready but charming. There was a small restaurant with wobbly wooden tables and benches, serving hearty rustic cuisine: game terrine with baby pickled onions and home-made Scotch eggs and thick chewy bread and pots of pale butter studded with sea salt. The bar had a stone floor, a huge inglenook fireplace, and a collection of bold paintings by a young local artist depicting stags and hares and pheasants. It was frequented by locals and weekenders alike and you could turn up in jeans or jewels: it didn't much matter.

Dillon had been coming here ever since he could remember. His dad used to bring him and his brothers in on a Sunday while his mum cooked lunch, and it had become part of his life now. There was always someone he knew at the bar. If you didn't know anyone, it wouldn't be long before you did, because the atmosphere was convivial and everyone mucked in. It was easy to strike up a conversation.

That evening Alice was in there with Hugh and a horde of their friends. Dillon immediately felt tense.

Dillon loathed Hugh Pettifer with a vengeance. He could tell how difficult Hugh found it to treat him with politeness. He knew that if Hugh had his way, Dillon would never be allowed to speak to any of the Basildons and would bow and scrape and tug his forelock all day long. But that wasn't how the Basildons worked, and whenever Alice saw Dillon she threw her arms around him and chattered away, teasing him in a manner some might consider flirtatious but that Dillon knew was just Alice.

Hugh would look at him with distaste, just about managing to acknowledge him with a nod and a smile that didn't go anywhere near his eyes, and would draw Alice away at the first opportunity. It was all Dillon could do not to put two fingers up to Hugh's retreating back.

Once, Sarah had asked him what he thought of Hugh. He wanted to say what he thought, but he would never say the c-word to Sarah.

Of course Hugh wanted to marry Alice. She had social standing, which Hugh didn't, and was due to inherit quite the prettiest manor house in the county. She would be a wonderful wife, and a wonderful mother. Dillon could imagine a clutch of sturdy blonde-haired moppets stomping around Peasebrook in their wellies, with puppies and ponies galore.

Dillon couldn't help wondering what was in it for Alice. Good genes? Hugh was pretty good-looking, if you liked that minor-royalty-polo-player sort of look: thick hair and year-round tan. Was it money? He was wealthy, certainly, but Dillon didn't think Alice was that superficial. Maybe Hugh was a demon in bed? Maybe it was a combination of all three?

He made Dillon's teeth go on edge. He told himself he was jealous. He would never have that kind of pull. A mere underling, on a fairly paltry salary, with no power or influence.

He and Alice got on like a house on fire when they were alone at Peasebrook Manor, but he felt awkward when she was out with her gang. They were spoilt and loud and drank and drove too fast.

'They're all really lovely,' Alice would protest.

'I'm sure they are,' said Dillon. 'But when they're in a big crowd they come across as tossers.'

Alice looked wounded. Dillon knew he had to be careful. There was a limit to how horrible you could be about someone's friends without it being a reflection on them.

So he tried to slink up to the bar and get a pint without her seeing him, but she did. She leapt out of her chair and came to give him a big hug.

'Hello, Dillon! We're all a bit sloshed. We've been to the races.' She beamed and pointed over to a crowd of her friends around a big table by the window. 'Come and join us.'

Dillon declined, as politely as he could. 'Got to see a man about a ferret.'

This wasn't a lie. He had a pair of ferrets at home, and the jill had just had a litter of kittens. He wanted to get shot of them before too long. A mate of his was interested.

Alice wouldn't give up. 'Come on. Come and meet everyone. I bet they'd all love a ferret. How many are there?'

Dillon sighed. Alice just didn't understand, God bless her. Her friends were no more interested in him than he was in them. They had absolutely nothing in common except Alice. And they certainly wouldn't want a ferret.

Alice was a little sunbeam who loved everybody, saw the bad in no one and treated everyone the same. To her, life was one long party. She fizzed with fun and bonhomie and that was why she was so good at her job. She understood what her clients wanted and did her utmost to get it for them. But she was shrewd underneath it. She knew how to get the best price for everything, and how to get the effect her clients wanted without paying over the odds.

That was how Dillon had really got to know her. She had become tired of paying astronomical sums for flower arrangements. After every wedding she looked at the florists' handiwork and sighed. So she came to Dillon and asked him to plant her a cutting garden.

'I'm going to do the flowers myself from now on,' she declared. 'Everything has to be grown at Peasebrook. That's our selling point. If they don't like it, they can go somewhere else.'

So she and Dillon had spent hours poring over florists' websites and leafing through seed catalogues. He told her what they could grow: tulips, narcissi, peonies, dahlias, roses, of course, sweet Williams, sweet peas, alchemilla... She sent a couple of the girls who worked for her on a floristry course, and by the next wedding season they were doing the bouquets, buttonholes, table arrangements – everything.

'I want that freshly-plucked-from-the-garden look,' said Alice. 'Not those awful stiff formal arrangements. I want it all frondy and feathery and Thomas Hardy-ish.'

In the end, Dillon had suggested a polytunnel, to get the biggest seasonal range, and Alice had declared him an utter genius.

So they had got quite close, and sometimes they ended up in the White Horse having a drink, and Alice bobbed about the pub like the butterfly she was, chatting to everyone. And then she'd met Hugh, at a friend's party in London, and Dillon backed off. He could tell it was time for him to cut the ties, because there was absolutely no way a man like Hugh wanted the likes of Dillon cosying up to his girlfriend. And he tried to make it so that Alice didn't realise he was deliberately avoiding her, because he knew the minute she twigged she would be insistent about including him, and Dillon simply couldn't face the humiliation or the power struggle.

This was the first time he had been cornered in public, and he didn't have a watertight excuse. He felt the prickly panic of a socially awkward situation.

'You've got to meet everyone,' Alice urged him. 'They'll all be at the wedding. Come on.'

She was tugging at his arm. Across the pub, Dillon saw Brian Melksham come into the bar for his Friday pint. Relief flooded him, just as Hugh walked over and put a proprietorial arm around Alice. There was no mistaking the underlying message.

'I can't,' said Dillon. 'There's Brian. He's having my ferrets off me.'

Alice's face fell.

Hugh smirked and gave an unpleasant laugh.

'It's like the bloody *Archers* in here.'

Dillon grabbed Brian's arm and walked him over to the bar. 'Don't look over. Just pretend we're deep in conversation.'

'What's going on?'

'Alice wants me to go and sit with all her mates.'

'Is she here with that knob?'

'Yep.'

No one in the White Horse thought much of Hugh. They all thought Alice deserved better.

'I seen his white tart trap in the car park,' said Brian. 'Nothing that a squirt of slurry wouldn't put right.'

He pulled a fiver out of his pocket for his pint. That was what Dillon loved about people in the White Horse. They didn't suffer fools.

At the end of the evening, the landlord called time. Dillon had stayed on for a game of pool in the back room but he decided he'd leave now, before the traditional Friday night lock-in. You had to be in the mood and he wanted a clear head for the weekend.

He walked back through into the main bar and saw Alice and her friends getting ready to leave. Most of them were unsteady on their feet, draped all over each other, braying and swaying. He looked at Hugh, who was holding his car keys. His face was flushed red, his eyes slightly glazed. He couldn't possibly be fit to drive. Dillon looked at the empty champagne bottles littering the table. They'd had shots too. Someone had set up a Jäger train – shot glasses of Jägermeister balanced on glasses of Red Bull.

There had been much hilarity as the domino effect pushed each shot glass into the next one.

But Dillon knew Hugh's type. He wouldn't let a small thing like being over the limit stop him. Dillon had only had two pints over the course of the evening. He wasn't going to risk his licence. Besides, drink driving was illegal for a good reason.

He walked over to Alice, who was just coming out of the loo. He could see she had drunk too much to have any common sense left.

'You shouldn't get in the car with Hugh. You shouldn't let him drive.'

Alice waved a hand. 'It'll be fine. It's only the lanes.'

'Please. I'll give you a lift.'

Hugh came looming up behind Alice. He was waving his keys. 'What's up, ferret boy?'

Dillon didn't falter. 'You shouldn't be driving.'

Hugh's stare was flat and hard.

'Mind your own bloody business.'

'Come on, man,' said Dillon, distressed. 'I can give you guys a lift.'

Hugh prodded him in the chest. 'Butt out. I'm fine to drive.'

Dillon bunched his fists and stepped forwards. One of Alice's mates spotted what was going on and started shouting, 'Fight! Fight!'

Alice looked worried. 'Honestly, Dills – he's fine.'

Dillon scowled. It went against all his instincts to let Alice get in the car with Hugh.

'Piss off, Mellors,' said Hugh. 'Come on, Alice.'

Dillon could see her falter for a moment. As Hugh led

her away she turned, then shrugged, as if to say 'What can I do?'

Dillon stared after them. His jaw was set. His heart hammered in his chest. He should grab Hugh and stop him; take away his keys. But he could see the look in Hugh's eyes. He'd try and punch his lights out. And if he got physical with Dillon, Dillon would fight back and there was no doubt who would come off the worse. Dillon worked outside all day; Hugh sat behind a desk and went out for boozy lunches. He couldn't beat up Alice's fiancé. Sarah would be horrified.

He pulled his own keys out of his pocket. He would follow them home. Make sure Alice didn't come to any harm. It was his duty. If anything happened to her, how could he ever look Sarah in the eye again? He headed out into the car park. The night air was crisp and cold; frost was starting to settle on the branches.

Hugh's car was waiting in the car-park exit, the engine idling.

Dillon got into his old Fiesta. He drove up behind the Audi, waiting patiently. He wasn't going to pip his horn. He knew that was what Hugh wanted him to do. He was goading him. The seconds seemed like minutes. Dillon tapped his fingers on the steering wheel, trying not to get wound up. He wondered what Alice was thinking, if she knew what game Hugh was playing. She probably wouldn't have a clue. Dillon was pretty sure she had no idea of her fiancé's true colours.

Finally the Audi shot out of the car park and into the road, accelerating at a terrifying rate. He could imagine Hugh at the wheel, laughing his head off. There was no way his little car could keep up with his high-powered vehicle. Dillon's lips tightened as he joined the road and followed in Hugh's wake.

The lanes back to Peasebrook Manor were inky black at this time of night, with trees looming on either side. Dillon dropped down a gear and put his foot down, taking the bends carefully. And then he turned the blind bend half a mile before the entrance to Peasebrook Manor and saw his worst fear in front of him. The massive oak tree that loomed over the corner was pierced by Hugh's car.

The driver's door was open. Dillon could see Hugh in the road, hands at his head. The passenger side had taken the full impact.

There was a horrible silence.

Dillon pulled out his phone. Thank God there was a signal here. He pulled into a gateway, flicked on his hazard warning lights, dialled the police and opened his door in one fluid movement, jumping out into the road.

Hugh came running up to him. There was panic on his face.

'Have you got your phone? I can't find my phone.'

Dillon pushed him out of the way and spoke into the phone. 'Ambulance, please. And police.'

He strode past Hugh, who pulled at his arm. 'Not the police—'

Dillon pushed him away. 'There's been an accident at the Withyoak turn. Car's gone right into the tree. I don't know how many casualties yet but definitely one!'

Dillon hung up and ran towards the car, jumping into the driver's side.

Alice was slumped over the airbag, unconscious. Her side of the car was crushed. There was broken glass, and blood on her face and her hands and in her hair. He could see that her legs were trapped. Dillon couldn't begin to try and get her out. He might do more harm than good. He realised he was crying. He should have stopped her.

Hugh poked his head through the door.

'Shit. Is she all right?'

'No she fucking isn't! There's blood everywhere.'

'Oh Jesus. Jesus Jesus Jesus.'

'Alice! Can you hear me?' Dillon put a tentative hand on her shoulder. 'You're going to be OK. The ambulance is on its way. Alice?' Dillon felt sick as he realised there was no response. He took her wrist and felt for a pulse. It was still there, and now he knew she was still alive he could see her breathing.

What should he do? Dillon was racking his brain for first aid rules, but he couldn't think of anything. Her legs were trapped. He couldn't pull her out. He didn't want to move her in case he did more damage. All he could do was reassure her. He was shaking. With shock and fear and anger.

'It's your fucking fault,' said Hugh. 'You were following us. I saw you pull out right behind me. You were harassing us.'

'Don't talk crap.'

'I'm going to make sure they have you for dangerous driving.'

'They'll think you're having a laugh. My car doesn't do over sixty.' Dillon pointed a thumb over to his ancient car by the nearby gate. 'And they'll see the tyre tracks.'

Hugh looked at the road in the moonlight. Dillon was right. There was a pair of black lines imprinted on the road where he'd lost it on the corner. They'd be able to work out his speed.

'Fuck's sake. I'll lose my licence. I'll lose my job. I won't be able to support her.' He grabbed Dillon's shoulder. 'You do realise that's all they want me for, the Basildons? My money. They think it's going to save Peasebrook. They need me.'

Dillon looked at him. What a bloody state. But now he thought about it, it explained a lot. Hugh was loaded. It would take the pressure off if Alice married him. A source of ready cash.

That was how these families worked, wasn't it? It wasn't so far from an arranged marriage. He felt ill at the thought. Was Alice having to pretend to love Hugh, in order to save Peasebrook?

'If she dies,' Dillon told Hugh, 'I'll kill you.'

'She's not going to die,' said Hugh, but he looked as pale as the moonlight as lights appeared around the bend accompanied by wailing sirens.

Next to him, Alice stirred and moaned. She reached out a hand. Dillon took it.

'It's all right,' said Dillon, squeezing her hand as hard as he could. 'It's all right, Alice. The ambulance is here. You're going to be all right.'

In no time, there were people swarming everywhere, shouting instructions, the elaborate choreography of an emergency procedure taking shape.

Dillon and Hugh were taken to one side, removed from the scene of the accident.

'I lost it on the bend,' Hugh was telling a policeman. 'I'm not used to this car, and there was some black ice.

I was taking Alice home to Peasebrook. We're due to get married in three months...'

He was trying his best to look the modicum of respectability.

'Come and sit in the car with me a moment, sir,' said the copper to Hugh.

'No problem,' said Hugh, but he looked daggers at Dillon.

Dillon didn't know what to think as he watched Hugh follow the policeman. He didn't want trouble for Alice, but the man was an idiot. He'd got what was coming to him. Dillon hoped they locked him up and threw away the key.

It seemed to take forever for the ambulance men to get Alice out of the car. The minutes seemed like hours. Eventually they lifted her gently onto a stretcher. She looked so small, so still, as they carried her over to the ambulance.

'Who's coming with her? Is anyone coming with her?' one of the paramedics asked.

'Yeah. I'll come.' He didn't want Alice turning up to the hospital on her own. He climbed into the back.

'Are you her husband? Boyfriend?'

'No – I work for the family. Is she going to be all right?'

No one answered. Someone was taking her blood pressure. Someone else was wiping away the blood.

Then suddenly Hugh was banging on the door. Someone opened it to let him in.

'Is she all right? I'm coming with her.'

'There's only room for one.'

Hugh looked at Dillon. 'Out.'

Dillon was astonished. It looked as if Hugh was in the

clear. How on earth could he be? Dillon had seen him with his mates. They were all roaring drunk. What had he done? Had he bribed the policeman? Or was he genuinely not over the limit? Dillon couldn't understand it.

'Can you blokes sort yourself out?' asked a paramedic. 'We need to get going.'

Hugh's eyes met his. There was a message in them to say his card was marked. Dillon didn't care. Hugh couldn't touch him. All he cared about was Alice.

Without another word, Dillon climbed out of the ambulance.

Another policeman walked past.

'Somebody get on to Peasebrook Manor,' Dillon heard him say into a radio. 'Best for them to meet us at the hospital.'

Dillon felt sick at the thought of Sarah being given the news. She would be distraught. He couldn't imagine there was anything worse than being told your child had been in a car accident. He wished he could be with her, to reassure and comfort her, but it wasn't appropriate. It wasn't his place. Even though Dillon spent hours with her every day, it was Ralph who would and should be with her. He didn't even feel entitled to go to the hospital. This was a family matter. He was staff. It was his duty to step away, and wait until he was needed.

The ambulance doors slammed shut and the driver turned on the siren. Dillon wondered if Hugh would hold Alice's hand and tell her it was all going to be all right. He thought probably not. All Hugh would be worried about was saving his own arse. How was he going to explain the accident to the Basildons?

He looked up into the night sky. He couldn't believe

the stars were there, twinkling happily. How was it possible, when Alice lay there so still and small?

The ambulance drove off and Dillon was left there, watching Hugh's car being hoisted onto the tow truck. There was the sound of hydraulics and clanking chains, the mechanics shouting instructions to each other. A remaining policeman removed the accident sign.

And suddenly, everyone was gone and it was deathly quiet. It was as if the accident had never happened, except for the scar on the old oak tree. Dillon stared at it and wondered how fast Hugh had been going. He felt sick thinking about it. He felt totally helpless. What could he do? Pray, he supposed, but he'd never been a praying man. As far as he was concerned, nature took its course, man interfered from time to time, and what happened, happened. No greater force had any influence.

He went back to his car, still parked in the gateway. He drove slowly home, seeing ghosts in the shadows as the light turned from granite to gun-smoke. If he phoned the hospital, they wouldn't give him any information: he wasn't family. Was Alice a cadaver, under a white sheet, eyes shut? Was she on an operating table, waiting for a surgeon to perform his magic? Was she sitting up in bed, pale and shaken but laughing, drinking tea and chatting to the nurses? How was he going to find out?

At Peasebrook Manor, when Sarah Basildon heard the sound of a bell drill through the house, she sat up in bed and thought, Oh God, no. Please. Not so soon after Julius. Not someone else. I can't take it.

9

Sarah sat upright, her hands pressed between her knees, staring at an awful painting of a wood in autumn hung on the pale green wall of the hospital waiting room. Waiting, she thought. Waiting for news. A diagnosis. A prognosis. Suddenly nothing else in life held any import or urgency. Eating, sleeping, drinking – all were irrelevant. They'd been here since two o'clock in the morning. Alice was having a brain scan, or an X-ray, or was in theatre, or something – she couldn't remember which, or in what order. The information was a jumble and Alice was the staff priority, not giving out information. And they couldn't give information until they had answers. Sarah kept telling herself everyone was doing their best, but it was agony.

Ralph came in with a mug of tea in each hand and held one out to her. He'd gone off to find the friendly Scottish nurse with the bleached blonde hair and the smiling eyes, to see if she had any idea what was going on.

Ralph, for all the blundering blustering hopelessness he usually used to dissemble, had come into his own. His mantle of fecklessness slipped away, and out came a man of integrity and grit. It must have been his army training. He'd only had a couple of years in the Blues and Royals, but it must have been lying dormant in him. Maybe that was what had been lacking in his life over the past few years? A proper crisis.

Sarah stared down at her tea.

'Come on,' he said. 'Drink up, darling. We're going to need all our strength.' He fished in his pocket and brought out a brace of digestives. 'Not much of a breakfast, but they'll see you through. An army marches on its stomach.'

Sarah took the mug and one of the biscuits. A tentative sip told her the tea was too hot, so she dunked the biscuit in.

'The consultant should be here in a few minutes,' Ralph added, and their eyes met. It was the moment they had been longing for and dreading, the consultant's verdict. Ralph put a hand on her shoulder. 'We'll get through this, darling. She's a fighter, Alice. That spirit of hers . . .'

He trailed off and his voice caught on his words. Sarah put up her hand and squeezed his arm. He needed reassurance too. He looked down at her, surprised and grateful, and she realised with a start that they barely had any physical contact any more. It hadn't been a conscious decision, but a gradual withdrawal. Sarah wondered for a moment if he had noticed, or, indeed, if he minded. She felt a rush of regret, tinged with guilt.

The door opened and they both stood to attention, Sarah sliding her arm into Ralph's. Now she had touched him, she felt the need to be close. They both stood there, clutching their mugs of tea, staring at the young doctor in the maroon jersey.

He smiled. 'Mr and Mrs Basildon?'

They nodded, mute with dread. They couldn't read into

his smile. Was it just a greeting, or a barometer? If it was bad news, would he bother smiling?

'Well, she's in a bit of a pickle, I'm afraid.' He grimaced. 'But the good news is we've done a brain scan and there doesn't seem to be any great injury. Obviously we need to keep her monitored. There's never any guarantee. Bleeds can occur unexpectedly after trauma. But so far, so good.'

'Oh, thank God.' Sarah leant against Ralph, limp with relief.

'It's not all good news. Her left leg is in very bad shape. There are multiple fractures, and we're going to have to operate and pin it all back together. It's a bit of a mess. It's going to be a while before she can walk. There'll be a lot of rehab work. A lot of physio.'

'We want the best people,' said Sarah. 'We can pay, if necessary.' God knows how, but they'd find the money. Sell a painting. She'd sell her soul if necessary.

'You don't need to worry about that just yet. She's in the best hands at the moment. Although there is more.' He cleared his throat and Sarah looked at him. Somehow she knew this was going to be the bad bit. 'Her face is badly lacerated. There's a very nasty cut on her left cheek. She may well have to have some cosmetic surgery.'

'Oh God,' said Sarah. 'She's getting married in November.'

'We'll do our very best for her.' He paused. 'Look, there's a lot to take in, and we don't know yet which order we are going to be doing things. But in some ways she's been very lucky—'

'Lucky?' Sarah looked appalled. Beautiful Alice, who was the least vain person Sarah knew.

'We should tell Hugh,' said Ralph. Hugh had gone out

160

for fresh air. He said he was feeling odd after the crash. But he'd probably gone for a cigarette.

Sarah stiffened slightly at the mention of Hugh's name. 'It's all his bloody fault.'

'Darling. It was an accident. Black ice . . .'

'Yes.' Sarah didn't sound convinced.

'It must be awful. Imagine how he feels.'

'He drives too fast. I know he does.'

More than once Sarah had had to brake in her Polo, meeting Hugh coming the other way in the narrow lanes leading to Peasebrook.

'Boys will be boys.'

'How can you *say* that?'

'Come on. We should be celebrating the fact that she's not got a brain injury—'

'As soon as she comes back from X-ray, you'll be able to see her,' said the consultant.

'She's going to be as right as rain. I know it,' said Ralph. 'She's made of stern stuff, my daughter.' He managed a smile. 'Like her mother.'

Sarah looked up from her seat in the waiting room when Hugh walked back in, smelling of freshly smoked cigarette and Wrigley's. He gave a tentative smile. He was, quite rightly, wary of Sarah.

'The nurse just told me. She's going to be all right—'
Sarah cut him off.

'You were driving too fast,' she said flatly.

'Sarah!' Ralph stood up.

Hugh looked down at the floor, then sighed.

'I know I was,' he said, quietly. 'And I'll never forgive

myself. But there'd been a bit of an incident in the pub. I was trying to get Alice home as quickly as I could.'

'What do you mean – incident?'

There were fisticuffs in the White Horse sometimes. Not often, but it was inevitable sometimes after a few too many beers.

'It was your gardener chap. He was being a bit . . . aggressive.'

'Dillon?' Sarah was incredulous.

'Yes,' said Hugh. 'I should have taken him outside, but I didn't want trouble.'

'What do you mean – aggressive? That doesn't sound like him.'

'Everyone's different after a few.' Hugh put on a pained expression. 'I think he's got a bit of a thing about Alice. It was pretty embarrassing. He was following us. In his car. I put my foot down to get away from him. It was just instinct.'

Sarah shook her head. 'I don't believe you. Dillon wouldn't put Alice in danger.'

'Well, I can assure you it happened.'

'Following you and then what, exactly? What was he going to do then?'

Sarah was staring at Hugh, her eyes hard. He shrugged.

'I don't know. Beat me up? I think he'd had a few too many. Maybe I should have reported him. Stopped him from driving. In retrospect, that would have been the responsible thing to do—'

'I don't think any of this is true.'

Ralph stepped forwards. 'Darling, I don't think this is the time.'

Hugh looked distressed. 'I'm sorry. I was trying to protect Alice. And yes, I put my foot down—'

'So it *was* your fault.'

'Sarah – this isn't an inquisition.'

'I want to get to the bottom of what happened. And I'm not convinced Dillon had anything to do with it. It sounds completely out of character.'

Ralph and Hugh shared a complicit look.

'Oh, Sarah,' said Ralph. 'You always see the best in everyone.'

'Not everyone.' She looked at Hugh. 'I don't always see the best in everyone.'

Hugh attempted a disarming smile. 'Look, we're all a bit upset. We're bound to be. The great thing is Alice is going to be all right. Let's not lose sight of that.'

'All right?' said Sarah. 'She's going to be scarred for life.'

'Sarah.' Ralph's tone was sharp. 'This isn't helping.'

The door swung open and the three of them looked towards the nurse. She was smiling.

'If you want to come and see Alice, just for five minutes...'

'Just me,' said Sarah. 'I want to see her. Three will be too much for her.'

Neither Hugh nor Ralph dared to remonstrate.

Alice was a tiny bundle in a bed in the middle of intensive care, a mass of bandages and wires and bruised flesh. There was barely a bit of her Sarah recognised. Even her voice was just a croak.

Sarah didn't want to say much. She didn't want drama. She didn't really do drama. The confrontation in the waiting room was as high as her voice had been raised for years. She was the epitome of calm, brought up to be serene and gracious.

She held Alice's little paw, the one without the cannula, and stroked it gently.

'Poor sweetheart,' she whispered.

'How bad is it?' asked Alice. 'I can't move anything and my head hurts. I can't *think*.'

'You've bashed your poor leg up a bit,' said Sarah. 'They'll need to pin it back together.'

She swallowed. She couldn't look at Alice's face. She couldn't say anything about her face. Not yet.

'We'll have to cancel, won't we? The wedding?' Alice's voice was a quaver.

Sarah looked at the floor. Something inside her said yes. That would be the answer to everything. Cancel the wedding. She had a bad feeling about it. About Hugh. But she didn't want to upset Alice by agreeing, because it would imply that things were terribly serious. Which indeed they may well be, but Alice had been through enough already. She needed soothing.

'We don't have to worry about that at the moment. It's a long way off.'

She suddenly felt drained, and incredibly emotional. She didn't want to cry in front of Alice.

'What happened, darling?'

'I don't know. I can't remember. There were loads of us. In the pub . . .'

'Was Dillon there?'

'Dillon?' Alice was trying hard to recollect the events. 'Maybe.'

'Did he and Hugh have a row?'

'I don't think so.'

'Only Hugh seems to think they did.'

Alice shook her head. 'I can remember the Jäger train...'

Sarah wasn't going to push it. She didn't want Alice distressed.

'Would you like to see Daddy?'

'Yes, please. I'm sorry, Mummy.'

'Sorry? What on earth are you sorry for?'

She could see Alice struggling with a thought, a memory.

'I don't know,' answered Alice, and her eyes filled up with tears.

It was eight o'clock before Sarah and Ralph got back to Peasebrook Manor from the hospital. The nurse had insisted they go in the end, had assured them repeatedly that Alice would be comfortable, and that they would end up being a nuisance if they stayed any longer.

Hugh had gone to stay with a friend. He had sensed, quite rightly, that he was best out of Sarah's line of fire for the time being.

Sarah sank down into her chair at the kitchen table. Yesterday morning seemed a lifetime away, when she had sat here preparing for Julius's memorial. You never knew what lay ahead.

'Shall I make scramblers?' asked Ralph. She shook her head. She couldn't bear the thought of food. 'You've got to eat.'

'Not now. Honestly. I'm beyond it.'

'Tea.' He grabbed the kettle and put it on the Aga. 'That hospital tea was definitely made from scrapings off the factory floor.'

How could he be so jovial?

She stared at the dresser on the wall opposite. She could see Alice's Noddy egg cup. It had been hers when she was small: a Noddy cup with a little blue felt hat with a bell on, to keep the egg warm. She thought about all the boiled eggs she'd made her daughter.

She could feel it coming. The grief. It was gathering speed, and was going to smash into her any moment. And this time, she didn't have to brace herself to withstand it. This time, she could let it engulf her. She'd been through every emotion today. Shock. Fear. Anger. Fury. Worry. Relief. Then more worry, doubt, fear, anxiety... There was only so much you could take.

And being at the hospital had reminded her. Of the day she had said goodbye to Julius at the cottage hospital. It was two weeks before he had finally slipped away. She'd been in to see him; brought him the new Ian Rankin, which she was going to read to him because his eyes kept going blurry and he couldn't concentrate.

She hadn't been prepared for him telling her he didn't want her to come in to see him again.

'I feel OK today. But I know it's just a temporary respite. Tomorrow I might be out of it. Or gone altogether. I want us to quit while we are ahead. I don't want you here when I don't know you are there. I don't want you to watch me die. I want to say goodbye to you while I am still me. A pretty ropey version of me.' He managed a self-deprecating smile. He was thin; his skin had an awful pallor; his hair was wispy. 'But me.'

'You can't ask me to do that,' she had whispered, appalled. She stroked his cheek. She loved every bone in his poor failing body.

'Please,' he said. 'I don't want to argue about it. It's for the best.'

Their fingers had been entwined while they spoke. And she knew him well enough to know that he had thought this through, that what he was saying was right. Emilia was on her way home to be with her father. Sarah couldn't be seen with him any more.

She held his hands in hers and kissed them. She kissed his forehead. She leant her cheek on his and held it there for as long as she could bear. She looked deep into his eyes, those eyes she had looked into so many times and seen herself.

She couldn't see herself any more. He had shut her out. It was time for her to go, and he was preparing himself.

'You're the love of my life,' she told him.

'I'll save you a place. Wherever I'm going,' he said back. 'I'll be waiting for you.'

He gave a smile, and then he shut his eyes. It was his signal for her to go. She recognised that he couldn't take any more. If she loved him, she had to leave him.

She drove home, staring at the road ahead. She felt nothing. She had shut down. It was the only way to cope. There was nothing in her that was able to deal with the horror of that final goodbye. She had wanted to climb into his bed and hold him forever. To die with him, if that were possible. Drift off into that final never-ending sleep with him in her arms.

She went to the folly when she got back. She curled up on the sofa with a cushion in her arms, folding herself into the smallest ball. There was a copy of *Anna Karenina* she had been reading. It was the last book Julius had given her. She tried to read it but the words were too small. She shut her eyes and prayed for sleep. She couldn't bear to be awake. It was Dillon who found her, hours later, and shook her awake. She had looked up at him, wide-eyed, confused for a moment.

'Are you all right?' he asked, and she nodded, slowly. She had to be. She had no choice.

But now, here, in the kitchen, she embraced the grief when it finally hit. She put her head down and sobbed. Great big heaving sobs that threatened to choke her and take her very breath away. She could hear them, resounding around the kitchen: a primal keening, ungodly and harsh. She melted down into them until she almost became her own tears. In the midst of it all a small voice told her she was hysterical; that she needed to pull herself together.

But she'd waited a long time for this chance. The chance to purge herself of her grief. The chance to cry for the loss of her lover; her best friend. She wondered if she was wicked to hide behind Alice's accident for the chance to have this outpouring. She wondered if Alice's accident was a punishment for what she had done. Neither of these thoughts helped her regain control. On the contrary, she felt reason slipping further and further away. It was the sort of crying that would never stop.

Until she felt Ralph take hold of her arms. He took hold of her arms and shook her.

'Sarah.' His voice was firm but kind. 'Sarah. You must stop this. This isn't doing you any good at all. You or Alice.'

She juddered to a halt. He looked at her, concern in his eyes.

'Listen to me. I've never told you how magnificent I

168

think you are. How grateful I am for the way you stood by me. I wouldn't have blamed you for walking away after everything I did. But you got us through that bloody awful time like the fighter you are. And you're going to get us through this as well. Because you're a brave and wonderful woman, Sarah.'

He trailed off, looking a bit embarrassed. Ralph wasn't one for gushing speeches. He wasn't sure where the words had come from. But he had meant them, of that there was no doubt.

Sarah shut her eyes and breathed in deeply. Her breaths were jagged but her sobs eventually stopped.

'I'm sorry,' she said, but of course he had no idea what she was sorry for.

'Come here,' he said, and folded her into his arms. And although he wasn't who she wanted him to be, she felt safe, and knew that he was going to be there for Alice, and that they would get through it, that she would be able to live without Julius . . .

And that she wasn't going to cry again.

SARAH BASILDON

LITERARY COUNTRY HOUSES

Manderley – *Rebecca* Daphne du Maurier
Pemberley – *Pride and Prejudice* Jane Austen
Wuthering Heights Emily Brontë
Thornfield – *Jane Eyre* Charlotte Brontë
Gormenghast Mervyn Peake
Blandings P. G. Wodehouse
Cold Comfort Farm Stella Gibbons
Brideshead – *Brideshead Revisted* Evelyn Waugh
Howards End E. M. Forster
Godsend – *I Capture the Castle* Dodie Smith

10

Bea Brockman loved Peasebrook on a Saturday. It seemed to be fuel-injected: it was faster, busier, more animated than it was during the week. The market was full of interesting stalls: people selling berry-bright liqueurs made from local fruits, tables piled high with artisan bread, handmade beeswax candles in hot pink and emerald green and cobalt blue. She was ever on the lookout for the next new thing. It was – or had been – her job for so long, she had never lost the habit.

She dressed up on a Saturday more than she did during the week – though there was no point in doing full-scale London-style dressing. Monday to Friday she wore her casual-trendy mum-uniform of Scandi chic – asymmetric jumper, black skinny jeans and black trainers. Today, though, she had on a pretty dress, red suede boots and an Alexander McQueen scarf. Her hair was tied in a messy knot, and she'd painstakingly painted her mouth a luscious dark pink. She knew people looked at her. She was a tiny bit vain, Bea, and she missed the attention she'd had as a single girl. Though she loved being a mother. She adored Maud, who was proudly showing off her new beaded moccasins to anyone who cared to look from the depths of her fashionable all-terrain pushchair.

Bea had done the market, her favourite café, The Icing on the Cake, for a blueberry friand, and the butcher for a French-trimmed rack of lamb. She decided to head up to Nightingale Books for something to read. She had lists of all the paperbacks she should be reading to keep in the know, but there was nothing like a good browse in a book shop to broaden your horizons. She rolled the pushchair along the pavement, relishing the autumn sunshine that turned the buildings in Peasebrook to golden treacle. She was looking forward to their first winter in the country. London was so drab and bitter once the chill wind got a grip, chasing litter along the streets and alleys. Here, the air would be rich with the scent of woodsmoke, and there would always be a pub to hunker down in, and game from the butcher to be transformed into a warming casserole. She'd already spent the happiest of days that week making damson jam and apple chutney from the windfalls in the garden, with fashionably minimalist labels she'd designed herself.

She was quite the country mouse.

Nightingale Books was like stepping back in time. She loved its bay windows, the ting of the bell as she walked in, and the smell — a rather masculine smell, a combination of wood and parchment and pipe tobacco and sandalwood and polish that had accumulated over the years.

She hadn't been in for a while, because there hadn't been much time to read over the summer. Autumn and winter were for reading. She remembered seeing in the local paper the owner had died. Nevertheless, the shop was busy. Someone must have taken it over. They'd made a few changes: the displays were a little less haphazard, and it definitely looked less dusty, although the dust had been part of the charm.

Her eyes were immediately drawn to a display at the front of the shop. It was a huge coffee-table book, of photographs by the iconic Riley. It was lavish, beautiful, and at a hundred and thirty pounds, eye wateringly expensive. She picked up the display copy – all the others were shrink-wrapped to protect them – and leafed through the pictures.

An assistant passed by her and smiled.

'Stunning, isn't it?'

Bea sighed. 'It's gorgeous. I love his work.'

'Who doesn't? He's a genius. You should treat yourself.' Then she coloured. 'Sorry – I'm not trying to do a hard sell. Well, I suppose I am. It's a limited edition.'

Bea shook her head. 'I can't afford it.' She smiled. 'It's a lot of jars of organic baby food.' She put her hand on the handle of the pushchair by her side. Maud was gazing up at them as if fascinated by their exchange.

'She's adorable,' said the assistant.

'She's taking up all my money.'

'Oh my goodness. I love the shoes. Teeny little moccasins.'

Bea wasn't going to tell the girl how much they had cost. It was embarrassing.

'Me and Maud are going to choose a book together. You can't start them too young.'

'Absolutely. Get them a book habit. We've got lots of lovely new stock. I'm trying to build up the children's section.'

Bea was curious.

'Is this your shop, then?'

'It was my father's.'

'I heard he'd passed away. I'm so sorry.'

'Thank you.'

'It's great that you've taken it over. I love it in here.'

'Good. Just let me know if there's anything you want. I'm Emilia.'

'I'm Bea.' They exchanged smiles, then Emilia walked away.

Bea looked down at the pile of Rileys.

In a trice, she took the top one off the pile. Then she pushed Maud over to the children's section, and they spent the next ten minutes browsing through any number of board books until they chose just the right one.

'*I Love You to the Moon and Back*,' said Bea. 'It's true, darling Maud. I do.'

She pushed Maud over to the counter.

Maud stared up at Emilia, the board book clutched in her hands.

'Ah, that book's lovely. She'll adore it.'

'If she doesn't eat it first.' Bea smiled. 'Everything goes straight in her mouth at the moment.'

'Is that all?'

'For today. Yes. Thank you.'

Afterwards, Emilia watched Bea go. She was just the kind of customer she needed. Young and vibrant, with a disposable income. What else could she do to attract people like her? Cards and wrapping paper? Women like Bea were always buying cards and wrapping paper, because they had friends galore. She made a note on a pad, and turned to her next customer.

*

Bea walked briskly up the high street, her heart pounding. She didn't stop until she came to the church, where she swung into the churchyard. She strode on until she reached a bench and sat down. She put her head in her hands momentarily, then looked up. She reached over and pulled up the hood of the pushchair.

There, nestled in the folds, was the copy of Riley's book, still in its shrink-wrap. She picked it up and sat with it in her lap, staring at it.

What the hell was happening to her? What on earth had she become? What was she *doing*?

It had seemed the logical thing to do at the time. She'd wanted the book and she couldn't afford it. It had taken her two seconds to lift one off the pile and slide it into the hood of the pushchair.

A single tear trickled down one cheek. She wanted the book, yes. She wanted to sit at home and leaf through the photographs, studying them, analysing them, wondering at the skill and the talent and the artistry. She could have afforded it if she'd really wanted it. Bill wouldn't have minded if she'd put it on their credit card.

But more than the book, she'd wanted a thrill. She'd wanted to feel alive. She'd loved the adrenalin the feat gave her. It had been the most exciting thing to happen to her in months.

Bea sat back on the bench and looked up at the sky. A few swallows were circling overhead and the breeze rustled the last of the leaves in the trees that lined the path. The church reminded her of her own wedding only three years ago. She remembered the vintage Dior dress she'd had shipped over from the States, pale blue silk taffeta, with its tight bodice and covered buttons and full skirt. She'd been a perfect bride at their perfect wedding.

They had thought they were so clever, she and Bill. Selling up their trendy warehouse flat to start a life in the countryside. They'd agreed they didn't want to bring up their kids in London. Peasebrook had been the answer, with its brilliant commuter service, its cute shops and gorgeous houses. They had felt very pleased with themselves when they bought the gingerbread cottage in one of the back streets, with its tiny walled garden. It was idyllic; the ideal place to start a family. Bill carried on commuting to his ludicrously well-paid job as a digital guru and Bea did up the house and garden. And popped out Maud. Their friends all exclaimed in wonder and envy at how cunning and brave they had been, and came down in their droves to stay in their spare bedroom with its white floorboards and chalky walls and silk curtains and the high bed with mounds and mounds of feather-light bedding.

But now Bea thought she was going mad. She missed work. She had been exhausted when she left. As art director for a women's magazine, she had lived on black coffee and deadlines, working right up to the wire on each issue, dealing with a crazed editor who changed her mind every two minutes and expected her to be psychic. When she left, she never wanted to lift another finger.

Now, she was psychotic with boredom. She adored Maud, of course she did, but once she'd pureed some organic carrots and free-range chicken breasts and frozen them into portion-sized blobs, and hand-washed Maud's little cashmere cardigans in lavender-scented washing powder, and taken her for a walk in the flower-filled meadow down by the riverbank on the outskirts of Peasebrook – what more was there? Apart from cooking a Mongolian fish curry for when Bill cycled back from the train station at seven o'clock at night.

She was living the life she had depicted so many times in the magazine. She thought of all the spreads she'd done outlining bucolic bliss: girls in tea dresses and wellies pegging out washing. Wicker baskets and picnic rugs and muddy vegetables and home-made bloody jam. She had pots of it. Pots and pots and pots.

From the outside, she was living the dream. Inside, she felt bored and empty and meaningless. How on earth had she thought that full-time motherhood was going to be enough for her? She stroked Maud's fat little hand and felt her heart shrivel with the ugliness she was feeling. She was an ungrateful cow. How could this little bundle not be enough?

Maud was looking drowsy, one hand clutching her little towelling blankie with the rabbit in one corner. What would her daughter think, having a kleptomaniac as a mother? Bea knew she'd always been impulsive, but she'd never put her impulsiveness to bad use until now.

What would Bill think if he knew what she'd done? He was under enough pressure, with the travelling and the job. He could barely speak in the evenings when he came home. He just ate and went to bed, then got up at six to set off again. He wasn't much fun at the weekend either. For the past two months he'd refused to let them have guests down. He didn't do much. Slept. Watched a bit of telly. Opened his first bottle of beer at midday and drank steadily until he fell asleep again at about nine. If she complained, he snapped at her.

'You're living the dream, remember?'

OK, so it had been she who had orchestrated the massive change. She'd found the house, sold theirs, organised the move. Taken voluntary redundancy so she had a lump sum to live on. Arranged their finances so they could manage the drop in salary. Found ways to make savings so their weekly outgoings dropped by half but without a drop in standards. She'd saved them two hundred pounds a week by stopping them going out to eat or getting takeaways and getting a more economic car and not having a cleaner. Saving money had become her hobby, a point of pride.

She thought now she would do anything to be standing in a crowded train, with a takeaway latte in one hand and her iPhone in the other, brainstorming for a breakfast meeting. She would kill for an impossible brief or a draconian deadline or a crisis. These days, a crisis constituted running out of milk or nappies. Neither of which she ever did, because she had infinite amounts of time on her hands and so was the most efficient housekeeper on the planet.

But was she really so bored she'd resorted to shoplifting?

She walked back through the winding streets and by the time she got home Maud had fallen asleep. She pushed the pushchair into the living room, then sat on the pale grey velvet sofa that exactly matched the one opposite. In between was an antiqued mirrored coffee table that bore nothing but the occasional fingerprint. She spent most of her life polishing them off, and didn't want to think about the day when Maud began to cruise around the furniture.

She put the copy of the Riley in the middle of the table. It was the perfect book to have on display. She admired the black and white graphic on the front cover. She itched to take off the wrapping and look inside, to feast on the images and imagine herself to be one of his models.

Before she had a chance to remove the wrapping, she heard Bill come in the front door. He'd been to the garden centre, to get some posts and some wire for some fruit trees he was planning to espalier in the garden. It was a serious business, espaliering. She wasn't entirely sure what it was . . .

She jumped up and grabbed the book. She slid it under the cushions of the sofa just as Bill came in.

'Hey!' She smiled at him, trying her best not to look like a thieving lunatic. 'How are you? Me and Maud have had a lovely morning.'

'Good.'

'We bought a book. Didn't we, darling?' But Maud was still fast asleep, the book on her lap.

'Great.'

'How about you?'

'I bought a chainsaw.'

'How much was that?'

'Does it matter?'

'No. Of course not.'

'Good. Because we need one. I'm going to hack that old pear tree by the back gate down. It's blocking the light into the kitchen.'

'Great. We can have a gorgeous pile of logs. Make sure you chop them up evenly, so we can stack them by the fire.' She held her hands eight inches apart. 'About this long would be perfect.'

Even as she said it, she knew she sounded like a control freak.

Bill looked at her. 'Does everything have to be a fucking design statement?'

Bea opened her mouth to reply, but couldn't think of a good answer. She was puzzled, though. It wasn't like Bill to be so grumpy. What on earth was eating him?

She had to take the book back. She couldn't live with herself otherwise. She would confess all to the girl in the book shop. That was the only way to shock herself back to normality.

II

After a busy week, Emilia was looking forward to her first rehearsal that Sunday with the Peasebrook Quartet, although she was nervous too. It had taken hours of practice for her to get just one piece of music fit for human consumption. She knew she would have to get up to speed on dozens of new pieces, and she was terrible at sight-reading: it had always been her weakness. No doubt she would know some of the music, but there would be plenty that was new to her, and she was terrified of letting the side down.

Marlowe had been around earlier in the week to drop off some sheet music. She had been surprised at how pleased she was to see him – there was something reassuring about his presence. He hadn't stopped, though. He'd been in a hurry to get somewhere else.

'Work your way through this lot. Practise as much as you can. We can iron out everything at the rehearsal, so don't get into a panic. We've got loads of time.'

Emilia tried to be reassured, and went through as much of the music as she could in the evenings. She was pleased no one could hear her as she stumbled through, and when Sunday came she wasn't sure if she'd done the right thing, agreeing. She wasn't nearly as confident in her ability as Marlowe seemed to be.

They were rehearsing in the old church hall at the back of St Nick's. She walked down with Julius's cello on her back, not sure whether she was relieved to have something completely different from the book shop to focus her energy on, or whether she should be catching up on all the things she didn't get a chance to do when the shop was open. Dave had jumped at the chance to man the shop on Sundays for the interim: she'd left him in sole charge, with instructions to phone if it got too hectic.

They'd been really busy. Autumn seemed to bring with it a hunkering-down feeling that drew people back to reading, and the town was filled with people indulging in a weekend break in the countryside. With its Cotswold charm and inviting inns and welcoming shops, Pease-brook wore the colder months well and had become quite a hotspot, and Emilia and her team were working hard to raise the shop's profile. Dave had started them a Facebook page and a Twitter account; she'd been talking to several reps about supplementary merchandise; June was starting a monthly book club sponsored by the local wine merchants: for ten pounds you would get a copy of whichever paperback was going to be discussed over two glasses of specially chosen wine.

Of course, the main issue was cash flow. Andrea was still uncovering the extent of the shop's debts, they were waiting for probate, and in the meantime, the bills and the staff still needed to be paid. There was no shortage of ideas for making Nightingale Books the best book shop in the world, but to do that Emilia needed money. And there were plenty of boring things that needed to be done before the exciting things: the computer system badly needed updating; security was non-existent; and the roof was only held on by a wing and a prayer. The autumn winds were gathering strength and Emilia fully expected to find it no longer there one morning, the contents of the attic exposed for all to see.

In the church hall, four chairs were laid out in a semi-circle in front of four music stands. There was much discussion as to the best seating order, but in the end Marlowe dictated that Emilia and he were best at either end, so that she could see him and vice versa.

Any nerves Emilia had were doubled the moment she saw Delphine. Emilia knew the viola player, Petra, from old, but she had never got to know Delphine properly; only by repute from what Julius had said. She was wearing PVC drainpipes, brothel creepers and a frilly white blouse. She had Paris written all over her, with her asymmetric bob and red lips. Emilia felt dowdy in her jeans and hoody, with her hair in plaits.

'Do you two know each other?' Marlowe asked, his casual tone not giving anything away.

'Hello,' said Emilia, feeling a nasty burning sensation in the pit of her stomach. 'Thank you so much for playing at the memorial. It meant a lot.'

'We miss your father very much,' said Delphine. 'He was a beautiful player.'

Emilia immediately felt under pressure to be as good as her father, which she knew she wasn't.

She panicked even more when she heard Delphine play. She picked up her violin and played a snippet of Vivaldi's 'Autumn', in honour of the leaves turning to orange outside the window and the fact the sun had had little warmth in it that day.

It was the musical equivalent of a sketch. The bow barely touched the strings, just danced over them, picking out the few notes she wanted to give an approximation of the piece. The notes were pure and perfect and stunning in their simplicity. Delphine was a player at the top of her game.

Was she showing off? Or did she just feel the need to send Emilia a warning shot? A message to her that said you can never be as good as me, as long as you live, as often as you practise.

She finished the piece with a flourish. Petra clapped in delight. Emilia knew she would look churlish if she didn't join in. Her face ached as she smiled. Delphine gave a tiny self-deprecating shake of her head and a shrug as if to say 'it was nothing'. But Emilia knew she knew how good she was.

And then she sauntered over to Marlowe and slid a hand around his neck, stroking the back of it with her thumb. Marlowe was busy tightening his bow and didn't react, but it was such a familiar gesture, Emilia was left in no doubt: of course they were going out. She could imagine them having sex. French sex. French sex where Delphine was on top with her head thrown back and her eyes half-shut but her lipstick still perfect. Delphine was Juliette Binoche, Béatrice Dalle and Audrey Tautou rolled into one, and a musical prodigy to boot.

That answered that query, then. They were an item. Why did she feel disappointed?

She snapped the locks open on her cello case and stood up.

She was surprised how unsettled she felt.

Marlowe came over as she took out her cello and pulled out the spike.

'I hope you're not too nervous.'

'No! Well, yes.'

'You'll be fine. We're concentrating on the wedding music for the first half, then we'll start looking at some carols.'

'I should know most of them.' Emilia suddenly felt less daunted. She had spent her school years in the orchestra, after all.

She took her seat and began to tune her cello, pulling the bow across the A string. It sounded discordant and ugly, badly out of tune. It sounded how she felt. Swiftly, she adjusted the pegs until the note rang true.

And then they were off. They were starting with 'Arrival of the Queen of Sheba', the music Alice Basildon had chosen for her wedding entrance. It was a joyous and upbeat piece of music that Emilia loved, but it was extremely fast and extremely fiddly.

She played atrociously. Her fingers felt stiff and unyielding. Her mind couldn't concentrate. She missed the dynamics. She lost her place. She forgot what key signature they were in and played several wrong notes. And because there were only four of them playing, she couldn't hide behind the others. It made the piece sound dreadful.

Eventually Marlowe stopped.

'Shall we go back to bar twenty-four?' he asked. He didn't look at her or say anything else, which made it worse.

Red with humiliation, Emilia took in a deep breath and

studied the sheet music again. Petra gave her an encouraging smile and she felt as if she had one ally, at least. Marlowe raised his eyebrows and gave the signal to start again. She concentrated with all her might, but it was a huge effort. Nothing came naturally. She was playing like a robot, programmed to follow the black marks on the page, not feeling it with her heart or in her soul.

All the time, she was keenly aware of Delphine taking note of every tiny mistake she made. She wanted to throw down her cello and tell her to bugger off. She had never felt so threatened, and it was a horrible feeling.

At last, thank goodness, they got to the end.

'Well done, everybody,' was all Marlowe said.

Emilia kept her head low. She felt as if she had let everyone down. Her eyes felt peppery with unshed tears, but she wasn't going to let them out. Not with Delphine gloating in the corner. There was no point in apologising or drawing attention to herself. They all knew. She would just have to do better next time.

'Let's try the Pachelbel,' Marlowe said, and they shuffled through their sheet music until they found the right piece and put it on their respective stands. Emilia felt relieved. She knew this piece well, and could play it blindfolded; she could make up for her earlier debacle and prove herself to Delphine.

Afterwards, Marlowe gave her a nod and a smile that said she had redeemed herself. Just.

'Are you coming to the Cardamom Pod?' he asked. 'It's where we always go after Sunday rehearsals.'

Emilia wasn't sure if she could face it. Having to be

polite to Delphine, and feeling self-conscious about her lacklustre performance.

'I've got paperwork,' she lied. 'Mounds of it. The accountant will shoot me if I don't get it in to her tomorrow.'

There was a flurry of protest but Emilia didn't miss the flash of triumph in Delphine's eye. And suddenly she wondered why she should be made to feel bad when she had done her best, and been thrown in at the deep end.

'But why not?' she said. 'I've got to eat, after all.'

She lifted up her cello and hoisted it onto her back with a bright smile.

'Excellent,' said Marlowe.

The Cardamom Pod was housed in one of Peasebrook's oldest buildings, with wonky floors and low ceilings, but it felt funky and modern, with the walls painted a hot dusty pink and the beams whitewashed. It smelt exotic, of warm spices, and Emilia swooned as her mouth began to water, realising that she had been existing on sandwiches and muffins from The Icing on the Cake. She was too tired to cook properly for herself. They ordered bottles of Indian lager and dunked poppadoms into the Cardamom Pod's home-made mango chutney while they chose their food.

'Your father always ordered for us,' said Marlowe. 'He made us be adventurous. And he always had the hottest dish he could stand.'

'He loved Indian food,' said Emilia, gazing at the menu.

'I think we should propose a toast.' Marlowe raised his glass. 'To welcome you to the Peasebrook Quartet. I know how proud Julius would be.'

Even though she'd played abysmally, thought Emilia, but she didn't say it, because it was ungracious.

'I hope I can live up to him,' she said, raising her glass too. 'I don't think I made a very good start.'

'Two hours' practice a day, remember.' Marlowe gave her a playful stern stare. 'I'll be on to you.'

'Marlowe is terribly strict,' murmured Delphine, ladling as much innuendo into the statement as she could.

Inwardly, Emilia rolled her eyes – she'd got the message – but smiled as brightly as she could as she raised her glass and chinked it against the others'.

MARLOWE COLLINGHAM

12

On Monday morning, when Bill had safely gone off to work and before she could think twice, Bea stuffed Maud into her pushchair and walked into Peasebrook, marching up the high street until she reached the bridge by Nightingale Books. The sign outside was swinging gently in the autumn breeze. Through the bulging bay window, she could see Emilia talking to a customer.

A sign on the door, written in beautiful copperplate writing, said: *Open Monday Till Saturday 10ish until the last customer goes.* Bea smiled, pushed open the door with her bum, dragging the pushchair inside, then waited until the shop was empty. The great thing about a book shop was nobody thought it was odd if you lingered for ages. That was what you were supposed to do after all. So she hovered between the cookery and the art section, all the while keeping an eye on the other customers, until the last one drifted out of the door and there was her opportunity.

She walked up to the till before she could change her mind, and laid the book on the counter.

'I need to bring this back to you.'

Emilia looked up and recognised her.

'Oh! You bought *To the Moon and Back*.' She frowned. 'I didn't realise you'd bought a Riley.'

Bea looked down at the floor.

'I didn't.' She paused. 'I nicked it.'

Emilia looked from the book to Bea and back.

'Nicked it?'

Bea nodded. She took in a deep breath.

'I don't know why. I had a really weird moment. I don't know what came over me. It's not even as if I couldn't afford it. Not really. Not if I'd really wanted it.' She looked at Emilia, bewildered. 'I'm so, so sorry. I had to tell you. To stop myself ever doing anything like that again.'

'I don't know what to say.' Emilia managed an uncertain laugh. 'Except I probably wouldn't have noticed. You could have got away with it.'

'But I didn't want to get away with it. I had to bring it back. To scare myself. I sort of wonder if I might be going mad. It's such a stupid thing to do.' She gave Emilia a smile, half rueful, half scared. 'If you want to have me arrested, then so be it. I deserve it.'

'Of course I won't. You brought it back. That's not the behaviour of a repeat offender.'

'It's the behaviour of someone who needs help. Don't you think?'

'I don't know.'

'Thank you for being so understanding.' Bea thought she might cry. 'I just don't feel like myself any more. Shit. I'm sorry. I'm going to cry. No, I'm not.'

She gave a snort and a gulp, a half laugh, half sob, then pulled herself together.

'Are you OK?' Emilia was intrigued, but concerned.

Bea gripped the handles of the pushchair. She was struggling to speak.

'I thought I was. But maybe I'm not. It's been tough.

This whole... motherhood thing. This whole... not having a job thing. This whole moving to the countryside to live the dream.' She was getting more worked up. 'This whole... not having anything to do all day thing. Except, you know, mash up carrots and change nappies.' She looked down at Maud in her pushchair. Maud beamed up at her. 'Not that I don't utterly adore Maud. Of course I do.'

'I can't imagine what it's like,' said Emilia. 'I suppose one day I'll find out.'

'It's lovely. But it's...' Bea took in a gulp of air. 'I'm not allowed to say it.'

'Boring?' offered Emilia.

'Yes! And of course it's the most important job in the world, blah blah blah, and I should be grateful, because I've got friends – more than one – who've been trying for ages and had no luck. But...' She stared at Emilia. She shook her head in disbelief. 'Oh my God. I didn't come in here to dump on you. I'm sorry. I don't know what's the matter with me. I don't really know anyone in this town. And you look... nice. Like you might get it.'

Emilia didn't know what to say. 'Thank you. I think.' She put her hands on the book. 'I'll put this back on the pile and we won't say anything more about it.'

'Who nicks stuff from a book shop? That is just so wrong.'

Emilia pointed a warning finger at her. 'We're not saying anything more about it. Remember?'

Bea stood up straight and nodded obediently. 'Thank you. For being so understanding. How's it all going, anyway?'

'I'm panicking a bit, to be honest.'

'Why? I'd have thought this would be the least stressful job in the world.' Bea looked around the shop. 'I'd love to spend every day here.'

'Yeah, but it's losing money hand over fist.'

'What with people nicking stuff and all. That can't help.'

The two girls laughed.

'So what did you used to do? Before the little one?' asked Emilia.

'I was an art director. For *Hearth* magazine?'

'Oh wow. I love *Hearth*. It's how I want my life to be.'

'That's exactly why they sell so many copies.'

Studying Bea, Emilia thought she looked just like the poster girl for *Hearth*. Beautiful and on trend, with all the latest accessories and the perfect baby. And she must be smart. *Hearth* was one of the bestselling women's lifestyle magazines, dictating what any modern woman with even a hint of style should be putting on her wall or on her plate or in her plant pots, leading the zeitgeist in interior design and food and gardening. But clearly something was not right.

Bea shrugged her shoulders. 'Anyway, I've brought the book back and I promise I won't darken your door again.'

'Don't be silly.' Emilia felt drawn to Bea and her self-deprecating honesty. 'Actually, you might be able to help me.'

'Help you?'

Emilia grinned. 'Yes. It could be your punishment. You can give me some advice.'

'Advice on what?'

'I need to turn this place round. Make it appeal to a wider customer base. But I haven't a clue where to start.

Oh, and the kicker is – I don't really have any money to do it. Maybe you could give me some ideas?'

Bea put one hand on her hip. She grinned.

'And in return you won't have me banged up?'

'Something like that.'

Bea looked around her, thoughtful. 'I love it in here. The shop's got great atmosphere. It's really warm and welcoming. But it is kind of...'

She screwed up her face.

'Dickensian? Out of the ark?' offered Emilia.

'Not out of the ark. I like that it's old-fashioned. But you could make more of it. Keep the spirit, but open it up a bit. Lighten it. Create some little sets, maybe – you know, dress it up? And that mezzanine?' She pointed upwards. 'That is totally wasted on boring old history and maps. Does anyone ever really go up there?'

Emilia looked up. 'Sometimes. My father used to. He keeps his special editions locked in a glass case. But you're right. It's wasted space, really.'

'Maud goes to nursery two mornings. What if I come back and measure up. Take some photos. Then draw you out some ideas.' She frowned. 'What is your budget, exactly?'

Emilia made a face. 'Um – I don't really have one. But I suppose it will be an investment. I can use my credit card.'

Bea put her hands over her ears. 'Don't let me hear the word credit card. Don't worry – I'm used to creating magic out of muck. The great thing is you have lovely architectural features. Like a woman with good bone structure. You can't go too far wrong.' She smiled. 'I know all the tricks. And I've got great contacts. I can get you all sorts of things at trade prices. Lighting.' She looked up at the ceiling. The red velvet lampshades were dusty and she could definitely see cobwebs. 'And paint.' She looked at the floor, at the old red carpet, almost worn through in places. 'And carpets.'

Emilia looked amazed. Bea seemed to have blossomed and flourished right in front of her eyes.

Bea stopped mid flow.

'Sorry. I don't mean to be rude.'

'You're not! It's good to have an objective eye. I've lived with this shop for so long I don't notice that it's a bit old and tired.'

'We won't throw away the spirit of the place. That's vital. The ambience in here is what makes it special. But look – the old fireplace, for example. You should be using that as a feature. It would be wonderful opened up, with a squashy armchair next to it so people could read.'

Emilia stared at the fireplace, which had been bricked up.

'If you get cold feet, and start thinking what on earth am I doing asking that crazy girl to help me, just say. I won't be offended. Or surprised.'

'No. Weirdly, I feel as if this could really work.'

'Window displays,' said Bea with a sigh, looking over at the windows on either side of the door. 'Those windows are just waiting for stories to be told! Can you imagine? Valentine's Day, filled with love stories? Or ghost stories at Halloween? As for Christmas . . .'

Bea clapped her hands in excitement.

Emilia thought Bea was possibly a little bit mad. But she didn't care. Bea's enthusiasm had lifted the fug of the past few weeks and given her life. She had felt weighed down since her meeting with Andrea, not sure what to address first. It was exciting to hear someone brimming with enthusiasm. For the first time since her father had died, she felt a glimmer of hope.

She told June about her encounter with Bea later that afternoon.

'I feel as if things are falling into place. I've got a vision of what the shop could be like. I know I mustn't get carried away because I can't afford to wave a magic wand and have it how I want it, but at least I don't feel so overwhelmed.'

'I think once you start making changes, things *will* fall into place,' agreed June. 'In the meantime, what do you think about this?'

Emilia looked at the press release June handed her.

There were months of them, piled up under the counter. Endless missives from publicists wanting their book to be given pride of place. Julius never read them, because he wanted to make up his own mind about which books to give preference. He had a brilliant instinct for what would sell well, and he hated gimmicks and hype.

Emilia knew, however, that if she was going to increase Nightingale Books' profit by any significant margin, she had to raise her game. She needed publicity and a raise in profile as much as the authors and publishers of the books she was selling. So why not use them?

Two blue eyes were staring at her from the middle of the blurb. Mick Gillespie. Even a photocopy of him at seventy years old still had it. His expression made you feel as if you were the centre of his universe. Emilia wondered what it was like to be under his gaze in real life.

He was doing a pre-Christmas book tour to promote his no-holds-barred autobiography, which promised any number of secrets and scandals and behind-the-scenes indiscretion. He would give a talk, answer questions, sign books. Not that he needed to do anything, Emilia thought. He just needed to breathe.

Mick Gillespie was the perfect person to kick off her new campaign. No one was immune to his charms. Men and women, young and old, would be intrigued. She imagined the shop bursting at the seams, the queue snaking out of the door. He was a legend. An icon. As cool as Steve McQueen and James Dean and Richard Burton all rolled into one. Handsome and devil-may-care and charismatic.

'June – that is a genius idea.'

'I knew him once,' admitted June, with a twinkle in her eye.

'No way!'

'Yeah. I was an extra on one of his films. For my sins.'

'An extra? I didn't know you were an extra.'

'Not for long. I was no good at it.'

'But you met Mick Gillespie? It must have been in his heyday.'

June nodded. 'Yes . . .'

'What was he like?'

'Absolutely out of this world. Unforgettable. Magical.'

'Do you think you can pull strings?'

June laughed. 'No. Absolutely definitely not. There's no way he'd remember me. I played a barmaid. If I'd been an *actual* barmaid he might have paid me more attention.'

Mick Gillespie's love for the drink was legendary.

'Well. Nothing ventured,' said Emilia. 'This would

bring everybody to the shop. We'd be in the papers and everything.'

She picked up the phone to his publicist. He was probably fully committed already. No book shop in the country was going to pass up this opportunity.

Luck was on her side. Peasebrook would fit neatly in between Mick's current commitments.

'It'll be a chance for him to have a little rest. We've given him the next day off, so where better to spend it than in the Cotswolds?' the publicist said.

Emilia grinned to herself as she hung up the phone.

'Nightingale Books is added to the tour. Mick Gillespie is coming here, to Peasebrook.'

'Goodness!' June looked rather taken aback.

'I think we should get Thomasina to do the food,' Emilia went on. 'An Irish theme. She gave me a card the other day in case I needed any catering. What do you think?'

June was away with the fairies.

'Stop daydreaming, would you?' Emilia teased. 'What drinks should we serve?'

'I'd keep him well away from the drink if I were you,' said June darkly.

'But he must be getting on a bit.' Emilia looked at his picture. 'And they wouldn't let him out on tour if he was trouble.'

'Careful who you're calling old,' teased June. 'He's not much older than I am.'

'Well, we all know you don't look your age.' Emilia gave June a hug. She was so grateful for the older woman's advice and help. She almost felt like a maternal presence, something Emilia had never had, or, to be honest, felt the need for. But with her father gone, June's presence was comforting, and she thought perhaps she didn't appreciate her enough.

She was only too aware how important the people in this town had become to her in such a short space of time. Without their support, she'd have thrown in the towel weeks ago.

'Mick Gillespie,' she sighed, looking at the press release again.

By four thirty in the afternoon, there was just one man in the shop. It was getting dark outside and he was hovering, looking uncertain. This wasn't unusual. Emilia found people were either totally at home in a book shop, or felt a little out of place. He had a dog with him, a shaggy lurcher who looked as awkward and out of place as his owner.

Dogs were a good icebreaker.

'Hi.' She walked over in a friendly but unobtrusive manner, holding a book in one hand so she looked as if she was on her way to put it somewhere rather than accosting him. 'Look at you. You're a lovely boy, aren't you?'

'Thanks,' joked the man, and Emilia laughed, bending down to rough up the dog's ears.

'What's his name?'

'Wolfie.'

'Hey, Wolfie.' She looked up at the bloke. 'Were you looking for something in particular, or are you just browsing?'

He grinned at her and gave a little shrug of his shoulders. She could tell he was on unfamiliar territory. People unused to book shops had an awkwardness about them. An apologetic awkwardness.

'It's a bit . . .' He trailed off as he searched for the word. 'Embarrassing.'

'Oh.' She tried to sound reassuring. 'I'm sure it's not. I'll help if I can.'

She watched him move his weight from one foot to the other. He was cute, she thought. Faded jeans and a white T-shirt, with a soft red plaid shirt undone over the top. His hair was dark and scruffy, and he had a five o'clock shadow, but both of these things were by design rather than neglect: she could smell baby shampoo and something else more manly.

'Don't tell me – your girlfriend's sent you in for *Fifty Shades of Grey*.' She grinned on impulse, because her mind had suddenly gone that way.

He looked startled. 'God, no.'

'Sorry. Only you wouldn't believe how many women send their boyfriends in for it. Or how many men think they might spice things up a bit.'

'No. It's even more embarrassing than that.' He scratched his head and raised his eyebrows, looking sheepish. 'The thing is, my little boy asked me the other day what my favourite book was. It was for his homework. And I realised – I've never read one. I've never read a book.'

He looked at the floor. It was as if he was waiting for a punishment.

'Never?'

He shook his head. 'No. Books and me just don't get on. The few times I've opened one I just glaze over.'

He made a glazed-over face and Emilia laughed. Then stopped.

'Sorry. I'm not laughing *at* you.'

'No, I know. It's OK. Anyway, I've decided. I'm a really bad example to him. I want my son to get on and do really well. And I don't want to die never having read a book. So I want to start reading with him. So I can encourage him. But I don't know where to start. There're bloody millions of them. How do you start to choose?'

He looked around at all the shelves, baffled.

'Well, I can sort you out with something, I'm sure,' said Emilia. 'How old is he, for a start? And what sort of thing do you think he might like?'

'He's five, nearly six. And I don't really know what he'd like. Something short, preferably.' He laughed, self-conscious. 'And easy. I mean, I can read, obviously. I'm not that thick.'

'Not reading doesn't make you thick.'

'No. But his mum's going on at me for not getting involved with his homework.' He looked sheepish. 'She likes any chance to have a go. I'm not with her any more.'

'Oh,' said Emilia. 'I'm sorry.'

'Don't be. It's a good thing. Mostly.' He ruffled his hair, looking awkward. 'But I just want to show her I'm not as rubbish as she seems to think I am.'

'Well, let me see what I can come up with. Give me a couple of minutes.'

Emilia walked slowly up and down the children's bookshelves, turning over possibilities in her mind. Every now and then she would stop, pluck out a book, study it, then put it back. She wasn't sure she had ever met anyone who had never read a book before. Which made the choice even more difficult. She was determined not to put him and his son off for life. She had to hook them in. And she didn't want to patronise him. He might not be a reader, but he clearly had a lively mind. She mustn't judge.

'What's his name? Your son?'

'Finn.' The bloke smiled proudly.

'Ah,' said Emilia. 'That makes the task a whole lot easier.'

She picked out a book, and walked back over to her new customer, who looked at her with an eager curiosity.

She laid it on the counter in front of him.

'This is one of my absolute favourites of all time. *Finn Family Moomintroll*.'

'Yeah?' He picked the book up and eyed it warily.

'I think you'll both like it. It's a bit mad, but it's cool.' She paused. 'It's a bit quirky. It's about this family of Moomintrolls who live in a valley, and all their crazy friends.'

'Moomintrolls?'

'They're kind of big, white creatures who hibernate in the winter.'

He turned the book over to read the back, not saying anything.

'Honestly, it's really cute. I'll give you your money back if you don't like it.'

'Really?'

'As long as you don't spill your tea on it.'

'I promise.'

She slid the book into a blue paper bag with Nightingale Books emblazoned on it. He gave her a tenner and she gave him his change.

'I'll let you know how I get on.' He lifted the bag with a smile. 'Cheers.'

Emilia watched him go. She wondered if she would ever see him again. She thought she'd probably flirted with him a little bit. It was wrong, really, to flirt with customers, but she didn't care. She'd had a tough time lately. At least this proved she was still alive. And it took away the sting of Delphine's hostility the evening before, and her proprietorial attitude towards Marlowe – as if Emilia had been a threat. Which she absolutely wasn't.

As the door shut behind her newest customer, she felt a tiny thrill, and hoped he'd read the book and fall in love with reading. That was the whole point about Nightingale Books. It cast a spell over its customers by introducing them to the magic. And how wonderful for her to open up a whole new world—

She realised she was being utterly ridiculous. She was romanticising. This wasn't some Hollywood movie where she unwittingly changed someone's life. Get real, Emilia, she told herself. He's had a bit of a row with his ex and he's trying to prove himself. He probably won't even open the bloody book. And he definitely won't come back.

Jackson walked along the road with the book tucked under his arm. That had been easier than he thought. He was a good actor. At school, acting was about the only thing he'd been good at, but because he'd been so naughty they hadn't let him have the lead roles in the annual play. The plum parts always went to the swots. Which was one of the reasons Jackson had hated school so much. It wasn't fair, how it was run. You couldn't be good at everything. And why were you punished for not being clever?

Actually, going into the book shop hadn't been as daunting as he thought. Emilia had been really helpful, and hadn't laughed at his desire to read to his son, or his admission that he'd never read a book. She'd been really sweet and hadn't made him feel like an idiot at all. In fact, he was positively looking forward to reading it. Moomintrolls.

He didn't want to think about the real reason for going in there. The fact that he was supposed to be charming the pants off Emilia Nightingale in order to get her to sell up. Although he thought it was going to be easy. She'd definitely flirted with him. It was impossible not to flirt with Jackson, unless you'd been officially pronounced dead. Even men flirted with him. Straight men. It never got him anywhere, though.

But he had to keep Ian Mendip happy. For the time being anyway. Else he'd be out of a job.

He knocked on the door. Finn answered and barrelled into him.

'Dad! It's not your day, is it?'

Jackson usually had Finn on a Sunday, but he didn't see why he couldn't see him every day if he wanted to.

Finn knelt down and started hugging Wolfie.

Mia appeared, looking wary.

He held up the book.

'I thought I'd come and read to Finn.'

'Read?' She looked very dubious.

'Yeah. It's important. Reading to your kids.'

'It is. Yes. You don't have to tell me that.'

She watched him as he came in. He flopped down on the sofa. He remembered them going to choose it, from the big out-of-town retail park. Five years' interest-free credit. That was another thing he was still paying off. So he might as well get some use out of it.

'Come here, buddy.' Finn was still small enough to sit on his lap. 'I got this crazy book. *Finn Family Moomintroll.*'

Wolfie muscled his way in too. Jackson trapped him between his legs so he didn't jump up on the sofa. He suspected Mia wouldn't approve.

He cracked open the spine and began to read.

He was astonished to find that both he and Finn were soon under the spell of the Moomins and their funny little world. He read two chapters. Three.

'Shall we stop there? Carry on tomorrow?'

'No,' said Finn. 'I want to know what happens.'

Mia was standing in the doorway, watching them. She almost had a smile on her face. Almost. To Jackson's surprise, she came over and sat on the sofa next to him. She reached out for the book and had a look at the cover.

'Looks to me like the Moomins have BMI issues,' she said.

Jackson looked at her. If anyone had BMI issues, it was Mia. She'd lost even more weight. There was nothing of her. But he didn't mention it.

He pulled Finn closer in to him and carried on reading.

While she was cooking a sage and butternut squash risotto, Bea outlined the afternoon's events to Bill, omitting the bit about taking back a stolen book, obviously. Just telling him she was going to do some plans for Nightingale Books.

Bill frowned. 'What's the point of that?'

'I owe her a favour.'

'What favour?'

Bea didn't have a clue what to tell him. She could hardly tell him the truth. She wished she'd never started the conversation. She concentrated on pouring the stock onto the rice while she thought of a suitable reply.

'Maud had a meltdown in her shop. She was really kind to her.'

'That's not like Maud.'

Bea felt awful, blaming her gorgeous daughter who rarely had tantrums.

'She was a bit tired and hungry. Emilia gave her a biscuit.'

'A set of plans in return for a biscuit?'

Bea frowned at him. 'Look, I want to do it. OK? It's nice to use my brain.'

She felt unsettled. It wasn't like Bill to be so ungenerous. Did he feel left out? She had read somewhere – not in *Hearth*, because in *Hearth* life wasn't allowed to be anything less than perfect – that men could get jealous of new babies, and resent the attention their partners lavished on the newborns. But if anything, Bill was the one who lavished attention on Maud. He spoilt her far more than Bea did.

Maybe he was just tired.

'Shall I see if I can get a babysitter for tomorrow?' she asked. 'We could try one of the new restaurants in Peasebrook? It would be nice to have a night out.'

Bill poked at something on his iPad. 'Nah. Let's stay in. I don't want a hangover midweek.'

They could never go out for dinner without demolishing a bottle of wine each. For some reason they were never as profligate at home. Bea supposed it was because if they started drinking like that in their own kitchen they would be heading for rehab in a month.

Unless guests came, of course. Then the bottle count was shameless. But they hadn't had so many people to stay lately.

Maybe Bill was lacking stimulating company. Guests were hard work but it was always fun, and now Maud wasn't getting up quite so horrifically early, it would be easier.

'Shall we ask the Morrisons down for the weekend?' she asked. 'Or Sue and Tony? We've been a bit unsociable lately.'

Bill gave a sigh. 'It's non-stop washing up and sheet changing.'

'Not really. Everyone gives a hand.' And he never did the laundry. It was Bea who stripped the beds, washed the linen and sprayed it with lavender water before ironing.

He didn't answer.

Bea frowned.

Maybe he was bored. Maybe he was missing their London life? And the London her? Maybe stay-at-home-in-Peasebrook Bea was too dull for him? She was back into her jeans and was carrying hardly any baby weight, but she knew they didn't have sex as often as they used to. And certainly never those up-against-the-wall sessions they used to have when they first met, when the need for each other overcame them. They were both exhibitionists. Both admitted the thrill of possibly being seen or caught turned them on.

But somehow, what seemed OK in a London alley didn't seem appropriate in conservative Peasebrook. There would be consequences to being caught. A city was anonymous. Here in a small provincial town, wanton behaviour would be frowned upon. She could imagine the gossip already.

Still, Bea was never one to resist a challenge. When they went upstairs to bed, she rummaged in her underwear drawer and took out her best Coco de Mer satin bra and knickers, pulled her Louboutins out of the cupboard, and slipped into the bathroom to get changed. She put on red lipstick, backcombed her hair slightly, and slid into her femme fatale combo.

She sashayed into the bedroom and stood in the doorway, hands on her hips, with a wicked smile.

'Oi!' she said. Bill was lying under the covers, eyes closed.

'Oi!' she said, louder.

She thought she saw his eyelids flicker. She frowned. She walked over to the bed, picked up his hand and put it between her legs, letting his fingers feel the warmth of the silk.

He rolled over, mumbling, and pulled his hand away.

Her mouth dropped open. Never, in all the time she had known him, had Bill turned down an opportunity. She sat down on the bed, looking down at the bright red shoes with the pencil-thin heels and the spaghetti-thin ankle straps, thinking how many times he'd watched her in them, eyes laughing as she walked towards him.

She didn't know whether to be cross or hurt or puzzled.

13

June had taken the press release about Mick Gillespie home.

She poured herself a glass of cool Viognier and sat at the kitchen table to look at it.

His thick hair was now white and cropped close to his head. Those infamous slate blue eyes had no doubt been hand-tinted to enhance that hypnotic gaze. His face was carefully airbrushed to emphasise his bone structure, with just a few judicious laughter lines left, because it would be silly to pretend he was wrinkle-free at his age – whatever that was exactly, but older than her, certainly. He'd kept his exact age shrouded in mystery for so long, but now, it seemed, his venerable years were a useful marketing tool rather than something to be hidden. An opportunity to monetise his dotage.

His autobiography had been much heralded in the press. There would be countless television and radio appearances, for despite his advancing years, Mick (or Michael, as everyone now called him) was good airtime. He was guaranteed to make an outrageous remark or drop a piece of juicy gossip. His lawyers were always on standby, but he was clever. Hints and innuendoes hadn't landed him in court yet, largely because what he claimed was grounded in truth. The lilting accent had long gone, replaced by a RADA/Hollywood hybrid delivered with mellifluous perfection and just the merest hint of Kerry. His voice was famous: from a whisper to a mighty roar, it was instantly recognisable.

His book promised a searing exposé of his entire career, complete with every dalliance and indiscretion he'd ever had. The lawyers had been through it with a fine-tooth comb and it was said there were many women waiting in trepidation for its release. It was destined to fly off the shelves, for not only were its contents shocking but it was remarkably well written. Witty and observant and colour-ful. The rumour was he hadn't employed a ghostwriter, but had been responsible for every single word himself.

June didn't doubt it. He'd always had the gift of the gab. She imagined him in his Hampstead conservatory – the go-to resting ground for luvvies – scrawling out his bon mots while a discreet assistant brought him coffee, then wine, then brandy later in the day.

June reflected that if he wrote as well as he talked, if he painted pictures as pretty and convincing with his written as his spoken words, then he was a gifted writer indeed.

She put a hand to her heart to feel how fast it was beating. After all this time, he was coming to Peasebrook. To Nightingale Books.

Maybe she shouldn't have suggested it to Emilia. Nightingale Books was the place June felt happiest in the world. She'd had no hesitation about stepping in to help Julius when he started deteriorating, for she wor-shipped him, too. He had filled a void in her life. Not romantically at all, but intellectually. And socially. They'd often enjoyed a drink out or supper together or gone to concerts. He was her absolute dearest friend at a difficult time. Retirement had been tougher than she thought. She was a hugely successful businesswoman, and to go from schmoozing and wheeling and dealing to doing almost nothing had been a massive shock. And moving to the cottage that had been her weekend retreat had been strange. It took a long time for it to feel like a permanent home. She still sometimes felt as if she should be packing up on a Sunday night ready to drive back to London.

She loved her cottage, though. The wall-to-wall shelves, groaning with the tomes that had seen her through two failed marriages and several dodgy affairs. She read voraciously, and the cottage was perfect for that, whether tucked up in front of a log fire or sitting in the garden with a glass of wine. She scanned the bestseller lists, flagged up reviews in the newspapers, and every week she would pop into Nightingale Books for the latest biography or prize-winning novel.

She'd seen Mick Gillespie's book previewed in the *Sunday Times*. She simultaneously longed and dreaded to read it.

She'd tried to forget him. Time had betrayed her. It hadn't been a great healer at all. It had made no difference. She had tried a million different distractions. Other men. Drink. Drugs, once or twice (it had been the sixties, after all). Charity work. Australia. Then, eventually, a kind of release. Two husbands. And motherhood. That had helped her heal. But her boys were off and gone, though they would be back eventually when they'd found wives and had children. The cottage would come into its own then.

The memories were still there, vivid. It had started as a dream come true: a silly competition, to become the 'legs' of an exciting new brand of tights – a necessity as hemlines grew shorter and shorter. Little June Agnew had won and convinced herself she was going to be propelled into a lucrative modelling career, hurled from oblivion in Twickenham to a giddy life of glamour. Through it she had got an agent, Milton, (who appeared from nowhere, but was extremely kind and helpful), who had changed her name from June to Juno and told her she was going to be a star.

With her white-blonde hair, huge eyes and skinny, endless legs, Juno was the queen of mini skirts and kinky boots and white plastic macs, all sugar-pink lipstick and spidery false lashes. There was money (to her it seemed a fortune, but now she knew that other people had been creaming it off and just giving her the bare minimum), a Chelsea flat-share, parties, cameras, late nights – and then a screen test. Everyone had gone into ecstasies. She was, it seemed, a natural. And she had to admit it came easy to her. She memorised the lines they gave her, and pretended. It seemed that was how easy acting was. She could sense Milton's excitement and the stakes getting higher. She was told to watch her weight and her behaviour, and had to have her hair done every morning before she left the flat.

Milton told her to be patient. The big jobs would come. But she had to do the small ones first. He got her a job on a sweepingly lush romantic film set on the west coast of Ireland, about a young girl who gets pregnant by the local aristocrat and wreaks her revenge. The script was by an acclaimed playwright and the director was renowned for savagely beautiful productions. Mick Gillespie was the star. Juno was to play the barmaid in the local pub. She had two lines.

Juno had devoured the script and loved it. She dreamt about the actress playing the heroine getting pneumonia, and them casting Juno, because they'd spotted her talent. The actress remained robustly healthy throughout. But Mick Gillespie noticed her. He noticed her all right.

In Ireland, she'd never known rain like it. It was there all the time. Yet it was soft. It was like having your skin kissed endlessly.

'Does it ever stop?' she asked him, and he laughed.

'Not in my lifetime.'

And the smell. She loved the smell of the burning peat that sharpened the damp. And the colours, smudgy and muted, everything in soft focus, as if you'd forgotten your glasses.

He lent her his cream Aran sweater. It swamped her, but in it she felt safe and loved and special. She wore it to the pub with jeans, her hair tousled and not a scrap of make-up, and they sat by the fire with glasses of Guinness and she thought she had never been happier. She wanted time to stop.

And then, on the last day, her dream was ripped apart. She had been so sure of *them* that it came as a huge shock. She had assumed they would carry on. There had been no indication this was temporary.

He was standing behind her on the cliff, his arms wrapped around her. She fitted just under his chin. The wind was buffeting at them, but he was strong and sure, so she didn't fear falling. Everything was grey: the clouds, the sky, the rocks. As grey as Donegal tweed, apart from the white-tipped waves, which were as skittish and playful as overfed horses, chasing each other into shore, kicking up their tails.

'Well,' said Mick. 'It's been fun, all right.'

'It has,' she replied, thinking he meant the shoot.

'Ah well.' His voice was tinged with regret; a fifth-glass-of-Guinness melancholy, though he hadn't had his first yet.

'We can always come back another time.' She put her hands over his. 'Mrs Malone would always make us welcome, I'm sure.'

Mrs Malone was the landlady of the guest house they'd been billeted in.

She felt him tense as she leant further into him. Every muscle in his body.

'Darling,' he said, and she felt her heart plummet. 'There won't be another time. This is it.'

She whirled around to face him.

'What?'

He had a strange smile on his face. 'You must understand. You know the rules. Didn't anyone tell you, when you signed up for the film?'

'Tell me what?' She was confused.

'This is just a . . .' He searched for the words. He found one, but he could sense she wouldn't like it. 'You know.'

'A you know?'

He shrugged. 'Fling?'

She stepped back. He reached out to pull her back. They were very near the cliff edge.

'Fling.' She could barely say the word.

'You knew that!' His eyes were screwed up in consternation.

She shook her head.

'What did you think this was?'

She could hardly breathe. She took in gulps of air to

quell her panic. She clutched her middle. It felt as if a surgeon had gone in with a knife and was cutting out her vital organs. No anaesthetic. The pain burned in her gullet.

'Darlin', darlin', darlin' . . .' He put a concerned hand on her shoulder. 'Come on, now.'

She flung his hand away. 'Get off.'

'There's no need for this. We've one last night. Let's make the most of it.'

She ran. She ran and ran and ran, through the rain, down the cliff, down to the road. They had one more scene to shoot but she didn't care. The whole film could go to hell.

She stumbled along the road. The mist was closing in, filling her lungs with its viscosity.

She pulled at his sweater as she ran, tugging it over her head, hurling it into the fuchsia bushes, until she was just in the long-sleeved vest she'd worn to stop it scratching. She'd left everything behind. Her purse. Nearly all her clothes.

She stopped at the crossroads, a crooked signpost giving her a choice.

A car drew up. It was the make-up girl.

'Get in, sweetheart.' Juno just hugged herself tighter. 'Come on! You're miles from anywhere and you'll catch your death. I'll take you back to my place.'

The girl made her retrieve the sweater from the bushes, then went to fetch Juno's things from her digs. She put Juno to sleep on her sofa with a spare blanket. Juno didn't sleep, but got up early to catch a bus to the airport, where she got the first flight back to London so she didn't have to travel with the rest of them. She hid in her flat for days, until Milton came to dig her out. He'd got the whole sorry story from someone else on the shoot. She was mortified, humiliated and swore she would never leave the flat again.

She was gaunt and had lost her sparkle. She couldn't get the chill out of her bones from getting soaked when she ran away and she feared she would never feel warm again. Her fingers had chilblains, but the pain of them was nothing compared to the empty gnawing inside her.

She'd been living off the money from *The Silver Moon*. She'd been frugal but now there was nothing left. For a moment, panic overruled pain. But actually, she decided, she didn't care. She would starve to death in her flat. At least then the horrible feeling would go.

'Do you want my advice?' asked Milton. 'Go and do a secretarial course. Everyone needs a good typist. Even me. Actually, especially me. Go and learn typing and shorthand and I'll give you a job.'

She stared at him. She supposed he was being kind, but did he know what he was suggesting? One moment she was on a trajectory to stardom and had found love. Now she had come crashing down and her agent wanted her to be his typist?

She had no fight left in her to tell him what she thought. She should be screaming at him to get her back in the loop, to get her some auditions. But she could see her reflection in the mirror on the wall. Gone was the luminous bombshell with the glowing skin and the eyes filled with promise. In her place was a bag of bones, with lacklustre hair and a blank gaze. Who would employ her looking like this?

'And for heaven's sake,' added Milton, 'eat something. In fact, come for lunch with me.'

He took her to a tiny Italian on the corner and filled her up with pasta and bread and creamy pudding.

She felt a little stronger when she finished. Starving was a miserable business. So miserable that she did as Milton suggested and signed up for a secretarial course. She was guaranteed employment at the end of six weeks, as long as she attended every lesson and practised every night. And she went back to being plain June Agnew.

She'd done all right for herself. She had gone back to work for Milton. She'd become his right-hand girl, and then realised that there were many Miltons who needed a right hand in the office to organise their lives, so she left him to set up her own agency, providing top-notch administrative staff, and the agency had grown and grown. She'd retired three years ago, handing the reins over to two of her sons. She had plenty of money, plenty of friends, and was as happy as anyone had the right to be.

She had unfinished business though.

She looked back down at the press release and it hadn't changed. She could remember those eyes burning into her as if it were yesterday. She hadn't really entertained the thought that she might ever see him again. Of course, she might have passed him on a street in London, or spied him across a crowded restaurant one day. But he'd fallen right into her lap. She wouldn't sleep between now and then.

For heaven's sake, she told herself. You're not a skinny little wannabe actress any more, and he's an old man. Get over yourself.

JUNE AGNEW

TEN NOVELS SET IN IRELAND

Good Behaviour Molly Keane
The Country Girls Edna O'Brien
Troubles J. G. Farrell
Ulysses James Joyce
Circle of Friends Maeve Binchy
The Last September Elizabeth Bowen
The Gathering Anne Enright
The Commitments Roddy Doyle
Nora Webster Colm Tóibín
Cashelmara Susan Howatch

14

It had taken Andrea a few weeks to plough through all the paperwork and get a clearer picture of the kind of shape Nightingale Books was in financially. Several more worms had crawled out of the can.

Emilia had unearthed a pile of pro-forma invoices that didn't seem to have been paid. They were from some of their main suppliers. She wouldn't be able to order any more books until she'd paid them.

Then a credit card bill had arrived with the morning post. She opened it and was horrified by the balance. There were no purchases for that month, of course, but neither had any minimum payments been made, because Emilia hadn't been aware of the card's existence. It hadn't been in Julius's wallet.

She searched through the piles of paperwork on the desk, and found two copies of previous bills in unopened envelopes. The withdrawals were all cash. The interest was compounding due to the lack of payments.

She phoned Andrea, who told her to bring the bills around straight away.

'That must have been what he'd been using to pay the wages,' Andrea sighed. 'This is one of those cards with six months nought per cent finance. He must have taken it out to cover his cash flow. But of course now the interest is going to kick in big time. I'll phone the company and put them in the picture. And I'll have to pass it on to your solicitor for the probate.'

'It's nearly four thousand pounds.'

Andrea sighed again. 'It's easily done. He's not the first and he won't be the last.'

Emilia felt disconsolate. She was just getting her head around the existing debts and feeling she could manage.

'The debts are just getting bigger and bigger.'

'We can consolidate them.' Andrea tried to sound reassuring. 'Don't worry – you're sitting on a goldmine. You can take out a loan if you need to.'

'I suppose so. I'm just not used to such big sums of money.'

'I wish all my clients felt like that. Honestly, this is nothing in the grand scheme of things.'

'Easy for you to say.'

'I wouldn't say it if I didn't mean it.'

Andrea took Emilia off to the bank in the high street where Nightingale Books had had its account since the day Julius arrived in Peasebrook. There, they negotiated a generous overdraft facility with the bank manager.

'Now you don't have to worry about how to pay the wages.'

Emilia shuddered. 'I've never been in this kind of debt. I don't even go overdrawn usually.'

'It's good debt. It's debt you're investing in the business. It's not Louboutin debt.'

Emilia looked down at her battered old sneakers. 'No,' she said ruefully. She eyed Andrea's shoes – high and shiny and undeniably expensive.

Andrea grinned. 'I've earned them. It's my one indul-
gence. And there is some good news. Look – your takings
are up, week on week this month. You must be doing
something right. Not that your dad did anything wrong,'
she added hastily. 'But it's obvious his eye wasn't on the
ball.'

Emilia looked at the last couple of weeks' spreadsheets.
Something *was* working. Dave had turned into a social
media guru, tweeting book reviews and special offers,
and they'd seen an upturn. They had opened the last few
Sundays, and had done rather well, yet the in still didn't
cover the out.

'But the shop isn't making enough to cover its outgoings now, let alone a monthly payment if I take out
a loan.'

'But you need to do that to grow the business. That's
how it works.'

Emilia put her hand to her head. 'I understand it all in
theory – of course I do. But it's making my head spin. It's
the decisions; the *commitment*. The responsibility! Maybe
I should just walk away.'

'Are you mad? Don't give up after all this.' Andrea
checked herself. 'Sorry. I shouldn't try and influence you.'

Emilia looked at her.

'When I first came in, you said I shouldn't be sentimental.'

'I know.' Andrea gave a rueful shrug. 'But I was walking
along the high street the other day. I went past the shop. I
saw you in there and you looked as if you belonged there.'
She laughed. 'Listen to me! I'm supposed to be Miss
Ruthless and Pragmatic. Now *I'm* being all sentimental!'

Emilia sighed. 'I've just booked Mick Gillespie to come and do a book signing.'

Andrea's eyes gleamed behind her glasses. 'Mick Gillespie? Wow!'

'If I sell a hundred copies of his book, it still won't pay the electricity bill.'

'I know it's a big decision for you. It's down to you, Emilia. Whether you want to make Nightingale Books your life. Like your father.'

'I don't know yet. In my heart, of course I do. But in my head . . .'

Andrea gave her a kind smile. 'We can play for time. Let me see what I can do with the figures. I can find ways of offsetting some of the debt.'

'Bloody money,' said Emilia.

'Yes. Well. It makes the world go round. Don't worry. Nightingale Books isn't on the scrap heap yet.'

Emilia walked back along the high street, her hands in her pockets. Just when she thought the shop was on the up, reality kicked in. And it was all new to her. She'd never really got involved in the behind-the-scenes machinations, and now she was cross. She should have paid more attention, but it all just seemed to tick over without her needing to know any of it.

She'd foolishly thought running a book shop would be easy, and that she knew everything. But of course there was more to it than finding someone the perfect read for their upcoming cruise, or recommending a christening gift, or tracking down a book when someone said, rather vaguely, 'It's got a blue cover . . .'

Andrea had done her best to keep her spirits up, but Emilia felt that keeping the shop open was becoming less and less viable: something she was just doing because she didn't want to let her father down.

She passed The Icing on the Cake, its windows crammed with sugared doughnuts oozing wine-dark jam and shiny chocolate cakes and golden custard tarts. She went in and bought a sausage roll – she was more of a savoury than a sweet person – and devoured the melting pastry and herby sausage meat in three bites.

To cheer herself up, she called Bea with the news about Mick Gillespie. 'You'll never guess who I've got coming to the shop.'

Bea squealed when she heard the news. 'Oh my God – he's my favourite actor of all time. That Aran jumper he wears in *The Silver Moon* – I bought Bill one like it.'

'Do you think people will come?'

'Of course! And we'll dress the shop.'

'Not leprechauns and shamrocks?'

Bea laughed. 'No. I'll think of something clever.' She gasped. 'Do you think we can take him out for dinner afterwards?'

'I'm booking him a room at the Peasebrook Arms.'

'You'll have to give me his room number.'

'Bea – he's an old man!'

'I know. I'm only kidding. But that's great. You'll have them queuing round the block. We'll make it a night to remember.'

Emilia hung up, smiling to herself. Suddenly all the problems of the past few weeks began to recede. She felt a little shoot of hope. Maybe she *could* turn the shop around, with a bit of help and a bit of imagination?

*

Sarah managed to find a rare parking space on the high street in Peasebrook. She was en route to the hospital for her daily visit but there was something she really needed to do. She locked her car and took a deep breath. She wasn't sure if she was ready for what she was about to do, but if she waited until she was ready she would never go.

She could feel him as soon as she walked into Nightingale Books. The very essence of Julius. The shop *was* him. She looked around, expecting to see him bent over a table of books, looking up to meet her gaze, smiling at her over his spectacles.

The memory, the longing and the sadness were overwhelming. No one had ever made her feel like Julius. That meeting of the mind and the soul. And the body... She chastised herself. That wasn't why she was here – to wallow in her memories of what would never be again.

Emilia was hanging up the phone as she walked over to the counter.

'Emilia? It's Sarah. Sarah Basildon.' She wasn't sure Emilia would recognise her, necessarily. Sarah was modest. She never assumed people knew who she was, even though they usually did.

'Sarah. How lovely to see you. Hello.'

'How are you?'

'Oh... you know. It's been tough but I'm getting there.'

'You must miss your father dreadfully.'

'Oh God yes.' Then she remembered. Marlowe had told them about Alice at the last rehearsal. A car crash. She'd been taken to hospital. 'But how's Alice? I heard about the accident. I'm so sorry.'

'Well,' said Sarah. 'The great thing is she will be all right. Her leg was very badly injured. But she's in very good hands. We're hoping she'll be back on her feet for the wedding. Literally! Otherwise she'll be going up the aisle on crutches.' Sarah tried to laugh. It was obvious she was being brave.

'Would you give her my love?' Emilia didn't know Alice well, but she liked her. They'd both been at Peasebrook Infants. Alice was a few years below her, but Emilia remembered her in the playground, with her flaxen hair and duffel coat. Emilia had gone on to the high school, and Alice went off to boarding school somewhere, so they'd drifted apart, but Emilia was looking forward to playing at her wedding. It was bound to be a fairy tale.

'She's why I'm here, actually. I wanted a copy of Alice's favourite book – I can't find it anywhere at home. But I thought it would be nice for her to have something to read.'

'Of course. What is it?'

Sarah gave a smile. '*Riders*. Jilly Cooper. Do you have it in stock?'

'Of course! A book shop's not a book shop without *Riders*. Especially round here.' Emilia walked over to the fiction shelves. She could see a range of fat paperbacks in the C section. The comfort of Jilly Cooper. She'd read them all herself: it was always a celebration when a new Jilly came out. 'Here we are.'

'That's wonderful – she'll love that. I remember when she first read it. I didn't get a word out of her for about a week.'

Sarah handed over a ten-pound note. As Emilia wrapped the book in a bag, she hesitated, as if she wanted to say something. Eventually, she cleared her throat.

'Emilia, I wondered if you would come and have tea with me? There's something I'd love to talk to you about.

In confidence. Something your father and I had been discussing.'

'Oh!' Emilia wondered what it could be. Her father hadn't ever mentioned talking to Sarah Basildon about anything. Well, not specifically. The Basildons were great customers. They were very good at supporting local businesses in general, and they always bought a lot of books, especially at Christmas. They were very popular in the area. They didn't think they were better than everyone else because they lived at the Big House. 'Of course. When would you like me to come?'

'What about Thursday? About three? That gives me time to nip to the hospital in the morning – I like to go and see her every day.'

Emilia had a quick look at the calendar and the staff rota. There'd be one person in the shop, which was fine at the moment.

'Of course. That's perfect.'

Emilia watched Sarah go, intrigued. It would be good to get out of the shop and go to Peasebrook Manor. She'd had enough of uncovering nasty bills today. After this morning's meeting, she actually felt a bit cross with her father. It was no way to run a business, leaving accounts undealt with. But she was starting to realise Julius hadn't really seen Nightingale Books as a business, more a way of life.

The question was whether it was to be a way of life for her as well.

Sarah left Nightingale Books with a sense of relief and headed off to the hospital. She had been putting off going in there because of the memories, but she couldn't spend the rest of her life avoiding the book shop. And she wanted to see how Emilia was. She felt she owed it to Julius to keep an eye on her. After all, Emilia was on her own, with no mother.

Sarah remembered the day Julius had told her about Rebecca, and the terrible start he'd had to fatherhood.

'It was an awful shock,' he admitted. 'But I was very young. I suppose at the time, I thought Rebecca was the love of my life. Things happened very quickly: her deciding to stay in England, then getting pregnant, so we hadn't really had time to fall *out* of love. I don't know how long we would have lasted in the real world, a young couple with the pressure of a baby. It's very easy to romanticise it.'

'You must have been very lonely, after she died.'

Julius gave her a cheeky grin. 'Oh, don't worry. There's nothing women find more attractive than a single man in charge of a baby. I coped.'

Sarah had pretended to be outraged. 'And there was me thinking I was the first person to melt your frozen heart.'

He looked at her seriously. 'You're the first person I've really cared about.'

She remembered the woozy sensation of realising how much she meant to him. Though despite his declaration she knew she would only ever come second to Emilia, and rightly so. Sarah had a strong maternal instinct. It was an awkward situation, but she wanted to make it clear to Emilia that she was there if she needed her. That if she ever wanted to talk about her father, or just to come up to the house for supper because she wanted to get out, then Sarah's door was wide open.

It was the least she could do for her lover.

It was delicate, though. She could tell by the way Emilia greeted her – polite but warm, with definitely no hint of knowing in her eyes – that she had no inkling of their relationship. And she couldn't just say, 'By the way, your father and I were long-term lovers, so please do consider me your surrogate mum...'

She thought she had found the ideal way for them to start a conversation and possibly develop a relationship. She smiled when she thought of her brainwave: it really was a brilliant idea. She'd spent a lot of time in the car lately, driving backwards and forwards to the hospital, and car journeys were the perfect catalyst for light-bulb moments. And here she was again, driving out onto the Oxford road. She looked at the book on the passenger seat. Goodness knows where the original copy had gone – she'd given it to Alice for her fourteenth birthday – but it might cheer her up.

'That is the best present ever,' Alice told her as she took it out of the bag. 'Thank you. But what I really want you to do is bring me my laptop.'

'No way,' Sarah said firmly. 'You need to rest, Alice. You've got enough to deal with just getting better. Everything's under control. Your dad's taking charge and being really helpful.'

She didn't add 'for once'. Ralph really had stepped up to the plate. Usually no one was quite sure where he was or what he was up to, and unless he was given a really specific task he did his own thing, but he had been magnificent.

Alice giggled. 'I bet he's driving everyone mad. But honestly, Mum – the thing is I just lie here and worry. If

I've got my laptop I can keep up to speed on everything. Otherwise Christmas is going to be a nightmare. It's all in the planning.'

'Darling, we've done it often enough. The girls in the office have all your lists and timetables—'

'But it's the small things. And there were lots of new things I wanted to do this year—'

'It's out of the question.' Sarah cut her off. 'And if things aren't perfect this year, it doesn't matter. Anyway, we need you better for the wedding. That's your big day.'

Alice gave a dismissive wave of her hand. 'The wedding will organise itself. I'm not worried about that.'

'But I want you to enjoy it.'

Alice looked stubborn. 'I won't enjoy it if I'm worried about work, will I?'

Sarah laughed. 'Look – I'll get one of the girls from the office to come in and talk everything through with you. Then you can see how well they are managing.'

'Are you saying I'm replaceable?' Alice looked indignant.

'No. I'm saying you need to look after yourself otherwise you'll end up in a worse state.'

The thing with Alice was that she never stopped. And now she'd been forced to, she didn't like it.

'Who's organising the flyers to hand out at the farmers' market? Who's doing our tweets? Who's ordering the presents for the Father Christmas visits? Who's talked to the reindeer man about the reindeer?'

'It's all under control,' repeated Sarah, who had no idea of the answer to any of Alice's questions. But she wasn't going to let her know that. All that really mattered was that Alice got better. If no one tweeted for a few weeks, or the reindeer didn't turn up, it wasn't the end of the world.

*

After visiting Alice, Sarah drove back home, observing how the first of the leaves were now leaving the trees. Of course Peasebrook Manor was glorious in summer, an abundance of colour and greenery, but she rather liked being able to see the structure underneath, the bare branches, the absence of colour, the golden stone of the walls and balustrades and terraces dulling to a more subdued grey. The starkness certainly suited her mood, as she watched a flock of starlings scatter themselves across the sky.

She got out of the car. She could see Dillon moving some of the lead planters on the terrace. She'd been avoiding him rather since Alice's accident, because she wasn't sure what to think about what Hugh had told them about the events leading up to it. She didn't want to believe that Dillon could have been instrumental in the accident, yet she could hardly ask him for his side of the story. So it was easier not to think about it. There was too much going on in her head already.

But she was fond of Dillon. It wasn't fair of her to give him the cold shoulder. He'd been devastated to hear about Alice, but was that because he felt guilty? Did he know he was responsible for Hugh's fast driving?

She walked along the terrace to the French windows that led into the morning room. A light autumn breeze caressed her. It lifted her heart just a little. To the right and left of her the velvety lawns of Peasebrook had just had their last cut before the winter and she breathed in the grassy scent. Clusters of great oak trees lined the horizon. The grey ribbon of the drive stretched out into the distance: she could just see the gates.

Dillon looked up as she approached. He stood up, his hands smothered in rich peat. He was planting the bulbs for her favourite tulips: dark purple, almost black.

'How is she today?' he asked.

'She's not too bad,' Sarah told him.

'Will you tell her I said hello? Next time you go in.'

'Of course.'

'When will she be back home?'

'It depends on her leg. She's just waiting for one more operation. We're hoping not too long. But at the moment she's best off in the hospital.'

Dillon looked away for a moment. He looked troubled. As if he was about to say something.

'Is there something the matter, Dillon?' Sarah wondered if he wanted to confess. She would prefer everything to be out in the open.

'No. No, it's fine. I was just wondering... would... would it be all right if I went to see her?'

Sarah thought for a moment. If what Hugh had said was true, maybe Alice wouldn't want to see him. On the other hand, Dillon and Alice had always been friends. Who was she to stop him seeing her?

Alice's mother, that's who. It was her duty to make sure her daughter wasn't put into any more discomfort than she already was.

'I think perhaps not, at the moment, if you don't mind.'

She turned and stepped into the morning room. She felt awful. Dillon had looked crestfallen. But she couldn't deal with what Hugh had told her at the moment, because there would be too many consequences. She couldn't manage without Dillon, therefore she didn't want to investigate any further. But in case it was true, she needed to keep him away from Alice. For the time being, anyway.

Dillon was furious with himself. Why was he such a coward? Why couldn't he just come out with it and tell Sarah what had happened in the White Horse? It wasn't as if they weren't close. Or as close as they could be. Dillon didn't fool himself that Sarah thought of him as an equal. Of course she didn't.

He'd talked to Brian about the Hugh thing, in the pub.

'I don't understand why he didn't get done. You saw how much they'd all been drinking, and he was partying with them.'

Brian chuckled. 'You are a bit green sometimes, Dillon.'

'What do you mean?'

Brian tapped his nose.

'What does that mean?'

'He's a little bit fond of the old Bolivian marching powder, isn't he?'

Dillon still looked puzzled.

'Didn't you see how many times he nipped off to the toilet?'

'For a slash?'

'No, idiot. For a line of cocaine.'

Dillon blinked. 'Cocaine? Bloody hell.' He thought about it. 'So he *wasn't* drunk?'

'No. Just high as a kite.'

'How come the police didn't notice?'

'He'll have charmed them, won't he?'

'You mean they turned a blind eye?'

Brian shrugged. 'Just gave him the benefit of the doubt

236

when he passed the breathalyser. They wouldn't suspect him, would they? He's marrying a Basildon.'

'So the bastard got away with it.'

'Yep. And it's too late to grass him up now.'

'Do you think Alice knows what he gets up to?'

Brian shrugged. 'Probably not. She's a nice girl. He wouldn't want to blot his copybook with her.'

'How do you know, anyway? That he takes cocaine?'

Brian scoffed. 'You ask Pogo. That's where all Hugh's money goes – in Pogo's pocket. Pogo supplies him and all his mates.'

Pogo was the local drug dealer who skulked about in the dodgier pubs in Peasebrook and thought he was a bit of a gangster, with his dreadlocks and gold front tooth. Dillon had been at school with him and thought he was an idiot. He wasn't going to lower himself to ask Pogo for corroborative evidence to incriminate Hugh. Pogo would say anything if he thought it would save his own sorry arse.

'Why haven't you told me this before?'

'I thought you knew.'

Dillon shook his head. He felt shocked. He hadn't thought much of Hugh in the first place, but this was even worse. But what could he do?

If he told Sarah that Hugh had been off his head on cocaine the night of the accident, Hugh would deny it. And no one would believe Dillon over Hugh, because Hugh had passed the breathalyser test. They'd just think Dillon was trying to cause trouble. They wouldn't want to think anything bad of Hugh, because he was the saviour of Peasebrook Manor. The one with the deep pockets. And one of them.

Yet if he said nothing, Alice was going to end up marrying him – a manipulative, amoral coke-head.

He kicked a clod of earth into a flowerbed. It was frustrating, being the lowest of the low. When it came down to it, he was just a nobody.

He walked back to the garden room. He felt angry with Sarah, even though she had done nothing wrong. But he was hurt she didn't want him to go and visit Alice. It wasn't as if she was whiter than white. What would Ralph say, if he knew the truth about her and Julius Nightingale? Not that Dillon would ever say anything, not in a million years. But that made it worse, not better. And Ralph himself was no role model. Dillon had worked out what had been going on years ago. Which was why he was so cross with himself for not seeing through Hugh.

He clenched his teeth. What was the point in behaving with loyalty to people, when they showed *you* none? He pulled off his wax jacket and put the kettle on. Was he the only person in the world who wasn't a bloody hypocrite? Well, him and Alice, of course. If anyone was the innocent party in all of this, it was Alice.

Dillon sat and drank his tea, and as he drank, he came to a decision. He'd go to the hospital and see Alice himself. He didn't need Sarah's permission. If Alice didn't want to see him, she could tell him herself. He swilled out his cup and picked up his jacket. There was no time like the present.

Dillon had been to A&E often enough. As a gardener, it was an occupational hazard and tetanus injections and stitches were par for the course. But he'd never been onto one of the wards. The hospital was a maze, of arrows to different floors and places with different colour codes and letters, of lifts that went to different sections.

Eventually he found his way to the right area. He pushed open the double doors and asked for Alice at the nurse's station. They pointed him towards a private room off the main ward.

He knocked gently and heard her voice. As he peeped around the door his heart leapt as he saw her. She was bundled up in bed, her leg in a cast outside the sheets, her face bandaged up, the one eye he could see still black with bruising.

'Dillon!' There was no hiding her delight.

He came in and held out the Terry's chocolate orange he'd brought her.

'I got you this.'

'My absolute favourite! Let's open it right now.' She shuffled over and patted the bed next to her. 'Come and sit down and tell me everything.'

He sat and started opening the box. He tapped the chocolate orange on the bedside table so it fell into segments, and fed them to her one by one as they talked.

'I'm so bored cooped up in here. I really want to go on a ward, so I've got people to talk to, but Hugh's insisted on a private room. It makes me feel as if people think I think I'm something special.'

'Well, you are,' said Dillon, smiling.

'No, I'm not. And there's so much to do at Peasebrook – Mum refuses to let me know what's going on and tells me not to worry, but I worry more *not* knowing. What *is* going on?'

'Everything's under control, I think. Your mum's doing a lot. And your dad, actually.'

Alice perked up as she had a sudden thought.

'Could you do me a favour?'

'What?'

'Could you bring in my laptop? So I can check up on everything? I've asked Mum but she keeps forgetting. Accidentally on purpose, I think.' Alice put her head to one side and looked at Dillon, eyes bright. 'It's in the estate office. The girls will know where it is. And don't forget the cable.'

'OK,' said Dillon, pleased he could do something for her. 'But should you be worrying about work?'

'I can't not worry. It's impossible.'

'You should try. Or you won't get better.'

'Honestly, you're just like Mum. She's worried I won't get better in time for the wedding. To be honest, I'm starting to wonder if I should just cancel it. But if I do, I won't be able to get married until next year, because Christmas will get in the way.'

'What's wrong with waiting till next year?' Dillon felt a leap of hope. Given another year hideous Hugh might show his true colours.

'No. We've got plans in place. Hugh wants to give up his flat and move into the cottage as soon as possible. We'll forge ahead.' She looked at her leg. 'I've just got one more operation on this and then ... then they've got a consultant coming to look at my face ... They said it could be much worse. I could have lost my eye. So I'm lucky really. Aren't I?'

She smiled at him, and he wanted to scoop her up in his arms because she was so brave, sitting there with her face all battered, thinking she was lucky. He didn't know what to say. Yes, in a way she *was* lucky. He shuddered when he thought about what could have happened. But the whole thing could have been prevented. If it wasn't for the awful man she was about to marry.

He wondered about telling her his suspicions about Hugh on the night of the accident. But Alice was so sweet-natured, so trusting, she wouldn't believe a word of it. She would give Hugh the benefit of the doubt. Dillon would just sound spiteful. And, of course, he didn't have any proof, except Brian's hypothesis. He had nothing to go on except speculation and gossip.

Alice pointed to a book on the bedside table.

'Read to me for a bit, would you?' she said, changing the subject. 'Mum brought me this in earlier. And I'm getting tired. That's the thing that gets me. I feel all right and then I get exhausted.' She sighed.

'Snuggle down then,' he told her. He picked up the book. *Riders*, by Jilly Cooper. It was huge. He flipped it open.

'I'm not a very good reader,' he warned her.

'It doesn't matter,' she said. 'I almost know it off by heart. I've read it about twenty times.'

'What's the point of hearing it again, then?'

'It's literally the best book in the world.' She managed a smile. 'There are some rude bits, though. Really rude.'

He laughed, and began to read. He felt awkward at first, but he began to get into the story: a bunch of colourful characters vying for hearts and trophies. The room was warm, a bit stuffy, and after a while he could see Alice was falling asleep, so he stopped.

She opened her eyes as soon as he stopped.

'I'm not asleep.'

'Maybe you should go to sleep.' He patted her.

She closed her eyes again. 'That's who you remind me of,' she murmured.

'Who?'

'Jake Lovell. The gypsy boy. Everyone else at school loved Rupert Campbell-Black, but I always liked Jake best. You remind me of him.'

'Oh.' Dillon looked down, not sure if this was a compliment.

'It's a good thing. Rupert Campbell-Black was a beast. But Jake was lovely.'

It was as if she was talking about real people. He closed the book and put it back on the bedside table.

'I better go,' he said. 'Visiting time's nearly over.'

'You'll come again, won't you?'

'Of course.'

He wasn't sure whether to kiss her goodbye. She put up her arms.

'Give me a hug. I need a big hug.'

He bent down and hugged her awkwardly.

'You be good,' he replied, and walked out of the room.

As he left the hospital, he could feel himself clenching and unclenching his fists. He'd hated seeing her like that, obviously in pain but still so bloody brave. Hugh didn't deserve her. But there was nothing he could do to stop the wedding. Even a smashed-up leg and a smashed-up face wasn't deterring Alice.

15

The morning room at Peasebrook Manor was the prettiest room Emilia had ever seen. It had primrose yellow walls and pale green silk curtains and two rose velvet sofas in front of a small fireplace. Over it was a Victorian oil painting of a girl feeding cabbage leaves to a fat bunny rabbit. The girl, with her rosy cheeks and blonde hair, reminded Emilia of Alice.

Emilia wondered what it was like to live in the Basildons' world. Not that hers was gritty reality – she was only too aware it was rarefied – but this was quintessential country life at its most appealing. This was the room where Sarah took tea or coffee with her guests, and wrote letters and saw to her business. She thought of the back office at the shop and resolved to make it a more pleasant place to work in. Her father had rarely spent time in there; just banished anything he didn't want to look at into its depths. It was cold and damp and dingy. It would have to change.

Sarah came in with a tray bearing tea: a proper china teapot, and dainty cups and saucers and a milk jug and sugar bowl. And a plate of shortbread, thick with caster sugar. She laid it on the table between the sofas.

'Milk?' she asked, and Emilia nodded.

Sarah somehow managed to look dishevelled but devastatingly attractive. She must be in her fifties but looked far younger. She had on jeans and a faded Liberty lawn shirt and pale blue loafers. Her hair was a mixture of honey and grey that looked as if a top London hairdresser had painstakingly streaked it, but was probably the result of Sarah not having been to have her roots done for months. Her hands were red and chapped from gardening, and her nails ragged, but the most enormous diamond glimmered on her ring finger: it was so large it almost couldn't be real, but Sarah wasn't the type to wear costume jewellery. She wore no make-up but a dab of pink lipstick hastily applied in the downstairs loo just before she answered the door. She was the archetypal English rose.

'I've just got back from visiting Alice,' she said as she poured the tea. 'The traffic out of Oxford was awful.'

'How is she?'

Sarah sighed. 'She's in a lot of discomfort, poor thing. And of course all those painkillers make one so fuzzy. But she's making progress.'

She sat down on the sofa opposite Emilia.

'I asked you here because I wanted to talk to you about something your father and I had been discussing for a while.'

Emilia nodded. Sarah clasped her hands. She seemed slightly nervous, not quite meeting Emilia's eye. She fiddled with the diamond ring. Her fingers were so slender it spun around and around.

'We had become quite good friends, your father and I. We spoke – met – often.' She lifted her gaze. 'Ralph is not a great reader and it was good to have a decent conversation with someone about books. Julius was always

244

so brilliant at recommending. He had a feeling for what I wanted to read and I don't think there was one book he suggested that I didn't love. Sometimes he'd make me read things because they were good for me and I always took something away from them. He widened my world . . .'

She drifted off, immersed in her eulogy.

'He was extraordinary,' she finished, and Emilia could see the glitter of tears in her navy blue eyes, as bright as the diamond on her ring.

'I know,' said Emilia.

For a moment, Sarah couldn't speak. Emilia was touched. She could see how difficult Sarah was finding this. She was still astonished by how deep people's feelings for her father ran. They still came up to her in the street or in the shop and told her how much he had meant to them.

'I'd love to do something. To remember him by. He often talked about organising a literary festival. It was a dream of his and I'd suggested that we could do one here, at Peasebrook. We have so many rooms here that could be used. We were starting to think quite seriously about it when he became ill.'

Here, Sarah looked down at the floor. Emilia could see she was struggling.

'He did mention the idea to me, once or twice,' she said. 'There are so many authors and celebrities within striking distance of Peasebrook, and we're not so far from London. It could be a real draw. Especially in a setting like this.'

Sarah had recovered her composure. 'Exactly! We felt we could attract a good calibre of speakers. The thing is, it was his dream, but it was starting to become a real possibility. We're very well set up for putting on events here. And I think it would be a shame to let the opportunity slip. I thought about doing the festival in his name.' She swallowed. 'The Nightingale Literary Festival.'

'Oh!' said Emilia. 'That would be a wonderful tribute.'

'I would need your help, though. And the support of the shop. We'd need you to supply the books, of course. And advise on who to ask. I mean, there's masses and masses to think about, but I wanted to see what you thought. Because I couldn't do it without you. It would have to be a team effort.'

Emilia took a piece of shortbread and bit into it. It was a wonderful idea. She could see it all in her mind's eye. Literary lions and lionesses holding forth in the ballroom, the audience hanging on their every word. A glittering programme; the Glastonbury of book festivals. It would be a wonderful boost for the town too – people attending the festival would want accommodation and would go into the pubs and restaurants. And they could get sponsorship from local businesses...

But she had to be cautious. She didn't want to get Sarah's hopes up. It was such an enchanting idea, but she couldn't show too much enthusiasm.

'The thing is,' she said, 'I'm not sure what I'm doing with the shop yet. I'm afraid it's not in very good shape financially. It's not making money at the moment: I'm struggling to cover my overheads. It needs a lot spending on it if it's going to even begin to make a profit and I haven't decided yet if that's what I want to do.'

Sarah looked horrified. 'You can't let it close, surely?'

'I don't want to. Of course not. But I can't just keep it

going out of sentiment. That would be foolish. And I've got my staff to consider, as well as myself.'

Sarah considered her words. 'I understand.' She sighed. 'Julius never mentioned the shop being in trouble.'

The way she said it gave Emilia the impression they spoke often, and that Sarah was hurt by his omission.

She smiled. 'I don't think Dad quite saw that it was. It's all a bit of a muddle. I've only scratched the surface. But he ran it by the seat of his pants, rather.'

'So was he in debt?'

'Nothing awful or to be ashamed of. But there are quite a few outstanding invoices.'

'Gosh.' Sarah looked perturbed. 'He never implied he was in trouble.'

'As I said, I don't think he thought he was. My father's famous line was: *I don't do numbers.*'

'Oh dear.' Sarah leant forwards. 'Between you and me, I have rather more experience of getting out of hideous debt than you might imagine. A while ago now we nearly lost Peasebrook. I won't go into it, but it was pretty frightening. So I understand how you feel. And if I can help at all ...'

'I have Andrea, my accountant – I was at school with her. She's like a walking calculator in Louboutins. She's been wonderful. But even she can't wave a magic wand. I've got some tough decisions to make. And if I do go ahead, it's going to be hard work. Not that I'm afraid of that, of course ...'

'It just goes to show you,' said Sarah, 'that you can think you know someone, but you have no idea.' As she said it, her cheeks flushed pink. She put her face in her hands, and in that moment Emilia recognised that her father and Sarah must have been closer than she realised. She wasn't sure how she felt about this realisation. She liked Sarah very much, but there was no getting away from the fact she was very firmly married to Ralph. Should she press Sarah for more detail? Did Sarah *want* her to realise? She thought she perhaps she did. She had more than hinted.

Maybe today wasn't the day. Everything was still a bit raw. They were feeling their way with each other. If they went ahead with the festival, and worked together, maybe the whole story would come out at some point, when they were both ready.

'I think the festival is a wonderful idea,' she said finally. 'And if I do decide to stay open, I think we should do it. As you say, it would be a perfect memorial. My father would be proud.'

Sarah's smile was a bit wobbly. 'He would . . .'

Emilia put her teacup down. 'I'll let you know as soon as I've decided what I'm doing.'

There was a pause. Sarah was twisting her ring around again. Something unsaid was hanging in the air.

'Emilia – there's something I'd like to share with you. But it's totally confidential. It can't go any further.'

Emilia could see Sarah was struggling with what she was about to say.

'Is it about you and my father?' she asked gently.

There was a spot of colour on each of Sarah's cheeks. 'I loved your father. Very much.'

If she thought about it, she could still feel that love now. A burning heat that went into her very bones; a ball of warmth where her heart sat. They had never known what to do with their love. Acknowledging it in public would have taken them into another realm; a set of circumstances Sarah knew she couldn't manage. Her duty was to her husband, her family and Peasebrook. She couldn't compromise that duty. It wasn't fair on anyone, but most of all it wasn't fair on Julius. He protested that he didn't mind, but Sarah did. She always felt terrible, that he had got the raw end of the deal, and that she was somehow having her cake and eating it.

But if she ever talked about ending it, which she did from time to time when the guilt gnawed at her in the darkness of dawn, he would pull her to him and kiss her. Oh, how they had kissed. Endless kisses that reached deep inside her. Was there anything more momentous, she wondered? To kiss someone so hard you could feel your soul fuse with theirs?

She wasn't proud of her relationship with Julius, for it compromised the two men she loved. For she still loved Ralph in her own way, despite everything he had put her through. Though the two of them lived very separate lives they still had much in common, not least Alice. Never in a million years would she have walked out on what they had.

But she had needed Julius. She knew it was selfish, to carry on, even though he insisted it didn't matter to him. As long as he could have a little bit of her, it didn't matter to him.

She couldn't explain all this to Emilia. Emilia was young. She wouldn't understand the subtleties and compromises and dilemmas that came with later life. And she didn't want to sully Emilia's memory of Julius by making him out to be less than morally upright.

So she chose her words carefully.

'I loved your father, but of course, I'm married, and he was very aware of that. He was a very understanding and considerate man. He respected my situation. But we became very close...'

She hoped what she was saying made sense. She wasn't actually lying. She hadn't denied anything as such. It was equivocation, if anything. She didn't need to go into details about the intensity of what they had. The extraordinary passion, even if it had felt pure.

Emilia didn't say anything for a while. When she finally spoke, her voice was gentle.

'I'm glad,' she said. 'I'm glad he had someone as lovely as you. To care about him. To think about when he woke up in the morning.' A tear slid out onto her cheek. 'Sorry. It's just... I miss him.'

She rubbed her eye with the heel of her hand. Sarah jumped to her feet. She could never bear to see anyone cry – it might be her duty to keep her emotions in check when it came to herself, but when it came to others, she was open and caring. She sat on the sofa next to Emilia and hugged her.

'I miss him too,' she said. 'Dreadfully.'

'I'm just glad he wasn't lonely.' Emilia's voice wavered. She sounded like a small girl trying desperately not to cry harder. 'I always worried that he was lonely. He was such a wonderful man. He deserved to be loved.'

'Oh, he was loved. Be sure of that.'

Emilia leant into Sarah. It was wonderful to be comforted by someone who had loved her father.

'Nobody knew about us, of course. We could never tell anyone. But I'm taking the risk of telling you because I think you'll understand. And because I want you to know that I'm always here if you need me,' Sarah told her. 'I know Julius would have wanted me to look out for you. And if I can be of support, in any way, just let me know. Even if it's just to talk about him. Or just to come up for tea. Or wine. Or anything. Anything.'

Emilia held Sarah's hands and looked at her. She could see now the depth of sadness in Sarah's eyes. And she could feel the warmth and kindness that Julius must have been drawn to. And she was grateful to Sarah, for her compassion and honesty. It must have been a painful confession. She felt honoured to be trusted with the secret. She supposed when she had time to think about it, she might be shocked, but she wasn't going to judge. She found it a comfort, that Julius had this woman's devotion. And she knew, from all the books she had ever read, that life was complicated, that love sprang from nowhere sometimes, and that forbidden love wasn't always something to be ashamed of.

16

A few days later, Bea laid a presentation folder in front of Emilia with a proud smile.

'I tried really hard not to get *too* carried away,' she said.

She had made it into the shape of a book. On the front it read *Nightingale Books*, in silver writing on navy blue. She'd designed a logo – N and B entwined, with a tendril of roses and a tiny nightingale perched amongst them.

'This is the logo – you can use it on all your social media, your bags, the sign outside. A really strong visual that people can recognise and identify with.'

'It's sweet. We could have T-shirts.' Emilia felt a swirl of delight.

'Exactly. This is about creating a brand as much as creating a really immersive shopping experience.'

'OK...' Emilia wasn't used to jargon, but Bea thrived on it.

The first page was a CAD drawing of the shop divided up into sections, using double-sided bookcases. There was a four-sided counter in the centre of the floor space, allowing whoever was serving to see all around the shop.

'I wanted it to feel as if it's got different rooms. Different rooms with different feels,' Bea explained. 'There's so much wasted space, but this gives you twice as much shelf space as well as more room to browse.'

Each section had a page and Bea had created a mood board for each one. The pièce de résistance was the café area on the mezzanine, which also had an area selling cards and wrapping paper and small gifts. There were just three wooden tables, and a marble-topped table with three cake domes.

'Oh!' breathed Emilia. 'Do you think we can do it? It looks absolutely gorgeous. Sort of the-same-but-different.'

'I wanted to keep the spirit of what your dad had here, but move it on a bit. Make it modern but nostalgic. Somewhere people can explore their imaginations: step back into the past if they want, or into another world, or into the future. That's what a book shop should be, after all – a gateway to somewhere else. But books aren't enough – you have to give people a helping hand.'

Emilia leafed through the drawings. Bea really had been clever. She had kept everything that was important, but showed it off to much greater effect. The colours were softer: the walls pale grey, the shelves painted white, which made the shop seem bigger.

'I love it all. I love the lights!'

At the moment, the shop was lit with old-fashioned strip lights, harsh at best. Bea had put in some very cool chandeliers: white twisted glass with red wire threaded through them.

'Well, those are probably very expensive, but it gives you an idea of what could be done.'

Emilia sighed. 'How much do you think it will cost? Because, of course, that's the rub. None of this looks cheap.'

Bea made a face. 'Well, you get what you pay for. But

some of it can be done with MDF and magic. And we can work with what we've got already. If we rip up the carpet, we can use the floorboards – put a nice chalky paint effect over them. And then painting everything pale colours will give the illusion of more space. And you don't have to do it all at once!'

'But I want to do it all at once,' laughed Emilia. 'And how long do you think it would take? We'd have to close while it was being done.'

'I've done a timetable,' said Bea. 'I reckon two weeks, with all hands on deck. As for price, we'd have to get quotes. It's mostly carpentry, a bit of wiring. Decorating. But, of course, as we all know, once you start taking something apart, then you uncover all sorts of horrors.'

'It's a total refurb,' said Emilia, shaking her head. 'There's no point in being half-arsed about it. We'd have to take all the books out and put them somewhere. And I need to put in a new computer system while I'm at it. And security.' She put her face in her hands. 'I'm so excited. But I'm scared. I've got to make the decision and I don't know what to do. It would be so easy to walk away and go back to my old life. Or sell up and start a new one. Either of those would be easier!'

'But not as rewarding?'

Emilia looked around the shop. She imagined everything Bea had outlined brought to life, and how exciting that would be.

She just had to find the courage from somewhere.

And the cash . . .

'I'll get some quotes. There's no point in getting excited until I know what it's going to cost.'

'I've got some good guys who did my house. They're

254

reliable. And fast. And good. They have to be, to work for me.' Bea laughed. 'I'll ask them for a quote.'

'And will you help me do a window display for Mick Gillespie? He's coming at the weekend, remember.'

'Of course!' Bea's eyes sparkled. 'Can I have carte blanche?'

'Carte blanche and a fifty quid budget,' said Emilia. 'And as many copies of his book as you can stuff in the window.'

'It'll be glorious,' promised Bea. 'Maud is at nursery on Thursday afternoon. I'll come and do it then.'

'I can't pay you much.'

'Listen, it's stopping me going mad with boredom. Just give me a signed copy.'

'You're amazing.'

'I know.'

Emilia smiled as her new friend left the shop. Bea made her feel as if things were possible, then put a layer of glitter on the top. She was one of those special people. She was lucky to have her goodwill and her talent, but she wasn't going to be able to rely on her long-term. Bea was way out of her league.

Later that week, Jackson came back to Emilia with his verdict on the Moomins.

'I've decided, I'm going to try and be more like Moomin-pappa,' said Jackson.

'Well, that's a very good resolution,' said Emilia. 'But you might need to put on a bit of weight.'

'Don't! My ex kept going on about how fat they all were. But at least they're happy. Not making kale smoothies and freaking out if they have an extra raw almond.'

'Is she a bit of a health freak?'

'She's turned into one. She never used to be. She's doing a triathlon and she's obsessed with her heart rate and her body fat and how often she can go training.'

'Sounds awful.'

'I don't mind. It means I get to have Finn more while she goes on endless bike rides. So – what shall I read next?'

'I've just got the perfect book in. I'm trying to build up the children's department and I think you should read this.' She led him over to a display table and held up a picture book. 'I don't know anyone who can't learn something from *The Little Prince*, though you probably need to read it a few times to get the full meaning.' She handed it to him. It was a slender book, with a picture of a little blond boy dressed in blue on the front, standing on a planet. 'It's a funny book,' she went on. 'Funny peculiar. But it explains things. It's my favourite book in the world.'

'I thought the Moomins were?'

'After the Moomins.' She grinned. 'OK. I admit it. I have lots of favourites. That's the trouble with books. You can never choose your favourite. It changes depending on your mood. But I really think you'll like it.'

'I'll give it a try.' He handed over the money. 'Finn's really loving being read to. It's made a big difference to our relationship. I think he just saw me as the one who messed about with him in the skatepark, but we've been having some really good chats.' He looked a bit emotional. 'It's good, after everything that's happened. I don't feel like such a bloody failure...'

'I'm sure you're not a failure,' said Emilia.

Jackson looked embarrassed. 'Sorry. I'm oversharing…'

'Listen, it's part of the job. Everyone comes in here to overshare. I'm part bookseller, part therapist.'

She handed him the book. As he took it, Jackson spotted the poster behind the counter, advertising the evening with Mick Gillespie.

'Mick Gillespie? Is he actually coming here?'

'I know, right? I'm so excited.'

'Have you still got tickets? How much is it?'

'Five pounds – but you get nibbles and a Silver Moon cocktail for that. I've got someone doing special Irish canapés. It's going to be amazing.'

'Mia would love that. She's obsessed with Mick Gillespie. She bought me one of those Aran jumpers for Christmas one year. I looked like an idiot in it.' Jackson shrugged ruefully. 'Can I have two tickets?'

'Of course!' She took two tickets from the drawer.

'She is going to be so made up,' grinned Jackson, pulling out a tenner.

Bea emerged from the window, dressed in a boiler suit, a glue gun in one hand. She smiled at Jackson, and looked at Emilia, enquiry in her eyes.

Emilia had no choice but to introduce them.

'Bea, this is Jackson. Jackson, this is Bea. She's doing a window display for the event.'

The two of them nodded hello at each other.

'If you ever want anything done,' said Jackson, 'I'm quite handy.'

Bea held up her glue gun. 'I'm good. But thanks.'

Jackson turned to go, putting a farewell hand up to Emilia.

'Thanks for everything. See you soon.'

Bea watched him go out of the door. 'I bet he's handy all right. What are you waiting for?'

'Bea!' Emilia feigned shock. 'He's not my type. Although he is cute. But he's totally obsessed with his ex. He's just bought tickets to the Mick Gillespie event for her.'

'She's his *ex*!' said Bea. 'Come on! You need to have some fun. And he needs to get over her. Ask him out.'

'He's a customer! I'm not going to ask him out.'

'Why not? It's not like you're a doctor. You're not breaking some Hippocratic oath. There is nothing that says you can't have a relationship with one of your customers.'

Emilia was suddenly reminded of her father and Sarah. So many questions had been whirling around in her head. How had their affair started? In the book shop? Sarah might tell her one day, she supposed.

In the meantime, she needed to get Bea off her back. Jackson wasn't an option. She could see it in his eyes.

'You've got glue in your hair,' she said, and walked away.

Dillon had been in to see Alice every day after work. He'd brought in her laptop and she was jubilant.

'Don't tell my mum,' she warned him. He didn't think it really mattered, her having access to her emails. She had nothing much else to do in the hospital.

'To be honest, it takes my mind off the pain,' she told him.

He was steaming ahead with *Riders*. He was actually starting to enjoy the story and wanted to know what happened next. It was like being in a little bubble, just him and Alice in her private room. The nurse brought them pinky-brown tea in green cups, and he brought in more chocolate.

'I'm going to get so fat,' complained Alice. 'I won't fit into my wedding dress.'

Good, thought Dillon. He wanted Alice to get better, but he'd been hoping and praying that the wedding would be postponed because of her injuries. She seemed determined though. Even though she was in terrible pain, she pushed herself to do her physio.

'I'm walking up that aisle without crutches if it kills me,' she told him.

It exhausted her, though she tried to pretend it didn't. She was lying with her eyes shut as he read. He wasn't sure if she was asleep but it didn't matter. He could always go back and read the chapter again.

He stopped.

She opened her eyes.

'Do you want me to carry on?'

'No.' She sat up. 'I want you to do something for me.'

'Anything, you know that.'

'I'm going to take off the bandage on my face and I want you to look at my scar and tell me how awful it is. I can't look at it myself. But I need to know if it's too bad to get married.'

'OK.'

She picked at the tape holding the gauze in place.

Dillon tried not to show his distress. 'Careful.'

Gently she pulled back the dressing. Underneath was a livid red gash, a v-shaped wound on her cheekbone.

'It should go down and the redness should go and it will fade a bit,' Alice was gabbling. 'But is it really horrific? Is it Frankenstein stuff? Do I look like Herman

Munster? All I'm worried about at the moment is not looking awful at the wedding. If it's really bad I'll have to call it off. I want you to be really honest.'

Dillon looked long and hard at the wound. His mind was racing. If he told her it was terrible, then maybe, just maybe, she would postpone the wedding. And in the meantime, he would get a chance to bury Hugh, somehow. Get him to show his true colours so the wedding would be called off for ever and ever. Maybe he could get some coke off Pogo, then offer it to Hugh. Offer him a better deal. He wasn't sure he'd make a very convincing drug dealer, but he thought it would probably suit Hugh to have a supplier on the premises at Peasebrook...

No, thought Dillon. He wouldn't be able to pull it off. Hugh would be instantly suspicious.

He couldn't do it to her, though. To him, it wouldn't matter if her whole face were scarred: she was beautiful.

'It's just a bit red and swollen,' he told her.

'Really?' she said. 'I mean, I can have my hair over my face and I'll have a veil...'

'Honestly,' said Dillon. 'No one will notice it.'

She sighed. 'You're the only person I can trust to tell me the truth. Everyone else is just lying to make me feel better. And none of them wants the wedding to be cancelled. But I know it doesn't matter to you either way.'

That couldn't be further from the truth, thought Dillon. If anyone wants that wedding stopped, it's me.

'Hugh keeps telling me not to worry and I don't want to go on about it because it just make him feel more guilty about the accident.'

Dillon felt so angry he almost couldn't breathe. The bastard hadn't felt a moment's guilt.

'Are you OK?' asked Alice.

'Fine. It's just a bit stuffy in here.'

'I know. It's awful at night. I can hardly sleep. But I should be out of here soon.'

'That's good news.'

'I'll go mad if I have to stay in here much longer. I'd go mad if it wasn't for your visits. Mum nips in every day, but she and Dad are so busy with Peasebrook, and Hugh's working like a lunatic so he can get time off for the wedding and the honeymoon—'

'Please,' he interrupted her. 'I don't want to hear any more about the wedding.'

Alice looked startled.

He reached over and touched her face gently.

'You're beautiful. You do know that?'

She was staring at him. Time stood still for a moment. He stroked her cheek with the back of his fingers.

'You poor little chick.'

He knew he was touching her for longer than was necessary. But she didn't seem to mind. She seemed frozen to the spot.

'Oh Dillon,' she said.

'What?'

Her face scrumpled with confusion. 'You make me feel funny. That's what.'

'Funny.' He smiled. 'I was trying to make you feel better.'

'You do! That's the point – you make me feel as if it doesn't matter how I look.'

'Well, of course it doesn't.'

She bit her lip. 'Thank you . . .'

She leant forwards. She smelt of antiseptic and baby

powder and chocolate. Dillon's heart thumped. She was going to kiss him.

Then suddenly they heard Hugh's voice in the corridor, exchanging idle banter with the nurses. Alice pulled back sharply, and Dillon got to his feet, moving away from the bed. Dillon usually left at half six, because Hugh came in at seven and he wanted to be long gone. But today, because of the bandage and the conversation about the scar, he was running late.

The door opened and there was Hugh, in his City suit, his hair slicked back, self-important. He glared at Dillon.

'What the fuck are you doing here?'

'I've been visiting Alice.'

'He's been reading to me.'

'Isn't there gardening to be done?'

'Don't be so rude!' Alice was indignant.

Hugh turned to look at her.

'Jesus Christ,' he said, when he saw her scar.

'Shut up,' said Dillon under his breath.

Hugh looked appalled. 'Look, it's OK. We'll get the best people. There must be something we can do.'

He leant forwards to take a closer look.

Alice looked between Dillon and Hugh. 'Dillon said it wasn't too bad.'

'What is he – blind? He's just told you what he thinks you want to hear. We'll talk to the consultant. We've got time to sort it before the wedding.'

'I think what Alice needs is support,' said Dillon. 'Not a plastic surgeon.'

Hugh stared at him. His eyes were dead, thought Dillon.

'I better be going,' he said.

'You had.'

'You don't have to go,' said Alice. 'Just because Hugh's here.'

'My parking's running out any minute.' Dillon made his way to the door. Hugh followed him and opened it for him.

'I don't want to see you here again,' he said, sotto voce.

'Fine,' said Dillon, thinking: you won't see me, because I'll be gone before you get here.

'I mean it,' said Hugh.

And it turned out he did, because when Dillon went to see Alice the next day, the nurse at the reception desk stopped him.

'I'm really sorry, it's close relatives only for Miss Basildon.'

'But she's expecting me.'

The nurse looked sympathetic.

'I can't let you through.'

Dillon went to push past her. 'Let's see what Miss Basildon says.'

The nurse put a hand on his arm. 'I'm sorry. If you go any further, I'll have to call security.'

Dillon stopped. He looked at her. 'It's that bastard, isn't it? He's told you not to let me in.'

'I have to obey the wishes of the family.'

'Not the patient?'

The nurse sighed and Dillon knew he couldn't push it.

'Could you tell her I came to see her? Dillon. Could you tell her Dillon came to see her?'

'Of course.'

He turned to leave, knowing full well the message wouldn't be passed on.

DILLON GREENE

17

On the day of Mick Gillespie's book launch, Thomasina went to the cheesemonger to get some Irish cheese. She stood outside, looking in the window at the display, keeping half an eye on the queue inside until she could be sure that she would be served by Jem. It was the most calculating thing she had ever done.

'I want some Cashel Blue, for some baby tartlets,' she told him. 'And some Gubbeen, so I can make little cheesy choux puffs.'

'Sounds great.' Jem lifted a wheel of Cashel Blue out of the refrigerator and grabbed the end of the cheese wire. 'What else are you doing?'

'Potato cakes with smoked salmon. And Clonakilty Black Pudding with pan-fried apple on skewers. And miniature chocolate and Guinness cakes.'

'Wonderful.' Jem handed her the two cheeses, wrapped in wax paper with the shop's logo printed on it.

There was a silence.

'Twelve pounds seventy,' he said eventually.

She paid him quickly and scurried off. She'd wanted to ask him, because Emilia had given her two tickets. But she didn't have the courage. This was exactly why she didn't push herself forward when it came to men, she thought. She didn't have the guts.

She got back home and started to instruct Lauren on how to prepare the canapés.

'I'm going to teach you how to make flaky pastry,' she told her. 'It's time-consuming, but it's worth it.'

The two of them spent the afternoon rubbing butter into flour, kneading the dough, rolling it out, cutting up cubes of butter, folding the dough and rolling it out again. The mixture was smooth and soothing beneath Thomasina's fingers, and Lauren was a natural pastry maker and had an innate understanding of the process: her results were as neat and professional as Thomasina's. As she looked at the results of their afternoon's work, she felt hugely satisfied.

Thank God for cooking, she thought. Cooking never let her down.

'You look fantastic,' Jackson told Mia, and it was true. She did. She was only in jeans and a silk paisley top, but she looked much healthier than she did in all the fitness gear she wore these days, which just made her look like a shiny stick insect.

She'd been wary when Jackson had flourished the tickets. She had looked at him as if it was some sort of trap. He'd hoped she couldn't resist, especially as he had arranged for his mother to come and babysit Finn. He was pretty sure that, except for her ridiculous training sessions, Mia hadn't been out for a long time.

'Are you guys going on a date?' asked Finn. He was in his pyjamas, all ready for Cilla to put him to bed.

Jackson didn't know what to reply. Mia put him straight.

'No. We just happen to be going to the same thing. So we're going together.'

'Cool.'

Outside, on the way to the book shop, Jackson turned to her.

'So this isn't a date then?'

Mia made a face. 'No. That would be weird.'

'Oh.' Jackson was a bit stung by her vehemence.

'We're going to a thing together,' Mia reiterated. 'But not *together* together.'

Funny, thought Jackson, I thought I'd bought tickets for something you'd like and invited you out. It was typical of Mia to completely recalibrate the gesture and throw out the original intention. But then, that was partly what he loved about her. Her relentless goalpost moving.

'You'd be annoyed if I buggered off to the pub, though, wouldn't you?'

Mia sighed. 'Go if you want. When has what annoys me stopped you doing anything?'

'I don't want to go to the pub.'

'Then don't!' She looked exasperated.

Jackson kept quiet. They were going around in circles, like they always had done. It was how their relationship worked. They arrived at the book shop. Inside, it was heaving. There were silver moons hanging from the ceiling. And behind a table, a figure with white hair surrounded by a stack of books.

'Mick Gillespie,' breathed Mia. 'Actual Mick Gillespie.'

'He's about ninety-seven!' Honestly, thought Jackson. There was no accounting for women, or pleasing them.

*

The window of Nightingale Books took June's breath away. She'd seen it in progress, but now it was all lit up from the inside it looked incredible. She pulled her coat around her, standing in the chill air. The window display was crammed with shots from his most famous films. Fifty years of Mick Gillespie playing heroes and villains and sex symbols and icons. He was an icon himself. And amidst them hung silver moons, the symbol from the film that had made his name. *The Silver Moon*...

It was almost a shrine.

There were thirty-seven of them in the window. She counted. Thirty-seven Mick Gillespies. And she shivered. He could still do that to her.

Just before she stepped over the threshold, she stood and measured how she felt. It still hurt, even now. That dull tug deep inside her, the one that never left. She imagined it, her feeling: a tangle of scar tissue that would never be allowed to heal.

She was here tonight as a guest, not a member of staff, because she still wasn't technically a member of staff – she just did what she could to help as and when she was needed. She refused to take payment, so Emilia had insisted tonight was for her enjoyment. Mel and Dave were holding the fort, and Thomasina and Lauren were passing around the food and drinks.

They'd sold seventy tickets – the shop wouldn't fit many more – and Mick was sitting behind a wide table, surrounded by copies of his book. Bea had made a veritable throne for him to sit on: a golden high-backed chair that was to be the shop's special signing chair for visiting authors. At the back of the shop, Marlowe was playing

Irish tunes on his violin, adding to the atmosphere. It reminded June of the tiny pub in the village they'd filmed in where the locals had often taken over in the evening, entertaining them with their fiddles and whistles and drums.

June took a Silver Moon cocktail. She wasn't sure what was in it, but it tasted delicious and there was a glittery moon perched on the side of each glass. She needed a drink to take the edge off her jitters, although she wasn't quite sure how to identify what she was feeling, or even what she was expecting from the evening. Just to be breathing the same air as him felt momentous.

She picked up a copy of the autobiography and joined the queue for it to be signed. June never usually queued for anything... The shop was buzzing, and she felt pleased. Julius would be so proud of what Emilia had done. She'd rolled up her sleeves and got on with making the book shop work. She was there, behind the till, hands-on, smiling and laughing with the customers he had built up over the years, but also the new ones who'd been drawn in by the lure of a legend. June hoped more than anything that things would fall into place and the shop would stay open.

It was her turn. Mick Gillespie looked up at her, his eyes as dazzling as they had ever been, his smile making you feel special... even though you weren't. June knew that well enough. And as she smiled back and handed him her book, open at the flyleaf for him to sign, there was no recognition. Not a flicker that he had any memory of her.

'Who will I sign it to?' he asked.

'To June,' she said, waiting for a moment, but there was no reaction. He wrote her name and signed his with a flourish before handing it back to her with another smile. He was so practised. She managed a smile back, although inside she felt fury. How could she still be furious? It was a lifetime ago.

She joined the till to pay.

'Don't be daft,' said Emilia. 'There's no way I'm going to make you pay after everything you've done for me.'

At the back of the shop, Mick Gillespie turned to Marlowe with a glint in his eye.

'Do you know "Whiskey in the Jar"?'

'Of course.'

'Come on, then, boy. Let's show them how it's done.'

He stood up and, as Marlowe struck up the tune on his violin, Mick began to sing. And the delighted crowd gathered around and clapped their hands.

'As I was goin' over the far-famed Kerry mountains...'

June abruptly turned and left the shop. After all, she'd heard him sing that song herself, all those years ago in a tiny pub with a dirt floor and an equally appreciative audience.

June walked the short distance to her cottage. There, in the sky above, was a full moon, as if it had known about the evening and made a special appearance. She got home, slipped off her high-heeled boots and put on the slouchy cashmere bedsocks she used for padding over the flagstones. She threw some logs on the wood-burner, poured a glass of wine and sat with her legs curled up on the sofa in her living room.

She leafed through his book until she reached the section about *The Silver Moon*. It had been his turning point, and was an historic film, so there was a hefty chapter.

There was no mention of her. Not a word about the blonde-haired extra who'd played the barmaid and his affair with her. Not a hint of the passion he had professed to feel at the time. She was insignificant. The scenery was discussed at length, the genius writer, the visionary director – even Mrs Malone, the landlady of the cottage they'd stayed in during the shoot, was given a namecheck. But as far as the rest of the world was concerned, she didn't exist and had made no contribution.

She went upstairs. In her sparest spare bedroom she had stored a box in the wardrobe.

She pulled it out. Inside was his Aran sweater and the script from *The Silver Moon*. Beer mats from the pub they drank in. Shells and pressed flowers. She could smell the air if she breathed in deeply enough. She was there, in the drizzle, the scent of damp wool, the taste of his mouth, tinged with whiskey . . .

And the photographs. Faded and curling now, but here was her evidence. Irrefutable evidence. The two of them, arms around each other, laughing into the camera. You could see the chemistry between them, crackling and fizzing, evident even in yellowing black and white. She remembered the little old man with the donkey and cart looking at the camera in consternation but taking the pictures nonetheless. Not exactly David Bailey, but it had been a memory not a work of art.

And she remembered holding the camera at arm's length, back to front, and the pair of them lying on their backs, smiling, as she took what would now be called a 'selfie', his dark hair tangled up in her platinum blonde.

They had been so beautiful, she thought. There was a purity to the photographs that you never got today. It was the real them, no filter, no fiddling, and she'd worn no make-up, yet their beauty shone through nevertheless.

She laid everything out on the bed. It was all there, their story, in the few artefacts. All the proof she needed.

That had been another her. She'd stopped bleaching her hair, going back to her natural brown, and had put on some weight. No one would ever have known she was Juno.

She suddenly felt angry. He had ruined her for anyone else. She had loved her two husbands in a low-key way, and the divorces had been amicable rather than acrimonious. But she'd never felt the same way about anyone as she had Mick Gillespie.

There was a large brown envelope too, that she hadn't opened yet. She lifted it: it was heavy with paper. She opened the flap and pulled out a manuscript: pages and pages typed onto cheap flimsy paper.

In 1967, Michael Gillespie ripped out my heart and dashed it onto the rocks at Coumeenoole Beach. To my amazement, I managed to live without it. And I'm here, living, breathing, and able to tell you the story of what happened when an innocent young girl fell in love with the world's greatest star. It's a fable, really. A warning.

It was her story, of what had happened to her. She remembered writing it, two years after she had come back from Ireland. She'd sat at her typewriter and written, long into the night, the words tumbling out at a breakneck pace, so fast she couldn't keep up with them.

June smiled as she remembered the sound of a real typewriter. Somehow the gentle *tip tap* of the computer keyboard didn't have the same satisfaction. She began to read the words, the words of a wounded young girl.

Halfway through, she stopped reading. She found it too sad, the memories. She wasn't that girl any more. She was a part of who she had become, but she didn't need to go back and revisit the pain. She knew now that everyone had heartbreak in their life at some point. What had happened didn't make her special or unusual. It was part of being human. A broken heart was, after all, the source material of a myriad books. Some of those books had become her comfort, and had made her realise she was not alone.

She slid the papers back into the envelope and sealed it back up again.

Mick and Marlowe were in full swing. Mick had produced a bottle of Paddy whiskey and was topping up the audience's cocktail glasses in an expansive 'one for you, one for me' gesture, then calling up ballads for Marlowe to play: 'The Irish Rover', 'Molly Malone', 'The Rising of the Moon' . . . The atmosphere was bordering on riotous.

Eventually Emilia had to call a halt to the proceedings. She could sense Mick getting slightly out of hand, and she wasn't sure about the legality of getting all her customers insensible at this hour of the day. So she gestured discreetly to Marlowe to wind things up, and despite Mick's protests – he would have gone on all night given the chance – the shop gradually emptied, and after much effusive hugging and kissing, Mick headed off to the Peasebrook Arms. Emilia had no doubt he would waste no time making friends in the bar, but she was too exhausted to accompany him herself.

She was cross when Marlowe refused to let her pay him for playing.

'It's the best fun I've had for weeks. Playing the fiddle for Mick Gillespie? I'd have given my right arm for that. I don't want payment.'

'But I wouldn't have asked you if I thought you wouldn't let me pay.' Emilia hated the thought of exploiting anyone's better nature.

'I know. Which is why it's OK.'

'But I won't ask you again.'

'You can pay me next time. But this time: gratis. It was a pleasure. And I did it for your dad.' Marlowe smiled kindly. 'You have his magic, you know. People want to do things for you, like they did him. You're going to be all right.'

'Well, thank you.' Emilia was very grateful. Marlowe had certainly helped make the evening a memorable one. 'People are going to be talking about it for weeks.' She laughed. 'I thought things were going to get out of hand. He's a handful even at his age.'

'He's a legend all right,' said Marlowe in a mock Kerry accent, buttoning up his coat.

Bea went home after the event feeling slightly high on the buzz. Everyone had raved about her windows; she'd had her photo taken in front of them with her arm linked in Mick Gillespie's, and she felt like her old self. She hadn't felt like Bea since the day she'd left *Hearth*. Mummy Bea was a slightly alien creature she still didn't feel comfortable with.

So she was full of it when she got back home, babbling on to Bill, who had got home from work early for once in order to babysit. But he just seemed grumpy and disinterested.

'For heaven's sake,' said Bill. 'Stop wittering on about that bloody shop, will you?'

Bea's mouth dropped open.

'Wittering?' she said. 'I try very hard not to witter, thank you very much.'

'I'm sorry. But it's not as if you're even being paid. And I don't think I can listen to another word.'

'Well, in that case, you can listen to me witter about what Maud ate for lunch. And what shape or consistency her poo is. Because that's what most new mothers talk about. I'm not as lucky as you. I don't have reams of people to talk to about interesting things. So I'm sorry if I seem a bit obsessed, but Nightingale Books is the most exciting thing in my life right now—'

She hadn't realised her voice was getting higher and higher with indignation. Bill put up a hand to stop the flow.

'I'm off to bed. It's nearly midnight. And I have to be up at six. Sorry.'

And he walked out of the room.

Bea was astonished. She crossed her arms. She wasn't going to let Bill get away with this behaviour. She wouldn't tackle him now, but she was going to call Thomasina in the morning. Book them dinner at A Deux, and have it out once and for all, on neutral territory, in private. She was not going to stand here and watch her marriage go down the pan.

Mia and Jackson walked back from Nightingale Books in the lamplight.

Mia had drunk two cocktails and was quite garrulous.

Jackson supposed that as she barely ate anything these days they must have gone straight to her head. She was a little unsteady on her feet, and as they reached the edge of the town he took her arm. She didn't seem to mind. She leant on him as they walked up to the house. He thought it felt a bit like the old days, when they'd first got together and had gone out on the town with their mates.

But the minute they got inside the door of the house, Mia went quiet and cold.

'Thanks for a lovely evening,' she said, but it sounded automatic rather than genuine. 'I'm off to bed. Thank you for sitting, Cilla.'

And she was gone.

Jackson was flummoxed. He looked to his mother for an explanation.

'Ten minutes ago she was babbling about what an amazing evening she'd had. Suddenly she's like an ice queen.'

Cilla looked knowing.

'She's scared.'

'Of what? Not me, surely.'

'She feels a fool,' said Cilla. 'She knows she was wrong to kick you out, but she doesn't know what to do about it.'

'Why can't she just say she was wrong?' Jackson was puzzled.

Cilla sighed. 'You don't understand women, do you?'

'No,' said Jackson. 'But if that's what she feels, what am I supposed to do?'

'Woo her back.'

'That's what I thought I was doing.' He shook his head. 'Sometimes I think I didn't get the instruction manual.'

'You'll be all right.'

'How do you know?'

'I just do.'

Jackson hugged his mum. 'Come on,' he said. 'I'll just go up and give Finn a goodnight kiss, then let's get home.'

Ten minutes later he bundled his mum into his jeep, popped Wolfie in the boot and walked around to the driver's door. At the last moment, he looked out and saw Mia peering out of her bedroom window. As soon as she saw him looking, she dropped the curtain and was gone.

In the quiet of the empty shop, Emilia gathered up the last of the cocktail glasses that were scattered around and took them upstairs to wash them and put them back in the box to be taken to the wine merchant.

It had been a wonderful evening. It had lifted her heart. So many people had turned up to see Mick Gillespie, old customers and new. There had been a real buzz in the air.

Of course, Emilia knew that she wouldn't get a star like him to come along to the shop every week. And the novelty would probably wear off. But it had given her a glimpse of what could be done, and they had rung more through the till that evening than they did in a week because people had bought other books as well as Mick's. Dave and Mel had worked hard to make the display tables as enticing as possible so people would make impulse purchases, and they had.

Of course, there had been one thing missing. Her father would have loved it. But she was determined not to think like that any more. Julius was gone, and she was clomping about in his shoes, trying them on for size.

Sometimes they felt either too small or too big as she stumbled around.

Nights like this, though, made her feel as if his shoes fitted perfectly.

Just before midnight, June heard the wind get up and the rain begin. It was wild. She shut the curtains tight, grateful that she'd had her little cottage double-glazed when she moved in full-time. She went into the kitchen to make a cup of camomile tea, then heard a mighty rapping on the stable door. She froze, wondering who on earth it was at this time. It wasn't as if she was on the way to anywhere. She decided she would ignore it.

Then she heard shouting. An indignant roar that carried through the gale. A roar she would have recognised anywhere.

'For the love of God, would you open the door?'

She marched across, slid back the bolts and turned the lock. She just opened the top half, in case. And there, framed in the doorway, was Mick Gillespie, soaked to the skin.

'Thank Christ for that. Will you let me in?'

'Give me one good reason why I should?' She put her hands on her hips.

'Because it's pissing with rain and I'm soaked through and I'll get pneumonia. I'm an old man.'

She couldn't help smiling. What a bloody fuss. She stood back and he bowled in through the door. She smelt wet wool and him. She took his coat – cashmere and no protection from the rain – and hung it on the Aga.

'They told me at the hotel it was only ten minutes' walk,' he grumbled.

'How did you find me?'

'You don't need to be Sherlock Holmes. And the people in this town aren't very discreet, you know.'

'You recognised me, then?'

'Of course I did,' he said. 'But I didn't know what to say. You didn't say anything so I thought it was best left, maybe. But then I thought: you wouldn't have been there if you hadn't wanted to see me.'

'You're a better actor than I thought. I didn't think you had a clue.'

'I'm trained, remember.' His smile was teasing. Those bloody crinkly eyes . . .

June smiled and handed him a towel to dry his hair, then poured two glasses of red wine. They sat down at the kitchen table, looking at each other.

He looked around in approval. June knew the cottage looked good. She'd spent a lot of money making it comfortable and stylish, and she had a great eye for art and antiques. She'd perfected the designer farmhouse look: the gleaming pink Aga, the flagstones warmed by underfloor heating, the French kitchen table, the chunky wine glasses stamped with a bee.

'You've done well,' he said.

'I have,' she said, not ashamed to be proud of her achievements.

'I was a shite,' he told her. 'But it was the best thing for you. I'd have played merry hell with you and you'd have ended up hating me. Or killing me. I really wasn't a very nice person in those days.'

'And are you now?'

He tipped his head to one side to consider her question. 'I don't think I'm all bad.'

'That's good to hear.'

'You're a nice person, that's for sure. You always were. People like you don't change. Unless they get damaged by people like me. I hope you weren't.'

'Nobody as awful as you, no.'

They grinned at each other.

Mick raised his glass.

'Well, here's to old times' sake. It's very nice to see you.'

'I suppose you were just bored in your hotel room?'

He looked a bit taken aback.

'No. I wanted to see you. I've very fond memories of our time.'

'I wrote a searing exposé,' June told him. 'About how cruelly you treated me.'

'Really?' He made a face. 'It would be the perfect time to publish it. Everyone seems to be obsessed with my past at the moment.'

'Ah, no – it's staying firmly locked away. It was just a therapeutic exercise.'

'Writing's therapy, for sure. I was amazed what I dredged up when I did the book.'

'So you're trying to right wrongs now?'

'Jesus, I haven't enough time left on this earth to do that.'

He roared with laughter. Then stopped and looked at her.

'Just one wrong will do me for now.'

She held his gaze. She wanted to laugh. He was incorrigible, even at this age. He couldn't help himself. She realised that the spell she had been under for so many years was broken. He no longer had a hold over her.

How many times had she dreamt of this moment over the years? She couldn't begin to count.

Yet to turn him away would be boring. She couldn't remember the last time she'd been propositioned. She deserved some fun as much as the next person. And he hadn't been a selfish bugger in the bedroom, that much she could remember. She felt her cheeks pinken slightly at the memory as she picked up her glass. She was going to make him work for it.

'What are you suggesting, Mr Gillespie?'

18

Two weeks later, Thomasina and Lauren were tucked away in the kitchen at A Deux. Lauren was putting the finishing touches to a chicken and pear tagine, chopping almonds and coriander to scatter on the couscous.

'You mark my words – this is a crisis dinner,' Lauren whispered. 'This is the last resort. It's written all over them.'

Thomasina, who was cutting out lavender biscuits to go with the panna cotta, nudged her to be quiet. Discretion was the watchword at A Deux – it was the whole point.

A Deux was booked several nights a week now, and Thomasina had grown in confidence. She and Lauren had become quite a team, catering outside events. She'd had masses of enquiries since doing the canapés at Nightingale Books and it was almost getting to the point when she might have to give up the day job, though she probably never would.

Seeing Lauren blossom and flourish under her tuition had been incredibly rewarding too. That was the joy of teaching: capturing someone, inspiring them, giving them a purpose. Lauren was a different girl. She was focused, conscientious, full of initiative. If Thomasina hadn't seen her potential and tapped into it, she would be excluded from school by now, on a one-way ticket to nowhere.

In the dining room, clusters of candles gave a rosy glow to the two guests at the table. Thomasina's cottage was small – just one main room, which you walked straight into from the front door, and where the table was laid. She had bought the best cutlery and china she could afford: knives and forks with mother-of-pearl handles, and pale cream china with an ornate French pattern. The snowy white linen tablecloth and napkins gave an air of formality, but other than that the room had a warmth that wrapped you up, with its dark red walls and the rich Egyptian-style carpet.

Bill sighed, and looked down into his Jerusalem artichoke soup, as if the answer might lie in the swirl of cream on the top.

'I'm sorry. I'm sorry. It's just . . .'

'It's just what?'

'I think I'm going mad.'

He looked up, and Bea saw a bleakness in his eyes that scared her.

'What do you mean?' Bea crumbled up some of Thomasina's walnut bread in her fingers.

'I understand it's been hard for you. Giving up your old life and starting anew. But I'd give anything to be in your position.'

'Oh.'

'I don't think I can carry on.'

'What do you mean?' Bea panicked. 'With what? Do you mean us?'

Oh God. He was asking for a divorce. She'd bored him into wanting a divorce with her 'wittering'.

'No! Of course not. I mean this way of life.'

Bea took a gulp of wine. Then another. They were walking, so they didn't need to have the driving conversation.

'I hate it. I hate leaving you and Maud. It's bloody exhausting, getting up at stupid o'clock and going to catch the train. By the time I'm back home, I'm too knackered to have a conversation or enjoy my food and the weekends go in a flash. By the time I've had a lie-in to get over the fact I've had hardly any sleep, it's Sunday. And from midday on Sunday my stomach is in a knot, dreading Monday morning.'

'I had no idea you felt like this.'

'I thought it was going to get easier. But I just want a normal life, Bea. I love it here in Peasebrook. I want to be a normal bloke. Join the darts team in the pub. Muck about in the garden. Enjoy my family. Maud looks at me sometimes as if I'm someone she thinks she should recognise but isn't quite sure...'

He rubbed his face and Bea suddenly saw how terrible he looked. Haggard and red-eyed. She'd put it down to too much red wine.

He looked over at her.

'I don't want to be a high-flyer any more. I don't want to be part of the commuter club, an absentee husband and father.'

Bea fiddled with the knife and fork on either side of her bowl. She had lost her appetite all of a sudden and couldn't finish her soup.

'What do we do about it?' she asked, her voice very small. 'I'm so sorry, I had no idea...'

'I don't know, Bea. But I can't carry on. If I'm not careful, I'm going to get sacked. I'm tired and I'm stressed and I'm resentful and I'm making mistakes and being a pain in the arse to work with.'

Bea reached out a hand and put it on top of Bill's.

'I'm sorry,' she said. 'I've been stuck in my own little world, trying to play the perfect wife and mother. And to be honest, I haven't been that happy either. It's as if we've both been forced into a way of life we don't want, in order to sustain this fantasy lifestyle.'

'Exactly,' said Bill. 'I know you're bored. I know you adore Maud, but I can see you trying to find ways to get through the day.'

'Handwashing cashmere cardigans just isn't doing it for me.' Bea managed a laugh. 'Not even when I get to hang them on the line with fancy artisanal wooden clothes pegs.'

She had a mental image of herself, a veritable layout from *Hearth* magazine. But she wasn't going to be defeated by this. Bea was a strategist. She always had a plan.

'What about if we do a swap?' she said.

Bill raised his eyebrows.

'Swap?'

'I could go back to work. I get people calling me all the time offering me jobs I really, really don't want to turn down. I would love to go back and be a proper grown-up in London. And you could hang out here with Maud.'

'Be a house husband?' Bill frowned. 'I'm not sure about that.'

Bea wrinkled her nose. 'No! You can do some freelance work from home while Maud's at nursery. Though you would have to do a *bit* of house stuff – get food in, bung the washing on every now and again. But it's not hard, Bill. Why do you think I'm so bored? I think you're way better suited to this country life than me. I just don't see myself as a jam-making, WI sort of person. But I think you'd really like the gardening and the log-cutting and the endless trips to the pub.'

'Do you really think it could work?' asked Bill. 'I've got loads of people who want me to do consultancy for them.'

'Yes!'

'You'd have to be the breadwinner. You won't mind the commute?'

'No! I am soooo jealous whenever you head off for that train.'

'Really? You're welcome to it.'

'It will take a bit of time for me to find the right job. But I think it's a great solution. Don't get me wrong. I don't want to move back to London. I think here is perfect, and right for Maud.'

Bill looked as if the weight of the world had been taken off his shoulders.

'I'd love that, Bea. I feel as if life's whizzing past, and I don't have time to enjoy the things I want to enjoy, and any minute now Maud will be sixteen. I want to slow down. I know I'm only just forty, but I don't want to spend the next ten years slogging my guts out. And if it means cutting back on crap that doesn't matter—'

'Like hundred quid candles?'

'Yes!'

'You've got yourself a deal, mister.'

Bea shook hands with her husband over the table.

As Lauren brought out the tagine, Bea sat back in her chair with a sigh of relief. She had been terrified Bill was going to give her some ultimatum. Or tell her he'd found someone else. The thing was, Bea quite liked playing at country mouse, but really she was a town mouse through and through. It would all be here at the weekends, the trugs and the Peter Rabbit carrots and the eggs still covered in chicken shit.

And this time, when they got back home, after the two bottles of ruinously expensive wine they'd drunk to celebrate their decision, Bill was still awake when she came out of the bathroom in her Coco de Mer. Wide awake.

19

The following Sunday, Emilia gave herself the day off. She had worked flat out for weeks, and Dave was happy to run the shop for the day.

Marlowe had offered to give her a cello lesson, to get her up to speed on the pieces she was unfamiliar with and to practise the Handel. Of all the pieces she had to get that right, as it heralded Alice's entrance.

'It's renowned for being a bitch of a piece for the cello,' he told her, 'but we'll nail it, don't worry.'

It was one of those autumn days that take you by surprise. Although there was a sharpness in the air on waking, warm sunshine and a cloudless sky belied the season. Emilia put on a yellow dress and a pale green cardigan and drove to Marlowe's house, a tiny Victorian lodge on the outskirts of Peasebrook. It was like a cottage out of a fairy tale, all pointy windows with a gabled roof and an arched front door.

Inside, it was chaos. Books and sheet music and empty wine glasses and two smoky grey cats stepping amongst it all. John Coltrane was playing and she could smell fresh coffee. With a pang, she realised it reminded her a little bit of the flat when her father was alive: he was always in the middle of twelve things at once; there was always music, something cooking.

'God, I'm sorry. I meant to tidy up.' Marlowe kissed her. 'Meet Crotchet and Quaver.'

He scooped one of the cats off a chair and patted the seat. 'You sit here. I'll get you a coffee while you set yourself up.'

Emilia got out her cello, and as she looked around the room she spotted evidence of Delphine: a silk Hermès scarf on the sofa; lipstick on a glass; a pair of Chanel ballet flats.

'Delph's in Paris for the weekend – some family knees-up. So we've got all day if you need it.'

OK, thought Emilia. I've got the message. 'Delph'. That was fond familiarity if ever she'd heard it.

After two hours, she was exhausted. Marlowe was a brilliant and patient teacher, and not once did he make her feel inferior. He helped her with her posture and her bow hold. At one point he put his hand on her shoulder. His fingers dug in until he found a muscle.

'You need to relax that muscle. Drop your shoulder.'

Emilia tried desperately to relax, but she found it difficult. The feeling of his hand on her was making her think about things she probably shouldn't. Eventually she managed to untense.

'That's it!' Marlowe was triumphant. 'If you relax that, you'll be able to play for longer, and much better.'

By half twelve, she was exhausted.

'Come on,' said Marlowe. 'Let's walk to the pub and get some lunch.'

They walked to the White Horse and bought hot pork ciabatta rolls with apple sauce and bits of salty crackling, sitting at a table outside next to a patio heater. Emilia didn't want to leave the sunshine, the easy company, the half of cider that was making her sleepy and made her want to slide into bed...

'Let's go back through the woods,' suggested Marlowe. 'It's a bit further than the road but we can walk our lunch off.'

The walk through the wood meandered alongside the river. Sunshine and birdsong lifted Emilia's heart: she'd spent far too much time inside recently. She must make the effort to get out and enjoy the countryside around Peasebrook. It was truly glorious, with the trees ablaze with crimson and coral and ochre, and the rich smell of dead leaves underfoot.

Eventually they came to a section of the river that was deeper than the rest, the banks widening to form a bowl-shaped pool. The water was crystal clear: Emilia could see the smooth stones at the bottom, covered in moss, and there was a willow on the far bank, trailing its branches in the water.

'Fancy a swim, then?' asked Marlowe. 'Doesn't get wilder than this.'

'You have to be joking. Surely it's too cold?'

'Nah. I swim here all the time, even on Christmas Day. It's invigorating.'

'Invigorating?'

Emilia looked doubtful. Yet part of her couldn't resist the challenge.

'Does Delphine swim in this?' She couldn't imagine she did.

'God, no. She's a total chicken.'

That was all the encouragement Emilia needed. She was

going to prove to Marlowe she was no wuss. There was only one thing stopping her.

'I haven't got any bathing things,' she said, but she had a feeling that wasn't going to inhibit Marlowe.

'We can go in our underwear,' he said. 'No different to swimming trunks or a bikini.'

Emilia laughed.

'You're on,' she said, and kicked off her shoes and began to unbutton her dress.

Marlowe needed no encouragement. He ripped off his shirt, undid his jeans, and she saw a flash of surprisingly toned skin and a six-pack before he dived straight in.

He came to the surface spluttering and whooping with the shock of the cold.

'Whoa!' he shouted. 'Come on! Don't hesitate or you'll never do it.'

She dropped her dress on top of his clothes and before he had too much time to examine her in her bra and knickers she leapt in too.

The iciness took her breath away. But it was exhilarating.

'Oh my God!' she said. 'It's giving me brain freeze.'

They trod water for a while.

'I love it here,' said Marlowe. 'It's where I come when I've fucked things up. It clears your head.'

Emilia nodded, but her teeth were starting to chatter.

'You don't strike me as someone who ever fucks up.'

He gave a hollow laugh.

'You know, when you get yourself into a situation you can't get out of?' His tone was dark.

Emilia wondered what he meant. Was he referring to Delphine? But he didn't elucidate.

'Come on,' said Marlowe. 'You're getting cold.'

They climbed back out onto the bank. Marlowe picked up his shirt.

'Use this to get yourself dry,' he said. 'I can go without. We're nearly at the cottage.'

She felt self-conscious, wiping herself down with his shirt, but it took away the worst of the water before putting her dress back on. She found herself riveted by a tattoo on his chest – a line of music on his taut skin.

She bent forwards to inspect it. She wasn't great at sight-reading, but even she could work it out.

'Beethoven's Fifth!' she exclaimed in delight.

'Well done,' he said. 'You passed the test.'

'Test?'

He looked at her. His eyes were teasing. 'I never sleep with anyone who can't read what it is.'

Her eyes widened.

He looked embarrassed. 'Not that—'

'No! Of course not.'

She walked on, confused. Why had he said that? It was a bit unfair, given his relationship. He'd definitely been flirting with her, just for a moment.

Back at the cottage, she felt shivery: the water had been freezing and the cold had got into her bones. Marlowe made her a hot chocolate, and lent her a grey cashmere sweater. As she slipped it on, she breathed in the smell of him. She immediately felt warmer, as if she'd been wrapped in a hug. That was cashmere for you, she supposed.

'Stick some of this in it.' Marlowe held out the bottle of Paddy she'd brought him to say thank you for play-ing. He poured a generous slug into her mug. As she drank it, curled up on the sofa, she felt her eyes close.

The morning's playing, the walk, the lunch, the swim, the warmth of the fire and the whiskey . . .

'Well, well, this is cosy.'

She started awake to see Delphine standing in the doorway.

Marlowe got up off the sofa in a fluid movement. Emilia had had no idea he was sitting next to her.

'Hey, Delph.'

Delphine's eyes took in the scene. Luckily Julius's cello was still out, in front of a music stand. It was all the excuse they needed.

Not that they needed an excuse. They'd done nothing. Though Emilia was conscious of wearing Marlowe's sweater.

'You're back early,' said Marlowe. 'Have a whiskey.' He took a glass off a shelf.

'I should go,' said Emilia.

'Not because of me,' said Delphine, taking the whiskey off Marlowe and sinking into the sofa. She was in a red sweater dress and matching beret. She looked unbelievably smug, and Emilia felt a sudden flash of intense dislike.

'Do you mind if I keep your jumper on?' she asked Marlowe, knowing she was being provocative. She only did it because she knew they had nothing to hide. She had a clear conscience.

Delphine didn't flinch. Marlowe nodded. 'Sure. Give it back to me at the next rehearsal.'

Emilia drove home, trying not to feel nettled by Delphine's hostile presence. She concentrated instead on what she had achieved. She felt so much more confident after Marlowe's tuition. Maybe she wasn't going to let the side down after all.

*

Jackson couldn't settle that Sunday.

Ian Mendip had called him to hassle him about the book shop.

'It doesn't usually take you this long to get into a girl's knickers,' he complained, and Jackson hung up on him. He'd blame the bad signal in Peasebrook.

He didn't want any more to do with Ian's twisted plan. He really admired Emilia for what she was doing at the shop and hated the thought of Ian getting his hands on it. Nightingale Books was a force for good, and Mendip was a greedy monster. If he sacked him, then so be it.

He walked over to his house. Mia was heading out on a twenty-mile bike ride as part of her triathlon training, and he'd offered to look after Finn. He didn't see it as a chore – why would he?

'Nice bike,' he said, as she got everything ready – gel packs and water bottles and repair kits.

She looked at him. 'It's all I've got,' she said. 'I don't spend money on clothes.'

'I didn't mean anything by it,' said Jackson, because he hadn't. Why was she so defensive? Why did she make it so hard for him to be nice to her?

He looked at her, in her ridiculous tight black Lycra and the helmet that made her look like an alien, and thought how vulnerable she looked. His heart gave a little stumble.

'Good luck,' he said. 'Call me if you get tired and need picking up.'

'I'll be fine,' she said, clearly not wanting to show any dependence on him whatsoever.

He went back into the house.

He felt as if he was in limbo, halfway between being an upstanding person and a waste of space. It was as if he was in the bottom of a dark well, and there was a light at the top, and he had to climb up to it. He wasn't sure what he was going to find when he got to the light, but if he did get there, things would be better, he felt sure.

He leafed through the book Emilia had suggested he read with Finn. *The Little Prince* was a curious book, and a lot of it he found puzzling. It seemed to have all the wisdom in the world in its pages.

She cast her fragrance and her radiance over me. I ought never to have run away from her. I ought to have guessed all the affection that lay behind all her poor little stratagems. Flowers are so inconsistent! But I was too young to know how to love her...

It was true. He had been too young to love Mia properly. He had driven her away with his behaviour. He could see that now. She didn't trust him. Of course she didn't. He'd been immature, and feckless, and selfish.

He stared at the wall in the living room. He'd given up, he realised. He'd given up on his hopes, his dreams, his relationships. He'd become involved in something that made him hate himself more than he did already.

He closed the book. So that was why people read. Because books explained things: how you thought, and how you behaved, and made you realise you were not alone in doing what you did or feeling what you felt.

He took Finn out to the skatepark, a million thoughts whirling around his head, not sure how to make sense of them, but knowing that he needed to, and that somewhere there was an answer. He didn't just have to stumble along, making mistakes, doing things he didn't want to, at the will of everyone else.

Suddenly everything seemed so clear in his mind: what he wanted from life. He wanted the chance to be a good husband to the woman he loved and had never stopped loving. He was a good father, he knew that, but he wanted to be a father in a proper family, not a single dad kicking a football or standing in the skatepark.

What would she say? How could he convince her he had changed? He had no proof, except for the fact that he felt different. That someone – Emilia – had, without knowing, shown him the way. Mia would laugh if he tried to explain it. She would think he was trying it on, trying to get his feet under the table because it suited him.

He had to ask her. He had to man up and fight for what he wanted. His wife and his child to be together with him. He'd learnt by his mistakes. He wanted responsibility and security.

He picked up a couple of takeaway pizzas for him and Finn from the corner shop on the way home. They scoffed them in the kitchen, not even stopping for plates, eating them right out of the cardboard box.

Jackson was in the middle of tidying the kitchen when Mia got back from her bike ride. She looked exhausted.

'Are you OK?'

'Fine,' she said brightly, and looked askance at the remains of the pizza, one eyebrow raised in disapproval of its fat and carb content.

It was now or never, thought Jackson.

'I miss you.'

Mia blinked. 'What?'

'I miss you. I miss us. I don't understand why I'm stuck

in a caravan with my mum – much as I love her – and you're obsessed with ...' he waved a hand in the air, 'driving yourself into the ground with all that fitness and healthy eating. We should have gone out today, as a family.'

She crossed her arms. She looked away. She looked as if she was going to cry. Eventually she looked back at him.

'But we're not a family any more, Jackson.' She walked away to put the kettle on, turning her back on him to indicate the conversation was over, and Jackson felt a lurch of disappointment. So much for being brave.

He sighed. 'Oh.' He frowned. 'Is there ... someone else?'

He imagined some sinewy cycling fanatic planning endless bike rides on a fitness app.

She gave a bark of laughter. 'No. No, there isn't. I don't want somebody else, Jackson. I'm trying to figure out who I am, after everything you put me through. Build a new life.'

Without him in it. That much was clear.

He nodded. 'OK ...'

He walked out of the kitchen and went to find Finn, who was playing on his Wii in the lounge.

'See you soon, mate.' He hugged his son to him. As long as he had Finn, that was all that mattered. If Mia couldn't find it in her heart to forgive him for his transgressions, that was fair enough. But he was still Finn's dad. She couldn't take that away from him.

He walked back to the kitchen to say a final goodbye. Mia looked up, startled and guilty. She was eating a piece of their cold pizza as if it was the last slice on earth.

'Bye,' said Jackson, resisting the urge to say something cutting. Because he didn't feel bitter. He just felt sad. But he thought perhaps the pizza showed a chink.

20

Bea took Emilia out for breakfast to tell her what she and Bill had decided.

Emilia was feeling terrible. She hadn't felt right since her wild swim with Marlowe. She was fighting off a cold, but losing. She ordered eggy sourdough with roasted vine-ripened tomatoes to give her some strength. Bea was feeding Maud discs of banana.

Emilia scooped the froth off her cappuccino. The café roasted its own coffee, and she always swore never to drink instant again when she came in here.

'There's something I need to tell you.' Bea finished her granola. 'I didn't want to say until it was definite, but I'm going back to work. In London. I got the official offer through this morning.'

'Oh.' Emilia tried to look happy for her. 'That's a bit of a life change.'

'Bill's going to work from home and have Maud when I'm in London. We both realised we'd got our lives the wrong way round.'

'But I need you!' Emilia was joking, but she realised she had become dependent on Bea's vision and advice. She really valued their friendship.

'I know. But I can still help you with the shop. It was

getting involved with you that made me realise how much I miss work.'

'If I stay open.'

'What do you mean?'

'It all seems like a bit too much effort at the moment.'

Bea punched her arm. 'Shut up! I won't listen to that negativity. You've got plans, Emilia!'

Emilia couldn't be bothered to argue. Her throat was on fire and her head throbbed. So she just smiled. She was happy for her friend. Of course she was.

By Sunday, she felt like the walking dead. Emilia wanted nothing more than to stay in bed, but she was scheduled to spend the day rehearsing with the quartet. The wedding was getting closer and closer. She stayed under the duvet as long as she could get away with, then scrambled into her clothes without having a shower and rushed to the village hall.

She knew she looked rough in her jogging bottoms and hoodie. To add to her malaise, Delphine was looking particularly stunning in an electric blue silk blouse with a pussycat bow, which she wore with a tiny leather miniskirt.

Marlowe went to give her a hug, but she dodged out of his way.

'Don't come anywhere near me. I'm full of germs.' She thrust his hand-washed cashmere sweater back at him.

Usually, playing the cello took Emilia out of herself. Music soothed her soul, and playing music soothed it even more. They were playing 'Salut d'Amour' by Elgar, one of the tunes they would play for the congregation while waiting for the ceremony to start. It reminded

Emilia of the Elgar piece the quartet had played at her father's memorial service: 'Chanson de Nuit'.

She couldn't play for toffee. Her fingers were all over the place, her bow kept slipping and she lost her place.

Marlowe stopped them all and looked at her.

'Are you all right?' he asked. 'You did know we were doing this?'

His tone was even, but she sensed he was hiding his annoyance. The unspoken accusation was that she hadn't practised. She had. But she was a human being. Not a bloody robot.

She put down her bow on her music stand.

'I'm sorry. I've had a lot on. And I don't feel well...'

Everyone was looking at her. Only Petra looked sympathetic. Delphine looked inscrutable.

Marlowe just looked exasperated.

'If you're feeling that bad you should have cancelled. We're just wasting time.'

Emilia got up and headed for the door. Marlowe followed her outside.

'I'm sorry,' he said. 'I always get stressed before events. I just want us to get it right and I know you can do it. You were amazing when you came to my house. You'd cracked it. What's going on?'

'It's my father's birthday today.' Emilia looked down at the ground.

'Oh, you poor baby.' Marlowe softened immediately. 'Oh shit – I'm a bastard. I'm sorry. Come here.'

He was about to pull her into his arms when Delphine appeared by the door.

'We've only got the hall till four,' she told him.

Marlowe backed away from Emilia as if she had the plague. Which she felt as if she did.

'I can't do this any more,' said Emilia. 'I thought I was good enough but I'm not. You'll have to get Felicity back.'

'Don't be silly,' said Marlowe.

'Honestly. It's much better that I pull out now than mess it up on the day. Felicity knows all the music, I know she does. I'm sorry.'

She hurried back in and packed up her cello. She didn't want to talk about it. Nor, it seemed, did the others, which confirmed she was doing the right thing. They'd obviously been longing for her to pack it in, but hadn't had the heart to tell her. She left the hall as quickly as she could, so they could get on with their rehearsal. Without her messing it all up for them.

She walked past Delphine. Delphine tried her best to give her a smile of sympathy, but she really wasn't that good an actress.

When she got home, she didn't even stop to go into the shop and see how Dave was getting on. She didn't feel like pretending she was all right. He'd be closing up in a couple of hours – they shut at four on a Sunday.

Instead, she went upstairs to the flat and felt plunged into stifling gloom. She decided to phone Sarah Basildon. Maybe they could have a glass of wine, share some memories of Julius, and raise a glass to him.

'I'm really sorry,' said Sarah. 'Any other time, but Alice is coming home from hospital today. Ralph and I are just going to collect her. You're welcome to come here, of course: we're doing a celebration tea to welcome her back.'

Emilia lay on her bed. Even Sarah Basildon had moved

on. She hadn't even mentioned his birthday. She stared at the ceiling. She missed her dad more than ever.

Maybe staying in Peasebrook was the wrong thing to do? Maybe keeping the shop open was a romantic gesture, but a foolish one? She shouldn't be trying to live her father's life. She should be living her own.

She decided to run a bath, get warm and put clean sheets on the bed and fresh pyjamas and get an early night. She poured half a bottle of Badedas into the bath and turned the taps on, then went into the kitchen to make a Lemsip, adding two spoons of honey to soothe her throat. She sat on the sofa while she sipped at it: it was scalding hot, but she knew it would do her good. By the time she reached the unmelted honey at the bottom of the cup, her eyes felt heavy and were closing. She curled up in the corner of the sofa and let sleep take over.

Alice was packing up the last of her things before going home. She couldn't wait. Her room was starting to drive her mad. Although all the staff had been wonderful, she'd had enough. The last operation on her leg had been deemed a success and it was up to her now to build up her strength. It still hurt horribly, and she got very tired, but she longed to be at home, at Peasebrook, and felt sure she would heal more quickly there.

She shut her case and looked around the room to see if there was anything else. Her book, *Riders*. She picked it up. It reminded her of Dillon. She had loved him reading to her. It had been so comforting, lying there listening to him, and if she drifted off it didn't matter, because she knew the book so well. He hadn't been in to see her recently and she wasn't sure why. She supposed he was busy putting the garden to bed for the winter.

Hugh had refused to read to her. It wasn't his thing, reading. He was always on edge when he came to visit. He hated hospitals, he told her. Alice wasn't sure anyone liked hospitals all that much, but she didn't say anything. She chatted to him and he pretended to listen and spent most of the time on his BlackBerry. He was doing a few deals he wanted to get out of the way before the wedding, so she understood he was under pressure.

'You don't have to come and see me every night if you don't want to,' she told him, but he insisted. He never stayed long, though.

She tucked the book into her case and zipped it up. She couldn't wait to get back to Peasebrook. There was so much to do. Not just for the wedding, but to get things ready for Christmas. And there was the Christmas garland to make. A sixty-foot rope of flowers from the gardens at Peasebrook. Dillon had been cutting and drying them in one of the potting sheds all year. It was going to be a labour of love to assemble it, but Alice was determined. It was going to be a celebration of everything that had grown at Peasebrook over the year. She was itching to get it done.

Her door opened, and there were Ralph and Sarah, beaming with excitement. She felt a lurch of love for her parents, who had been so caring over the past few weeks.

'Come on, then,' said Ralph, picking up her case. 'The car's waiting.'

As they drove up the drive to Peasebrook, Alice could see all the staff gathered outside the front door waiting for her return – not just the ones who worked there on a Sunday, but the girls from the office as well.

'Oh God,' she said. 'Everyone's here.'

'Of course, darling,' said Sarah. 'They've all missed you.'

She got out of the car and made her way up the steps to the front door. Everyone was clapping and cheering. She felt a mixture of delight and embarrassment – surely she didn't deserve this attention?

In the hall, Ralph opened champagne and everyone was given a glass.

'To a speedy recovery,' said her father, and everyone echoed his wishes.

Alice went and stood three steps up on the staircase, so everyone could see her.

'I just want to thank everyone for holding the fort while I've been away,' she said. 'I know all of you have gone the extra mile to keep things together. And I expect you've enjoyed not having me breathing down your necks!'

Everyone laughed. Alice wasn't a neck-breather at all.

'But now I'm back I want to make sure that this Christmas is the best one ever. So if you've got any ideas about how to make it even better, please come and see me. If you've got any problems, please come and see me. Peasebrook is what it is because we all work together. So I just want to say thank you for being the best team ever.'

She raised her glass with a smile and everyone joined in the toast.

As she sipped at the bubbles, Alice looked around the hall and thought how lucky she was. It was only then that she realised there was one person missing. Dillon. Where was Dillon? Suddenly she wanted to see him more than anyone. The front door opened and she looked eagerly to see if it was him.

It wasn't. It was Hugh.

'Darling.' He pulled her into an embrace. 'Welcome home.'

'Thank you,' said Alice. And it was at that moment she realised she hadn't even noticed Hugh had been missing from the proceedings.

Emilia started awake a while later. She had no idea how long she had been asleep, or why she had a horrible feeling of unease; a sensation that there was something wrong. She tried to gather her thoughts in the muzziness of her head.

And then she remembered. She'd been running a bath. She shut her eyes, praying that she had turned off the taps before she fell asleep. Maybe she had forgotten she'd done it? She couldn't remember doing so. She got up off the sofa and walked with dread towards the bathroom, where she was greeted with the sight of the bath overflowing, oceans of water surging over the side and onto the wooden floorboards.

She flew across the bathroom and turned off the taps, then grabbed her keys from her coat pocket and ran down the stairs, opening the door that led into the shop as quickly as she could. An unexpected burst of common sense told her not to turn the lights on, but the glow from the lamplight outside told her all she needed to know.

Water was pouring through the light fitting above the mezzanine in a merry torrent, all over the books below. And as she watched in horror, the ceiling collapsed slowly, leaving a gaping, jagged hole.

She couldn't do it. She couldn't deal with this on top of everything else. She almost felt grateful it had happened, for at least she didn't have to try any more. She could give in, and no one would think any the worse of her.

She went behind the counter and fished out the card Ian Mendip had given her and looked for his address. She picked up her car keys and went out to the car, not looking back. If she stopped to think, or spoke to anyone else, things would become muddled. At this moment in time, she had absolute clarity.

She drove to Mendip's house, two miles outside the town down narrow lanes. She swished in through an impressive set of gates and up the drive to his swanky new-build, lights automatically illuminating her way.

She banged on the door. Ian Mendip answered, frowning, not recognising her in her bedraggled, distraught state.

'Emilia Nightingale,' she told him. 'Can we talk?'

'Emilia. Of course. Come in.'

He stood aside to let her in. She stepped into a cavernous hallway, hung with an over-the-top chandelier, a sweeping staircase rising up, carpeted in dark purple tartan. Normally she would have enjoyed inspecting his lack of taste, but today she was on business.

'I've just come to say I've decided to sell up,' she said. 'The shop is yours if you still want it.'

A smile spread across his face.

'Well, that *is* good news.'

'I want to exchange contracts as soon as possible.' She wanted to be out of Peasebrook by Christmas, only a few weeks away. She wanted to be on the other side of the world.

'I'll get my people onto it.' He stood to one side and

gestured she should come into the kitchen. 'Do you want to come and have a drink on it? I always keep some Bollinger in the fridge for occasions like this.'

'No, thank you,' she said, recoiling at the thought.

'Well, at least shake hands on it.'

He was the traditional type. A deal wasn't a deal unless you'd shaken hands.

Emilia hesitated for a moment. She didn't really want to touch him. It felt as if she was doing a deal with the devil. But she had to look after her own interests, and get the best price, so she braced herself and shook his hand.

She tried not to wonder if she was betraying Julius's memory: what would he do if he knew she was selling to Mendip? She told herself she had done her best, and it was not to be. There was no point in her trying to carry on with Nightingale Books as some sort of infinite tribute. He had loved the shop, but it was time for her to move on. And it was silly not to get the best price possible.

'Let me have your solicitor's details,' she said, 'and I'll get mine to draw up the contracts.'

He saw her out and she went and sat in her car. She wanted to feel victorious, as if she'd achieved something by letting go of the past. Instead, she just felt incredibly sad.

And alone. She rammed the key in the ignition, not sure where to go.

She had no job, no commitments, no ties to anyone or anything, and she'd just done a deal that would see her pretty well off. She slammed the car into reverse.

Cuba, she thought. She'd book a month's holiday in Cuba and go and find herself. Drown herself in rum daiquiris and dance till dawn, feel the sun on her face and the music in her soul. Havana would be crazy and dirty and noisy: about as far away from Peasebrook as you could get. And she would be about as far away from herself as she could get. In fact, she could leave Emilia Nightingale at home and come back as someone else. She imagined a girl with a tan and a red ruffled dress and a flower in her hair. *That's* who she was going to be for now.

Jackson's phone rang. It was Mendip. His heart sank.

He was going to badger him about Nightingale Books. He steeled himself. He was going to tell him where to get off. He didn't want any part in the duplicity any longer. If that meant he lost his job, so be it.

He answered, cautious. 'Hello?'

'Well done, my son.'

'What?'

'You could make a good living with your powers of persuasion. It's a skill.' Mendip laughed a horrible laugh.

'What are you on about?' Jackson asked.

'Miss Nightingale is selling me the shop. Contracts are being drawn up as we speak. Soon as we've all signed on the dotted line, you're in charge at the glove factory. We should be in there by the New Year. Good work, Jackson!'

He hung up.

'What was that all about?' asked Cilla.

'Nothing,' said Jackson. 'Just Mendip's usual bollocks.'

He felt sick. He should feel happy, that Emilia had decided to sell up without him putting any pressure on her. After all, he was going to have a plum job as a result. Head gaffer at the glove factory – that was something to get excited about. But Jackson didn't feel excited at all.

The last thing he wanted Emilia to do was sell the shop.

21

Alice was sitting in the polytunnel, wrapped up in her duckdown ski jacket and her Uggs, wearing a pair of fingerless mittens. The two girls who helped her with wedding flowers were sitting with her.

They had a long piece of rope lined up on trestle tables in front of them, and were attaching bunches of green foliage to the rope with pieces of wire. Once the rope was covered, it would be hung up on scaffolding so they could start adding individual flowers, stripping the leaves by hand from each stem so they could be easily inserted. Blooms of yellow, pink, blue and purple were mixed in with the foliage until the garland was complete, ready to be hung up in the chapel. It was a labour of love, but the Christmas garland had become a Peasebrook tradition.

Alice looked at all the dried flowers waiting in boxes. Dillon had cut every single one of them, choosing only the very best, and had put them away carefully to dry. She still hadn't seen him properly since she got back. She had glimpsed him in the grounds, but every time she got to her feet and went to call him, he had disappeared.

He was avoiding her, she thought. She wasn't sure why. Had she done something to hurt him? She needed to find out. She was going to go and find him. She stood up.

'Can you two carry on with this?' she said to the girls. 'I'll be back later.'

Dillon had purposely stayed out of the way when Alice had come home from hospital. It was like something from *Downton Abbey* – all the staff lined up to greet her when Sarah and Ralph drove her back in the Range Rover. He'd watched from a distance as everyone hugged her. Everyone loved Alice. There'd been champagne in the hall and Hugh had been there, of course, watching her fondly. Alice looked so happy, even though she still used a stick when she got tired.

He'd stay out of the way, if he could. At least until after the wedding. If he had the nerve, he'd find another job, but his loyalty to Sarah was greater than his awkwardness at the situation. Just. And a stubborn part of him wanted to prove to Hugh that he wasn't intimidated by him.

So it took him by surprise when Alice cornered him by the entrance gate where he was clipping the box hedges into perfection before they were decorated for the wedding.

'Hey,' he said with a smile.

'I've found you at last,' she said. 'Have you been avoiding me?'

'I've been busy. There's a lot to do.'

'So much you couldn't even have a cup of coffee?'

He couldn't look her in the eye.

'Never mind,' she went on. 'I want to go and choose the tree for the hall. I want you to come with me. Make sure I've picked the best one before everyone else gets there.'

There was a small field on the edge of the estate where

they grew Christmas trees to sell. People came in early December and picked the one they wanted. It was marked with a label indicating the date they wanted to pick it up, then Dillon would dig it up fresh on the day. The trees made enough money to pay for the estate's decorations and a staff lunch.

'Are you sure you'll make it?' Dillon looked concerned but Alice waved her stick at him.

'I'll be fine.'

He took her arm and they walked across the soft ground around the edge of the estate.

'Why didn't you come back and see me in hospital?' she demanded. 'You promised you would.'

He hesitated. 'It wasn't appropriate.'

She frowned. 'Appropriate? I don't understand.'

No, he thought. You don't. And that's why I love you.

'I don't think Hugh would have liked it,' he said eventually.

'That's ridiculous.' Alice frowned. She stopped. 'Dillon. I need you to be honest with me. You don't like Hugh, do you?'

Dillon felt cornered. This was his chance to tell her what he really thought.

'It's more that he doesn't like me . . .' he said finally.

'But why? Why would anyone not like you?'

'Because . . . because he thinks I know the truth about him?'

'What truth?'

Dillon hesitated. He had to be very careful. Whatever he said now could very easily backfire on him. But he owed it to Alice to tell her his suspicions. He couldn't just say he thought Hugh was an arrogant cock, but he could warn her about what he'd heard. That might be enough to give her second thoughts.

'It's probably just rumours. But the word is he's a bit of a coke-head.'

'Hugh?' Alice laughed. 'He can't be. I'd know, surely?'

Dillon shrugged. 'I'm just telling you what I've heard.'

Alice thought for a moment. Then she looked at him with a bright smile. 'Pub gossip, probably. People say things. What they don't know, they make up. And Hugh wasn't brought up round here, so they've just tried to fill in the gaps. It's because he works in the City and he's got a flash car. It's just ... stereotyping.'

She trailed off. Dillon could see she was desperate for reassurance. He didn't have enough evidence to contradict her.

'Probably.'

'It's important to me that you two get on. You're very dear to me, Dillon. And I know you're being protective, but Hugh's all right, really. He's just very different from you. But he'll be a good husband. He loves Peasebrook and he's going to help us take it forward. And you're going to be part of that too.'

Dillon didn't reply. He understood. It was all about money and power. Hugh had cash and influence and contacts. Of course he was going to take Peasebrook forward. He couldn't wait to be lord of the bloody manor. That was how it worked. He couldn't force Alice to see the truth, because it *was* her truth. He had no power to change that.

'I just wanted you to be aware what people are saying. And you're right. It's because I want to protect you.'

Alice hugged him. 'Thank you,' she said.

314

Then she pushed her hair back and showed him her scar.

'Look,' she said. 'It's got much better. You can hardly see it now.'

I never did see it, thought Dillon.

'And I've got some special make-up. It shouldn't show at all. For the wedding...'

She looked at him. He really wasn't sure what he was supposed to say.

She stopped to lean on the gate he had put up to stop members of the public going up to the folly. It was just starting to rain: a spiteful squall that reminded people not to be seduced by bursts of fine weather and bone-warming sunshine that could easily be whisked away in a trice.

She looked white, an awful grey-green white.

'Bloody hell,' she said. 'My stupid leg. I thought I could do it, but I can't. I haven't got the strength.'

He looked at her. He could carry her back to the house, he thought, give her a piggyback or hold her in his arms, but it was half a mile from here and the ground would be slippery.

'Tell you what,' he said. 'I'll go and get the quad bike.'

'That would be brilliant. You're a star. I'm sorry to be a nuisance.' She shivered. 'I'll wait here.'

'No,' he said. 'Let me carry you to the folly. You'll catch your death if you wait here. You'll get soaked through. Here.'

He held out his arms to pick her up, sliding one arm under her shoulders and the other under her knees. He lifted her easily.

'I must weigh a ton. All that chocolate you fed me.'

'Don't be silly.'

He pushed open the gate and strode along the path to the folly, pushing through the undergrowth. When he got to the folly, Alice gasped.

'My goodness! Look at it!'

Dillon managed a smile. It had been his secret project. He hadn't told anyone what he was doing. It was taking him a while, because he just did half an hour here and there when he had a moment. But gradually he was restoring it to its former glory. He'd cut away all the overgrown ivy and brambles, revealing the golden stone underneath. He'd pointed up the brickwork, sanded down the windows and the door and repainted them the same teal blue the estate used on all its wood. Inside he'd sanded the floorboards too.

'It's a surprise,' he said. 'For your mother.'

'Oh Dillon,' said Alice. 'What a wonderful thing to do.'

He put her down on the old sofa. He'd been going to take it away, because it was old and damp and musty. He took his scarf off to wrap around her neck and keep her warm. She protested, but he insisted.

'I don't want you getting a chill. Just wait here. I won't be a tick.'

Alice lay back on the sofa. She felt terrible. She'd been trying so hard not to let her leg get the better of her, but her bones were aching; her painkillers were wearing off, and she was freezing. Darling Dillon, she thought. He was so lovely. She couldn't believe what he'd done to the folly. Her mum was going to be so touched.

She tried to get comfy on the sofa. She thought about what Dillon had told her and felt a squiggle of panic. She knew some of Hugh's friends were a bit on the wild side, and probably indulged in a bit of party powder – she wasn't totally naïve. But Hugh had never hinted that he took part and she'd never seen any evidence. Not that she'd know what to look for, she thought. She was a bit green, she knew that.

But why was Hugh marrying her if that was his scene? He'd go for someone more flashy and glamorous, surely? He had plenty of friends who were, after all, but he'd chosen her. He loved her. She knew he did.

She shut her eyes and her mind wandered. Dear old Dillon: he was so anxious to look out for her. She remembered that moment in the hospital, when she'd thought Dillon was going to kiss her. She couldn't pretend she hadn't wanted him to, but it would have made things a bit tricky. She'd always had a bit of a thing for Dillon, but he'd never shown any interest until that afternoon. Though now she realised he hadn't been interested at all, really. The painkillers must have made her imagination run away. Luckily Hugh had turned up just in time. She felt herself blush at the thought of what might have happened. What was she like? Having fantasies about lovely, kind Dill. He was obviously totally embarrassed about it all. It was why he'd been avoiding her. She was an absolute nit.

She laughed at herself, then put her hands behind her to try and shift around a bit. She felt the corner of a book that had fallen down behind the sofa cushion.

She tugged it and pulled it out. *Anna Karenina*. A big fat Penguin classic. She flipped it open. The pages were damp and yellowing.

There was an inscription on the flyleaf. Written in fountain pen.

You are braver and more beautiful than Anna, and I hope I am a better man than Vronsky.

That was it. No indication who it was from or to. No date. Alice turned the page and began to read.

All happy families are alike. Each unhappy family is unhappy in its own way.

Well, thought Alice. At least my family is a happy one. She didn't know where she'd be without them. And she began to read.

Dillon was reversing the quad bike out of the yard when Sarah came up to him, her Barbour coat flapping behind her. This was just what he didn't want. But he couldn't ignore her. She looked worried.

'Have you seen Alice? She was helping with the garland and then went off somewhere but she hasn't come back. She's been ages and it's raining.'

'I found her up along.' Dillon was deliberately vague. 'I was just going to go and fetch her on the quad.'

'Is she all right?'

'Just a bit wet. And tired, I think.'

'Have you left her in the rain?'

Dillon paused for a moment. 'She's in the folly. She's in the dry.'

Sarah eyed the quad bike. 'I'll come with you.'

He could hardly protest. But he'd wanted to save the surprise, until the job was properly finished. She wasn't going to see it at its best – there was still a bit to do. But he couldn't keep it a secret forever.

'Hop on, then.'

He drove as quickly as he could across the lawns and cut up through the top of the woods along to the folly. He was the only person who'd been up here for the past few weeks. He drew up and killed the engine.

Sarah climbed off and stared in astonishment. 'Did you do this?' she asked, and for a moment Dillon thought she was angry. That he had overstepped the mark with his gesture.

'I didn't want it falling down. It was in a bit of a state. So I thought I'd do some repairs.'

She stared, and there were tears in her eyes. The folly looked loved and cared for again. It had gone to seed, like a middle-aged woman who had stopped bothering. Now it stood proud and gleaming, its paintwork immaculate, intriguing and inviting.

'It looks wonderful,' she said softly. 'Thank you.'

'Let's go and see if Alice is OK,' he said, gruff with embarrassment.

Sarah took in a deep breath and pushed open the door. She hadn't been inside since Julius died. Again, Dillon had worked his magic. The walls were painted, the floor sanded, the woodwork repaired.

On the sofa, Alice was engrossed in *Anna Karenina*.

'Darling!' Sarah rushed over and started to fuss over her. 'Your hands are like ice. You silly girl – what were you thinking? Come on, let's get you back to the house.'

Alice held up the book. 'Look what I found down the back of the sofa.'

For a moment, Sarah stood stock-still, as if she'd been turned to stone. Then she took the book from Alice. 'Oh yes. I bought it in a charity shop. I was halfway through. I wondered where it had gone.'

'Here you go,' said Dillon, scooping up Alice again. 'There won't be room for all of us on the quad, I'm afraid.'

'That's OK,' said Sarah. 'I'll walk back. Take her to the kitchen and make her a hot chocolate. I'll be just behind you.'

Dillon strode out of the door with Alice in his arms as if she weighed no more than a bag of flour.

Sarah stood in the middle of the folly. The musty familiar smell of it took her back. She looked at the sofa, grey with dust, and remembered all the times the two of them had sat there, wrapped up in each other, while the rain, and, on occasion, the snow, fell outside. It had been so cosy. Their little hideaway.

If she turned, she might see him pushing his way through the undergrowth, his face breaking into a smile as he saw her.

She clasped the book to her chest. She'd never see him again. Would it get any easier, she wondered? The gaping hole in her heart where Julius had been?

She looked around the folly, touched to the core by Dillon's kindness and thoughtfulness. He must have spent hours. She'd have a wood-burner put in, she decided, and get some decent furniture. She could come here and read whenever life got too much. It could be her little hideaway once again.

It made her realise something else. Whatever Hugh had said about Dillon, whatever claims he had made, they couldn't be true. He cared for Alice, she could see that. He was loyal and trustworthy and stalwart. How could she have doubted him, even for a moment?

That evening Alice plucked up the courage to confront Hugh. She had to say something. It was eating away at her, what Dillon had told her. They were sitting in the little drawing room before dinner. Hugh had lit the fire and was pouring himself a gin and tonic. Alice just had the tonic – she still couldn't face spirits.

'I need to ask you something.'

'Of course,' said Hugh, popping a couple of ice cubes into his glass.

'Do you ever... do coke?' Alice asked, feeling awkward even just using the word. It sounded so stupid when she said it. 'Cocaine, I mean.'

Hugh looked at her in astonishment. 'What on earth's made you ask that?'

'I just... heard something. A rumour. And it's been worrying me.'

'A rumour? Where? From who?'

'Oh, just... just in the pub. Someone said you did.'

Hugh was silent for a moment. He looked down into his gin and tonic. When he looked up his face was grave.

'Do you want the truth?'

'Of course,' said Alice, feeling her stomach flip with fear.

Hugh sighed. 'I used to. I was in with a bad crowd and, for a couple of years, I dabbled a bit. It was what people did.'

'Oh.'

'But we all do stupid things when we're young. It's all behind me now. I wouldn't touch it with a bargepole these days.' He smiled. 'I'm glad it's out in the open. I don't want there to be any secrets between us. But it's not the sort of thing you can just bring up out of the blue, so I'm glad you asked me.'

Alice nodded. 'Thank you so much for being honest with me. I was worried to death!'

Hugh chuckled. 'You thought I was going to snort Peasebrook up my nose?'

'No. I just wanted to know the truth.'

'Well, now you know my murky past. But I'm a reformed character. So you can tell the rumour-mongers to put a sock in it.' He grinned. 'How about you? Have you got any confessions? Any dark secrets you think I should know before it's too late?'

Alice found herself going red. She told herself it was the heat from the fire.

'To be honest, I don't think I have, no.'

'Are you sure?' teased Hugh. 'You look a bit guilty to me. No cheating at Pony Club camp?'

'Certainly not,' said Alice stoutly. 'I got every single one of my trophies fair and square.'

'Well, I'm glad to hear it,' said Hugh.

Alice took a gulp of her tonic.

She wasn't going to tell him about wanting to kiss Dillon. She didn't think that would go down very well at all.

22

On Monday morning, Emilia phoned the staff and told them each about the flood but asked them not to come in. She made up an elaborate excuse about a difficult meeting with the insurers, otherwise she knew they would all be there helping to clear up and she couldn't face them yet. She knew she was betraying them by selling, and although she knew she didn't need to keep the shop open just because of them, it still sat uneasily with her.

She stood in the middle of the shop and looked at the damage. It was a sorry mess. Sorting out the books that hadn't been damaged was going to be a job in itself and she wasn't sure what to do with the remaining ones. Have a big sale? Donate them to a library? Let the townspeople come in and help themselves to whatever they wanted?

She'd been stupid to try and keep Julius's dream alive. It wasn't her dream. Or her world. Nightingale Books was hers in name only. Trying to keep it open had been more trouble than it was worth. She'd been keeping it open from a sense of duty. Out of sentimentality. She had to let go.

She'd have to find the courage to tell Sarah Basildon what she was doing as well. She knew Sarah would be upset, not least because that would mean there was no chance of the literary festival she had dreamt of going ahead. Was she being selfish? No, she told herself. She couldn't keep the shop just because she didn't want to upset Sarah. If Sarah wanted to set up a festival in the future, she could find someone else to run it for her. There'd be loads of people in Peasebrook ready to help.

She felt popped, as if someone had taken a pin to her. Deflated. As if her spirit had evaporated. She wasn't sure she deserved to feel like that, but she supposed it was partly grief, partly stress and partly not being sure what to do with her life.

She wanted a new chapter. She smiled at the metaphor. If only you could just rewrite things, she thought. Where would she go back to, if she were going to rewrite her life?

There was somebody in the doorway. She hoped it wasn't one of the staff. She didn't have the heart for a conversation about the shop's future.

It was Jackson.

'Bloody hell,' he said, surveying the chaos.

'I left the taps running.' Emilia made a face. 'The bath overflowed.'

'I can get you some dehumidifiers. That'll help dry it out.' He looked up. 'And I can patch up the ceiling for you if you want. Temporarily.'

'Thanks, but there's not much point. I'm just trying to rescue as many books as I can. The next person can worry about the damage.' She looked at him. 'I'm selling the shop.'

Jackson didn't tell her he already knew.

'You can't sell up. You know that, don't you?'

'I haven't got any choice.'

324

'But it's wonderful. The shop's wonderful. What you do changes people's lives. For the better.'

'Oh, don't romanticise.'

'Seriously. You changed my life, with those books you gave me. You made me see things as they should be. You've made me see what *I* should be. It's too late for me and Mia, but... well, I understand where I went wrong now. I'm not going to make the same mistakes next time. And that's down to you.'

'Well, that's great. That's wonderful.' Emilia tried to smile.

'But if you close the shop, you'll never be able to do that for anyone again.'

'Of course I will. In some other way.'

'I think you'll regret it.' Jackson's eyes were burning with intensity. 'When I came into this shop you seemed so happy with what you were doing. You couldn't wait to find me something to read. You were made up when I came back and I'd liked it. What other job would give you that?'

'I don't know yet!' Emilia shrugged.

'Don't sell it,' said Jackson. 'It's part of who you are.'

'Oh God,' said Emilia. 'Jackson, it's really sweet of you, but the shop's in debt. I can't afford to give it the refurb it needs. There's... there's about a million reasons why it's not a good idea. Anyway, I've shaken hands on the deal. I can't go back on it.'

'You can,' said Jackson. 'I've got a confession.'

'What?'

'I didn't really come in here to buy books. I was under cover.'

Emilia frowned. What was he on about?

'You're not from the Inland Revenue?'

'No.' He took a deep breath. 'I work for Ian Mendip. I was supposed to try and persuade you to sell the shop to him.'

Emilia tried to take in what he was saying.

'Bastard!'

'Who – me, or him?'

'I don't know. Both of you.' She looked furious. 'So you didn't want to read to Finn at all? That wanting to be a good father line was just a bluff—'

'No! It was to start with, I suppose—'

'Get out,' said Emilia, pointing to the door.

Jackson stood his ground.

'Look, I don't feel good about it. Once I'd met you, I couldn't go through with it. I didn't realise you were going to give in.'

Emilia shrugged. 'Well, it's too late. I can't afford to stay open. Not now. Look at it. It's completely ruined. It's going to cost a fortune to fix the damage.'

They both looked at the mess.

'I've got a suggestion.'

Emilia rolled her eyes. He wasn't getting the hint.

'Thank you for your interest, Jackson, but can you please just leave me alone? I'm not in any mood to listen.'

'Just give me one minute, will you?'

The two of them stared each other out. Emilia sighed. 'One minute.'

'I've looked at the plans for the glove factory,' Jackson told her. 'I've looked at the car park and measured it out. I've done the maths. If you knock down that flat-roofed extension at the back, where the office is, and sell Mendip a third of the car park, it gives him the parking space he needs for four more units, which will make him an extra two hundred grand.'

'Two hundred grand?' Emilia's eyebrows went up.

Jackson nodded. 'So he could afford to give you half that.'

Emilia took what he'd said in. 'A hundred grand? For a bit of car park?'

'I know you'll lose the extension the office is in, but I don't think that's a problem, because you could put the office down in the cellars. They'd probably need a bit of work, but as long as they're solid and dry...'

'You've really thought this through, haven't you?'

'Yes. Because I don't want the book shop to go. And I don't want you to miss the opportunity to make a few quid out of Mendip either, if it's there to be had. He's a greedy bugger.'

'Are you sure he'll agree to it? He'll be furious if I don't sell, surely? He's not going to want me to make money out of him.'

Jackson grinned. 'If he doesn't have that bit of car park, he'll end up losing money. He'll give in eventually. I know him. He's more interested in profit than pride.'

'He's not going to be very happy with you, is he?'

'Well, that doesn't matter, because I'm not going to work for him any more. I'm giving in my notice. I'm setting up on my own.' He grinned. 'In fact, you can be my first client, if you like.'

'Ah. So there is something in it for you!'

'I was kidding. Sort of...'

Emilia folded her arms. She looked around the shop. It was a disaster. It smelt terrible and she'd had to pull up most of the carpet. She couldn't imagine order restored.

'You're going to have to empty the place anyway, to repair the damage. So while you're at it, you can get it replastered. Do a bit of rewiring. Put in some smart lighting...'

Emilia looked at him evenly. 'Why should I trust you? You've already admitted trying to stitch me up.'

Jackson put up his hands. 'Fair enough.'

There was silence for a moment.

'How long would it take?' asked Emilia.

'Don't you want a quote first? And it depends what you want. What sort of finish.'

Emilia walked over to the counter and found Bea's plans. She handed them to Jackson.

'That's what I want.'

Jackson started leafing through it. 'This is really cool. But you could do it, no problem. Three weeks would do it, I reckon.'

'Give me a price. Let's make it happen.'

'Seriously?'

Emilia pulled out her phone.

'Do you want to listen while I tell Mendip...?'

Mendip was livid, but as Jackson predicted, he capitulated eventually. Knowing the extent of his skulduggery, Emilia played hardball with him. She secured a hefty cash deposit from him for the deal, which would allow her to finance the repairs.

Andrea was open-mouthed with admiration. Even though Mendip was her client, she was jubilant.

'Don't feel too bad about pressuring him,' she told Emilia. 'He'll do well out of the glove factory. Everybody wins this way.'

Mendip was surprisingly calm when he heard that Jackson was leaving him. Though he didn't know that it was Jackson who'd given Emilia the inside info.

'I knew I'd lose you one day,' he told him. 'You just had to find the balls.'

'I'm doing a quote for the book shop refurb,' Jackson told him, hoping he wouldn't put two and two together.

Mendip nodded and held out his hand. 'You're a good lad,' he said. 'You'll be all right. I'm sorry to lose you.' He cleared his throat. 'I wouldn't mind using you. For a bit of sub-contracting.'

Jackson walked Wolfie home that night filled with glee. Things had worked out even better than he expected. He had his first job, and a promise of more work. And it was all on his terms.

'Would you babysit for Finn tomorrow night?' he asked his mum. 'I want to take Mia out for a meal.'

'Of course, love,' said Cilla, sensing a sea change in her son. Sometimes she had worried he would go under and lose his way completely, but he was getting it together.

The next day Jackson told Mia he had something to talk to her about.

'I need to tell you over dinner. I've booked a table at the Peasebrook Arms.'

She was reluctant, but she finally agreed.

'What's this all about then?' she asked him, brittle with wariness.

'I'm setting up on my own. I've left Mendip. Finally. It's going to be tough, but I think in the long term I'm going to be better off.'

'Oh. Is that it?'

'It's a pretty big deal. For me.' Jackson was disappointed she wasn't more impressed.

She sighed. Jackson frowned. He thought she had tears in her eyes.

'It's not something to cry about. Don't worry. I'll still give you your money.'

This wasn't going quite how he expected. He'd wanted to ask her to start again. But obviously all she was worried about was where the money was going to come from. She wasn't interested . . .

She *was* crying.

'What? What is it, Mia?'

'It's OK. I just thought . . . you were going to tell me you were seeing someone else.'

'No!' Jackson frowned. 'Not for a minute.'

'Good.' Mia nodded. 'Because I don't think I could handle that.'

'Me seeing someone else? Why would you even care?'

Mia looked down at the tablecloth.

'I . . . I miss you.'

'Miss me?'

She nodded. A big tear rolled down her cheek.

'I'm sorry for throwing you out. It was wrong.'

'What?' One glass of wine on an empty stomach – did she know what she was saying?

'I was too hard on you, Jackson. But I was scared. Being a mum . . . being a mum really freaked me out. I know I was difficult. Impossible. Neurotic.'

'You weren't that bad!'

Why was he fibbing? She'd made him feel like the worst husband and father on earth.

He was fibbing because getting Mia back was more

important than proving a point. He was fibbing because life was too short and he *had* been irresponsible and let her down, occasionally. But he'd learnt, and he loved his son with a passion, and more than anything, he realised he wanted Finn to have a family. The family he already had.

'I thought you hated me,' said Mia.

'What?' Jackson was horrified. 'No!'

'I thought you couldn't wait to get away from me.'

He looked at her. 'I thought *you* hated *me.*'

Mia shook her head. 'I hated *myself.*'

'Me too.' He remembered the feelings of self-loathing, after one too many beers.

The two of them looked at each other.

'Come back,' said Mia.

Shit, thought Jackson. He was going to start blubbing now.

They walked back home, hand in hand.

Mia unlocked the door and led him inside. Inside his home – *their* home.

'Come here,' said Jackson, and she walked into his embrace.

Jackson stared over her head as he held her. He saw the big black-and-white photos they'd had taken of Finn when he was tiny. The coat rack, with the white coat he'd bought her the Christmas before he left. He heard Finn bound down the stairs and saw him leap off the bottom step, then come to a standstill as he saw his mum and dad in an embrace.

'Mum?' He stepped forwards, protective, and Jackson felt pride. He held out an arm.

'Come here, you,' he said, and for a few moments the three of them stood together in a group hug.

Cilla appeared in the doorway of the lounge. She felt a surge of pride for her son. He was a wayward boy, but he'd found his mettle.

'You'd better drop me home,' she said with a smile. 'And pick up your toothbrush.'

A week later, Thomasina made preparations for that evening's dinner: a young couple that had not long had a baby wanted to celebrate a birthday.

She was in Peasebrook for half past eight, collecting her meat from the butcher, selecting the best vegetables from the farmers' market, and finishing off at the cheese-monger, where she bought a trio of French cheese: one soft, one hard and one blue. She was disappointed not to be served by Jem but by one of the other assistants, though he gave her a cheery wave and a thumbs up from the far end of the counter. He was too busy serving to speak. Thomasina left before he became free.

She got back to her cottage where Lauren was ready and waiting: she'd prepped the kitchen and it was gleaming, all the utensils ready and waiting. They divided the work up between them. Lauren made the celeriac soup with a gloriously rich chicken stock she'd made earlier in the week, and she strained it and sieved it until it was silky smooth, then set it aside and fried some crispy strips of pancetta ready to put on top.

The main course was a loin of venison, coated in mushroom duxelles and wrapped in puff pastry. With it went little copper pots of potato gratin, sliced paper thin on a mandolin, and a smooth cauliflower purée.

Dessert was a delicate pear mousse, light and fluffy, with a warm rich chocolate sauce in the middle.

By half past four, everything that could be prepared in advance had been, the kitchen was cleaned, and Thomasina put the finishing touches to the dining room.

At quarter to five, the phone rang. It was the husband who had booked the table. Their baby was coming down with a cold. They couldn't leave it with a babysitter. They would pay, of course, but they wouldn't be coming.

Thomasina put the phone down. She looked at the table for two and then went into the kitchen, where her perfectly wrapped loin of venison was chilling. And she knew this moment was a test. She knew that if she didn't do what she thought she might, that she would stay on her own forever, that she would spend the rest of her life cooking for other people's birthdays and anniversaries. That she would watch them gaze into each other's eyes. That she would never look at anyone else across her own table.

She *deserved* to look into someone else's eyes. She knew she did.

'What are you going to do?' said Lauren. 'It's a terrible waste.'

'Wait there,' said Thomasina.

She walked into the kitchen and poured a glass of wine from the bottle she used for cooking. She drained it in one gulp. Then she dialled the cheese shop. It might be closed. She didn't know what time it shut. It was ten past five. It could easily shut at five. The phone rang and rang. She was about to hang up when it was answered.

'Peasebrook Cheese.'

'May I speak to Jem?'

'I think he might have gone, love. We shut at five.'

'Oh.' She couldn't ask for his mobile number. She just couldn't. 'Never mind.'

Disappointment, she discovered, was cold and lumpy and stuck in your chest. Like leftover tapioca.

'No – hold on. He's just coming out of the storeroom. Jem – phone call for you.'

She heard the phone being put down, and voices and footsteps. She could hang up and Jem would never know. She would spare herself the humiliation. She imagined that would be as hot and burny as the disappointment had been cold.

'Hello?' Jem's cheery voice came down the line, and she felt his warmth. It gave her courage. She wanted to feel that warmth again, in person. She craved it.

'It's Thomasina,' she said. 'From the book shop. From A Deux.'

'Oh!' Jem sounded delighted. 'Hello.'

Thomasina summoned up the last of her courage. 'The thing is, I've had a cancellation. Ten minutes ago. For tonight's dinner. Which is all prepped and ready for the oven. I can't freeze any of it, really. So I wondered . . .'

'You want to return the cheese?'

'No! Of course not. No . . .'

'Ah. You want me to come and help you eat it?' asked Jem.

'Yes.'

'Oh.' There was a pause. 'I was only joking.'

'There's celeriac soup and loin of venison and pear mousse.'

'I don't need persuading,' he said. 'What time?'

Thomasina was almost struck dumb. He was coming for dinner. And he sounded pleased about the idea. What on earth had she done?

'Half seven?' she managed. 'For eight o'clock.'

'I'll be there! I'll bring some wine. See you later.'

He rang off and Thomasina stared at the wall with the phone still in her hand.

Lauren was in the doorway, grinning at her.

'What are you going to wear?'

'I'm not going to dress up.'

Lauren pointed at her. 'Oh yes you are. You wait there.'

She came running back in twenty minutes later with a bulging make-up bag, a magnifying mirror, a hot brush and a bag full of jewellery.

'Come on,' she said. 'Upstairs.'

Thomasina followed her into her bedroom obediently.

'Right,' she said, sitting Thomasina down in front of the mirror and handing her a towelling headband. 'Put that on.'

Thomasina protested. 'I don't want too much make-up on!'

Lauren ignored her. She squeezed a blob of foundation onto the back of her left hand, then started dabbing it onto Thomasina's face until she was satisfied she had a perfect base.

'There,' she said. 'Not an imperfection to be seen. Not that you have many – you've got lovely skin.'

Thomasina thought she looked as if she had a mask on, but she didn't say anything. She sat in silence as Lauren pulled out endless palettes of colour and various brushes. She applied a thick black line of eyeliner to her eyelids, then coloured in the sockets with a sparkling charcoal grey. She coloured in her eyebrows, taking them up into a graceful arch, then applied a row of individual false eyelashes. She highlighted her cheeks with pale coral. Her mouth was outlined in pale pink then coloured in nude, with a little shimmer on the bow and the plumpest part of her lower lips.

Then she took the hot brush and worked her way through Thomasina's hair until it was straight and glossy, then backcombed it and pinned it into a half-up, half-down tumble. She put two large silver hoops in her ears.

'What are you going to wear?'

Thomasina shrugged. 'Just my usual black trousers and T-shirt.'

Lauren shook her head. 'No, you're not.'

Lauren stood in front of Thomasina's wardrobe and flipped through everything, tutting and sighing. When she found something that was to her satisfaction, she put it over her arm.

'OK,' she said. 'I think we can improvise with this lot.'

She rolled up a stretchy black skirt until it was just above the knee, then put a red cardigan over it, leaving the first two buttons undone, tying it with a black patent belt – taken off an old dress – around Thomasina's waist. Then she cut the feet off a pair of black tights and made her put them on with a pair of flat black ballet pumps.

Then she let Thomasina stand in front of the mirror.

Thomasina clapped her hand over her mouth.

'You look amazing,' said Lauren.

'That's not me,' said Thomasina, and made to do the buttons of the cardigan up. Lauren slapped her hand away.

'Leave it,' she commanded. 'You look totally gorgeous. Like a French—'

'Tart?' suggested Thomasina, looking at herself from all angles.

'No! Film star.'

'I'm going to feel really uncomfy. I won't be able to cook in this.'

'You're not going to cook.'

'What?'

'*I'm* cooking tonight. I've watched you often enough.'

'I was going to send you home.'

'Uh-uh. You're going to be the guest. I'm going to do all the work. If I get stuck, you can tell me what to do, but I don't want you to lift a finger. I've seen you run around people so often, making sure everything is perfect and they are having a great time. It's your turn for once.'

'But I don't know how to behave like . . .' Thomasina pointed helplessly at her reflection. The stranger with the big eyes looked back at her.

'Just be yourself.'

'But I'm so boring.'

'No, you're not.' Lauren shook her head. 'You're amazing. You're inspiring. OK, so you're not a loudmouth show-off like me. But at least what you say is interesting.'

'Interesting?'

'Seriously – you are the only person who keeps me sane at that school. I love your lessons and I come away feeling like I want to do something with my life. If it weren't for you, I'd have legged it ages ago. You tell stories when you're cooking. You make people want to listen. And learn more.'

'Oh.'

'I'm not the only one who thinks so, either. You're loads of people's favourite teacher.'

'You're just saying that.' Thomasina didn't know how to cope with all the unfamiliar praise.

'Yes, I'm just saying that cos that's what I'm like.' Lauren rolled her eyes. 'Shut up. And go and have a glass of Prosecco. Just one, before he gets here.'

She pushed Thomasina out of the bedroom.

Downstairs, the little table was laid, the cutlery shining, the glassware gleaming.

Tiny bowls were stuffed with creamy roses and burnt orange gerberas.

Tonight, as Thomasina lit the candles and dimmed the lights, it was for her.

Tonight, as she found a Chopin prelude and put it on, it was for her.

Her and Jem.

Dinner à deux.

When Thomasina opened the door to Jem half an hour later, he beamed at her.

'You look fantastic.' He breathed in appreciatively. 'And dinner smells great. I've brought two bottles – one red and one white. And ...' He proffered a bunch of red roses rather sheepishly. 'Not from the garage. I promise.'

Thomasina took the flowers from him.

Lauren took the bottles. 'I'll put the white in the fridge and open the red and let it breathe, shall I?'

Thomasina tried not to giggle at Lauren's solicitousness.

'I'm really glad you could come,' she told Jem. 'It would have been such a waste otherwise.'

Lauren came over with a tray, on which were perched

two flutes of Prosecco, the golden bubbles shooting up inside the glasses.

'We're being waited on tonight,' Thomasina told Jem. 'It's good experience for Lauren. It means I can write her a reference.'

'Awesome,' he said, taking a glass and raising it.

Thomasina raised hers too. She felt confident. Excited. Happy.

'Here's to last-minute cancellations,' she said.

THOMASINA MATTHEWS

BOOKS ABOUT FOOD

Chocolat Joanne Harris
Heartburn Nora Ephron
Quentins Maeve Binchy
Julie and Julia Julie Powell
Kitchen Confidential Anthony Bourdain
French Country Cooking Elizabeth David
Toast Nigel Slater
Charlie and the Chocolate Factory Roald Dahl
How to Eat Nigella Lawson
The Art of Eating M. F. K. Fisher

24

It was amazing what could be done in a short space of time, with all hands on deck and a willing team. Two days after the flood, Nightingale Books was stripped bare, all the undamaged stock boxed up and stored safely in June's garage. Emilia and Bea drove around the countryside picking up materials – shelving and lighting and paint. Jackson hired three lads to help him out with the plastering and the carpentry, and hired the best electrician he knew. Everyone worked long into the night.

The morning of Alice Basildon's wedding, the door of the shop burst open. Emilia looked up in alarm. She was helping to sand down some of the old shelving.

It was Marlowe.

They hadn't spoken since she'd walked away from the quartet. She thought she might have heard from him, that he might have called to see how she was, but he hadn't.

'I need you,' said Marlowe. His hair was wild, as if he'd only just got out of bed. By now he should be suited and booted with his hair slicked back – the wedding was at twelve.

Emilia sighed. 'What for?'

'Delphine's buggered off back to Paris and I need you in the quartet.'

'What? Why?'

Marlowe looked a bit shifty.

'Why, Marlowe? What did you do?'

'Look, I haven't got time to argue. The wedding starts in just over an hour, and we need a quartet to play "Arrival of the Queen of Sheba" no matter what. And we're only a trio right now—'

'It'll sound fine.'

'*Emilia*. It's Alice Basildon's wedding. You know what a lovely girl she is. We can't let her down.'

'She won't notice a missing cello.'

'Sarah Basildon will.'

Emilia looked away. She wanted nothing more than to refuse, but she thought about Alice walking up the aisle, after everything that had happened to her, and she wanted it to be perfect for her. She hadn't seen Marlowe since she'd walked out of the last rehearsal.

'Even though I can't play for shit?'

'You *can* play for shit. When you try.' He looked at his watch. He looked distressed. 'Come on, Emilia. Fifty minutes. It's not fair on Alice . . .'

She downed tools, ran up to her room, threw open the wardrobe, grabbed a long black dress and her cello and ran down the stairs, through the shop and out into the street, where she jumped into the back seat of Marlowe's car. He drove off and she wriggled out of her grubby clothes.

She could see Marlowe laughing in the rear-view mirror.

'Don't laugh at me!' She shimmied into the dress with its tight bodice, praying the fabric wouldn't tear in protest. Then she looked down at her feet.

'I've forgotten my shoes!' she wailed.

'There's no time to go back.'

'I can't wear sneakers with it.'

'Go barefoot. Like Dusty Springfield.'

'Who?'

Marlowe rolled his eyes. 'Call yourself The Barefoot Cellist. It's a good gimmick.'

'It's freezing out there!'

They were at the gates of Peasebrook Manor, which were decorated with holly and ivy and red roses and white ribbons and tiny pinprick fairy lights.

'Oh,' sighed Emilia. 'It looks stunning. Look, Marlowe.'

'Yeah, yeah, yeah,' he said with a cursory glance, and roared up the drive. Wedding guests were being directed to a roped-off grassy area, but he drove on to the official car park near the chapel.

Marlowe tied his bow tie in the mirror. Emilia poked her head in between the two front seats.

'Why did Delphine bugger off like that? What a rotten thing to do, on the morning of the wedding. It's so selfish.'

'Well, yes. That's Delphine for you.' Marlowe looked tight-lipped. 'Though I can't say I'm sorry. Things had been rocky for a while.'

'You don't need someone in your life who's going to let you down like that.'

Their eyes met for a moment. Then Marlowe looked away.

'No...'

Emilia bit her lip. He was obviously more upset than he was letting on.

'Felicity and Petra have already set up,' Marlowe told her. 'I've told them you'd be coming.'

'How did you know I'd say yes?'

Marlowe grinned and shrugged.

Emilia grabbed her cello and hitched up her dress.

Ten minutes later she took her seat at the front of the church, facing the congregation. She spread her skirt out, hoping no one would notice her bare feet. Thank goodness she had painted her toenails the week before, so they weren't a total disgrace.

Marlowe, Emilia, Petra and Felicity tuned up.

A sense of calm descended on Emilia as they began to play for the congregation. She felt focused, the music in front of her making perfect sense, and her fingers did everything they were told. She smiled as she grew in confidence and felt a tiny thrill as Marlowe gave her a nod of approval. It was almost like flying with the music as the notes soared and fell.

And then, on the most imperceptible of signals from Marlowe, they struck up 'Arrival of the Queen of Sheba'.

The aisle in front of Alice looked endless.

She had been awake since before dawn, millions of tiny wings beating in her stomach. But they weren't day-before-your-birthday butterflies, or Christmas Eve butterflies. These butterflies felt as if their wings had been dipped in acid. They were making her stomach roil with anxiety and gave her a sense of impending doom.

As Sarah buttoned her into her dress, she felt breathless, and not because the dress was too tight.

A fitted cream silk crêpe bodice, with three-quarter-length sleeves, buttoned up the back. Then a tulle skirt, on which was embroidered a trail of ivy and roses. Everyone had joked that Alice would probably be wearing wellies under her frock, but she'd found some of the prettiest beaded satin slippers with rosebuds on the front. She had her stick waiting for her in the front row in case she needed it, but she was determined to walk down the aisle without it.

'Oh darling,' said Sarah. 'You look out of this world. Hugh is the luckiest man alive.'

Alice looked out of her bedroom window. The drive was filled with cars, bearing wedding guests in all their finery, crawling along, perfectly wrapped presents on the back seats. She could see the hats; almost smell the perfume. Nearly everyone she had ever known in her life was going to be here today.

She could see Dillon moving a rope to allow a new slew of cars into the parking area. He was in his camouflage trousers and a hi-vis jacket. Why did her heart feel warm when she saw him, whereas when she thought of Hugh it felt as if it had been dipped in a bucket of ice?

Because you aren't marrying him, silly, she told herself. Of course she felt safe when she saw Dillon because there was no risk involved. He didn't represent change. He was solid and reliable and always there, that's all. And he always would be.

'I feel sick,' she told her mother.

'I remember feeling terrified the morning I married your father,' Sarah said. 'It's because your whole life is going to change from now on. But it's not a bad thing.'

'Have you always been happy with Daddy? Did you ever think it was a mistake?'

Her mother looked at her.

'I suppose I would be lying if I said there weren't moments I wished my life was different. But I don't think

I'm alone. There are always difficulties along the way. Times when you don't always agree with the person you are married to, or see things from their point of view. But all in all, I'm glad I married Daddy. He's a good person, a good husband. And a wonderful father.'

If Sarah chose not to mention that it was she who was the bad person, the bad wife – although she still considered herself a good mother – it was because she wanted to see her daughter enjoy her wedding day, to banish any doubts from her mind, to enter into her union with Hugh light of heart and fully committed.

She hugged Alice.

'You've had a hard time and you've been very brave. You deserve a wonderful day and a life of happiness. I'm so very proud of you. But I want you to know that whatever happens, Daddy and I will be there for you. *Whatever* happens.'

Alice had been shored up by her mother's words. Sarah was the one person in the world she respected. And trusted. And it was up to Alice to step up, take on the mantle of responsibility and make Peasebrook Manor her life, with Hugh at her side. The cottage was waiting for them, bright with new paint and freshly hung curtains.

And now here she was, at the top of the aisle, the quartet playing. She took her father's arm and stood as tall as she could. She could see Hugh's straight back at the altar, tall and true in his morning suit, his dark hair slicked back. He turned and said something to his best man, and she saw his familiar grin.

The quartet was halfway through the entrance song. Any minute and it wouldn't be an arrival any more. The congregation were turning around to see what the delay was.

Alice began to walk. No one could see her face yet, as it was hidden by the creamy lace of the Basildon family veil. No one could see her scar.

All they could see was Alice's smile.

Alice *always* smiled.

The notes of the music died away just as she reached Hugh's side. She carried on holding on to her father's arm, not wanting to let go. These were her last moments as just a daughter. In a short while, she would be a wife.

Dillon had told Sarah that he wouldn't be attending the wedding as a guest.

'I wouldn't feel comfortable,' he told her. 'I'd rather be on the sidelines, making sure everything's all right.'

'I don't want you to feel as if you're not welcome.'

'It's all right. I know I'm welcome. I'd just prefer not to, if you don't mind. And could you explain to Alice?'

'Of course,' said Sarah, but she was sad that Dillon felt like that. She prided herself on having a good relationship with her staff. Although she suspected there was more to Dillon's reticence than social awkwardness. There was no love lost between Dillon and Hugh, she could see that now.

Dillon was there first thing in the morning, to make sure the grounds were in perfect condition, that the logistics of car parking were under control and the ground staff knew exactly what they were doing. The guests were to walk from the chapel to the grand hall, where lunch was laid, and he had made sure that not one pale chipping was out of place on the paths. The adjoining marquee had been laid out with military precision, and the Portaloos were positioned discreetly behind a bank of trees.

He thought that once everybody had made their way to the reception he could make his escape. He didn't want to hang around and be witness to the sort of drunken revelry he'd seen the night of Alice's accident. It was going to be inevitable. And he didn't want to see Hugh's smug face.

Dillon walked straight to his car. He didn't look over at the chapel. Inside, he could hear the sound of triumphant processional music. He blocked the vision of Alice in her wedding dress out of his head. He started up the engine and drove to the White Horse, where he ordered a pint of cider and a Scotch egg.

'You played a blinder.' Marlowe smiled over at Emilia as she packed away her cello.

'It wasn't a football match,' she told him, but she was smiling. She *had* played a blinder. For some reason, everything had fallen into place. Her bow had danced over the notes, through every piece they had played. Even the pieces she hadn't rehearsed at all and had to sight-read, because they'd decided on them after she had left.

'Musical genius,' said Marlowe.

'Gifted amateur,' contradicted Emilia. She was miles away from being as good as him or, she hated admitting it, as Delphine. But they had done a good job, and now the guests were being seated for lunch they were no longer needed.

There was a slightly awkward silence.

'I better get back to the shop. It's all hands on deck at the moment.'

'Oh,' said Marlowe, and she thought he looked a bit

disappointed. Maybe he wanted to go and drown his sorrows? She couldn't go with him, though. She felt guilty enough about swanning off. She needed to get back.

'I'll give you a lift.' Marlowe offered.

'That would be great. Thanks.'

She put her cello in the boot of Marlowe's car and climbed in the front seat. She grabbed her sneakers and put them back on. She let her head fall back on the headrest as he drove through the lanes.

'Are you OK?' she asked. 'About Delphine.'

He shrugged. 'I will be.'

'Do you want to talk about it?'

Marlowe was silent for a moment. 'Not really, to be honest.'

'Well,' said Emilia. 'You know where I am if you need me.'

Marlowe nodded. 'Cheers.'

Of course he wouldn't want to talk to her about it, thought Emilia. He'd probably go home and drink the rest of the whiskey she'd given him. That's what boys did when their hearts got broken. She wasn't going to interfere.

She was married, thought Alice, a few hours later. Her face was aching as much from all the smiling as her leg. She needed to sit down. And she needed the loo. She slipped away from the reception. There was a gaggle of girls smoking outside who she didn't recognise. They must be Hugh's crowd. They were much more ritzy than her Peasebrook chums: long legs, long hair, expensive clothes and scent, blowing menthol cigarette smoke all over each other.

'Hello!' she said to them all, and they gathered around her in a cooing crowd, admiring her dress, telling her how lucky she was.

'You look just amazing,' said one, who'd introduced herself as Lulu. 'Hugh made out it was much worse than it is.'

'It's fine,' said Alice. 'It is starting to ache a bit. I'll probably have to sit down.'

'Oh, I don't mean your leg,' said Lulu. 'I meant your scar.' She indicated her own face. 'He said it was really terrible. Whoever's done your make-up did an amazing job.'

Alice stared at her, not sure if she was hearing right. Or if anyone could be so stupid and tactless. Or that her own husband could have been so horrible behind her back. To these shallow and vacuous girls.

'Excuse me,' she said, and made her way to the loos.

She shut herself into a cubicle and tried not to cry. She told herself that Hugh probably hadn't said her scar was terrible at all, that the girl had been a bit drunk and a bit tactless. She was over-sensitive, that was all. She needed to toughen up.

She could hear the clatter of high heels as the same girls clustered into the loos. She could hear Lulu's voice above the rest.

'Hugh said a wedding's not a wedding without a little goodie bag,' she said.

Alice could hear gasps of glee.

'Oh my God – amazing!' said another girl. 'He is *such* a party animal.'

'He says just wait for the parties he's going to have here.'

'Chop it out on the sink surround,' said another. 'I'm not snorting it off the loo seat.'

Alice stood up, rearranged her dress and came out of the cubicle. Lulu smiled at her brightly.

'Do you want some?' she asked. She held up a little bag of white powder.

They were too stupid and drunk to be careful, thought Alice, or to realise that she wasn't like them. They assumed because she was marrying Hugh she would be the same as they were. She held out her hand.

'Can I have it, please?'

Lulu blinked for a moment. 'Sure – if you want to do the honours.'

'Thanks.' Alice took the bag. She looked down at it.

'There's loads,' said Lulu. 'Enough for all of us to have a good time.' She giggled. 'Hugh said just because he's moving to the country doesn't mean he's going to turn into a bumpkin.'

Alice shut her hand around the bag. 'Sorry, girls,' she said. 'But this is mine.'

Lulu was outraged. 'You can't just walk off with it!'

'Watch me,' said Alice.

She felt very calm as she walked down the steps and across the lawn back to the reception. No one dared to follow her. She could see Hugh, holding court at their table. He'd looked her in the eye and lied to her, she thought. She could almost, *almost* have excused the cocaine, but not the lying. You couldn't be married to someone who was prepared to hide that kind of thing from you.

She walked over to their table. Hugh saw her and stood up with a smile.

'My beautiful bride,' he said.

She wasn't going to take issue with him about what he'd said about her scar. She couldn't be bothered.

Instead, she dangled the little bag in front of him. His face turned as white as the powder.

'Here's the deal,' she said to him. 'You leave this wedding reception right now. On Monday morning you call your solicitor and arrange for an annulment. For which you will pick up all the fees, yours and mine. And I never want to see you again.'

Hugh opened his mouth to protest. He put up his hand to take the bag off her, but she snatched it away.

'Either that, or I call the police. But then it would all be over the papers and, to be honest, we don't want the scandal.'

She could see her parents bearing down on her out of the corner of her eye.

'Darling?' said Sarah.

'Hugh will explain,' said Alice. 'Won't you, Hugh?'

Ralph loomed over his son-in-law. 'What's the story, Hugh?'

'It's not what it looks like. I think Alice is—'

'Alice is what?' asked Alice. 'Look, I don't want a fuss. I want everyone to carry on and enjoy themselves. It would be a shame to break up the party now. Daddy, perhaps you would get Hugh a taxi? I don't think he's fit to drive. And Mummy – there's someone I need to go and see. Could you be hostess for me? I'll be back later.'

Sarah hesitated for a moment. Whatever had happened, it was serious. Things weren't going to pan out as she'd thought they would. But she trusted Alice, and had made her a promise that very morning. She and Ralph would be there for her, whatever happened. And she thought she knew who it was Alice was going to find.

'Of course, darling.'

Alice gave her mother a hug and left the reception.

She was going to leave Hugh to explain. She smiled as she thought about his bluster. How he would try and squirm out of it. Her parents would deal with him appropriately, she was sure, and make certain there was as little fuss as possible.

She made her way to the courtyard around the back of the house, where her old banger was parked. She fished around for the key on the top of the wall. She always kept it there, because she lost it otherwise. She started up the engine and put the car into reverse. Luckily she'd only had one glass of champagne, because she was still on painkillers. She turned the car around and headed off down the drive.

Dillon was on his second pint of cider. He'd better stop at that, and maybe have something more to eat. Or maybe he should go home now. The trouble with drink was it could fool you into thinking it made you feel better.

Brian walked past him and patted him on the back. 'Not at the wedding of the year, mate?'

'No chance,' said Dillon. She'd be married by now, he thought. He took another sip of his pint, then put it down. It tasted sour. He didn't want any more.

There was consternation over by the door. He looked over and frowned. It was dark outside so he couldn't be sure. But the figure in the doorway was wearing a white dress. A wedding dress. The veil on her head had come loose and her hem was spattered with mud.

'Alice?'

She walked over to his table.

'I think I'd like a glass of elderflower cordial,' she said. 'And maybe some crisps. Salt and vinegar.'

She sat down on the wobbly bench.

'What have you done?' he asked. 'Shouldn't you be . . . ?'

'I've buggered it up a bit,' she said, 'but I expect a good lawyer will get me out of it. I should have realised earlier.'

'Realised what?' He looked at her, her mascara running and her hair falling out of its elaborate do and her lipstick all smudged.

'It's *you* I want to be with,' she told him.

'Me?'

'You're always there for me. We always have a good time together. You love Peasebrook as much as I do. And more than anything, I want you to kiss me.'

For a moment, he wondered if it was some sort of joke. If Hugh would appear with a shotgun if he did what he'd been wanting to do ever since that day in the hospital.

Well, kissing Alice was worth getting shot for.

Her veil had fallen back down over her face. He lifted it up, so he could see all of her: her beautiful eyes, her lovely mouth.

And then he kissed her. And as he did so, he swore he was going to look after her and protect her as long as he lived, whatever happened.

25

Two weeks later the refurbishment at Nightingale Books was complete.

The shop was still recognisable as its former self, but looked fresher and brighter. The walls were pale grey, the shelves white, with hand-painted signs.

Bea had dressed each section to feel like a room. Fiction had a pink squashy sofa and small tables either side, each with a jug of fresh roses. Crime was positioned by the fireplace, with a plaid armchair and a Persian rug, and you could almost imagine Sherlock Holmes reclining there with his pipe. Cookery was designed around a butcher's block displaying the ingredients from a particular recipe. She'd accessorised all the other sections too: an easel for art, a spinning globe for travel.

They reopened the first week of December, ready for Christmas. There was no time to organise a party, but Emilia had a small opening ceremony for everyone who had been involved: June, Mel and Dave, Jackson and his cohorts, Bea, Andrea . . .

'This means the world to me,' said Emilia. 'Thank you all. And I know my father would thank you all too.'

And she turned the sign to *Open*.

There were people waiting on the pavement, eager to

shop, and they carried on flooding in all day long. There were queues at the till and Emilia was relieved she'd had the foresight to take on three new members of staff to cover the Christmas period.

At the end of the day she had just thanked the staff and said goodbye to them, but hadn't locked the door, when the bell tinged. She would tell whoever it was they were closed for the day.

It was Marlowe. He was standing there with a smile and a bottle of Perrier-Jouët.

'Are you closed?'

'I can make an exception. Just for you.'

'I wanted to buy a book on your first day. To mark the occasion.'

'Well, come in and have a browse.'

He put the bottle down on the counter and looked around in admiration.

'It's wonderful, Emilia.'

She looked around and saw it with his eyes. It *was* wonderful. And suddenly she felt overwhelmed, because the one person she wanted to see it wasn't there. She felt tears well up.

'Hey!' Marlowe was at her side in a moment.

'I'm sorry. I just wish he was here to see it.'

'Of course you do.' Marlowe took her in his arms. He put up a finger to wipe away her tears. 'He'd be so proud. You know that.'

Emilia nodded. She should pull herself together. Go and open the champagne or something. But she didn't want to move out of his embrace. On the contrary, she wanted to move closer. She shut her eyes.

They stood there for a moment, closer than close, their breathing in rhythm.

'Which book was it you wanted?' she asked eventually, barely able to speak.

'Have you got a book about a man who takes ages to realise the person he loves has been right under his nose all along?'

'There's loads of those,' she said. 'Can you be more specific?'

'Well,' said Marlowe. 'He's a violinist. And she's got a book shop.'

She opened her eyes, suddenly realising what he meant. 'Oh,' she said. 'I don't think there is.'

'Someone should write one, then,' said Marlowe, smiling down at her.

Emilia swallowed, trying to take in exactly what this meant.

'Is it true?' she asked.

'Yes. Ever since I watched you play "The Swan" at your father's memorial. You were so scared but you were so brave and you did it with so much love ... I'd never heard it played like that before.'

'Oh.' Emilia didn't know what to say. She was overwhelmed, both by his confession and his comments about her performance.

'Delphine knew before I did,' said Marlowe. 'That's why she left. She was pretty good about it. She said she didn't want to stand in the way.'

Emilia felt overcome. She rested her head on his shoulder and felt his arms tighten around her.

'So how's this book going to end, then?'

'Oh, happily,' said Marlowe. 'Like all the best books.

And it would be called... *How to Find Love in a Book Shop*.'

They stood holding each other, tighter than tight.

'It sounds,' said Emilia, 'like the best book ever written. I shall order fifty copies at once.'

26

It was Christmas Eve in Peasebrook.

From early in the morning its streets were thronged. There were queues snaking out of the butcher as people came to collect their turkeys and their geese, and Peasebrook Cheese were busily handing over wheels of Cheddar and wedges of Stilton and boxes of Vacherin. A choir sang lustily around the Christmas tree in the marketplace. The air was crisp and cold; the blue sky filled with plump white clouds.

'There'll be snow before the day's out,' said Jem's father, gazing up with a knowing look in his eye.

The promise of snow added a sense of urgency to the day. Eyes were bright, noses were pink, smiles were wide as people hurried through the streets to finish their errands and head home.

In Nightingale Books, Emilia hadn't drawn breath since turning the sign to *Open* at nine o'clock and she'd been nearly trampled in the stampede. She had no idea how people had the nerve to wait so late to buy their presents, but she didn't complain. They were buying with gusto. Thomasina had made gallons of mulled wine to hand out to customers as they browsed and the air hung heavy with the scent of cloves and cinnamon. She and Lauren had also made gingerbread men for any stray children to chew on while their parents shopped.

Bea was in charge of the wrapping station. Books were such a pleasure to wrap, with their satisfyingly straight edges and sharp corners, but perfectionist Bea took it to a higher level. The books were covered in the plain brown paper Julius had always used, and tied with red ribbon, then carefully stamped with *Merry Christmas from Nightingale Books* in one corner.

June and Emilia were kept busy helping customers with recommendations: they were easily identifiable by the red velvet elf hats Bea had made them. Emilia sold *The Cat in the Hat* and Enid Blyton and *Thomas the Tank Engine* and Flower Fairies gift books; Sherlock Holmes compendiums and gardening encyclopedias and Agatha Christie box sets; endless cookery books and biographies and atlases.

A dashing man in a navy overcoat came in needing a book recommendation for his wife. Emilia imagined a pretty woman in a beautiful Georgian house and sold him the Cazalet Chronicles, on the basis that no one she had ever met who had read them had ever disliked them.

At four o'clock suddenly the shop was emptied as if by magic. Emilia put on her coat, shut the door and turned the key. She thought of all the books they had sold, and imagined them being opened the next morning, and people being transported as they sat on the floor surrounded by wrapping paper, or curled up on a sofa with a glass of champagne, or sitting by the fire while the chestnuts roasted.

And she turned and Marlowe was there, smiling.

'Ready?' he asked, and she nodded, and hooked her arm through his.

They walked up the high street towards the church as the rest of the shops in Peasebrook shut their doors. And then, in the coldness of the night air, with the crushed velvet sky above them, she saw a bright star, and although she knew it was nonsense she couldn't help feeling it might be Julius, smiling down and feeling proud of them all. And she let herself believe it *was* him, and she tipped her face up to the sky to smile back, and she felt an overwhelming sense of warmth and joy and belonging.

'What are you grinning about?' asked Marlowe.

'I feel happy,' she said. 'I didn't think I would, because this is my first Christmas without him, and of course I wish with all my heart he was here but... I feel happy.'

Marlowe put his arm around her and squeezed her into him. She didn't need to explain that he was one of the things that made her happy, because he knew without being told, and that was one of the reasons. Marlowe always knew.

The church was bursting at the seams, but Emilia saw June's red gloves waving at her and they wove and wormed their way past seated knees to a space near the front, whispering apologies and smiling hellos at the people around them. The Basildons were in the front row, of course: Sarah in a fur hat next to Ralph, then Alice leaning on Dillon, who was looking slightly overwhelmed at being in such a conspicuous position.

The church was as quiet as a mouse as Mick Gillespie took the lectern and read 'Ring Out, Wild Bells', his unmistakable timbre tinged with West Cork holding the congregation rapt.

'Ring out, wild bells, to the wild sky,
The flying cloud, the frosty light...'

Next to her, Emilia saw June's eyes fill with pride and fondness. With his hair now white, and his spectacles on the end of his nose, Mick was a million miles from the bright young star she had fallen for, but he could still hold an audience in the palm of his hands as Tennyson's words resonated around the church.

'Ring out the grief that saps the mind,
For those that here we see no more . . .'

Emilia felt Marlowe squeeze her arm and loved him for once more just knowing. She looked over at Sarah and wondered how she was feeling. In her pocket she could feel the soft package she was going to give her later. She'd found it in a drawer in the office when she was emptying it out. She knew it was meant for Sarah and that it was her duty to make sure she got it, even though she knew it would mean mixed feelings, both joy and sadness.

She watched Mick leave the lectern and make his way back to June's side, and watched her whisper well done to him, and she loved how he smiled his thanks and appreciation even though he was an Oscar-winning actor who didn't need to be told he was brilliant. And she felt pride that in some small way she had been responsible for bringing them together at a time of life where they may both have feared they could be alone forever.

And there were Jackson and Mia and Finn, and she knew that amongst all the footballs and skateboards and Nerf guns Finn was going to get the next day, there was also his first *Harry Potter*, and she hoped that late on Christmas afternoon Jackson and Finn would curl up together and begin the journey to Hogwarts.

Everywhere she looked she saw familiar faces.

Afterwards she and Marlowe went to Peasebrook Manor for Christmas Eve drinks in the great hall. There was the biggest Christmas tree by the stairs, reaching up two floors, and a roaring log fire, and Ralph rushing around with a bottle of wine in each hand making sure everyone was kept topped up.

Emilia slipped away from the party and found Sarah in the kitchen, pulling sausage rolls out of the Aga and tipping them onto a silver tray.

'I found something,' she said. 'In the bureau. I'm certain it's for you. And I know my father would want me to give it to you.'

Sarah stood up, holding the tray in both hands. Her eyes were wide with uncertainty.

'Oh,' was all she said. Then she put the tray down and wiped her hands on a tea towel.

'I can just leave it here . . .' Emilia indicated the kitchen table.

'No. Please. I'd like you to be here. While I open it.' Sarah looked around to see if there was anyone listening, but it was quiet here, away from the hubbub of the jollity. She took the little package. Emilia had stuck fresh tape on it after she'd opened it, but Sarah slid her finger under it carefully and took out a scarf: a long devoré scarf in midnight blue and silver grey, with silken tassels.

She nodded, as if in recognition that this was exactly what Julius would have chosen for her. She held it to her face and felt its softness on her cheek.

Her voice was slightly cracked as she spoke. 'I feel as if he's going to walk into the room any minute. And tell me he chose it because of my eyes.'

Emilia could imagine her father in the shop, comparing colours and fabrics, holding the scarves up to the light until he had found the right one.

'He was the most brilliant present chooser.'

'Thank you for finding it, Emilia. Thank you for bringing it to me.'

'It's what Dad would have wanted me to do.'

Sarah folded it back up and tucked it back into the tissue just as Ralph appeared in the doorway.

'Sausage rolls, darling? Everyone's ravenous. They need something to soak up all the booze.'

Emilia turned around with a smile and Sarah picked up the tray. 'Just coming.'

The two of them walked out together into the mêlée, then drifted apart amongst the throngs. They would always have a tie, because of their secret, but it didn't need to be vocalised. They knew they would be there for each other, if they ever wanted to share a moment's reflection, or memory, and they would give each other comfort.

It was an unusual situation, thought Emilia, but then – what was usual? The whole point of life was you couldn't ever be sure what would happen next. Sometimes what happened was good, sometimes not, but there were always surprises. She smiled to herself as she scoped the room, and spotted Marlowe standing by the fire, chatting up a pair of sprightly elderly ladies who were surveying him as a pair of foxes might a chicken who'd escaped its coop.

'Oh look!' someone cried. 'It's starting to snow!'

Everyone rushed to the windows and gazed out at the almost luminescent snowflakes twirling around in the golden glow of the garden lamps. Faster and faster they fell, tiny ballerinas in the spotlight.

'Do you think we should go?' Emilia asked Marlowe. 'We don't want to get snowed in.'

'Let's,' said Marlowe. 'I feel as if I might be eaten alive any minute.'

They slipped away as discreetly as they could – endless goodbyes and Christmas wishes would only hold up the jollity. Marlowe started up the car and turned on the heater, then drove carefully through the blizzard, windscreen wipers at the double. The carol service from King's College Cambridge played on the stereo. It was as if they were in cosy bubble, tucked away from the outside world.

'A white Christmas,' sighed Emilia, as the landscape around them transformed into a winter wonderland. Their first, she smiled to herself, and thought about waking up in his cottage the next morning, and the stocking she had filled for him hanging by his fireplace.

As they came into Peasebrook, Marlowe stopped the car just on the hump of the bridge and Emilia looked at Nightingale Books, the light from the windows still glowing inside, the roof already covered in white, and in her mind she said, 'Merry Christmas, Dad,' and then the car rumbled down the other side of the bridge and up the high street into the oncoming snow.

How to
Find Love
in a

BOOK SHOP

Reading Group notes

Q&A with Veronica Henry

OK, so which book shop was it that inspired your novel? Was it a real book shop, or is Nightingale Books totally imaginary?

It's a hybrid of all the book shops I have ever visited, with a dollop of imagination, and of course it had to fit architecturally into a Cotswold high street. It was the window that was most important – who can walk past a book shop window without pressing your nose up to the glass? – and Goldsboro Books in Cecil Court in London was one of the main influences.

How do you write? Do you get up super-early and work till lunchtime, for example? When is the best time of day to write, for you? Do you have a favourite place to write, and certain things you have to have around you before you start?

I'm definitely a morning person – I've never been able to work well at night. I have to get all my paperwork and emails out of the way before starting, so my mind is free from clutter. I used to need complete silence but now I can work with Radio 6 on as very often the songs inspire me – music and literature are all about evoking emotion. Before I start a book, I have a notebook full of ideas and character sketches and plot developments, and I also have a mood board to get me in the 'zone'. I try and write visually so readers can picture what is going on as vividly as possible.

A few of your books are set in specific and perhaps unusual places: the Orient Express, a beach hut, a boutique hotel and now a book shop. Is there a bijou location planned for your next novel? Is it important to have the location settled in your mind before you begin writing?

I always start with the location – once I know where my characters are, I can start working out why they are there and what they are up to. I choose places I would like to be myself: all my books have an escapist edge. My next book is called *The Forever House* – a forever house is the house of your dreams; the house where you want to spend the rest of your life. I think the quest for a 'forever' house is something many people can relate to – who hasn't spent hours browsing property websites?

Bea, the character who once worked as an art director at a London magazine, is very vivid. She seems to leap off the page and live as soon as you 'meet' her. Have you based her on a real person? Which, if any, of the other characters have you borrowed from real life?

My characters usually evolve from a single premise: for Bea, I had an idea about a woman who doesn't realise how unhappy she is until she finds herself shoplifting. Her whole personality came from the moment when she steals the book. Sometimes the ideas are tiny; sometimes they are bigger. So Emilia's premise is: what happens to a woman who inherits her father's book shop? With Sarah Basildon, it's how do you cope with secret grief? They are usually very simple ideas, but they have to be interesting so a complex character can emerge.

The descriptions of food in *How to Find Love in a Book Shop* – and in your other novels – are utterly mouth-watering. Do you love to cook, or do you prefer to be cooked for? Tell us about some of your favourite dishes, whether to cook or to eat.

I love cooking, and eating, and being cooked for, and writing about food, and shopping for food, and reading recipe books, and discovering new restaurants . . . ! My philosophy is one has to eat three times a day, so you might as well make it as pleasurable as possible. My signature dishes are crab linguine, tarte tatin and pommes dauphinoises. I don't think I'm a particularly brilliant technical cook, but I know a good recipe when I see one. I'm very drawn to people who like cooking. There is always something to talk about. My brother and I can talk for hours about food.

Do you have any friends or relatives who have found love in a book shop, and was it their story that inspired you to write the novel?

For me, the title is more thematic than specific – the idea that you will always find something to love in a book shop. It's about a love of books and reading as much as romance. Books will never let you down: they are there to provide escape, comfort, inspiration . . . What's not to love?

Questions for discussion

- In the novel, some of the characters seem to be repressing their feelings. Which characters did you expect to be more private about their deepest feelings, and which characters surprised you by keeping their feelings hidden? How does the repressing of feelings by different characters affect the story?

- More than one character seems to feel that misfortune in their life comes as some kind of punishment for something they've done or not done. Discuss which characters see life's events in this way, and why.

- Is *How to Find Love in a Book Shop* a traditional romantic novel? Are there any ways in which the characters in it don't follow a traditional path to love?

- 'And she knew, from all the books she had ever read, that life was complicated, that love sprang from nowhere sometimes, and that forbidden love wasn't always something to be ashamed of.' Discuss the theme of 'forbidden love' in the novel.

- 'Where would she go back to, if she were going to rewrite her life?' Which characters in the novel are trying to rewrite their lives? Where do they 'go back to' in order to start the process?

Further Reading

Weird Things Customers Say in Bookshops Jen Campbell (Constable)

The Bookshop Book Jen Campbell (Constable)

Books, Baguettes and Bedbugs Jeremy Mercer (Weidenfeld & Nicolson)

Bread Alone Judith R. Hendricks (Orion)

An Omelette and a Glass of Wine Elizabeth David (Grub Street)

The Christmas We Met Kate Lord Brown (Orion)